# THE LAST WITNESS

## MICHAEL SHAYNE

The Last Witness

Michael Shayne



ISBN: 979-8-9891894-4-1

www.michaelshayne.net
michael_shayne@yahoo.com

# CHAPTER 1



"*Haz que ese niño se calle!*"

Rolando ignored the coyote's whispered order to quiet the screaming child in his arms. What could he do but pat her on the back and whisper words she didn't yet understand? He couldn't give her back to her mother. The woman was two people in front of him in line, waiting her turn to climb the make-shift ladder from the tunnel to the earth above.

A second coyote climbed down, gave a thumbs-up, and all light was extinguished. Shushing sounds began as the line of twenty migrants lumbered forward, pressing together until Rolando could barely draw a breath.

When his turn finally came, he shut his eyes and grasped the splintered rung (which was little more than a mop-handle segment) and hugged the child tighter, willing her to stop crying while he shielded her from the falling debris. When it stopped and he could again look up, he saw the mother's silhouette against an oval starlit sky; she was waving her arms and clapping. Rolando tested the rung once more, remembered there had been nineteen rungs coming down, then started his climb.

At the eighth rung, loose earth from the boot of the man ahead pelted the brim of his new Dodgers baseball cap. By the twelfth rung, it had stopped. When his hand hit the twentieth rung, the wannabe engineer in him realized the tunnel had been constructed to slant downward (surely not on purpose). Then, after the twenty-third, the frantic mother's arms were within reach. Rolando pulled the screaming child's face from his chest, pressed his back against the wall of the hole, then passed the child up to its mother. The remaining rungs were easy, and Rolando scrambled up and out onto a strange desert landscape that could as easily have been the moon.

The group had exited the hole next to a large boulder by a dune that blocked their view of the distant town of Lukeville, Arizona. But the dune couldn't block the streetlights' illumination of a few stray clouds and the promise that lay a mere half-mile trek through the desert. Most had already started to walk around the dune, while a few others remained huddled together in the shadows, chatting among themselves and making plans, unsure what to do next.

Rolando didn't hesitate. He sent one last glance to the mother and her child and had just started his trek toward the lights when two uniformed men rounded either side of the dune and ordered everyone to the ground. Many migrants scattered into the darkness, while Rolando and a few others complied and were lined up side by side with their hands laced on top of their heads. His hopes sank at the thought of being arrested, processed, and sent back to Mexico only to pay another $5,000 to start the journey from scratch. But then, there was hope, as the two men in uniform began shining their flashlights into scared faces but letting them leave.

After a few minutes, the two officers had sent everyone on their way except for Rolando, the woman, and her child. Both agents drew their pistols—and the baby started to scream again.

Startled, Rolando raised his hands high in surrender. His eyes had adjusted, and he was able to recognize the men's uniforms and the all-too-familiar gold-on-black badges of the United States Border Patrol. The name tag sewn into one man's shirt reflected beams of moonlight and revealed that the pistol with the fat barrel belonged to *Z. Penn*.

Penn's partner stood behind him with his pistol trained on the mother of the child. The partner stepped over to ask Penn a question, and Rolando could make out the man's badge and name tag. *I. Gallagher* asked his question, received a whispered answer from Penn, then went back to the sobbing woman.

"Shut the child up," Gallagher commanded in Spanish, jabbing his pistol in the mother's direction. She pulled the child closer, then turned away, using her body as a shield.

"Please. Do not shoot," Rolando pleaded, this time in broken English. "We have no weapons."

A flashlight beam scalded his eyes, and Rolando lowered one hand as a shield. He wanted to plead once more, but the metallic click of a gun's hammer being thumbed back stopped him.

"Shut that kid up!" Gallagher demanded again, which caused the child to cry even louder.

Rolando turned toward the woman and pleaded with her, *"Puede hacer que el niño deje de llorar?"* (Can you please make the child stop crying?) Rolando shifted his gaze and now found both pistols aimed his way. He hugged himself in an act of submission and defense. That was when bad went to worse.

Gallagher turned to the woman and, in an almost fatherly tone, said, "Perhaps I can help." He then took two steps forward and fired the pistol. The explosion of the shot died in the expanse of desert, along with the cries of the infant. But not the screams of the mother.

"No! No, no, no, no, no!" the mother cried, gripping her dead child tighter against her breast, rocking back and forth and screaming at the top of her lungs as if the ritual might reverse time and bring her child back. She held the baby at arm's length, then hugged her again before laying the child against the dune. Then, turning toward Gallagher, she attacked; her arms flailed, hungry to connect with anything fleshy, but Gallagher brought the pistol down on the woman's neck, and her knees buckled. She lay in a sobbing heap on the desert floor.

"Oh God! Why? Why do you do this?" Rolando cried as Agent Penn hit him behind the ear with the grip of the pistol grip, and he collapsed in a heap on the ground, his new baseball cap spinning out of sight.

Rolando twisted to crawl away, his fingers clawing at the loose and uncooperative sand. Behind him, Penn took another step closer.

With his raw and cracked hands reaching ahead for more desert to grasp in a desperate attempt to remove himself from the inevitable, Rolando realized it was useless. And, with the death of the child he had carried to the top of the hole, he was fresh out of motivation. Penn was now feet away and looming over him. Rolando turned his head, and as he hoped and prayed and clawed forward, another shot rang out, one he would never hear. The bullet caught Rolando in the back of the head and exited below his left eye.

. . .

Agent Penn knelt and rifled through Rolando's pockets and sparse belongings. He found $523 in American cash, then dropped the wallet and the crucifix into the sand but kept the folded note and the business card stapled to it. After reading them both, his eyes widened, and he called Gallagher over, away from the sobbing woman, and said, "I need to go to Lukeville to use the phone. Stay here with her."

They had parked the agency Tahoe on the far side of the dune, and in minutes, Penn was standing at a phone booth outside the truck stop. Picking up the handset, he pumped a quarter into the slot, dialed zero, then waited for the operator. He gave her the phone number and told her to make it collect. As he waited, he checked his watch. It was 3:02 a.m. His contact would be asleep and pissed when he answered. Finally, the party he was calling picked up and accepted the charges.

Penn kept his words short and to the point—and in Spanish. *"Está terminado."* (It is finished.) "And you were right about the two bitches. I found the lawyer's business card in the man's pocket." He listened, then said, "We promised to take care of it, and we will, but—" He listened again. Longer, this time, as the voice dictated a change in plans. "What do we do with the woman and the kid?" He listened again, then said, "Our price just went to fifty thousand." After the other party agreed, he ended the call with, "Yeah, yeah." Penn hung up, and his quarter was returned. He pocketed the business card and the quarter, then drove back to the desert, where Gallagher was sitting against the dune. The woman was still on the ground, rocking her dead child.

Penn sidled up to his partner and whispered, "One more job, then it's Cabo time."

"What do we do with the woman?" Gallagher asked.

"Nothing. I was told it would be handled," Penn said coldly. At his feet lay the Dodgers baseball cap. Swapping it for his own US Border Patrol cap, he waved the business card in the air. "It's a long drive to West Virginia, and we need to cash in this lottery ticket."

# CHAPTER 2

Toledo, Ohio
Saturday, August 26, 1995
1:30 p.m.

Sheik Tariq Al-Jabori waited patiently for his limo to ease to a stop before two of his three Armani-clad bodyguards exited and flanked the rear door. From beneath their suit coats, they produced Steyr 9mm machine pistols and held them at the ready. The third guard then exited, held out his hand to the sheik, and helped the robed man to his feet. The guard then returned to the back of the limo, closed the door, and ordered the driver to their next position while the first two guards hurried the sheik inside.

Had this been Ankara, Turkey, the arrival of Sheik Al-Jabori would have been met with rising cheers from an admiring crowd. But in Toledo, Ohio, every precaution to protect his life had been taken. There were to be no stragglers outside the conference center or in the lobby, where more guards had been stationed. Once inside, the sheik would wait in a secure room until the moment of his introduction. Then, and only then, would he be escorted by Guard One and Guard Two from the secure room to the twin steel doors where a fourth guard had been posted. The doors would remain locked and could only be opened from the lobby side.

Inside the auditorium, Ibrahim Nassar—the sheik's chief of security—had given specific instructions to the crowd: cheer all you want, but no one stands. He waited until every person had been seated before delivering a knock on the door, signaling the guard to open it. Guard One and Guard Two stepped inside the auditorium first, scanned the crowd, tucked their Steyr TMPs beneath their coats, then let the sheik walk down the aisle as applause thundered. The door was closed and locked, and the sheik was escorted to the podium.

Fifteen minutes into his dedication speech for the new mosque—that *he* had funded—the shot rang out.

At first, the crowd remained seated, not certain of what to make of the shot and the wall clock that had exploded near the back of the stage. However, once Guard One and Guard Two dove onto the sheik to shield him from a second shot, the crowd knew exactly what to do. They panicked. And in a single, terrified mass, moved toward the locked steel doors at the rear of the auditorium, pinning Nassar.

Following the plan, Guard One and Guard Two picked up the sheik and ushered him stage right, behind the curtain, and out through the emergency exit. Then, the second shot came.

In the alley between the two buildings, the limo was waiting. The rear door was open, the driver raced the engine, and Guard Three was waiting in the back seat. Guard One came through the exit first, was immediately shot in the head, and dropped to the pavement before his second foot ever left the building. The sheik followed but froze in midstep until Guard Three reached from the limo, grabbed him by the robes, and yanked him into the back seat—the sheik's head catching the doorframe on the way. He was shoved into the forward-facing seat, completely shielded by green-tinted bulletproof glass. Guard Two was still standing between the open limo door and the chassis when his head exploded, and he dropped like a wet sack, almost on top of Guard One. Inside the limo, the guard took the backward-facing seat, then ordered the driver to leave.

A loafered foot stomped on the accelerator, and the limo squealed down the alley and across the parking lot, where people were now streaming out of the conference center. The driver took a right onto the main street, following the egress route, until the guard in the back ordered him to turn onto a dirt road that split a field of tall corn. The road took them to a clearing at the top of a knoll beneath a water tower stenciled with the words *WELCOME TO RIGA*. The limo came to a stop, its tires digging into the freshly tilled soil.

The sheik, still gazing through the rear window and nursing the bump on his head, was thrown forward against the seat. He flinched as two more shots were fired, this time from inside the limo, and when he spun around to find the source, he saw his driver slumped over the wheel, a mist of red painting the windshield. And Guard Three now had a silenced .22 caliber pistol leveled at him. When the sheik raised both hands in surrender, a third shot was fired, and the bullet tore off the top segment of his index finger, blood spurting out of his severed digit like a cherry fountain. Doubling over in agony, he wrapped the nub in a wad of his white robe; the blood spread through the linen in his grasp.

After catching his breath, the sheik stammered in Arabic, "What—what are you doing?" It was the first time he noticed the guard was wearing a pair of powder-white surgical gloves. It was also the first time he noticed this guard was not the same man who had first been in the limo. The first guard had worn his hair pulled back in a ponytail, as did this guard. But this guard's hair was thicker and wavier. His face was stronger and his jawline more pronounced. And he appeared to be bigger in his tailored Armani suit.

As bile rose in his throat, the sheik's heart skipped when the guard spoke a single word.

"Lilliana."

The sheik stammered in Arabic, "Lilliana? What is—? I do not know this name."

The guard said nothing. He crossed his legs and lay the pistol's barrel over a knee.

The sheik gripped his aching finger and stuttered, "What is it that you want? I do not—" But then he stopped. He *did* recognize the name, and it caused another series of heart palpitations as he recalled it was the name of a friend's dead daughter. And the friend was dead too. His gaze shifted to meet the icy-blue eyes of the guard, and he realized he was in deep trouble. He said, "All this for a dead little girl? A death I had nothing to do with. The man you are looking for died two years ago."

"Yes, I know," the guard said.

"Who are you working for? The dead man's estate?"

"Something like that."

"I will triple what they are paying you."

The sheik kept his eyes glued to the silencer's opening, willing it not to speak and wondering which was worse, waiting for the shot—or the shot itself? He swallowed back the bile, and his mind rewound to when he, too, had paid for the lives of many men to be taken. Money was power.

The sheik adjusted his grip on the throbbing shorter digit, willing it to grow back as a phantom pain from the missing tip sent pulses into his wrist. Then, his gaze wandered back to the guard and the now visible machine pistol strapped to the guard's shoulder, peeking from beneath the man's jacket. It was not his security team's standard issue Steyr TMP.

The guard noticed the sheik's interest in the machine pistol, and he pulled his jacket open, proudly displaying the Uzi 9mm.

"That weapon is made by Jewish dogs," the sheik said. When the guard didn't answer, he again asked, "Who is paying you?"

The guard shook his head, slow and deliberate.

"Why are you doing this?" the sheik asked.

"Lil-li-a-na," the guard repeated, letting each syllable drop like pebbles into a pond. Then, from his inside coat pocket, he retrieved a folded piece of white printer paper, which he then unfolded and lay on the sheik's lap.

"What is this?" the sheik asked, still gripping the bloody spot of robe shrouding his shorter finger. When the page came into focus, his mouth and throat went dry as he scanned the columns and the names of birds on the left and the human names on the right. Then, he understood what was happening and wished he had pulled the revolver from beneath his robes instead and taken his chances. The smell of his own urine filled the limo as his own name—and its bird equivalent—appeared next to the bottom, already crossed off.

Eagle        Unknown
~~Falcon~~      ~~Tim Branson~~
~~Hawk~~      ~~Don Cruxfield~~
~~Osprey~~     ~~Munir Kateb~~
~~Dove~~      ~~Bob Munson~~
~~Harrier~~    ~~General Al-Rasheed~~
~~Kite Tariq Al-Jabori~~
Owl Unknown

"Please. You have nothing to fear from this group. The NEST is dead. Commander Trevor Harmon is dead."

"And you put the contract out on Harmon two years ago," the guard said.

"But I didn't kill him. The IRA did. What you are doing serves no purpose."

The guard pursed his lips, then nodded in a diagonal motion. A little yes. A little no. Then, he pointed to the last name on the list and said, "Owl. Who is he?"

Al-Jabori said, "His name is Rufus Carmichael. Now, please, let me go. I am the only man on your list who has not killed anyone."

That's when the guard jabbed the barrel of the pistol at the top name.

"Eagle?" the sheik said. "You will never find this man. He is a ghost. Some say he isn't real. Even *I* have never met the man face-to-face."

The guard didn't speak. Instead, he jabbed a finger at the name *Eagle* again.

The sheik said, "I don't know who—" But he was interrupted by another spit from the .22 pistol, and his left ear erupted with fire. He screamed and grabbed at the organ to find a dangling piece of flesh that was once his lobe. Behind him, a spiderweb formed in the glass of the rear window. His finger and ear were both screaming, but not as loudly as the gun tucked in his waistband. He wanted it now—badly. And it wanted him. But it was buried beneath three layers of robes. How could he possibly reach the pistol without—

The .22 spat again, and this time, the sheik's right kneecap exploded beneath his robe. Shards of bone and flesh exited through the tiny hole poked in the fabric. Al-Jabori doubled over, gripping the injury in the crook of his elbow.

The sheik screamed. "I don't know Eagle's name. No one does! Please. Whatever name I give you will not be the truth." He squeezed the pain from his damaged knee, then gazed upward in defiance while his lips trembled. So, the guard shot his other knee, and this time, the sheik wailed in pain, giving all his breath to the scream. It took more than a minute before he could speak again. "I do not know his name. Please, please. The drugs in the darts had been switched. The general was the target. Not the little girl."

"I know," the guard said. He reached out, retrieved the list, and shoved it into a pocket. "The NEST used the CIA's asset to assassinate one of your own members. None of that matters. The child is still dead."

Beneath his robes, Al-Jabori's finger found the .45 caliber's trigger, and his thumb found the hammer. He cleared his throat and spat to hide the click as he thumbed the hammer back. Muscles tensed in his arm as he readied himself. He would rise slowly from hugging his knee and bring the barrel of the gun up, the movement hidden beneath his robe. He would then fire at the guard through the fabric, emptying all six rounds. The man would not know what hit him.

With his hand firmly on the revolver's grip and his middle finger on the trigger, the sheik slowly sat up and slid the pistol from his waistband, the silk of his ropes resisting against the gun sight.

The sheik said, "You do this for one little girl?"

"Lil-li-an-a," the guard repeated. "Say her name. I need to hear her name from your lips."

"Lilliana," Al-Jabori repeated. "Does it make you feel better?" Beneath his robes, the barrel of the revolver was now aimed in the general direction of the passenger door. A few more inches, and it would be aimed at the guard's gut. The sheik said, "If you kill me, you'll know not one more minute of peace. My people will hunt you down."

The guard let a thin smile spread across his lips, then said, "Peace? What's that?"

His fury no longer contained, the guard worked the pistol with pinpoint accuracy and let loose two shots. The first bullet went through the sheik's left eye. As the sheik's reflexes jerked his head to the right, the second bullet shattered the sheik's left cheekbone. Then, the sheik's reflexes took over, and his finger pulled on the revolver's trigger, sending a .45 round through his robe and creating an ear-crushing explosion inside the limo. The large round passed between the guard's legs, missing flesh as it punched a hole in the floorboard. A stream of smoke dripped out and upward from the new hole in the sheik's robes.

. . .

The guard leaned forward and pulled the sheik's keffiyeh over the man's blank and bloody face. He then opened the briefcase and took several credit cards, tore four checks from a portfolio, closed the case, stepped outside into the bright afternoon, then strolled easily along the dirt path to the rented SUV hidden behind the water tower.

A gray glob of sparrows, spooked by his approach, exploded from nearby trees, forming a rolling sheet as they left. He leaned against the back bumper, then retrieved a slim digital recorder from a pocket inside the suit coat, which he placed on the bumper while he changed into jeans and a T-shirt. He stuffed the Armani suit and gloves into a plastic garbage bag, then tossed it onto the floorboard of the SUV. If everything had gone according to plan, his partner would already be on the road and well ahead of him. He slipped on a new pair of gloves before climbing into the SUV.

Once he was on I-75 heading south, he took out the digital recorder and pressed the Play button, and the sheik's tinny voice said, *"Lilliana. Does it make you feel better?"*

"You know what?" he said to the empty SUV. "It actually does."

# CHAPTER 3

The White House
Same Day
7:22 p.m.

Chief of Staff Patricia Woodburn—Woody, to her friends and enemies—apologized to the dignitaries at her table as her aide, Connie Perdew, approached from behind and whispered in her ear. Woody's wine-tinted smile never faded as she listened to both the marine band and Perdew before excusing herself. The king of Jordan, gracious as always, stood as she rose. The president and Secretary of State Jerry Manchin did the same, although both did so with concerned expressions.

Arranged in what the staff called a seventeen-eight configuration, seventeen tables of eight chairs, the White House State Dining Room resembled the Battle of Waterloo, as 135 pairs of eyes from dignitaries and 30 more pairs from the staff hung on Woody's every move. No doubt, the president felt it as well. Woody smiled it all away. Her escort and partner, ex–Secret Service Agent Paul Kelvington, also stood, but she gently placed a hand on his shoulder, easing him back into his chair. "I'll only be a moment," she whispered, straightened his bow tie, then left him to entertain the group in her absence.

"I think I've been promoted," she heard Paul say to a snickering table as she bunched up the excess blue chiffon of her evening gown, trying hard to keep up with Connie, who had already left the State Dining Room. She followed Connie to the Blue Room, where a Secret Service agent stepped out and then closed the door behind them. She and Connie were not alone. The attorney general was there—waiting for them.

"There's been an incident," the AG said. Dean Rittenger took a long, deliberate step toward the two women, his vodka perched in a steady hand, though his smooth gait always made it seem as if he were about to fall forward. But when his jaw muscles worked the recently established gray at his temples, Woody had her first clue that whatever had happened was more than an incident.

"What's happened, Rit?" Woody asked. Beside her, Connie opened her mouth to speak but then closed it quickly, opting to let the two high-powered DC players take it from there. Technically, Connie Perdew, the deputy chief of staff, may have held the lowest rank in the room, but she and Woody had been together since the University of North Carolina nearly twenty years earlier. Many times, words from one were as good as words from the other.

Rit said, "Remember the temporary B-1 visa you pushed for—and the State Department approved—for Sheik Tariq Al-Jabori? There was an attack during his speech in Toledo. At least five known dead—so far."

"And the sheik?" Connie asked.

Rit shook his head. "We haven't found him or his limo yet. This could turn into a political—and diplomatic—nightmare."

The door to the Blue Room burst open, and another upset tuxedo arrived. Secretary of State Jerome Manchin closed the door as he yanked his tie loose and joined the others, empty-handed. "The king of Jordan is pissed," he announced. "Will someone please tell me—"

Rit stopped Manchin with a raised palm. "The FBI has people on the way right now, so everything we have is coming from the Ohio State Highway Patrol." Rit sipped his drink. "The limo, the driver, one guard, and the sheik are missing." Rit eyed the others, then finished with, "That's it. That's all we know."

Woody eyed Manchin. "If Al-Jabori turns up dead, it's going to appear as if we approved the visa to facilitate an assassination."

Manchin said, "The sheik requested the visit."

"That won't matter during a spin cycle," Connie said in almost a whisper, mostly to Woody.

Rit's cell phone rang again, and he stepped away.

Woody was about to ask a question. Beside her, Connie bit her lip and shook her head in micro-movements. It was her deputy's way of telling her to be careful. *Don't say too much yet.* Connie mouthed something Woody didn't catch when Rittenger returned.

"The sheik's chief of security survived, and we have him in custody. We're taking him to the Cleveland branch. His name is Ibrahim Nassar," Rit said, the phone still to his ear.

Connie shot a knowing glance toward Woody, who asked, "Any idea who did this?"

"Not a clue," Rit said. "The details are sketchy, and this Nassar character hasn't been a lot of help. He has functional immunity, and he's waiting on his attorney. He did tell us they had established a rendezvous point for the limo. We're checking it out."

"What about civilian casualties?" Manchin asked.

"Minor injuries," Rit replied. "Mostly from tripping over other people trying to break down the locked doors to get out of the building."

"Oookay." Woody drew out the word. "So, why is the king of Jordan bent out of shape?"

"Sheik Tariq Al-Jabori is Turkish by residency," Manchin said, "but he's Jordanian by birth. The king of Jordan is his first cousin."

"Oh shit!" Woodburn blurted out as her head impulsively turned toward the door. Her eyes burned through the centuries-old walls to the king of Jordan, who was sitting at her table in the State Dining Room being entertained by Paul.

Manchin's cell phone rang, and he took a couple of steps away before answering. He then closed his phone quickly and rejoined the group. "His Majesty has been ushered away by one of his advisors. It's hitting the fan and splattering all over the White

House guests."

"At least there's no press tonight," Rit said.

"Since when did that matter?" Woody asked. "There are congressmen and senators who are always looking to become anonymous sources. Especially if it makes a president from the other party look bad." Woody shook her head, then did the math. If the king of Jordan had left the table, it meant Paul was alone with the president and the first lady. Paul would be fine, but no doubt a few suspicious members of Congress would be salivating at the appearance of—something—now that the president's table was nearly empty.

There was a ringing sound again, and Manchin nearly dropped his phone as he fumbled to look at the screen. But it was Rit's phone this time, and he shook his head as he answered.

"When?" Rit asked. "How many in the limo?" He held up two fingers, then shook his head. "Tortured? Are you certain it's…? Okay. Give me the details." He listened for a few minutes more, then said, "Keep me informed." He closed the phone and examined the anxious faces. "Five of his guards were found dead at the conference center. They found Sheik Tariq Al-Jabori and his driver in a field three miles from the conference center, both dead. The driver was shot in the back of the head, and the sheik was tortured before he was killed. Seven total dead. Weather report: it's now an official shitstorm."

Woody lowered her gaze to the floor in thought as she considered what she would tell the president in the next few minutes. His table was slowly losing its guests, and she was certain he'd be here right now if he thought it wouldn't look even more suspicious if he abandoned his own state dinner.

"This had to be a professional hit," Woody said. "Except that limos aren't exactly low-key getaway vehicles."

Rit said, "Somebody needed to be alone with the sheik to get information. Or revenge."

"Or both," Woody said, then turned to Manchin. "I know what you're thinking, Jerry, but we don't know the shooters were American. It could have been anyone."

Manchin interrupted her. "Like the Israelis?"

Rit said, "Sheik Tariq Al-Jabori is a billionaire who donates millions to groups we know directly fund Islamic Jihad and Hezbollah. The only one we can't link him to is Hamas."

But Connie Perdew was shaking her head again. Faintly, so as not to draw anyone else's attention. Her eyes squinting a request for Woody to be patient. To wait. She had something to say, but not in this company. The door to the Blue Room opened, and the Secret Service agent poked his head inside.

"Ms. Woodburn? The president is asking for you."

"Thank you," she said, sending the agent back outside, and the door closed again. "Jerry, can you please find His Majesty and take him to the Oval Office? I'll brief the president first, and then we'll meet you there." Manchin nodded, attempted to retie his tie, then elected to rip it from his collar altogether as he left the room. Then, she turned to Rit. "Can you get with your folks again and have the freshest intel possible for us in, say"—she checked her watch—"fifteen minutes?"

"Sure," Rit said, then left the room.

It was the two of them now, and the Blue Room echoed with unspoken stress. Connie hugged herself, then patted down her suit coat in search of a cigarette. It was a symbolic gesture. Connie and Woody had both quit smoking the day they'd joined the White House staff. There was too much precious history here to risk damaging it with dropped ash.

"I hope I'm wrong," Connie said. "God, how I hope I'm wrong."

"Wrong about what?" Woody asked.

"Sheik Tariq Al-Jabori," Connie said and then paused to let her boss catch up. When she didn't, Connie started prompting. "Remember—two years ago? The Baghdad thing and the CIA agent everyone wanted dead? Sheik Al-Jabori was one of them and had put a contract out on the agent's life."

"So did I," Woody said. "I sent Paul, remember? But Commander Trevor Harmon died when the IRA planted a bomb in his plane." The night had started off so well, but now she felt like her most trusted friend had gut-punched her—and her filet and Cabernet might end up all over the Martin Van Buren rug. "It's a coincidence," Woody said in a prayer tone. "Sheik Al-Jabori had plenty of enemies with resources."

Connie said, "Maybe. But how many of those enemies could lay waste to his entire security team here in the United States?"

"They missed at least one," Woody said. She caught the breath she had lost as the memories from two years prior caught up. "Are you suggesting someone is picking up where Commander Harmon left off, and finished off the NEST?"

"It has to be," Connie said.

Woody said, "Ron Johnson is the AIC at the FBI's Cleveland branch."

Connie nodded absently. "You helped put him there. But if we start asking him questions that we don't want to know the answer to, we could run the risk of exposing yours and Paul's involvement in—" Connie paused midsentence, then asked, "Do we want to reopen that can of worms?"

Woody said nothing at first as she considered Connie's concerns and the potential consequences of reopening old wounds. But the fact remained that Harmon was dead due to no effort by her or Paul. And the only people who knew what she had attempted—to protect a president—were herself, Connie Perdew, Paul Kelvington, and—one other.

Her FBI contact in Cleveland owed her, but AIC Ron Johnson was a Boy Scout and couldn't be trusted with an issue so politically and legally delicate. She said, "We need to know as much as possible as quickly as possible, and I can't risk using the FBI right now.

What we need to do is confront Ibrahim Nassar directly."

Connie read her boss's thoughts and whispered, "You want to send Paul."

"Who else can I send? If this turns out to be—*something*—I don't want anyone else knowing. Paul will know what to ask and what not to ask."

"Something? Is that what this is?" Connie cocked her head. "Look, I'm practical, you know that. I don't believe in the tooth fairy or Santa Claus, but this has all the earmarks of Commander Harmon—again."

"The man's dead," Woody said.

Connie cocked her head. "Yes. But consider everything that's happened in the last two years, *after* Commander Harmon died. His enemies started to disappear—again." She started counting on her fingers. "CIA Director Walter Rehnquist, National Security Advisor Don Cruxfield, and CIA Chief of Station in London Whitey Garfield. Dead. Dead. Now, Sheik Tariq Al-Jabori. This isn't a coincidence. It has to be—"

"No! It doesn't have to be!" Woody blurted out. From the walls, suspicious portraits of long-dead patriots gazed back. Lowering her voice, she said, "Consider this an exercise to—exorcise—Commander Harmon's ghost."

"So, you agree it's a possibility?" Connie said.

"Do I believe the ghost of a dead CIA agent is murdering people from his past? Hell no! But is someone else continuing the cause? It's possible. But if anyone can figure it out, it's Paul."

"What will you tell him?"

It was a good question. If she asked Paul to go to Cleveland to investigate the ghost of the man Paul himself had been hired to kill two years ago—and nearly died trying—he might have Woody committed. Fiancé or not. And, if Paul suspected any part of that past was still around, he'd be like a beagle on a scent—never looking up until he either caught it or was hit by a truck on the way.

Woody said, "I'll tell him to question Ibrahim Nassar to head off a political nightmare, to see if it was an Islamic wacko or a Mossad hit. Either way, Paul needs to get there before anyone else has a shot at the guy. Nassar has functional immunity, so he may not talk. Will you please call our friend in Cleveland and get Paul cleared?"

Connie nodded, straightened her outfit, then said, "I'm on it." She crossed the room and opened the door and was immediately met by a Secret Service agent, who stopped her, recognized her, then let her pass before allowing the president of the United States to enter the room. Perdew smiled and then continued as the door closed behind her.

In the Blue Room, the president handed Woody a fresh glass of wine. "Care to fill me in on why the guests at my table are leaving?"

"Yes, sir," she said, then gave him the rundown. But only as much as the president would get from his AG or secretary of state in the next ten minutes, or the newspapers the next day. The part about a person taking revenge in the name of a dead CIA agent would not come up. He had his own issues to worry about. Which, coincidentally, happened to be hers too.

# CHAPTER 4



On the outskirts of the tiny Appalachian town of Princeton, West Virginia, Liam Curran chased the headlights of his blue BMW 325iC convertible over the curvy Route 7, then stopped at the twin brick pillars and black iron gate that marked the entrance to his driveway. He pressed a button on the remote over the visor, then waited as the gate swung upward like an executioner's ax. The tires rattled over the cattle stop, then he waited for the gate to lower before negotiating the winding drive to the two-story brick house on the hill. He eased the BMW into the three-car garage next to the black Ford Explorer parked in the center spot. After snatching the plastic garbage bag from the floorboard, he got out, felt the hood of the Explorer, found it was still warm and clicking, then hoped the owner was cooling off too.

He entered through the mudroom, blindly hanging his keys on a hook above the washing machine, then entered the kitchen, where he found the blonde woman waiting for him in the dim light, coffee in hand and leaning against a countertop, her legs crossed at the ankles in defiance. Normally at this time of night—or morning—Mika might be wearing one of his dress shirts, barefoot, with sleep or interest in her eyes. Tonight, she was in ripped blue jeans and an untucked white blouse. Her pageboy locks set off fiery blue eyes.

"You are late," she announced.

So—she hadn't cooled off as much as he had hoped. He let the plastic bag fall absently to the floor and said, "It took a little longer than I expected." He ran the faucet and drank with cupped hands.

Mika's gaze drifted to the plastic bag. "Your clothes, I assume?" she asked absently while biting into a sandwich. Her fake Southern accent faded with each syllable until her native Russian took over. Her blouse was open two buttons and showed enough to ignite Liam's interest, but he was smart enough to not even try. Not right now. She was still clicking.

"I'll burn them in the morning," he said. "It's a shame. I love Armani. Did you put your equipment in the safe room?"

She only nodded, then stared at her toes.

Approaching her as a zookeeper might a lioness, he gently took her hand and guided the sandwich to his lips, took a small bite, and when he received no blows to the head, he took another one. She turned away, but he wrapped his arms around her from behind and held her until the tension melted and her rigid frame gave in. After a few beats, she turned, putting her arms around his waist.

"You need to relax," Liam said, his chin tapping the top of her head as he spoke.

"I will. If you tell me you are finished with this madness. The NEST is empty."

"No. There are three more," Liam said. "But I know who Owl is now. It's Rufus Carmichael."

She pulled away, searched his eyes, then raised her hand and bit into her sandwich just as Liam tried to kiss her. She turned away, swallowed, almost choking, and mumbled, "Your timing is so bad, as usual." Her Russian accent was thicker now and made worse by the chewing of her sandwich.

He went to kiss her again and found the trace of a tear on her cheek. He touched it, and she turned away, taking her crumb-filled plate with her to the sink. There she stood, absently rinsing and staring through the kitchen window into the night. She pulled the drapes closed as Liam sidled up behind her. He pressed himself against her, wrapped his arms around her waist, and held her tight in hopes of a moment, but it was killed when the phone on the wall chimed. They both eyed the phone, then the clock on the stove, then the phone, and Liam felt her go rigid again.

"I've let her go. Why can't you?"

"Because she hasn't!" Mika barked. After a breath, she said, "It took the communists ripping me away from my you and our family and turning me into a Vympel to make *me* forget. But now, after all these years, we've found each other."

*Actually, you found me,* Liam thought.

Mika said, "We are all the family each other has left now."

*Not entirely accurate,* Liam thought again, then said—nothing.

The phone rang. Again, they ignored it. The caller gave up, but not before twelve rings.

Their eyes met. Hers burned with fury. His—fell away.

"It is her," she said. "Who else would call you at this time of night?"

"Morning," he corrected. "Maybe it's for you."

"You are my only friend," Mika said.

"I didn't answer the call."

"But you wanted to."

Mika was right. He had wanted to answer it, but not for the reason she suspected. "It's over and you know it is."

"For you, maybe," she said, spinning away and leaving him alone in the kitchen.

Liam followed her upstairs to the bedroom, where she had disappeared into the master bath. In the closet, he shed sneakers, a T-shirt, jeans, and socks. He listened to her run through her nightly rituals as he made his way to the bed, where he threw back the covers and fluffed the pillows. "Let me ask you something," he called out.

"No!" she yelled from the bathroom.

*Fine,* he thought, then changed the television to CNN and watched the breaking news with closed captions before turning it off. A minute later, Mika came out of the bathroom, switched off the lights, peeled back the covers, and dove in, pulling the sheets to her chin.

Liam reached for her, but she rolled away. "Can we get back to normal now?"

She chuckled. "When were we ever normal? That is why we belong together."

"Well, sis, you know how I love challenges. I've never been beaten. I think I'm somehow touched. You know—lucky."

Mika said, "We make our own luck."

"You saw that on a bumper sticker," Liam joked. "Can we change the subject?" He stroked her cheek. "We have a lot of catching up to do. Fifteen years of it. A lot of time to forget. The rest of our lives to make new memories. We have…" He kissed her neck. "Years…" He kissed an ear. "To make up." His hand traced her hips, then across her shivering abs. He said, "I'll teach you how to fish—sis."

"Stop it! Do not call me *sis*." Mika clung to his arms and closed her eyes while he kissed her cheek. "Your father and my mother were once married when we were very young. That does not make us brother and sister. That is—gross."

Liam chuckled, then felt a little guilty about his ongoing incestuous joke. "I'm sorry. I thought it was funny."

The phone rang. Ten times. Again, it was ignored. Liam waited for Mika to go cold again, but she didn't. Instead, she turned to him and they kissed. They made love, then lay in sweaty sheets.

*So much for her getting some sleep before driving in the morning,* he thought.

For several minutes, they lay still together, completely spent. Liam let his eyes drift to the clock. He had a field to mow in the morning but felt somehow exhilarated. He realized he could probably go again as he felt her kiss his forearm, her nails digging into the flesh. Punishment for something then, now, or yet to come.

She whispered, "The phone call was from *her*. The number

is also on your cell phone's display. She has been calling all night—and yesterday. If I am to now live here, I wish to avoid any—complications."

"She probably saw my headlights from her house when I pulled in," Liam said.

"The number is her cell phone."

Liam's eyes opened wide as he wondered exactly how Mika knew his ex-lover and neighbor's private number. But it wasn't a big stretch. Mika was the smartest person he knew. Which made her sexy *and* terrifying. "She's selling her house and moving, for shit's sake. Probably disconnected the home phone."

"Then her security system would not work," Mika said.

*Dammit*, he thought. He had a great mind for details, but hers was on steroids. His fingers splayed through her hair until he felt her eyes close again. It was time to lighten the mood, so he pulled tight against her again and asked, "And what if I were still seeing her?" He bit her earlobe playfully.

"Why don't you go to sleep and find out?" She waited for another beat, then said, "I do not believe you are a bad man. You have—demons. Lots of them. We both do. But yours are different. I chose mine. Yours, they come to you in the night, trying to get out. But you hold them in. Perhaps you cherish them. Maybe you believe the little girl is part of you."

"Change the subject," Liam said. This time, he turned away and gazed at the faint light spilling in from beneath the bedroom door. But Mika wouldn't let it go.

She rolled over and wrapped him up. Her chin rested on his shoulder. "Sometimes, I lay awake and listen to you dream. Mostly, it is only murmurs, but I already know the story. It's the little girl. Sometimes I want to wake you, but then I think you should let them play out. Maybe if you told me everything that happened in Baghdad two years ago, it would help."

"It won't," Liam said.

Again, the phone rang.

He said, "Let it go, Mika," then a tear hit his shoulder. "You're the cold one, remember?"

"I used to think so, but after working with you—I would not wish you to be my enemy." She pulled him over onto his back, then melted onto him until he came alive again. Afterward, they spooned like panting puzzle pieces until she tugged on his ponytail. "This must go."

"I kind of like it," Liam said. "Don't I remind you of a Russian gangster?"

"You watch too much television."

He draped his arm over her, and she squeezed as if hanging on in a storm. That was what they were—a storm. Two fronts merging into a tornado. When Mika showed up at his door almost a year ago, neither of them had ever expected to see the other again. Mika had thought Liam was dead, and Liam had wanted to keep it that way. But fate had a sense of humor, and in this case, fate had a name—Ginny Woodburn. Had she sent Mika to him to circumvent his vendetta with the NEST? Or to help him? The jury was still out. One thing was for certain: their relationship had always been one of youthful and blind passion (they were but teenagers back then), and now it needed nurturing and easing into. Like a swimmer entering a pool.

Liam let Mika drift off to catch at least a couple hours of sleep before her flight. He wanted to believe his insomnia was from the guilt of knowing she had made love to him tonight more as a favor than out of love. In truth, it was the animal passion of two people who doubted their tomorrows. But it wasn't the source of his insomnia. That came from the fear of sleep. The fear of dreams. The fear of watching a little girl die over and over and over again.

Finally, he drifted off. And at 5:31 a.m., the phone rang again for the last time… Liam never stirred.

# CHAPTER 5

---

Princeton, West Virginia
Same Day
8:12 a.m.

Liam awoke that morning with a start, in a film of sweat. He couldn't recall the dream, but he was certain it had been the bad one. He rose to one elbow, and even before rolling over, he knew he would be alone. The bed felt all wrong. It was higher on one side and cold to the touch. He started to worry that if he noticed such things, it could signal some growing dependency he couldn't afford. Those feelings came with expectations. And—at least for him—expectations were the seed of disappointment. When he finally opened his eyes, it was confirmed. Mika was gone.

There was no urgency to get up. No longing to trek downstairs to find her in the kitchen, scantily clad, making coffee and struggling to understand the American news media and his fascination with guitars and rock and roll. She was a stranger in a strange land but, in many ways, more comfortable than himself.

Liam was born in Enniskillen, Northern Ireland, but called America home. Mika was Russian and knew no home. She kept a few sweatshirts, three pairs of jeans, two rarely worn dresses, shoes, sneakers, panties, blouses, and socks in a drawer in the guest room. But, in the end, Mika didn't live here. Not really. Mika Gubina—or Casey Conner, as she was known on her passport and Georgia driver's license—lived nowhere and everywhere at the same time.

Liam checked the caller ID on the house phone and found that Lacey had called him again at 5:31 a.m. The call had come from her home phone this time, so once again, Mika was right.

In the kitchen, Liam absently flipped the switch on the coffee maker, then glanced toward the stove's digital clock to check the time. But a hundred-dollar bill had been taped over it. He peeled it away, spinning the bill onto the counter. A Post-it note read:

I pray I never win this bet. But I came close this time.

*What's that supposed to mean?* he thought. Mika was always betting he would one day get himself killed taking vengeance on the NEST, but she had yet to win. The problem with their running bet was, if he ever lost, she couldn't collect. Mika was an atheist, so he also found her use of the word *pray* amusing as he wadded up the note and dropped it in the trash.

For a farmer, the day was hours old. But Liam wasn't a real farmer. In southern West Virginia, though a person may own six hundred acres, the amount of land available for farming was less than a third. And should his land miraculously flatten, Liam had little interest in raising cattle or corn. Instead, he let three hundred acres of the forest grow wild for hunting deer and turkey. He kept ten acres for the homestead, then leased the rest to a man who knew the difference between a Barzona and Brangus. Cows and goats and horses roamed freely over fifty acres of the fenced-in property, with two hundred acres offering up soybeans and alfalfa. The remaining forty were left to hay, which Liam enjoyed cutting, raking, and bailing for his tenant. It was good exercise, and it kept him young. And distracted.

Today was Saturday, and Liam had made a promise to his tenant that he would mow the alfalfa field by the time he returned several days from now. But first, he had a call to make.

After dialing the eleven digits from memory, Liam listened to the odd ringtone for three cycles until a familiar and friendly voice answered in Greek. After a few pleasantries with the caretaker of his Lapta home, in a language Liam could pass with a B+, he told Marissa to expect Casey in the next few hours.

"Yes, Mr. Curran," Marissa said. "I have spoken with Miss Conner.

I am preparing the home for her. I assumed it would be okay."

"It's fine," Liam said. "But I need a favor. Could you let me know when she arrives? And please don't tell her I called. You know how she is about me fussing."

"Yes, I know."

Liam ended the call, and then, after a quick splash of water to his face, he dressed, then went to where he had dropped the plastic bag the night before. He found the bag empty and the clothes in a pile on the floor, except now, the pile was larger. Before leaving, Mika had added hers to the pile.

*She's always thinking.*

After stuffing the clothes into the bag, he made his way outside, where he took in a lungful of nature's fragrance. Cows and horses and sheep. He gazed across the field to the left as a whinny echoed and two horses raced by. One brown with a white star on its forehead and the other solid black. They were new.

*Shipman's been busy. I can't wait to see what he brings back from Oklahoma City.*

In the middle of the fading garden was a rusted barrel, and Liam dropped in several pieces of wood and kindling, then lit the pile. After it caught, he threw in the plastic bag, then drew in another satisfying breath before starting back to the house, when something near the pole barn caught his eye. It was blue with some red, whatever it was, so Liam detoured in that direction and found a soiled Los Angeles Dodgers baseball cap. Shipman must have dropped it when he was unloading the new horses.

Liam picked up the cap and stuffed it in the pocket of his overalls, then continued to the garage and retrieved the pistol and the Uzi he had taken with him to Toledo. In the kitchen, behind a set of louvered doors masquerading as a pantry, he punched a code into a keypad, spun the lock, then pushed open a second two-inch-thick steel door and stepped inside. The lights were automatic.

Liam referred to the area as his safe room, not because it was a place he would instinctively run to for protection—though it did have separate power and air-handling systems complete with backup food and water—but because it housed multiple stand-alone gun safes that held rifles, pistols, ammunition, and important documents on one side and communications equipment and his security system on the other. It was the one part of the property he had not paid for on his own but had been provided by his other employer. Liam found Mika's pistol and rifle on the workbench, and he placed his own beside them, reminding himself to return later to clean them and store them. Then, he spun the dial on the wall safe, opened it, placed the digital recorder inside, then locked it.

Afterward, he went back to the field of alfalfa and clover, where he waded through, letting the buds at the top of the grasses massage the bottoms of his outstretched hands. He examined one. Flowering had not quite begun. Then he checked the skies. Bright and blue.

After an hour of bouncing in the seat of the John Deere, he'd finished cutting the first two rows and had started on the third when he noticed the two cars in Lacey Sullivan's driveway. Her blue Audi A4 had been parked by the closed garage door, and her housekeeper's Volkswagen Rabbit was parked directly behind the Audi. Now might be a good time to walk up the hill and talk to Lacey and offer a worthless excuse for not calling her back last night, but his hopes were dashed when a third car topped the distant hill in a hurry, its tires briefly leaving the pavement. When it reached Lacey's driveway, it squealed sharply into the turn, then skidded to a stop behind the Volkswagen. It might be a Pontiac.

Two men in sport coats leapt out and immediately drew pistols. One man, slender and Black, disappeared behind the house, while the heftier white guy stayed in the driveway crouched behind the trunk of the car.

Shifting the tractor into neutral and turning off the blades,

Liam leaned on the steering wheel and watched the event unfold. After several minutes, a parade of emergency vehicles approached, topping the opposite hill, then briefly disappearing as the road dove into the draw only to reappear on the far side. They climbed the hill again until every emergency vehicle pulled into Lacey's driveway, where the white guy was still crouching and the thin Black man was sprinting from the back of the house. One hand was waving a wallet in the air, while the other was clumsily holstering a pistol. Cops in uniform spilled out, while the rescue workers stayed near the road.

*Oh shit! Now what?*

The dust cloud thickened on the ridge—so much so that the flashing lights appeared as crimson and blue heat lightning dancing between low clouds. A few moments later, the dust thinned and the lights were back. And even from this distance, he could make out a short, stout, and frantic Hispanic woman racing from the home toward the open arms of a crouching cop—whose gun was drawn. A knot rose from his stomach, and he swallowed it.

Leaping off the tractor, Liam raced into his house and to the safe room, where he retrieved a Nikon spotting scope. He took it upstairs to the spare bedroom and the window facing Lacey's place. He set the scope on a tripod, then quickly zeroed in on Lacey's place.

First, he zoomed in on Lacey's housekeeper, Louisa Perdomo. Wrapped in a blanket and sobbing, she was being led away by a female deputy while a swarm of state and county cops with pistols and shotguns poured into the house through every crevice available. A boot pushed in the front door as the side French doors leading from the deck to the dining room were smashed open. More cops disappeared around the back of the house.

Liam eased the window open and listened for the telltale pinging of gunfire and booming shotguns. But all was quiet. He blinked away the eyestrain, then went back to the Nikon as cops left the house. Guns holstered. Solemn expressions. A cop in a suit spoke into a walkie-talkie as he started toward a brown unmarked car with a bubble light on the dash. The light extinguished.

Louisa had been escorted to the farthest county squad car, where she sat in the back seat. Still sobbing, it appeared. A cop spoke to her, and her expression changed to one of horror. She rolled out of the back seat and bolted across the driveway as four men in white pajamas guided two gurneys out of the house, black cargo straps cinched tight across lumps beneath the sheets. A female rescue squad worker was hot on Louisa's heels and caught up with her before she reached the gurneys. Men in suits and uniforms waved arms and pointed in every which way, first toward the woods, then toward Lacey's house, then at the two screaming ambulances, the sky, the fields, and then—they pointed toward his house.

# CHAPTER 6

Princeton, West Virginia
Same Day

Liam pressed against the eyepiece as one of the suited cops was turning to another cop and pointing. He said something to another cop in uniform, then climbed into the driver's seat of the unmarked car he had arrived in. The two cops who had arrived first got in their car, and they backed out of Lacey's driveway.

*Shit! I'm about to get some company.* But he couldn't stop the thought that followed, and the chill hit him hard. *What time had Mika left for the airport this morning?*

The cops wasted no time in getting to Liam's gate. As he rounded the corner of the house, he spotted a cop leaning out the window and stretching for the intercom button. Liam took the remote from his pocket and opened the gate. A minute later, both cars had parked at the top of his driveway.

Liam thrust his hands deep into the pockets of his faded overalls as he lumbered slowly and purposefully toward the car. After all, he was a farmer-professor. He raised a hand in a country welcome. The skinny black cop raised one in return, then closed the front passenger door of the car Liam now realized was not an official police car. The heavier white cop, who had been driving, ignored Liam completely, opting instead to investigate his surroundings. Inside the unmarked police cruiser (complete with a flasher on the dash), the driver was working the radio mic button. Liam thought he might be running the license plates on the rusted pickup parked in front of the pole barn. The driver returned the mic to its clip, slammed the door, then caught up with the other two.

"Good morning," the skinny black cop called out in a warm tone as he unbuttoned his weathered blue sport coat. He raised a hand, exposing the sidearm nestled in a black holster fixed to a wide brown leather belt. A Smith & Wesson .357 revolver. Old school. Effective. This man was a veteran who used brains over brawn. But when he needed it—there was lots of brawn.

"Howdy," Liam said, stopping in the shade beneath the giant elm. He removed the red bandana from his head and wiped the sweat away as he eyed the activity at Lacey's. "Not such a good morning for some folks, I guess." His gaze dropped to the heavier, younger white cop, who had focused his attention on Liam. He was at least six five, coming in about 240, Liam guessed. His fresh-from-the-rack blue sport coat hung over beige trousers and a blue shirt. He wore brown shoes that were not high quality but not cheap either. And he wasn't a real cop. If he were, the soles of his shoes would be rubber and not leather.

The cop who had worked the radio caught up and had his ID and shield thrust forward. He was Detective Sergeant Wallace Taconelli with the West Virginia State Police. Taconelli wore jeans and a polo shirt. His sidearm bulged from his belt like a tumor. Glock, 9 mm semiautomatic. Taconelli returned the ID to his pocket, then held out his hand. Liam shook it and felt a strong, noncommittal grip.

"Mr. Shipman, I am Detective Taconelli with homicide. I'd like to ask you a couple questions—if you have a minute."

*Mr. Shipman?* Liam suppressed a smile, then let an eyebrow rise and fall. He waited for an introduction to the other two men, but it didn't come. Liam asked, "Something happen at the Sullivans'?"

"A shooting," Taconelli said. "A man and a woman."

"A man *and* a woman," Liam repeated.

As the younger man went for his notebook tucked into a back pocket, his sport coat shifted and Liam caught sight of his weapon.

A .40 caliber Beretta. Its wider grip accommodated a double-stacked clip. Twelve rounds. Volume over accuracy. Almost as common to cops as donuts. "How well did you know the Sullivans and—?"

"Please. Let me handle this," Taconelli interrupted. "My apologies. This is Agent Eugene DeVine and his partner, Agent Charles Gillespie."

"Agents?" Liam repeated.

The skinny black man said, "I'm Agent DeVine, but you can call me Bo." He flashed his badge. His partner did as well. Both IDs were identical, except for the names. Liam had been right. They were not cops. They were with the Immigration and Naturalization Service out of Chicago.

Liam shook DeVine's hand, trying hard not to let his grip reveal his coming anger. "Was the female victim short, five two, five three, slender, with jet-black hair? In shape? Like a runner? Dark-skinned?" He then paused as he eyed DeVine with some curiosity before finishing with, "Dark like—Pocahontas." When DeVine nodded slowly, Liam said, "Lacey Sullivan." Liam's eyes closed slowly, involuntarily, then clenched tight as memories of him and Lacey beneath this very elm flashed in his head. A dry lump formed in his throat as his soul prepared to experience the loss. But not right now.

"Yes," Taconelli said.

Liam then asked, "Was the guy about five ten? Surfer-blonde hair swept to the side? Professional? Most likely wearing Bermuda shorts and a golf shirt with the collar turned up."

Taconelli said, "Not even close."

"I just described Lacey's ex-husband, Scott Sullivan. But I don't see his Mercedes. The Audi is Lacey's."

"Perhaps Mr. Sullivan's car is in the garage," Taconelli said.

Liam replied, "The garage is full of boxes. Lacey was moving back to DC."

"But the maid said they were divorced," Taconelli said.

"That's true. But who can figure out women?" Liam said but knew damn well that Lacey was moving back because Mika had moved in.

Agent Gillespie glanced toward the Sullivan house on the hill. "Do you folks travel in the same circle?"

"The Sullivans are wealthy attorneys. Both lobbyists. He's involved with pharmaceuticals, and she does immigration. And I don't have a circle," Liam said. "I have a dot."

"Do you know who Miss Sullivan worked for?" Gillespie asked.

*Worked,* Liam repeated the past tense verb in his mind, then said, "Some firm in California. But her office was in DC near the big white buildings."

"Castille, Huerto, and Sullivan," DeVine said, gauging Liam's reaction. "She's one of the partners." He paused, clearly studying Liam's reaction.

"Who was the male?" Liam asked.

"I can't say yet," Taconelli said, taking over. At first, he asked mostly canned questions: Name, work, hobbies, notice any strangers around? He came off as professional and most certainly had a competent staff somewhere who would eventually look into Liam's background. Still, beneath the surface, Liam sensed that being nice was an effort for Taconelli. He had an edge about him and an unseen leash.

"My name isn't Shipman," Liam said. "It's Liam Curran. I guess you ran the plates on the old truck. It's his. Bill Shipman leases my property for his livestock."

Taconelli made a note. "Where is Mr. Shipman now?"

"Oklahoma City. I don't expect him back for several more days."

"Thank you for that," Taconelli said and made another note. Then came the first hard question. "Where were you between three o'clock this morning and now?"

"Asleep," he said, then thought, *Most of the time.*

Liam was relieved Taconelli chose that particular time frame, because if he'd gone much earlier, he would have had to lie about his whereabouts.

"Something the matter, Mr. Curran?" Taconelli asked.

Liam said, "Other than my neighbor being murdered?"

Taconelli nodded, then changed the subject. "The maid said you live with a woman."

"That's right," Liam said.

"What's her name? For the record."

Liam said, "Casey Conner."

Taconelli sounded out the spelling, and Liam confirmed it. He then asked, "Is Casey her given name or a nickname?"

Liam said, "It's her given name," then thought, *But given by someone else.*

"Where is Miss Conner now?"

"Out of the country. She left early this morning on a business trip."

"About what time?"

*Something I'd like to know too,* Liam thought, but said, "About six thirty this morning."

"I see." Then Taconelli asked, "And when will she return?"

"I'm not sure."

Taconelli eyed Liam suspiciously, made a note, then changed course. "Were you and Ms. Sullivan close?"

"Just neighbors."

"Do you know anyone who would want to harm her?"

Liam shook his head. "No. Not Lacey. At least not here. I don't know about DC."

"She has a home there too?" Taconelli prodded.

Liam said, "Yes. The place next door was mostly for weekends."

Taconelli scribbled as he asked, "Is her place in DC nice?"

Inside, Liam chuckled at the baited question, but he answered with a lie: "I couldn't tell you."

"Are you friends with her ex-husband?" Taconelli asked.

"I've spoken to him twice." Liam pointed toward the fence. "Mind if I ask you something?"

"Sure," Taconelli said as he wrote.

Liam asked, "What time did the nine-one-one call go out?"

Taconelli stopped scribbling, then flipped his notes. "Nine twenty-two this morning. The maid, Miss Louisa Perdomo, called it in. Why do you ask?"

"Curiosity. I wasn't aware Louisa was supposed to work today."

"Are you normally privy to her schedule?"

Liam said, "No. But Lacey told me she was cutting Louisa to one day a week and never on the weekends. Mostly, she comes in to keep the place realtor friendly. Have you checked the security system?"

"We can't get into it," Taconelli said as he wrote.

Liam said, "If the dead man wasn't Scott Sullivan, any idea who he was?"

This time, Agent DeVine spoke up. "I believe a Mexican named Gerardo Lopez?"

Liam's brow furrowed. "A Mexican? Illegal?"

Taconelli said, "We can't confirm the identity. It's John Doe for now." He paused, then added, "I'll need to check, but do you know if there was a restraining order against Mr. Sullivan?"

"No," Liam said. He knew Taconelli wanted to control the questioning, but it was time to throw a wrench into the process. The elephant in the yard was begging to be called out. He turned to DeVine and Gillespie and said, "You guys came from Chicago looking for an illegal, and you stumbled into a double murder. Hell of a morning."

Gillespie started to reply, but DeVine jumped in first. "We are here looking for two illegals. Angel and Gerardo Lopez. Brothers, we think." Taconelli cleared his throat, but DeVine continued. "I'm fairly sure the deceased male was Gerardo."

Liam asked, "You think Angel killed Lacey Sullivan and his own brother, then took off?"

After a deep sigh, Taconelli said, "Right now, we have a dead attorney named Lacey Sullivan, a dead Latino man with no ID, and no murder weapons at the scene. That's all we know for sure at this point." Taconelli put a period by his last note before turning tired eyes upward.

Liam suspected the detective didn't want to be here. The 911 call must have taken him away from something important on a Saturday. He wasn't wearing a wedding band, but he seemed to be in a hurry to leave—and Liam wasn't satisfied yet.

DeVine had effectively diverted Liam's question, but he couldn't let it go. "Why is INS chasing illegals in West Virginia?" Taconelli also turned to the two INS agents, a question mark wrinkling his forehead.

"That's our job," Gillespie answered.

"Oh. Are you a federal marshal too?" Liam asked. "My bad."

Taconelli sidestepped the comment, then took over the questioning. "Tell me about the Sullivans."

"Like I said, I've only spoken to Scott twice, and the guy's a jerk. But that's me," Liam said. "He's a few years older than Lacey and came from big money in Connecticut. Lacey grew up here—poor. Seriously poor. They met at Harvard."

"But you said she was poor," Gillespie said.

"Poor doesn't mean stupid. I think it's where the riff was in the marriage. According to Lacey, Scott was at Harvard because of family connections. She was there because she was brilliant. Scott graduated at the time Lacey was starting and went to work for a high-powered firm in DC. Lacey graduated a few years later and worked for a small firm in Virginia. Then, she was headhunted by—whatever firm she's with now—and they made her a partner quickly. Scott didn't make partner in his firm until several years after Lacey." He paused, then added, "That's all I know."

Gillespie started to speak, but Liam interrupted him. "If you're INS, why do you sound like homicide detectives?"

DeVine said, "INS is not as interested in Lacey Sullivan's death as we are in finding Angel Lopez."

"You were here, looking for an illegal," Liam said. "But not for murdering Lacey Sullivan. What did the illegals do worthy of a chase? Because I have to tell you, a Mexican would stand out like a zit on a supermodel in Princeton."

"Do you know if Ms. Sullivan might have owned a .40 caliber handgun?" Gillespie asked.

Curran pursed his lips and shook his head. "So, Lacey was murdered with a .40 caliber?"

Taconelli jumped back in. "We have to wait on ballistics. Did you happen to hear anything at all?"

Liam shook his head, but thought, *Unless you count my telephone, which I never answered.*

Taconelli jotted something down, then asked, "What is it you do, Mr. Curran?"

"I'm a professor at the local college," Liam replied, then went back to Taconelli. "What did your illegals do, Agent DeVine?"

DeVine said, "We believe they crossed the border near Lukeville, Arizona, three days ago, where they killed a man and a child."

"They killed a child?" Liam felt his hands begin to sweat with the pounding in his head.

DeVine said, "An infant girl. Less than a year old, I guess."

"Damn!" Liam said, his teeth grinding. Then, he asked, "Let me get this straight. Two illegals ran from Arizona to West Virginia to hide out with the good ole boys? Doesn't make much sense unless Lacey Sullivan was a target."

DeVine said nothing.

Liam said, "And you guys were sitting in Chicago, drinking your lattes, trying to figure out where your two murderers from Arizona had run to, threw a dart at a map, and hit Princeton.

And, luckily, you were the first on the scene of another murder, where one missing immigrant killed Lacey and his own brother. Seems like bullshit to me." He turned to Gillespie. "What do you think, Chuck?"

"My name is Charles, but you can call me Agent Gillespie," he said. "Or, as Bo likes to call me from time to time, Chaz. Do you have anything other than sarcasm that could help us, Mr. Curran?"

"No. Sorry," Liam said.

Taconelli had turned away. "That's a nice pole barn. What's in there?"

"A workshop. Wood. RV. Farm equipment. Animal stalls."

"Anything else you can tell us?" DeVine asked as he held out his business card.

Liam took it, then shook his head. "Nothing I can think of, but I'll keep my eyes peeled for a wandering Mexican." He exchanged an uneasy moment with DeVine, who eventually blinked and turned to leave.

"Thank you," DeVine said over his shoulder, but Gillespie glared at Liam before turning to follow DeVine.

"Sorry to have bothered you, Mr. Curran," Taconelli said. "I'll probably have some follow-up questions. Will you be around the next few days?"

"I think so," Liam said. "I'll help out any way I can." He followed Taconelli back to the unmarked. Gillespie climbed in the back. DeVine was in the front passenger seat, and Taconelli sat behind the wheel and fired up the engine.

Liam put his hands on the open passenger window and squatted until he was slightly lower than DeVine's concerned eyes. Liam said, "You know, Agent DeVine, this morning, you and Chaz showed up in your rental car. I'm guessing you got it from the airport. BLF won't take large planes, so you must have taken the INS jet or a prop job from Chicago. I'm not sure what time you landed, but it was early enough to put you at Lacey's house ahead of the cops."

Taconelli dropped the car into reverse but held the brake, paying particular attention to the conversation. "What are you getting at?" he asked.

Liam addressed Taconelli directly and said, "Bo and Chaz here came from the opposite direction as you and the EMS teams. When Bo and Chaz got out of the car, their guns were drawn, meaning they already knew something was wrong. Bo went around back and left Chaz to hold down the front. A few minutes later, Bo returned just as your team arrived. You had to check their IDs, meaning you didn't know them."

Taconelli let out a sigh as he tapped the brake, but Liam didn't move. His fingers gripped the window frame, his eyes never leaving DeVine. The man was holding something back. Something he didn't want to say in front of Taconelli.

Liam locked eyes with DeVine. "How did you know—Bo?"

DeVine didn't answer and set his jaw in defiance while Gillespie glared at Liam from the back seat. He started to speak, but DeVine silenced him with a raised hand.

"What are you insinuating?" Taconelli asked.

Liam only smiled, then said, "Nothing at all."

Taconelli eased the car backward as DeVine held Liam's gaze. At the bottom of the driveway, Gillespie made a dramatic show of getting out and checking the contents of Liam's mailbox. Liam shook his head, then waved as the agent returned the scant pieces of mail to the box, then continued back to Lacey's. Liam watched them park the car in the same spot, then blend in with the other suits and techs. Only then did Liam turn away to let the moment catch up.

The accusation had never come up, but Lacey had certainly been more than a neighbor to swap recipes with, which could complicate matters. A hundred questions raced in his mind, but a few floated to the top: What the hell happened, and did it have anything to do with Toledo? Or, had something else from his storied past caught up with him? Even worse, could Mika have been involved?

The sun was high and in full force. It was just after eleven o'clock and already hot. Liam, trying to put the murders in the back of his mind, climbed onto the John Deere and started the mower as the two ambulances carrying Lacey Sullivan and a dead Mexican disappeared over the hill.

He stopped the tractor, then lay his head against the steering wheel as his mind struggled with something he had to find the answer to: *How did Bo DeVine know?*

# CHAPTER 7

Liam forced himself to finish mowing. With each pass of the tractor, a new car arrived next door and a new forensic team was sent buzzing around Lacey's, getting closer and closer to his property, searching for clues and evidence, all while the murders and more questions ate at him. But there was one question he could answer on his own. One he had been avoiding—the Mika question.

After showering and eating a late lunch, he went to the safe room, hung the Dodgers cap on a nail, then booted up the computer system. He typed, clicked the mouse, and brought the security system log up first.

Every room in his house had a motion detector, and every window and every door had a sensor—constantly alert and recording. Only when the system was armed did it send out an alarm. But while most systems notified a monitoring company, Liam's system notified—him.

He brought up the log from earlier that morning and found no alarms after he and Mika had gone to bed. The first indication of any movement came at 5:45 a.m., triggered by the motion detector in the master bedroom. Mika was awake. The screen showed the activity.

5:45 A.M. MASTER BED MD

6:05 A.M. UPSTAIRS HALL MD

6:07 A.M. GUEST BR 1 MD

6:12 A.M. UPSTAIRS HALL MD

6:13 A.M. FOYER MD

6:13 A.M. DEN MD

6:13 A.M. LIBRARY MD

6:13 A.M. KITCHEN MD

6:35 A.M. MUDROOM BD

6:36 A.M. MUDROOM DOOR OPEN

6:36 A.M. SYSTEM PAUSED BY CASEY

6:36 A.M. MUDROOM DOOR CLOSED

6:37 A.M. GARAGE MD

6:38 A.M. GARAGE DOOR 3 OPEN

6:38 A.M. TURNAROUND MD

6:38 A.M. GARAGE DOOR 3 CLOSED

6:39 A.M. GATE OPEN

6:40 A.M. GATE CLOSED

Liam let go of a long sigh. Mika had awoken at 5:45 a.m., tooled around the house to gather her things, then spent most of her time in the kitchen before she left the house at 6:36 a.m., the garage at 6:38 a.m., and the property at 6:39 a.m. There it was, bigger than life—Mika had not left the bedroom before 5:45 a.m. or the house before 6:37 a.m. Mika couldn't have killed Lacey and still made her flight out of Roanoke, a ninety-minute drive at least. Now, all he had to do was confirm she made the flight.

He called the airline, but they would neither confirm nor deny the boarding status of Casey Connor. It was against their policy. But they did confirm the flight had left Roanoke on time and had landed at LaGuardia ten minutes early. They also confirmed for him that her flight to Cyprus had left on time. Liam thanked the woman and hung up, then stared at the telephone, wondering if he should make the hardest call.

For sanity's sake, Mika should be having her complimentary in-flight lunch by now and know nothing of Lacey's murder, which would make it pointless to call her cell phone. But, if she picked up, she could answer from anywhere, and Liam would be worse off than when he started. She'd eventually find out about the murder, then surmise he had called to check on her out of suspicion. His best play was to let the flights play out and leverage a friend for assistance.

The flight from Roanoke to LaGuardia had left at 8:55 a.m. The only flight from LaGuardia to Cyprus was scheduled for 12:20 p.m. If Mika had made the flight to Cyprus, there was no way she could have been involved in Lacey's murder. Liam had taken those same flights before, and the flight to Cyprus would arrive around 6:30 a.m., Cyprus time. Mika would rent a car, then drive the rest of the way to his villa in Lapta, and that would take at least an hour. Mika should arrive at the villa by 8:00 a.m., Lapta time, which was 1:00 a.m., Sunday-morning Princeton time.

Now, he had some time to kill.

With nothing to do now but wait, he decided to venture into Princeton for his weekly attempt to expand his dot of friends and meet a few of his fellow professors from the college at the local watering hole. Their modus operandi had always been to arrive early and leave by 8:30 p.m. before the dance floor was unfolded and the DJ started up his electronic jerk tracks. He was home by 9:15 p.m. with his Gibson Les Paul strapped on and an amp cranked.

He was in bed by 11:45, where he lay with the television on, gazing at the ceiling and checking the clock, willing time to pass. When the clock finally hit 1:00 a.m., he threw off the covers and rolled into a sitting position. After snatching the cordless phone from the nightstand, he let an angry finger pound *011357*, then the remaining eight digits, and the sweet Greek accent of Marissa Welsh answered after three rings. Mercifully, she confirmed that Mika had indeed arrived safely ten minutes earlier. No way around it—Mika must have made the 8:55 a.m. flight out of Roanoke. Only now did the notion of her involvement echo as absurd.

Liam thanked Marissa for her discretion, then hung up, knowing that, of all the people in his world not to trust, Mrs. Welsh wasn't one of them. She had been the live-in housekeeper since his mother was alive, and Liam considered her family. It was a sweet deal for Mrs. Welsh, as she kept up the home as if it were her own, and, in return, she received a salary from the estate and a free place to live overlooking the sea. At sixty-five, Liam hoped she still had a lot of living left to do.

After clicking off the call, he punched the pillow, rolled over, then pressed the buttons on the remote until the final minutes of an episode of *Cheers* came on, but he couldn't turn off his brain. Satisfied Mika was out of the picture, the likelihood Lacey had been the victim of a Latino criminal element, and not residue from his past, became more plausible.

As he closed his eyes, Lacey's face appeared. Not in a haze but more solid and condemning in a memory. An amazing, beautiful woman lying in bed next to him from the not-too-distant past. Here, in this bed. Her head resting on the same pillow that had held Mika's last night. Lacey's eyes were closed. Her lips were parted, tempting a taste. Glistening raven hair splayed out on the pillow like an explosion of ebony. She was at peace and safe. But she was lying next to him, and that had always proved to be risky. Had this time proved to be fatal?

Liam fisted his eyes and fought with the guilt. Was she one more innocent victim in the shambles doubling as his past? Neighbors and ex-lovers weren't murdered every day, so it couldn't just be a coincidence, and certainly not by a couple of illegals going on a murderous vacation in Appalachia. It had to be something from his past catching up to him. If it was, what was the tie? Arizona? Illegals? Lacey? Toledo? Iraq? Nothing seemed to fit.

*Damn it! Let it go, Curran!*

He sat up in bed, listening to the dark room taunt him with the faint brushing of the sheers as they battled the breeze. The window was open and crickets chirped. He left the bed and opened the

French doors leading to the wraparound balcony, then followed it to the far side of the house overlooking the driveway and the pole barn. He could see Lacey's place from here, and it was lit up as if a party were raging. Lights burned from every window broken by the shadows of passing forensic technicians. To the right, something caught his eye, and he turned to find a couple of men in the field, their flashlight beams sweeping the night. He gripped the railing as he watched in thought, wondering how Lacey's lobbying ties to Washington could lead to her death, but in the end, it had to tie back to Liam.

No, he decided. What would be the point of killing Lacey to get to him? Even if his past *had* caught up with him, if people had found Lacey, then they had found him. So why not kill him? And if killing Lacey was payback, its effects were benign if he wasn't aware of who did it. No. Lacey had gotten caught up in something completely unrelated to the gummy past stuck to the sole of his life. Had Lacey been bitten by the very vermin she tried to help? And if so, could he let it go? If he wanted to stay anonymous and live this life, he'd have to. Lacey had been murdered by DeVine's missing immigrant. He'd let the officials do their jobs, and he'd stay out of it.

Liam backed away from the railing, then caught his reflection in the glass of the second set of French doors leading to the guest bedroom. Mika's "mad room," as she liked to call it. The same room where Liam had set up his tripod and spotting scope earlier. Had Mika chosen this room *because* it faced Lacey's house? Was she even capable of killing over jealousy or passion? Wasn't that the antithesis of the Russian Spetsnaz and the Vympel code?

He raked fingers through his hair and whispered angrily to the night, "Christ, Curran! Mika didn't do it. Now you don't even believe yourself."

He went back to his bedroom, where *Cheers* had ended, replaced by *All in the Family* reruns. Liam surfed the channels as he let his mind drift to memories of Lacey Sullivan, and for the first time that day, he allowed himself to experience the emptiness from the loss. Yesterday, there had been a Lacey. Last night, there had been an annoying Lacey who wouldn't stop calling him. And now, he longed for it all to come back. And that's how he fell asleep.

. . .

At 5:52 a.m., Liam jolted awake, swimming in sweat-drenched sheets. His chest heaved and his heart palpitated as the recurring nightmare and the vision of a tiny Kurdish girl slowly faded. He couldn't recall much of it—this time—but it was so etched on his subconscious, it played like a perpetual horror movie in which he knew everyone's lines—even the extras'. From time to time, the lead-up to the final event was different in the dream, but in the end, Lilliana would always die.

"She's still here," he grunted, massaging his temples as if working a scar into healthy tissue. The television was on, and an infomercial played about knives that cut cans, then a workout machine pitched by a hot blonde supermodel and an actor-karate expert. The clock told him it was 5:52 a.m. and he still had some guiltless sack time coming. But something more than his nightmares was keeping him up—like noticing a clock in the room *after* it stopped ticking.

He tore the moist sheets from the bed and stuffed them into the laundry basket before heading downstairs. He fixed coffee, then headed to the safe room, where he fired up the computer and the camera system again. Surely, he had missed something else.

With eight cameras tiled as four squares on two monitors, he fast-forwarded through the videos, starting with the morning Lacey was murdered. He cycled forward to the time Mika backed out of the garage, but then he decided to go back further so he could ease the time forward in smaller increments in a detailed search for cause *and* effect. He started at 6:00 a.m., stepped forward, forward, forward, forward...

Finally, at 6:38 and ten seconds, Mika's Ford Explorer entered the frame of the camera covering the garage. At 6:38 and twenty seconds, she was looking over her shoulder, trying not to back into Shipman's truck. At 6:38 and thirty seconds, she was pulling forward. The next frame showed the rear of the Explorer and the taillights. Mika was leaving. Nothing was different than before. He then focused on the camera showing the field between his and Lacey's houses.

He cycled back to the time of Lacey's last call to him—5:31 a.m. A time he knew Lacey was still alive. Forward, forward, forward, his eyes scanning each frame. Dark, fuzzy shadows appeared in the uncut field he hadn't noticed the first time. At 5:45, a deer darted across and was gone in the next frame. There were horses and sheep and goats. Birds were everywhere, interrupted from their perches. Two of the horses had stopped, looking back to their right. What had they seen? Or heard? In the lower right of the frame were the top of Shipman's truck and trailer. Nothing unusual.

He went back to the pole-mounted camera looking toward the garage and the pole barn, then started the process over. Again, from 5:31, he stepped forward, forward, forward. He passed 5:45, 5:46, 5:47. Forward, forward, forward, but then, something at 5:51 a.m. caught his eye.

At the right-hand side of the pole barn, out of view of the camera, something had moved. It wasn't anything with mass but a tiny shift in light—a reflection from something else moving.

He backed up the video and stepped forward, forward, forward. Again, it was there. A smear of light across the doors of the three garage doors. The angle of the light told him it was being reflected off of something along the side of the pole barn out of view of the camera. But a reflection from what light source? It took a moment to realize the source was from the under-cabinet light in his kitchen shining through the window and reflecting. If the light from the kitchen was stationary, it meant something else had moved.

Liam turned off the computer, then locked up the safe room. He ran back upstairs, stepped out onto the balcony, and walked around to the side of the house overlooking the driveway, Shipman's truck and trailer, and the side of the pole barn the camera couldn't pick up. He examined the length of the pole barn from the back corner forward to the man door, the walkway, the corner, to Shipman's truck, and back. Nothing was out of place. But logic told him that, at 5:51, something must have moved. Then, he figured it out as his eyes settled on the steel man door and its window. The door opened outward and in direct line with the kitchen window. Then, he remembered the Dodgers cap had been lying nearby. He knew what had happened.

Liam raced downstairs to the safe room, chose a silenced Walther PPK from the pegboard, slipped on his sneakers, then stepped outside in the dew-covered yard.

# CHAPTER 8

North Canton, Ohio
Sunday, August 27, 1995
7:22 a.m.

A US Air Force C-20G Gulfstream IV passenger jet touched down at the Akron-Canton Airport, and the fourteen men and women who had boarded the shuttle an hour earlier in DC began fumbling for their belongings even before the jet disappeared inside the cavernous private hanger.

As thirteen passengers filtered from the plane, one stayed behind. His suit—Brooks Brothers. His shoes—Johnston & Murphy. His purpose—highly classified, and he smiled brightly at the flight attendant as she cleared peanut bags and plastic cups from the cabin. She took notice of his hesitation to leave the aircraft.

"We are returning to DC this evening. Will you be joining us, sir?" she asked, smiling at the pleasant face of the man who appeared boyishly confused.

"I'm not sure," Paul Kelvington said. He pursed his lips in thought, grabbed his leather bag, and started up the aisle. He stopped at the top of the airstairs and stared down at the concrete floor of the hangar—waiting until all the luggage from the belly of the plane had been unloaded, the attendant behind him mentally urging him forward. As he descended the stairs, one of the other passengers glanced at him, pausing long enough to form a question but not long enough to ask it. Paul ignored the man as he touched the hangar floor, turning to the left, while the others went right toward the main terminal.

HeirJet, a private charter firm owned by a German immigrant, occupied offices in the front of the hangar. Paul found the receptionist, who, after a brief conversation, passed him a set of car keys she had pulled from an expandable file. He smiled and thanked her again before leaving, found his Ford Taurus, and proceeded to I-77, then north toward Cleveland.

After settling into the drive, he dialed his cell phone. The one number he could remember was his most frequently dialed number, and any tech-savvy person would have consigned the number to a speed-dial button. But then again, most numbers didn't terminate in the blazer pocket of Patricia Woodburn, the White House chief of staff.

"You made it," Woody said after picking up on the first ring. "Where are you now?"

"Just south of Akron. In an hour, I'll get to the FBI field office. Did you make the call?"

"Connie did. Contact Agent Ron Johnson." There was a long pause as thoughts nibbled at the time. Woody finally added, "Rit told me the FBI is releasing him later today."

"You're joking! This man is the chief of security for a *known* terrorist with ties to Islamic terror organizations."

"So do a handful of mosques in this country."

"Whatever! They can't let that kind of intel go."

"Paul. Before you go in with accusations flying, we have to come to terms with facts. Ibrahim Nassar didn't break any laws and *does* have functional immunity. The fact he's still in custody is going to come back to bite us in the ass. Plus, he was the sheik's chief of security, whose entire team was slaughtered on our soil. You also need to remember Manchin and I lobbied for the sheik's visa. And the sheik was not only a billionaire Turkish art dealer but also the cousin of the king of Jordan." Then, under her breath, she added, "He's going home. The FBI has no grounds to hold him. If you think about it, professionally, he's not much different than you."

"Beg your *pardon*?" Paul barked.

"Pro-fes-sion-al-ly," Woody said again, emphasizing each syllable. "You know what I mean. Private security types."

He did know what she meant, and she was right. After leaving the Secret Service three years earlier, Paul Kelvington formed PeKay, Inc., a private security firm specializing in protecting corporate executives and government officials as they traveled to faraway lands with less than friendly inhabitants. On the side, Pekay, Inc. performed paramilitary functions. At the end of the day, PeKay's largest client was the US government and the State Department's Diplomatic Security Service. The DSS. Right now, he had more than two hundred men deployed around the world guarding people he loved and hated, with few in between.

"If they're releasing Nassar, I'll probably be home tonight," Paul said. "I'll call you when I'm done." He clicked off.

An hour later, Paul reached the FBI's Cleveland office. He showed his ID to the guard, parked, then entered the three-story brick building, where he was searched once more.

Regardless of his credentials, he was forced to surrender his sidearm to the guard, who tagged it, bagged it, then placed it in a small locker requiring two keys to open. He gave Paul one of the keys. In the lobby, on the far side of the floor logo, a tall, slender young man with gelled and parted short brown hair waved at him. The man was in a blue suit, red tie, and black shoes. Paul approached him, and they shook hands.

"I'm Agent Ron Johnson," the man said. "Good to meet you, Mr. Kelvington. I've heard a lot about you. Your service days, I mean. Guarding *the man*."

"You too," Paul replied, though he had heard little of the younger agent, who was dressed and groomed to impress—on a Sunday. He watched the man check his look in the reflection of the brass elevator door.

Ron pushed the Down button. "Do you miss the Service?" he asked, then glanced down at the Rolex on Kelvington's wrist.

"Silly question, I guess."

"Some days, I do miss it. But not the bureaucracy."

The elevator came and the two men stepped inside. The doors closed, and Ron swiped his badge in a reader slot, pressed a button, then waved off two other agents who tried to share the ride as the doors closed on them. The elevator dropped, and they rode in silence, both understanding the compartments were monitored closely. Audio and video. The doors opened to bright fluorescent lights and black letters on the cinder-block wall before them. Sublevel two.

In a low, hushed tone, Ron spoke while they walked. "Why is the White House interested in this guy?"

"Isn't it obvious?" Paul said but cautioned himself to stick with the story. One wrong word, and his visit would be over. Paul said, "Sheik Tariq Al-Jabori was a little more than an art dealer."

"Oh, the sheik was a bad guy," Ron fired back. "No argument there. But not his security chief. We can't find anything on him outside the normal stuff on his passport and paperwork at the UN. So, why does *he* ping the radar of the White House?"

Paul paused a beat as he eyed the acoustical tiles in the ceiling and all the workings above, then completely dodged the question. "How do you know Patricia Woodburn?"

"She and my mother go back. Plus, she helped me get into the academy and then this assignment to Cleveland. I'm from the area."

"Is your mother Marjory Johnson? The woman who once ran the CIA's DOI in London?" DOI was government-speak for the Directorate of Intelligence.

"One and the same."

Now, Paul understood the tie. "I remember your mother well," Paul offered. "When she worked for Whitey Garfield at Grosvenor Square—before he was killed."

Ron nodded his understanding, then said, "So, this isn't a national security issue?"

"I've seen the *Reader's Digest* version on Toledo. Can you add some color?"

Ron hesitated again as he weighed his response. When he spoke, his tone was hushed and tentative. "According to our guest, his security team arrived at the conference center the day before to survey the location, set up the entrance and exit strategies. They did a few dry runs, as any good security team should do. Every entrance and exit had been secured during the sheik's speech to the crowd. A safe area had been set up in a smaller room off the lobby in case they couldn't get out of the building. Access to the auditorium was tightly controlled, and the room had been sealed during the speech. Nobody was let inside after the sheik arrived. They set up two exits. The fire escape was the first choice, with the main doors secondary. A car was waiting between the main building and the caterers next door. The car was five feet from the door—and running. A driver and a guard were inside. The sheik was also wearing a bulletproof vest, the podium had been reinforced with steel plating, and he carried a pistol beneath his robes."

"Tell me about the gunshot in the auditorium," Paul said.

Ron shook his head. "It wasn't a gunshot." He chuckled, then said, "An M-80 had been taped to the back of a wall clock directly above and behind the speaker's podium. The trigger was a nine-volt battery, a model rocket igniter, and the metal hands of the clock itself. My nephew could have built it. What the hell? It worked. The M-80 went off, shattered the clock face, and the sheik's security detail went apeshit. They tackled the sheik and piled on to protect him while the crowd in the room scrambled to get out through the main doors, which were locked, and everyone on the other side was dead. The sheik was rushed out the emergency exit and into the alley, then shoved into the back of the waiting limo. And then the plan completely went to shit."

Paul asked, "It doesn't sound like there was any shit left."

Ron grinned. "Each of the two guards flanking the sheik were picked off as they left the building. One was taken out by a rifle shot that came from the roof of the catering business next door, and the other guard was shot by a small caliber pistol at close range from the front. Right between the eyes. Pop, pop. No misses. According to Nassar, he had placed a guard and a driver inside the limo. The guard in the limo was supposed to open the door and secure the path for the sheik as he exited the building. We figure the first guard to get shot got it from someone inside the limo, and the second guard bought it with the .300 Winchester round from the roof next door."

Paul considered the scenario, then said, "So the guard inside the limo was in on it?"

Ron shook his head. "Not the real guard. He couldn't have been. We found *that* guard in the dumpster behind the conference center with a bullet in his brain. The driver of the limo also took a bullet to the back of the head. Same caliber but different pistols. Six lands and grooves. Two Rugers, most likely. Probably two shooters. Amazingly, we didn't find a stray bullet casing anywhere, and almost everyone bought it."

"Everyone except our man in custody," Paul said. "Have you ever asked yourself, if someone could take out the guards so easily, why not waste the sheik in the alley?"

"It crossed my mind," Ron said. "The killer needed info from the sheik and a getaway car. That's why the driver wasn't killed until the limo stopped."

"I'll buy that," Paul said, which seemed to please Ron. "Has anybody checked the security cameras?"

"There were no cameras," Ron said. "Someone must have hated the sheik because they blew off both of his knees and shot a finger and an earlobe. Then, after two double taps to the head, they walked away. Not a print in the car. We did find some talc dust, though."

Paul said, "The killer wore gloves."

Ron nodded. "The limo driver was shot in the back of the head, twice. The trajectory of the bullet was low and upward. It matched the rounds found in one of the guards in the alley and the one in the conference room and the sheik. The sheik was shot several times with the same .22, but, as I said before, *not* the same .22 that killed the guard in the lobby and not the same one that killed the guard we found in the dumpster. Definitely two shooters. Two with silenced .22s and one or more with a .30 caliber rifle. Maybe three shooters. But it wasn't about money. We found the sheik's checkbook in his briefcase. Judging by the last check written, if the sheik kept good records, four checks were missing."

"Just four checks," Paul mused. "This was about revenge and conversation. But murder is not revenge unless the target knows why they are being murdered. Murder for revenge is as much about satisfaction for the killer as it is punishment for the target. Whoever killed the sheik wanted to talk a little. He needed to get the sheik away from the site."

"Or she needed to get the sheik off-site," Ron said.

"How's that again?"

Ron said, "A couple of workers at the caterer next door to the conference center mentioned that a new blonde woman showed up for work that day. She had the right clothing and an apron and indicated she had been sent by the temp agency the catering service regularly uses. We contacted the agency, and they sent over three people that day. All men. We had an artist do a composite, but it's pretty—generic. Small blonde woman. Athletic. Cute. Southern accent."

"A young blonde woman," Paul repeated. "Hmmm. I'd say you've found one of your shooters," Paul said. "I'll bet the blonde woman did the two guards in the lobby."

"You're kidding," Ron said. "A little blonde woman?"

Paul chuckled. "What did you do before the FBI?"

"Law school," Ron said, almost ashamed of his answer.

Paul sighed. "There are plenty of female agents in the FBI, CIA, DSS. Women make up some of the best shooters in the country. Ever check out the West Virginia University rifle team? Still, no one uses more female assassins than the Russians."

"*Vympel* agents?" Ron barked. "Why would the Russians care about an old Turkish art dealer? Better yet, why kill him here? On US soil, for Christ's sake. It would be easier to do him overseas."

"Maybe, unless…" Then he paused. "Never mind," Paul said, taking a step away. He glanced to the left, then the right, then walked down the hallway.

Ron took the hint, motioning for Paul to follow him to the right. Paul asked, "Does Nassar know what happened to his client?"

"We told him, and he hasn't said shit since. His phone call went to the Turkish embassy in DC, and he lawyered up quick." Ron checked his watch. "I hate to tell you this, but he'll be out of here in less than an hour."

They reached the interrogation room, and once inside, through the smoky glass of the two-way mirror, Paul watched an Arab man in Dockers and a button-up suck the devil from a cigarette as fingers raked through thick black hair. This man was anxious.

"You don't have much time," Ron said. "Our recorders and cameras are always on. I'm sure you know that. I'll be right here at this desk, watching through the two-way mirror, should anything go bad."

"It won't," Paul said. But then his gaze locked onto the Arab's face, and he thought, *Son of a bitch. Is that..?*

"Something wrong, Mr. Kelvington? You look a little—"

"I'm fine. Can I see the forensics report?" Paul's gaze never left the Arab.

"It's incomplete," Ron said as he slid a folder across the table to Paul, who opened it and perused the summary.

"Unbelievable," Paul said. "Not one unaccounted-for print in the limo. What about this .45 caliber bullet?" He pointed to a line on the page, showing it to Agent Johnson.

Ron said, "Yeah, that. Remember I told you the sheik had a pistol on him? Looks like he got off a shot, but it must have missed. Blew a hole in the floorboard of the car. We found the mangled round in the dirt beneath the limo and some shredded fabric with powder residue. And I know your next question. No blood, at least none we found. Smart guy."

"Yep. Smart," Paul repeated. He checked the summary again and the name printed on the file's tab. "Ibrahim Nassar," Paul said out loud.

Ron offered, "That's right. His passport checked out okay, and—"

Paul ignored Ron as he dropped the folder on the desk, twisted the doorknob, stepped into the hallway, and then through the adjacent door and inside the interrogation room, slamming the door closed behind him.

The Arab glanced up at Paul, and the bags under the man's eyes indicated he was exhausted. But Paul wasn't buying it. The man was a professional. Seasoned. And he was certainly not who the FBI believed him to be.

# CHAPTER 9

Princeton, West Virginia
Same Day
9:15 a.m.

The dark stall smelled of horse manure and straw. His hands and clothes did too, as he had been there for more than a day.

He came to his feet cautiously and took in the surroundings again, now that the sun was up. It was still very dark, but he could make out three other stalls, all empty; an RV parked in the far corner; a very nice workbench; and tools opposite of that. Venturing out further, the pole barn continued behind the wall of stalls and an even darker place.

Slowly, he eased across the barn to the window above the workbench so he could see the house next door. Cop cars were still in the driveway. Uniforms and white pajamas roamed between the house and the field and a forensic van. He thought he'd heard dogs last night. Glancing back at the stall, he decided it was still too hot to move. Maybe tonight.

At the corner near his stall was a faucet with a water hose attached. He twisted the knob gently, then drank the warm, rubbery liquid, letting what his hands couldn't hold fall onto the straw. After drying his hands on his jeans, he started toward the second stall, but when something caught the back of his shirt, he stopped and tried to pull free.

At first, he thought a nail had snagged his collar. But when he reached back to find it, something clamped onto his forearm like a vise. As panic grew, he used the grip as leverage and spun around to deliver a blow to whatever had him. His fist connected with something soft but rocky underneath. Fabric, then meat. Hard meat. Then, something fleshy and angry struck his nose, followed by a cereal-like crunch, and he went down hard. The connection with the concrete floor of the pole barn sent a current of pain from his tailbone through his neck. He tasted warmth and salt on his chin, then felt it leave in drips.

Pinching his nose and glancing up, he found a massive shadow looming. Large hands reached down and gripped his lapels, hoisting him up against the stall's railing and slamming his head against a wooden post. Something round and cold pressed against his temple, followed by a metallic click. He froze in place. Then, when the hiss of his own name in his native language tickled his ear, he pissed himself.

The voice said, "*Hola*, Angel."

. . .

"*Por favor, no dispares!*" Angel rattled off in Spanish. "*Yo solo tenía hambre y…*"

"Speak English," Liam hissed back, pressing the pistol deeper into the flesh of the man's temple as he patted him down from head to toe. The only lump he felt was in the man's front pocket, and when he reached in and pulled it out, he found a fold of bills: fifties, twenties, and lower. Liam stuffed the bills in his pocket.

"*No Inglés. Por favor, no dispares,*" Angel said.

Liam replied, "*Dónde está la pistola?*" (Where's the pistol?)

"*No pistola,*" Angel replied, his eyes wide with shock at hearing such good Spanish from a gringo. Angel said, "*Tú hablas español.*" (You speak Spanish.)

"Yes," Liam replied, staying in Spanish. "I also slobber in my sleep, fart in public, and chew my food with my mouth open—but I'm trying to quit." Liam detected the odor of urine blending with blood and the fresh paint on the new RV taking up most of the space in this half of the pole barn.

Angel slid down the post to the floor, fingers pinching a shattered nose.

"Why did you do it, Angel?" Liam asked.

"I needed a place to sleep."

The response caught Liam off guard. "No. Why did you murder my neighbor and your brother?"

"You will call the police now? Yes?" Angel's voice broke.

Liam inspected the shrunken Mexican tucked into a ball in the stall, rocking back and forth as blood dripped from his chin. A rag hung on a nearby hook, and Liam tossed it to the Mexican, who eyed it as if he had been given a new toy truck. Then he wadded it and dabbed cautiously at his matted nose.

"*Gracias.*"

Liam said, "I'm tired of you bleeding on my floor."

"When will the police come?" Angel asked.

Liam said, "If I were you, I'd be more worried about me. The police have to play pussyfoot with your rights. I don't."

As Liam hovered over the cowering man, Lacey's face appeared in his mind. Smiling. Laughing. Eating an ice-cream cone on Navy Pier. Pleading with Liam for vengeance. He was glad he never got to see Lacey's dead body, because if he had, this Mexican would have joined her by now. Liam raised his right foot high and let it hang over Angel's face. One well-placed stomp and the illegal was history, but Angel covered up and went fetal. Liam lowered his foot to the floor. How could this cowering piece of shit murder anything more than a plate of breakfast? Then again, cowards killed women and children every day.

Liam gripped the back of Angel's collar, lifted him to his feet again as if he were a doll, then removed the bloody rag from the man's face; his nose looked like chewed bubblegum. "Last time, Angel. Why did you kill them?"

"I did not kill anyone! What police will come now?"

"It won't matter if I kill you myself," Liam said, his rage building. But then: "Wait a minute. You *want* the police?" he asked.

"*Sí*. Police. Not INS, okay?"

Liam eased the hammer on the Walther forward, then dropped it into one of the oversized pockets of his cargo shorts. "Did you murder those people in Arizona?"

"No. It was the Border Patrol," Angel said. His tears had turned the dust on his face into streaks of mud.

"Don't move." Liam retrieved the water hose and shot a cold stream at Angel's forehead, careful not to hit the Mexican's nose directly. It didn't matter. Angle twisted away from the stream and caught his nose on the wooden post. He screamed. Liam dropped the hose to the floor and threw Angel a fresh shop rag.

Liam put a sneaker into Angel's chest, pressing him against the railing. "Okay. Arizona. Tell me what happened."

Angel drew in a breath. His voice nasal and shaking, he said, "My brother and I crossed the border in Arizona through a tunnel with many others. But when we came out, the Border Patrol was already there. They lined us up, like always, but then, they let us go. But not everyone. We heard voices behind the dune, so we went back to see who was hiding in the bushes. It was a man, a woman, and a child. And the agents had their pistols out. Then—" Angel stopped and covered his face before saying, "They shot the baby and the man."

Liam clenched his jaw. "Who was with you?"

"Gerardo. My brother."

Liam thought about the story for a beat. Something was off. "Did you know the man who was shot in the desert?"

"We spoke to him in the house. He said his name was Rolando."

"What house?"

"The house where the tunnel began," Angel said, but his gaze had drifted to the Dodgers cap on Liam's head.

"You dropped this outside," Liam said.

Angel shook his head. "It is not mine. Rolando was wearing a cap like that one. When the agents caught us next door, one of them was wearing it. They must be here." Kicking his legs, he pressed himself further into the corner. "It is only a matter of time before they find me," Angel sobbed.

Liam studied the man's broken face that had melted from pain to terror. Liam said, "Are you telling me it was the Border Patrol who murdered your brother and the lady next door?"

Angel nodded.

"Then they must have known you and Gerardo saw them in the desert and tracked you down." When Angel didn't respond, Liam asked, "Some men came to visit me yesterday morning. Did you see them?"

"I saw them."

"Did you recognize them?"

Angel shook his head, then dabbed at his nose.

Liam leaned against the railing in thought. Maybe Angel was telling the truth and maybe he was lying, but some things were starting to make sense, so it was best to keep the man talking, no matter how much his nose hurt.

"Walk me through this," Liam said. "What did you do after you witnessed the murders in the desert?"

"After the border agents were gone, my brother and I walked to the town and called the lady. We didn't know what else to do."

"What woman?" Liam asked. "Lacey Sullivan? How did you get her phone number?"

Angel's eyes drifted back to the cap on Liam's head. "In the house, Rolando bragged about his sister and how he knew a powerful lawyer here who would help him. He showed us her business card. I copied it down."

"I can't believe she actually talked to you," Liam said.

"We told her what happened, and she said she would help us if we could get here on our own. So, we bought bus tickets, and she picked us up at the station early yesterday. When we got to her house, the two border agents were waiting for us in the basement."

Liam tried to imagine the process. Lacey and two immigrants she had never met walked into her house greeted by two Border Patrol agents, who killed them. Except for Angel. "Why did they let you live?"

Angel lowered his head. "They lined us up against the pool table. One agent shot my brother first. When they did, I fell to the floor. The other agent tried to shoot the lady, but she ran, so he shot her in the back. But she did not die. They both turned to shoot her again, and when they did, I ran out the door and into the woods and hid. Then, I came in here."

"Okay. Why are you *still* here?" Liam asked.

Angel said, "The police are everywhere. And the killers—they are still out there." Angel dabbed at his nose. "What will you do with me?"

Liam ignored the question. He was struggling with the story. Not because it was complete bullshit but because it sounded real—and far more plausible than DeVine's notion that Angel would kill his own brother. Plus, if Angel was telling the truth and the agents had been waiting for them, it meant they must have gotten her information from the business card Rolando had. Or, they knew where she lived all along. If Rolando was a target, maybe Lacey was too. The shooters didn't follow Angel and Gerardo to Lacey's. The brother just happened to be in the wrong place at the wrong time—twice.

Liam breathed a controlled and guilty sigh of relief as he thought, *At least this isn't about me—this time. And Mika is definitely in the clear.*

Liam eyed the broken Mexican on the floor of the stall, realizing that he now had another problem. If Angel wasn't the murderer, and Angel's brother was resting comfortably in the county freezer, Angel was now the only witness to all the murders and a target for the two angry border agents who were still close by. It was a shit position Angel had accidentally put himself in. Liam couldn't afford to let Angel go to the cops or get caught by the border agents. On top of that, he had another problem.

If he did hold Angel, and the cops happened to find him, Liam could be charged with kidnapping or harboring a fugitive. Getting arrested would be bad, but getting his face plastered on the news would be worse. And quite possibly fatal.

Still, there were too many unanswered questions and inconsistencies between Angel's story, Taconelli's, and DeVine's. To the INS, Angel was the killer, and they had made no mention of rogue border agents. Taconelli was still undecided. The one item that stood out—what made Angel's story more believable—was the dead brother.

"Good news," Liam said. "You're going to be my guest for a few days." When Angel's face contorted, Liam added, "You'll stay in the RV, and I'll bring you food. But most of all, I'm going to protect you."

Liam found a box of lag screws on a shelf and a heavy-duty padlock in the drawer of the workbench. On a hook, he found a long length of chain Shipman always used to pull his truck out of the mud. Hovering over Angel, he yanked the man to his feet and shoved him toward the RV. With the chain in his grasp, Liam held it up to Angel's waist. "We need to get you fitted for a new belt."

# CHAPTER 10

When Paul closed the door to the interrogation room, the Turk glanced up from the table and into his eyes. "Who are *you*?" he asked in heavily accented English. He took a drag from a clove cigarette, tapped the ash on the table near the ashtray, then leaned back in his chair. His buttocks slid to the edge of the seat, and his back went rigid. "Are *you* my attorney?"

Paul said, "No. I'm not your attorney."

"Then I will not talk to you."

Paul knew their conversation was being recorded, so he had to be careful with his words. Careful to control what the FBI heard from both him and the man sitting at the table. "If you are Ibrahim Nassar, then you should not talk to me. But if you're not Ibrahim Nassar, you should change your mind while you still have a tongue."

The Turk eyed Paul curiously and said, "You are wasting your time. I am the victim." He poked his own chest, sending ash down the front of his shirt. "I am Ibrahim, a Turkish citizen, and I have immunity."

Paul stepped behind the Turk, and the man twisted to follow him. He gripped the Turk's shoulders, then leaned down to the man's ear, away from the two-way mirror. He whispered, "You are Malik Saliba. And you are an assassin."

"You lie!" the Turk screamed.

Paul chuckled. "Okay. We'll play it your way." He sat across from the Turk, then locked his gaze on the man. His eyes were sullen and wide. Sweat beaded on his brown forehead.

Paul said, "Two years ago, the sheik sent you to kill a man. But we both know you didn't."

Nassar's eyes widened but he said nothing. A serpent of smoke rose from the shaking clove cigarette between his fingers.

Paul said, "Have you ever wondered what that man might do if he found out you had been sent to kill him? Maybe that's what happened in Toledo. He just missed you." That's when Paul leaned on the man's shoulder and whispered in his ear again. "You remember him, don't you? Commander Trevor Harmon?" He felt the man stiffen in his grasp.

"I do not—"

But Paul interrupted him. "I also heard that man died two years ago. But maybe, just maybe, someone else is finishing what he started."

"You know nothing!" the Turk screamed, snuffing out his cigarette on the table. He lit another one with great effort, since his hands were shaking uncontrollably.

"But what if I'm right?" Paul said, leaning in further. "C'mon. You know what happened to your team. To your boss. You were supposed to die too, but the only thing that saved your life was the fact you never poked your head through that fire exit door. If you had, there'd be a neat little hole right here." Paul poked the Turk in the forehead, then added, "But a professional won't just quit. You're a professional yourself. What would you do?"

"These are lies!" the Turk screamed. "We are wise to your ways. I want my attorney."

"Don't get your turban in a bunch. Your lawyer will be here in ten minutes," Paul said. "And you'll be free to walk out of this building into the bright sunlight beneath all those tall buildings. Your lawyer probably parked in the garage across the street. If you get that far, he'll drive you to the airport. Cleveland Hopkins is a long way. What happens when you get back to Turkey, with your *ex*-employer and meal ticket dead? But you're a professional. You know all the tricks. That's why you know it's not in your best interest to leave here right away. If I were you, I'd give the boys in the other room a reason to hold me for a day or so. Then maybe you'll be transferred under armed guard to a different facility. Maybe then the DSS will watch your back until you leave American soil."

The Turk's lower lip trembled. And though Paul could not see through the two-way mirror from this side, he knew Ron Johnson was most likely standing up, his hands on the table, leaning close to the mirror, and turning up the gain on the microphones.

Paul continued. "Do you have another rich benefactor willing to pay you, hoping you do a better job for them than you did for Tariq Al-Jabori?" Paul pointed his finger at the Turk, who immediately dropped his eyes as the door opened and Agent Johnson stuck his head in.

"You and I need to have a talk," Ron said, then closed the door.

Paul fisted his eyes closed. *Great fucking timing, Agent Johnson.* He turned back to the Turk. "Three minutes—tops. You can go with the lawyer and take your chances, or you can work with us."

The Turk's eyes locked onto Paul's, then dropped. He pulled on a new cigarette, tapped ash, then said, "Commander Harmon died over the English Channel two years ago."

Paul nodded and smiled. "But it seems he has friends." After waiting for more than a minute until the color returned to the Turk's face, Paul whispered, "Ticktock, ticktock."

The Turk buried his face in his hands, shudders of sobbing evident in his shoulders. A beat later, he looked up at Paul, then to the camera in the corner, and said, "I *am* Malik Saliba."

Paul let a breath out. "You just saved your own life. Now, what I need to know is: Who did this?"

"I do not know," Saliba said.

"Then you better hope the FBI finds the shooters before they find you." Paul tapped on the door, and Agent Johnson opened it.

"So," Ron said, slamming the door closed, "that was—educational. I checked, and Malik Saliba is a person of interest, but neither the FBI nor Interpol has anything concrete. I'm not sure how long we can hold him. I'm glad you got him to come around. It saved us some time."

"And embarrassment," Paul said absently as he strolled toward the exit.

"About that," Ron said. "You had him shitting himself. Who was this guy he was sent to kill?" Another agent approached with an Arab man dressed in a suit and carrying a briefcase.

The attorney, Paul assumed. "Good luck," he said, then raised a hand in greeting as they walked by.

"Are you going to tell me what just happened?" Ron asked after catching up with Paul.

"You have the tapes."

"You did a lot of whispering."

Paul said, "I was fishing for something from the past, but I came up empty. So, I thought I would help you guys out by getting him to admit who he really was. You're welcome."

Just then, the agent who had escorted the lawyer into the holding cell caught up to them. He said, "Hey. Did you hear? A homeless guy in Oklahoma City cashed a check for five thousand bucks. It was made out to *CASH*, and some random guy dropped it in his lap. Guess whose name was on the check?"

"No idea," Ron said.

"Tariq Al-Jabori," the agent said. "Our dead Turkish sheik found out hell has no virgins and is trying to buy his way out." The agent chuckled, then darted back to the holding cell.

Ron asked, "What do *you* think?"

"Sounds like your killer is in Oklahoma City already."

"That's it? That's all you have?"

"Okay. It pays to be homeless? What more do you want? I struck out today and gave your team a win. Toledo is your problem, not mine."

"Why is the White House so interested in this case?" Ron asked.

"They aren't. Not anymore," Paul said, but thought, *I sure as hell am.*

# CHAPTER 11



The traffic light changed to green, and Liam eased through the intersection. Then, he pulled into the drug store parking lot for no reason other than to see how the two people tailing him would react. When they drove by and pulled into the gas station across the street, Liam went inside, bought a newspaper, returned, started the car, then kept his speed nauseatingly below the limit until he was certain they had caught up. When he reached the downtown area, he parked in front of a rundown movie theater now serving as a church. The marquee read:

*Salvation Str__t*
*All Ar W_lcom_*

Next door was a diner, and he tugged on the door, catching the reflection of his tail in the gloomy glass as they searched for a parking spot. The diner bustled this Sunday morning, and Liam took the one empty booth near the kitchen facing the front door. The air buzzed with conversation that quieted when the overdressed Black out-of-towner walked in. Liam raised a hand and waved Agent Bo DeVine over.

"You knew we were behind you, huh?" DeVine said as he removed his sport coat.

"Is that how they say *good morning* in Chicago?"

The waitress slid two glasses of water onto the table, then sprinted to another table.

"I'm surprised anything is open in this town on a Sunday. The food must be good here," DeVine said, glancing around at the crowd.

"The best," Liam said. "Greasy. Fatty. The real stuff. Are you going to sit down, or do you like the attention?"

DeVine slid across the red vinyl seat and removed the menu from the salt-and-pepper stand. "Chaz did a little light recon on you. He tells me you lost your parents in an accident when you were sixteen? You were living in Hills Yard, Ohio, then."

"Hilliard," Liam corrected, and was glad Chaz's research had uncovered his well-engineered cover story.

DeVine pulled out his notepad, then read: "You have two BS degrees, electrical engineering and mathematics, from West Virginia University, an MA in economics from Ohio State, and all by the time you were—what—twenty-two, twenty-three?"

"Why are you investigating me? I'm not a Mexican."

DeVine said, "Your past has more gaps than Morse code. No clubs or sports in high school. You took your GED before you got your driver's license. You finished college in '86, then—poof—gone. No history. No credit cards. Nothing until you rented an apartment in Columbus and started your PhD in history at Ohio State. Then you bought that huge house and farm and started working as a college professor. It's like Liam Curran died for nine years, then came back to life. Want to talk about the gaps in your past? Because you don't look like a history professor."

"What do history professors look like? Is there a uniform I'm not aware of?"

"You don't seem—academic."

Liam said, "I started at Concord as an adjunct this year. Last week was my first full week as an associate professor. I defend my doctoral thesis this December."

"What's the subject?"

"The economic and social impact of war on disenfranchised societies."

"Disenfranchised societies?" They held the other's gaze for several seconds before DeVine blinked. "Congrats, almost Dr. Curran." DeVine raised his water glass, and they toasted.

"What can I do for you, Agent DeVine?" Liam said. "You left Chaz in the car—which is rude. Nobody is that bad at tailing, so you wanted me to know you were watching. Oh—no one is named Bo. Is it short for Beauregard? Bocephus? Bojangles? You look more like a James or a Robert, but certainly not Eugene."

"Eugene was my grandfather's name on my mother's side. My father hated the name. He hated my mother too, so he started calling me Bo. It was short for 'boy,' which my father could never quite pronounce, as he was short on teeth."

Liam laughed as the waitress brought their salads, which drew the attention of a group of students sitting at a nearby table. Two boys and two girls all waved, and Liam waved back.

"Students of yours?"

Liam shrugged. "I think I played pickup basketball with one of them." He squirted Italian dressing on the salad, then said, "How's the murder investigation going?"

"Don't know. I'm INS, remember?" After Liam raised an eyebrow, DeVine said, "The ballistics report isn't back, but we have Lacey's phone records." DeVine paused, then added, "One person she called several times never answered."

*Now, he's baiting me,* Liam thought, but said, "What do the cops think?"

DeVine said, "Look—Taconelli jumped down my throat for talking to you. He thinks I'm tainting his investigation."

"If you tell me your theory, I'll tell you mine," Liam said. "Want to start with Gerardo?"

"Okay," DeVine said. "The blood-spatter patterns indicate his arms were outstretched when the first bullet was fired. There was powder residue on his wrists and forearms, but blood was on top of the powder. The second shot was fired upward, under his chin.

Do I need to tell you what the ceiling looks like?"

"I got it," Liam said. He could see Gerardo and Lacey standing in the line Angel had described. Gerardo raises his hand in defense but catches the bullet as blood and burnt gunpowder coat his forearms. He twists or turns or ducks or—something—then catches a shot to face. During the commotion, Angel bolts out the door and into the night.

"Tell me about Lacey," Liam said, mentally bracing himself.

DeVine said, "Lacey tried to run, but a bullet caught her in the lower back. The medical examiner says the shot severed her spinal cord before someone then put a bullet into the back of her head."

Liam fisted his eyes closed. *Why didn't I pick up the damn phone?*

"Are you okay? Your face is red."

"What else?" Liam said.

DeVine cleared his throat. "There were dirty sneaker prints on the patio, meaning that after Angel shot Lacey and Gerardo, he kicked a planter, stumbled, then ran away. Mostly likely, he's hiding in the woods." After pausing for a beat, he said, "But you aren't buying it."

Liam held both hands up and said, "Hey! I'm just a farmer." He bit into his salad and waited, but DeVine offered nothing. "The other day, Taconelli said the murder weapon was a forty-caliber."

"So?"

"I noticed Chaz carries a .45 Beretta. Standard INS issue, is it?"

"What are you suggesting?"

Liam chewed on his salad. "Just making an observation. Are you going to ask me about the calls from Lacey I didn't answer?"

DeVine said, "I was getting to that."

Liam said, "I was with my girlfriend at the time."

"If Lacey's just a neighbor, why not answer?"

Liam said nothing.

DeVine wiped his lips. "Your answering machine didn't pick up."

Liam shook his head. "I don't have an answering machine."

"You're kidding? What about your cell phone?"

"Nope. Go ahead and call it."

"I believe you," DeVine said. "At least we know you have caller ID." DeVine leaned on his elbows, his fingers tented beneath his nose. "It's the nineties, Curran. Pagers. Cell phones. America Online. Do you have an email?"

Liam said, "At the school. But I still have three rolls of Elvis stamps. When those are gone, I'll look into email."

DeVine said, "I'd rather talk about my missing Mexican."

Liam shook his head. "I think you are purposefully being myopic. Angel isn't the only possible suspect. And if that's the case, he's running for his life. And I don't think he'd shoot his own brother, and sure as hell not in the face."

"Speaking from experience?" DeVine said.

"I'm an only child. Born that way, in case you were wondering."

"Interesting theory," DeVine said as his attention diverted to the waitress at the counter, who was aiming a remote at the television mounted high in the corner. The volume increased, and every customer turned to watch as a Latino man in a double-breasted suit, gold watch, rings, and slicked-back hair stood proudly behind a podium and a thistle of microphones. Behind him, a skyscraper backdrop of LA. To the man's left sat a short Latino woman—her hands and legs trembling. To his right stood another Latino woman. Taller and slimmer, her chin tilted upward, lifting closed, pouting lips as if daring the crowd. And she was beautiful—and sad—as she dabbed a tissue at the corner of an amber eye while still clenching her jaw. Liam recognized her right away as the pop singer so famous, the world knew her by a single name.

Sierra.

. . .

On the television, the Latino man stepped to the sprout of microphones. His words were slow and deliberate. With no accent—

almost—he said, "Ladies and gentlemen, thank you for coming. My name is Manuel Castille, and I am the attorney representing both Ms. Catarina Guzman and Sierra."

Sierra put a comforting arm around the shoulder of the sobbing woman.

Castille said, "Four days ago, in the Arizona desert, Sierra's brother and Ms. Guzman's infant daughter were murdered by two—cowards! Their only crime—wanting to be Americans. Baby Esmerelda, not yet one year old, was shot—while still in her mother's arms. We buried the child this morning." Castille frowned as he glanced toward the openly sobbing Catarina Guzman while Sierra patted her back and whispered in her ear.

Castille continued. "Rolando Alvarez, the twin brother of Sierra, came to start a new life in Los Angeles. But he, too, was murdered. At first, the authorities refused to release the details of the investigation, and we couldn't understand why until Ms. Guzman told me the murderers had been agents of the US Border Patrol." After the oohs and ahs in the audience subsided, he continued. "Once this came to light, the Border Patrol finally admitted that evidence found at the scene suggested two of their agents may have fired the shots. We have since learned that two Border Patrol agents are confirmed missing and have not reported back to their posts since the day before the murders."

Castille continued. "Friends, there is a bill stalled in the House of Representatives called HR6363. Known as the Renner-Kline Bill, if it is passed, it would allow for a speedier path to citizenship, aid for those in need, and will prevent the deportation of parents whose children were born here. Rolando Alvarez had tried for many years to immigrate legally. Sierra offered to sponsor her brother, but the miles of red tape prevented it. Now, it will never happen. Not for him and not for little Esmerelda."

There arose roaring applause from the reporters and bystanders as makeshift posters stabbed at the sky. A Mexican flag was hoisted into a nearby tree. Castille smiled and lifted Sierra's arm in triumph. Sierra quickly lowered it, electing to rejoin Ms. Guzman and the aerobics queen.

Castille said, "I will be bringing a suit against the INS, the Department of Justice, and others for these murders. And I also ask you to join me in writing to your representatives of the one hundred and forth Congress to move HR6363 out of committee and to a floor vote. To keep Latino families together and streamline the process of becoming American citizens. I will now entertain questions."

A choir of voices rose in different keys and tones, and Castille pointed to a person in the crowd.

The reporter, a familiar network professional, asked, "Sierra, when was the last time you spoke with your brother?"

Castille said, "My client…" But Sierra was already approaching the podium, so Castille finished with, "…can speak for herself."

Sierra tiptoed to the mics. Raspy at first, her voice cleared as she spoke. "Rolando and I last spoke five days ago, on his birthday. He was somewhere between Santa Gertrudis, Mexico, our hometown, and Sonoyta when he called me from a pay phone. He was so excited."

Reporter: "Why was he coming here?"

Sierra: "To continue with his studies. He wanted to be a doctor."

Reporter: "So, he was accepted to a university?"

Sierra glared at the reporter before answering: "We never got that far, did we? I will be holding a series of benefit concerts honoring the lives of my brother and baby Esmerelda. All proceeds will go toward efforts to raise awareness of HR6363 and to fund the American Latino League. Thank you."

Reporter: "Ms. Guzman, Ms. Guzman, where were you—"

Sierra interrupted the man: "Unfortunately, Mrs. Guzman does not speak English."

Reporter: "What are the names of the missing border agents?"

Castille stepped to the podium as Sierra stepped aside. "The INS will not release the names. These men must be brought to justice, and with my last breath I will—"

The waitress aimed the remote at the television, and Jimmy Swaggart started preaching. The volume went down.

. . .

Liam shot a glance toward DeVine, who was playing with the condiment holder. "Manuel Castille is the managing partner at Lacey's firm, and he's now representing both Sierra and the child's mother. Coincidence?"

DeVine said nothing.

"Are you sticking to your theory, or did it just vaporize?" Liam paused for a beat, then said, "If Castille knows about the two missing agents, then you *must* have known."

DeVine let out a defeated breath. "You're right. But it doesn't mean the missing agents were the shooters at Lacey's, and it doesn't change the fact I still have a fugitive on the loose. But do you know what I don't understand?"

"Chinese arithmetic?" Liam said.

DeVine grinned. "I want to know how you came up with *your* theory—out of thin air? And don't give me that aw-shucks, lucky-guess-by-a-farmer shit."

"Will you answer my question from Saturday?" When DeVine didn't, Liam said, "Okay, play your game."

DeVine's face burned, and he'd started to speak when a bell tinkled in the background and the door to the restaurant opened.

Agent Gillespie entered and rushed to the table, out of breath and excited. "I got a call from the Chicago office," Gillespie said as he slid in beside DeVine. "They said—" But he paused and glanced at Liam.

"It's okay. Go ahead," DeVine said.

Gillespie said, "A BOLO went out for two of *our* guys. Isaac

Gallagher and Zach Penn. They are suspects in the Arizona murders. Can you believe it?"

Liam glanced at DeVine and raised an eyebrow.

DeVine shook his head. "That's Arizona. Not West Virginia. I still have an undocumented fugitive to find."

Liam wiped his mouth. "You may want to fill Chaz in on the press conference, but it looks to me like Penn and Gallagher are your murderers. Maybe Lacey Sullivan was helping Sierra to get Rolando into the country. Maybe—Angel and Gerardo witnessed the murders in the desert, made contact with Lacey, and ran to her for help. Penn and Gallagher tracked them here, but Angel got away. Now, Penn and Gallagher are looking for Angel to shut him up."

"That's very—imaginative," DeVine said.

Gillespie added, "And you're accusing our agents of murder."

"Your people started it," Liam said, "I'll bet ten-to-one that the ballistics report from the desert matches the ballistic report from Lacey's. Same grooves on the bullets, same guns. And—I'll bet those signatures match what the INS keeps on the weapons they issue to agents." When Liam pointed toward Gillespie's hip, the man's face bloomed crimson.

"How in the fuck do you know about that?" Gillespie asked through gritted teeth.

Liam said, "*Law and Order*. Season two, episode three." He turned his attention back to DeVine. "There's something else I'd like to know. Why wasn't Catarina Guzman murdered?"

DeVine stared into his food.

Liam said, "What do you want to bet there was a reason Sierra was having trouble getting her brother into the country?"

DeVine said, "You're right. Rolando Alvarez had a criminal record." DeVine let out a breath. "B and E. Resisting arrest. GTA. He's been to the US a few times and got deported each time."

"So, why would her law firm stick its neck out for an illegal with a rap sheet?" Liam asked the table.

"Because Rolando was Sierra's brother," Gillespie said.

"Maybe Castille and Huerto would—but not Lacey," Liam said. "She was too straightlaced. Too—by the book." When DeVine and Gillespie exchanged glances, he asked, "What?"

"Nothing," DeVine said. "Your relationship with Lacey Sullivan is none of my concern."

Liam studied the two men, regretting revealing so much of himself. He said, "Don't you find it odd that Castille didn't mention Lacey or Gerardo Lopez? As much as he hates the INS, he should have been chomping at the bit to tie Penn and Gallagher to those murders too."

"Maybe Castille doesn't know Lacey's been murdered," DeVine said.

Liam said, "Lacey's name was on the company stationery, for Christ's sake! Something's rotten." He slid across the seat, but then stopped. "And our conversations are over until you tell me what I need to know, Bo."

Gillespie's gaze volleyed between the two men. "What is this big question?"

DeVine tapped Gillespie's leg, and the man stood, a question mark wrinkling his brow.

"Bo?" Liam prodded as he dug into his pocket and placed a twenty on the table as if he'd played a trump card.

"You wouldn't believe me if I told you," DeVine said as he stood. "Thank you for your insights, Mr. Curran." He walked out, leaving Gillespie alone with Liam.

Gillespie said nothing but watched his partner leave as Liam stood.

"Chaz, I'll let you know if I see a stray Mexican or two nasty border agents floating around town." He winked and flipped Gillespie off before leaving the diner.

The sunlight stabbed at Liam's eyes as the pavement cooked

his shoes. Liam found his car, fired up the AC, but kept the car in park as he thought about the news conference. Castille, Huerto & Sullivan were now representing Sierra and the Guzman woman. A firm that primarily practiced immigration law and operated a powerful lobbying arm in DC. An arm that Lacey Sullivan used to head up. He recalled an earlier conversation where Lacey had briefly mentioned HR6363 and how she had been asked to lobby for the bill. Liam also recalled her mentioning that so much money was being dumped into DC by the pro-HR6363 lobby, the entire city could be carpeted in hundred-dollar bills. Liam had listened but, as always, had chalked it up to the normal course of the criminal process that was Washington politics. But now—it had hit close to home. He wished he had paid more attention.

And answered those damn calls.

# CHAPTER 12



After leaving the restaurant, Liam went straight to the pole barn to check on Angel. As he approached the RV, he could hear the sound of a television mixed with metal-on-metal grinding spilling out. When he opened the door, a surprised Angel stared pitifully from behind a foldout table, where he was working the chain back and forth against the table's aluminum edge. An episode of *Bonanza* blared from the television. Liam turned it off.

"You make too much noise," Liam said in Spanish as he plopped down on the sofa, unconcerned with Angel's efforts. *The world would end before he got through the chain*, he thought.

Angel stood, a section of chain in his hand. "Let me go!" he screamed and then slammed the chain against the table.

Liam said, "Hey, dipshit! If I can hear you from outside, the killers can too."

Angel adjusted the section of chain around his waist over the hem of the T-shirt and said, "They rattle all the time. How much longer will I be a prisoner?"

"You should be thankful. I was going to blow your head off."

"Do you believe me now, senor?"

Liam said, "I haven't decided. But I'll admit, the garage floor needs a good scrubbing."

"I will do it," Angel said. "I am bored."

Liam said, "I was joking. You're not my slave. More like a guest in my Hotel California."

Angel's face curdled. "What is this—Hotel California?" He then moved to the armchair across from Liam, who couldn't help but notice the telltale black eyes of a man whose nose had seen better and straighter days. He felt a little sorry for the guy. Busted nose. Wearing grade-100 chains used to hoist engine blocks and pull tractors out of mud pits.

Liam said, "You can look at this in a couple of different ways: as a prisoner, or an endangered species. Those chains are for your protection because those two border agents are out there. You've seen their faces, and you've seen them kill four people already. Plus, the two INS agents and the state police you saw earlier want you too."

There was another reason Liam didn't want to let Angel go yet. If INS or the cops picked him up, regardless of what Angel hadn't done, they'd find a way to make him the bad guy. And it meant they'd stop looking for the real ones.

Liam asked, "How's your nose?"

Angel touched it gingerly. "It throbs."

"I'll get some Tylenol," Liam said. Lacing his hands behind his head, he decided to change the subject. "How much do people pay coyotes?"

Angel said, "Gerardo and I paid five thousand dollars. We are pickers and were looking for farmwork. We were heading to Sells, where we would meet an American coyote who could find us work, but then—"

Liam interrupted him. "In the desert, did you happen to get the names of the agents?"

Angel shook his head. "No. It was dark and we were too far away." Angel paused, then said, "I know why you are asking me this. I saw the television. The singer Sierra and her lawyer. You saw this—yes?"

"And the mother of the child. Yes." Liam nodded as he restrained his burning temper. He held his eyes open to prevent the image of a murdered innocent child from appearing.

Angel said, "The lawyer said the Border Patrol had done this thing. It proves my story."

Liam said, "As I said, your story is believable. But I'm going to keep you safe until I figure this out."

Angel said, "And the man who was killed? He was Sierra's brother?"

"Rolando Alvarez. Yes," Liam said.

A hint of sadness blanketed Angel's face. "It is true, then, what Rolando told us? That he had important contacts? The lawyer lady would have been able to help us?"

"She *could* have." Liam's head throbbed with each beat and the desire to personally break the necks of the men who had murdered Lacey. He could imagine her there. Terrified. Fighting. Running away. There was no doubt in his mind she would have run to him for protection.

*Why didn't I pick up the phone when she called?*

Liam stood and said, "I'll be back."

"Where are you going?"

Liam said, "To check on some things. But you need to be quiet. Our Border Patrol friends won't give up until they find you. After all, you're the last witness."

# CHAPTER 13



Paul had taken the red-eye from Cleveland back to Dulles. In Alexandria, he turned into the gated condo community and waved at the sleepy elderly guard in the shack as he used his card to open the gate. Their place, his and Woody's, was in the back of the community, where the larger, more expensive units had been built. The button on the controller over the sun visor sent the garage door up, and he eased the black Chevy Trailblazer into its slot. He negotiated the lock on the door gingerly, then entered the condo's mudroom, trying not to wake Woody up. Light seeped from under the kitchen door with the smell of coffee. Quiet was a moot point.

"You're up late," Paul said as he closed the door behind him. He found Woody at the breakfast bar with a cup of brown steam in her hand, staring through the bay window at the darkness, shrouded in the red Victoria's Secret robe he had bought her last Christmas. She was right. It didn't suit her. She was more of a panties and a T-shirt girl—when the mood struck her. But that was not tonight.

"It's tomorrow already," Woody said.

Paul tossed his keys on the counter, then poured himself a black coffee and joined her at the bar. They sipped in tense silence, both of them aware of the other's position and how fragile these conversations could be. The White House chief of staff talking to her ex–Secret Service lover. Lions mingling with tigers.

Without looking at him, her eyes still on her reflection in the window, Woody said, "The FBI didn't release Ibrahim Nassar today."

"Good news travels fast," Paul said.

Woody nodded. "Connie spoke with Ron Johnson after you left, and he told her about a five-thousand-dollar check from Sheik Tariq Al-Jabori turning up at a bank in Oklahoma City."

Paul draped his jacket over the chair. "Yeah. Whoever offed the sheik is probating his will."

"An altruistic assassin? That's a small step in the right direction, I suppose."

"He's screwing with the FBI," Paul snapped. "Trying to throw them off the track."

"Who's screwing with the FBI?" Woody asked.

"You tell me," Paul said, his lips stretching into dimples. When she didn't respond, he asked, "Did Johnson mention that Ibrahim Nassar is actually Malik Saliba?" This time, her eyes went wide with surprise, but he wasn't buying it. "Don't give me that. Sheik Tariq Al-Jabori was once a member of the NEST. You and Connie would have both known that much before you sent me to Cleveland. Maybe you didn't know about Saliba, but you suspected someone was finishing what the late, great Commander Trevor Harmon had started."

"You're right," Woody said. "But we didn't know Ibrahim Nassar was Malik Saliba when I asked you to go. If the sheik was murdered by someone associated with Trevor Harmon, we knew you'd be the one to figure it out." She wetted her lips. "I hope you understand why I couldn't risk sending anyone else."

"I get it," Paul said. "No blood, no foul."

Woody paused a beat, then said, "You exposed him for a reason, and I know it wasn't to do the FBI a favor. What do you have up your sleeve?"

Paul chuckled. "I like the way you think, but I thought you'd be happy to get a known terrorist off the streets."

"He'll still get out. Johnson didn't seem to think they had enough on him," Woody said. "All you did was delay his release. You have plans for Saliba, don't you?"

"He could prove to be more useful alive—later," Paul said. "I have to admit, it felt a little hypocritical exposing the guy when he and I were both hired to kill Commander Harmon."

"It's not the same thing," Woody said as she spun around from the sink and pointed a finger at him. "Commander Harmon was a clear and present danger to the United States. He almost started a third world war." Her chest heaved, and she waited for it to calm before adding, "Besides, the IRA beat everyone to the punch."

"Think long and hard about this, Woody." Paul then filled her in on the details of the assassination he had learned from Agent Johnson. He said, "This hit on the sheik was professional—planned to the last detail. I mean, causing a panic in the auditorium and tricking the sheik's bodyguards into leading him to the slaughter? It was a brilliant move. But what happened to the sheik in the limo—that was personal."

"Are you suggesting the *dead* Commander Harmon is back?" Woody said, her face beet red now. "That's insane."

"Maybe," Paul said. "Still, I'm going to assign one of my men to watch the condo and to escort you to and from work."

"Don't," Woody said. "I was not a member of the NEST."

"Neither were the sheik's guards in Toledo, but they're *all* dead. Whitey Garfield was the CIA's chief of station in London, and he's dead. Rehnquist was the director of the CIA, and he's dead. C'mon, Woody. If a person could get to those guys, then they could get to any of us. That includes your mother." Woody fidgeted, then turned away. Reaching across the bar, he lifted her chin with a tender finger. "All of us were way too involved back then to take the chance."

Woody said, "I can request Secret Service protection from the White House."

"And what will you tell the president—a ghost is chasing you?" Paul asked. "What if whoever is doing this is caught and decides to talk? Fingers could start pointing our way."

Woody asked, "What do you have in mind?"

"I'm meeting Zilo at his hotel on Wednesday. I'll have him do a little checking. I'll also have one of my guys here in a couple of days. Okay?" When Woody didn't answer him, he snapped his fingers, and she blinked back to the present. "Okay?"

"Wonderful. Promise me Zilo won't do anything until you run it by me," Woody said.

"Agreed," Paul said.

After rinsing their cups and loading the dishwasher, they went to bed. Paul was worked up and wanted to make love but knew Woody was too wound up to enjoy it. Rather than put her in the position of having to turn him down, he simply held her and pretended to fall asleep. She was out soon after, and Paul lay awake for an hour longer, planning his next move.

# CHAPTER 14

Athens, West Virginia
Monday, August 28, 1995
8:05 a.m.

Even nestled in the tiny town of Athens, Concord College could draw students from around the world. Not in volumes to be considered international, but should a prospective student have the interest to seek it out, a microcosm of the world could easily be found. The operative word being *interest*, a quality most students lacked until it was too late and the mistakes of the past had once again taken root. As a professor and devout student of up-close-and-personal history, Liam Curran knew this all too well.

Liam closed the classroom door, then dropped his satchel by the desk. As he gazed across the sea of unmotivated students, and the occasional crest of hopefuls, he recognized a few tired faces from the bar Saturday night. Being the start of the first full week of classes, lectures were still little more than a review of high school, and the past weekend had been right to tie on a good one. And now, as he always feared, a few of the students remembered him from the bar. Especially the one sitting in the first desk in the second row. And *he* remembered her.

When Levi Strauss invented blue jeans, he had Rachel Cruise in mind. A strawberry-blonde beauty, she played her attributes well when the opportunity presented itself, and could also create an opportunity from scratch. The enigma of Rachel was that her scholastic record proved her to be a brilliant student. This morning, she fiddled with her pen but kept her eyes glued to Liam. He let out a heavy sigh laced with *here we go again* and *c'mon, Liam, control yourself.*

After a quick review of their Wednesday class (Friday's class had been with a sub), a few well-placed questions told him the students had not read the material. There was a difference between high school and college, and this was one of the big ones.

"You," Liam said, pointing to a stout young man wearing a football jersey. "What's your major?"

"Communications," the jock said.

"Great! So, why do you need to take a history class?" When a wave of hands went up, Liam then added, "Other than it's required?" Hands went down.

"I don't know," the jock said. "To help us understand the past?"

Now that he knew the hand he had been dealt, Liam lectured as most took notes; he had their attention, including Rachel Cruise's. She coaxed a strand of hair behind one ear with the stem of her glasses. The studious look was lost on her. Her beauty broke down those barriers, but for Liam, it was something more. She reminded him of someone from his past, adding to his struggles with himself.

After a half hour of drowning the class in animated dialogue, he was interrupted by a knock on the door and a familiar face peering through the glass.

Agent Bo DeVine.

Liam paused, but rather than stop the class, he waved the agent in. DeVine twisted the knob, cracked the door, then stepped inside beneath the inquisitive gaze of thirty-one students.

"Class, this is Agent Bo DeVine. Immigration and Naturalization Services. He and I are working on a project together. Give us a moment." Liam took a step toward DeVine, who stopped before they bumped into each other. Liam whispered, "This couldn't wait a couple more minutes?"

"I thought I would audit your course?"

Liam shook his head. "Fine. Have a seat."

DeVine elected to take the empty chair in the back left corner.

Liam continued lecturing and found DeVine hanging on his every word. He even took some notes. When the clock hit 8:50 and notebooks closed, Liam ended with, "Next time, we will be discussing Machiavelli's *The Prince* and the *Two Treatises of Government* by John Locke. Handouts are on the edge of the desk."

Liam dismissed the class and gathered his things as DeVine waited nearby. Rachel Cruise had also stayed behind, going to great lengths to be the last to leave.

"Dr. Curran," Rachel said. "Can I have a quick word?"

"It's 'Professor,'" DeVine said, drawing the young woman's gaze. She ignored him.

Liam shot DeVine a cat's grin before glancing at the attractive coed.

"I'll be in the hall," DeVine said, closing the door behind him. Liam wished he hadn't.

Rachel approached him, fingers twisting rings and adjusting hair. Her eyes lifted slowly to meet his, her flirting antics calculated and orchestrated to seduce. She wasn't nervous or a novice. She was dangerous but manageable. Still, the intrigue of the game and the unknown held Liam in place, against his better judgment.

Liam said, "I have office hours from one to three this afternoon, and I have an official from the INS waiting for me. What is it, Ms. Cruise?"

"I saw you at the bar the other night," she said. "I was with some friends. I waved."

"I waved back," Liam said.

"It's just"—she paused, measuring her words—"the whole campus knows about your neighbor. I was wondering if you were doing okay."

*Profs talk too much,* he thought, then smiled and adjusted the protruding books and notes in his satchel. "I appreciate your concerns, Ms. Cruise—"

"Rachel," she interrupted.

"Let's stick with Ms. Cruise. I assure you I am fine."

She said, "I'm applying for your open graduate assistant position."

"You're an undergrad, Ms. Cruise. I haven't posted the position yet. How did you know about it?"

"Julie. Your secretary. Still, I'd like to help. Grade papers, maybe. Get involved."

"Wouldn't you rather be drinking and partying with a sorority or something?"

"I'm not much of a joiner." She took a half step closer.

Liam said, "I can relate. I have a class on the other side of campus." He turned to leave, but her next words stopped him.

She said, "The man in the hallway—I saw him at the bar too."

"Really?" Liam asked, spinning around to face her.

"Mm-hmm. You were sitting with the profs, and he was on the other side of the club. I think it's strange he didn't join you. Are you two not friendly, or…" And she inched toward him. Her finger extended until it poked at his chest. "Wow! Do you work out?"

"I drink coffee. Drive a tractor," Liam said, taking one more half step toward her so he was now looking down and into her blue eyes. She backed against the desk, gripping it with both hands as her eyes closed and her lips parted. Waiting. Breathing him in. She rose on her toes to meet him.

To disarm the mood, Liam said, "You look a little sleepy. You should get some rest." He turned away and left her standing there. DeVine poked his head in the door, and Liam blew by, followed by a disappointed coed stomping off.

Liam said, "I hope you can jog and talk at the same time. I have a class in five minutes across campus." He took the stairs two at a time, then stepped out into the sunlight. A wispy breeze passed and leaves rustled.

DeVine caught up. "I want us to have a private meeting."

"I told you my price," Liam said. Ahead were three sets of

concrete stairs climbing the hillside with a black railing splitting the middle.

"Professor Curran!" DeVine called out. "Can you wait up?"

Liam stopped. "You're out of shape, Agent DeVine." He let a group of students pass, then added, "What is it you want from me?"

DeVine caught up, though his breath was still a few flights back. "This morning, the homicide team found shoe prints in the field next to your house. They figure a man's size eight or nine." He glanced down at Liam's shoes. "What are those? Elevens?"

"Twelves."

"Knocks you out of the running," DeVine said. "I don't think you had anything to do with Lacey's murder, and neither do the state police. But they don't have any real leads, so they'll want to talk to you again. Cooperation might help remove you from the person-of-interest list."

Liam took a step forward. "Are you threatening me, DeVine?"

"No. But the longer this case drags on, the more rocks Taconelli will turn over. Let's just say I'm educating you. I do think you and Lacey Sullivan were romantically involved, given the situation with her husband and the fact you two lived next door to one another."

"Nature." Liam grinned. "If you lock up a Bible study group in the church basement, they'll eventually start screwing, right?"

DeVine shook his head. "I could really use your help. You have a knack for details, you're local, and you're smart. It would—"

Liam interrupted him. "It would be beneficial—for me—if Angel were found quickly. Is that what you're getting at? You have Chaz."

"He's pretty green."

"Greener than me?" Liam turned to keep walking, but DeVine's words stopped him.

DeVine said, "All I have to go on is that Angel was in Lacey Sullivan's house."

Liam said, "You don't even know that. You *suspect* it because the corpse of Taconelli's John Doe—who you keep calling Gerardo—

was there, but you have no physical evidence placing Angel at Lacey Sullivan's."

*But I do*, Liam thought.

DeVine said, "We have a fingerprint from the basement we can't assign to anyone else. Most importantly, it doesn't belong to the missing border agents either. Or Scott Sullivan."

Liam asked, "Have you checked the mailman? The last owner? Even me. I've been in Lacey's house several times."

DeVine laughed. "I'm confident it will be Angel's, but I need his prints to compare."

"What about the ballistics?" Liam asked.

"Still in the lab," DeVine said. "Look. I agree Penn and Gallagher were the bad guys in the desert. But not at Lacey's. At least, not yet."

*Angel would disagree*, Liam thought. He said, "Let's wait on the ballistics report and see if you still feel that way. Finding Angel will be—secondary—in my book."

"But not in mine," DeVine said. "He's at the top of my to-do list."

Liam shook his head and started walking again.

DeVine called out, "You want an answer to that question—right?"

Liam spun around. "Keep talking."

"You want to know how I knew Gerardo's and Angel's names. How I knew to come to Lacey's house and how I know the dead man was Gerardo and not Angel. You were right. I didn't just throw a dart at the map and pick Princeton."

"I'm still listening."

"I'll give you one word, for now—Lacey."

"Lacey?" Liam stepped from the sidewalk to where DeVine was leaning against a tree and catching his breath. "Spill it, Bo."

"Quid pro quo. I'll tell you if you'll agree to help me."

"I'll agree to *hear* you out. It's all I can promise."

"It's a start. When?"

Liam made a show of thinking about it, then said, "I really don't have time, Bo."

"One question," DeVine said. "How do you know the INS keeps ballistic signatures on all of our weapons?"

Liam didn't answer.

DeVine said, "Okay. I get it. You think Penn and Gallagher are guilty all the way around. So, I'll tell you this: We don't have ballistics from Lacey's yet, but we have plenty from Arizona. The rounds from the victims prove the shots came from two separate .40 caliber pistols, and both had been issued to agents Penn and Gallagher. No doubt. And maybe they were the ones who murdered Lacey and Gerardo, but that's Taconelli's deal. I'm trying to find Angel Lopez."

"To protect him or to arrest him?"

"I have to find him first. Then I'll know."

Angel's story was gaining credibility by the second. Liam said, "Tell me about Lacey."

"Oh no. Tonight. Seven o'clock. Your place."

"Fine. Now I'm late for class." Liam turned to leave.

"Can I bring Gillespie?" DeVine called out.

"Is Gillespie a brand of beer I've never heard of?"

DeVine chuckled. "I'll leave him at the hotel. What kind of beer do you like?"

"I hate beer," Liam called back as he disappeared around the corner of a building.

# CHAPTER 15

Washington, DC
Same Day
3:15 p.m.

At the corner of L and Connecticut, an alabaster stone building stood majestically in a sea of identical structures. What set 1000 L apart from the other buildings was its somewhat circular design and the lack of information on its blue frontage sign. *No Federal Bureau of This* or *Department of That*. It simply read *1000 L Street* in bold white letters.

Its lobby was open twenty-four seven and contained several small shops, a credit union, fast food, a café, and even a post office branch. A popular health club chain took up the entire second floor, accessible by a set of escalators. Treadmillers could sweat while looking down on diners at orange Formica tables.

If one stood in the middle of the lobby and looked up, floors three through seven would seem to rise like a kaleidoscope of balconies trimmed in polished brass railings and spindles. Workers walked by, oblivious of those below. Capping off the kaleidoscope and doubling as the roof, a magnificent stained-glass oculus depicted Howard Chandler Christy's *Scene at the Signing of the Constitution of the United States*. It was possible to stand and admire the ceiling for hours. But if you tried to find the elevator or the stairs or the escalator leading to floors three through seven, you never would. Because it didn't exist.

Woody steered the black Suburban onto L Street, then turned down the delivery ramp to 1000L and stopped at the warning sign and the corrugated steel door. A guard in a blue uniform, badge, and sidearm, with serious biceps and broad, thick shoulders, appeared from a small door. She showed the man her driver's license, and he took the ID inside. When he returned, he said, "You've been cleared, Ms. Woodburn." The corrugated door rose, and he waved her through into the belly of the world headquarters of the Billings Institute for the Conservation of Americanism.

BICA—as it was known inside the secret circles of the DC beltway—had been founded in 1910 by immigrant Charles Edward Billings to counter the American Progressive movement in the early twentieth century and the overreach of government after the Teddy Roosevelt administration at a time when factories were replacing farms and city populations were booming. The Progressive movement, a relative of the Russian Socialist Movement and the German Workers' Party—though it wasn't known as the Nazi Party until 1920—had gained some national momentum as the tried-and-died ideas of Marxism once again reached the fertile and corruptible minds inside American universities. In Billings's mind, he was protecting his family's future by preventing America from becoming everything he had left behind.

Originally chartered as the Founder's Constitutionalists, a constitutional conservative political party—a more Jeffersonian Democratic-Republican Party—BICA's primary goals were to elect real statesmen devoted to the purity of America's founding principles of natural rights and the government's one purpose—to secure those rights. Not long after its founding, many of its earliest benefactors believed the organization could better serve the ideas of liberty—not as a political party—but as a nonprofit think tank advising America's leaders on intelligence and policy. Better to be the navigator than the captain.

When Billings died in 1965, the organization honored its founder by officially changing its name to the Billings Institute for the Conservation of Americanism. In every corner of government, it was considered one of, if not *the*, most influential foreign policy organization in the world, advising presidents, prime ministers, senators, representatives, and even revolutionaries. In the darker, quieter, and more intimate corners of national security, BICA had become an indispensable intelligence-gathering tool available to a worthy few in government.

Since its founding, BICA had three leaders. Beginning with Billings himself, the second chairman of BICA had been a Billings fellow at Oxford but had passed away in 1975, less than ten years after assuming the position. The third and current leader of BICA—Virginia Roosevelt-Woodburn—had not only been the first female dean of the Political Science Department at Brown University, but also held the distinction of being Patricia Woodburn's mother.

Until this year, Woody had barely spoken to her mother since 1982, the year her father had suffered a stroke and died. Woody never blamed Ginny for her father's death but felt the woman had betrayed him by choosing BICA over family by placing him in the care of twenty-four-hour nurses until his passing and leaving Woody in the care of a full-time nanny.

Woody had graduated high school with honors and attended the University of North Carolina for her undergraduate degree in marketing, then moved on to Stanford for her JD in law. After graduating, she formed Relational Excellence, a marketing company that not only positioned corporations and their products but also engineered the campaigns of politicians. Her most successful project had been to elect the current president of the United States. As far as Virginia Woodburn was concerned, her daughter had put a known enemy of Americanism in the White House.

After reaching the seventh floor of the parking garage, Woody passed a second guarded checkpoint, parked at an end spot, grabbed her things, chirped the lock, then paused between cars as she drew in a breath and wondered if she could accomplish what she'd come to do. Could she convince the great Virginia

Roosevelt-Woodburn to help her locate and destroy an enemy of the White House? If it were just for Woody, she knew her mother would walk through fire. But this would be helping the president, which would be like asking her mother to sleep with Satan.

Woody gripped the powdered brass handle and opened the set of heavy doors to the air lock. Embossed on the foggy glass at eye level was a quote she had been able to recite from memory since she was old enough to speak.

*"The tree of liberty must be refreshed, from time to time, with the blood of patriots and tyrants."*
*—Thomas Jefferson*

The doors parted and Woody stepped into the air lock. She braced for the puffs of air and ignored her reflection in the two-way mirrored door. On the other side, a smiling face would be waiting, chuckling at her dislike of the air lock and its cramped quarters. A happy ding sounded, and the mirrored doors parted, revealing the beaming face of a proud, regal woman.

"Good morning, Patricia," Virginia Roosevelt-Woodburn said brightly, annunciating each syllable with Southern-belle distinction.

Ginny, as she liked to be called by friends, stepped forward with stately grace, exuding the responsibility of great influence even as her long dress yielded to her still lovely femininity. Today, she was in solid blue, accessorized with a white belt and white pumps. Simple diamond stud earrings set off the gold in her necklace and the diamond-crusted cross lying flat against her breastbone—all good clues as to where she stood. Or where you stood with her. A single gold ankle chain betrayed her conservative nature.

"Hello, Ginny. You look well." Woody kissed both of her mother's cheeks.

Ginny held her daughter at arm's length as if she were a dress being chosen for a formal. "To what do I owe the pleasure—this time? Not that you need a reason to come by."

Woody smiled and turned from Ginny's inspection. "Is the snack cart stocked?"

"Of course."

As they navigated the circular hallway, passing workers whose noses were buried in reports, they spoke about the Redskins, then about Stanford and UNC, concerning the prestigious leaders and communists employed there. Then, as always, Ginny defaulted to her standard.

"So—how's Paul?" Ginny held the door for Woody, and they passed through the suite of desks. Two aides and a secretary smiled as they passed.

"He's fine. Still as funny as ever," Woody answered. Ginny loved Paul Kelvington but didn't care for their cohabitation. "He sends his love." Then she thought, *Even though he doesn't have a clue I'm here and would shit if he knew.*

They arrived at the sitting area of Ginny's office near a cart filled with muffins and bagels and coffee and juices surrounded by walls of mahogany shelves stuffed with volumes of books that—and Woody was certain of this—Ginny had read cover to cover.

Woody gathered goodies from the cart, picked a spot on the sofa, and bit into a muffin, washing it down with a sip of coffee, then wiping her hands on a cloth napkin. "I'd like to tell you this is a social visit, but you know me better than that."

"What's on your mind, Patricia?" Ginny asked, her voice low and calm.

"The murders in Lukeville, Arizona," Woody said, though this topic was but a lead-in to her real goal.

Ginny pressed on a smile, then wiped the corners of her mouth with dainty precision. "What a tragedy. But I imagine you're concerned about its effect on the Renner-Kline Bill. My guess is the murder of an infant and a pop singer's brother is causing reverberations through the capitol."

"Your guess is correct," Woody said. "The Renner-Kline Bill was stalled in committee, but now there's pressure to move it forward."

"Don't be evasive," Ginny said. "You and Connie put a full-court press on every congressman to vote *for* Renner-Kline once it hit the floor. What I'm hearing is that you would like to keep it in committee now."

"Yes—I worked with Congressman Trent to delay its debate," Woody said.

Ginny's lips pressed to a stitch. "I smell a Potomac two-step. What's going on, Patricia?"

Woody said, "I hate the bill, okay. After I read it—really read it—I realized the impact it would have on our country and the electorate. It's pure treason, plain and simple. But my hands are tied now because—and you're right—the White House initially backed the bill."

Ginny let out a sigh. "And how does your president feel about it?"

Woody lowered her gaze. "Unfortunately, that's irrelevant."

"I agree. He's a socialist importing votes. He'll sign it—the damned Progressive," Ginny proclaimed, and she turned away as if to spit a bad taste from her mouth.

Woody chose her next words carefully. She needed to bring her true purpose to the front but not directly. So, she said, "I think it's more than that."

"What? He's being coerced?" Ginny asked. "That's funny, because it's *his* bill. Renner and Kline are only the sponsors, so why would someone need to blackmail him to get his signature?"

*She said the word, not me,* Woody thought. *The perfect transition.*

Woody said, "At first, he wanted to let the Renner-Kline Bill battle it out with the Senate's TABS Bill. Whichever one pulled ahead, he'd get behind it. It's a coward's stance, I'll admit, but that's politics. But then, the Senate's TABS Bill actually started to pull ahead, and he seemed to panic and started whispering *veto* in the halls. I got the feeling that—" But then, she stopped herself.

Another tactical move to create a fill-in-the-blanks moment.

A silence born out of discomfort enveloped them. Ginny plucked a few crumbs from her lap and tucked them into a napkin, which she wadded up and placed on an empty saucer. Then, she said in a whisper, "Someone has something on the president?"

"Maybe," Woody said.

"Why not bring it out in the open?" Ginny asked. "Plenty of administrations have aired dirty laundry to give their blackmailers nowhere to go."

"All I have is conjecture. Whatever it is, he's guarding it like a child's toy," Woody said.

"Then maybe the president *should* resign. Or be impeached. Article One of the Constitution. It's there for a reason. So is Article Five, for that matter."

Woody's jaw clenched in a rock-shattering vise. "You know as well as I, if there's an inquiry, the president may not be the only casualty. Too many questions could lead to places a Senate hearing doesn't need to go."

"I see. You're afraid of the Commander Harmon fiasco from '93 biting you in the ass." Ginny pointed a newly painted nail at her. "I tried to tell you not to—" But she stopped herself and instead said, "You could plead the fifth."

Woody locked eyes with Ginny and said, "You know I can't sit back and just let things unfold on their own."

Ginny stood, turned her back, and said, "You want BICA to uncover the blackmail and who's behind it," Ginny said. "And keep *you* at a distance."

"Basically—yes," Woody said. "I'd do it myself, but if it were to ever leak that the White House chief of staff was investigating her own president—well—we don't need Blackmail-gate."

Ginny moved to the service cart and began refolding the cloth napkins. "BICA is the sworn enemy of *this* president, and we have contributed tens of thousands of dollars to defeat Renner-Kline.

In BICA's view, if the president is caught in a blackmail scandal and impeached, the American people win."

Woody's brow knitted. "If he's caught publicly, we *might* get a single win. But I certainly can't control the fallout. But if I catch him privately, then we can get multiple wins."

"We? Now you're on BICA's side?" Ginny asked. "I'm not sure what you're trying to pull on your own mother, but let me be the first to warn you: even *you* don't know the full resources available to the president, and you've never experienced ruthlessness until you've cornered the leader of the free world. Do you regret putting him in office yet?"

Woody nodded. "That's an understatement." Then, Ginny's next words hit her like a kick in the gut.

Ginny said, "I know about Sheik Tariq Al-Jabori. And that you sent Paul to Cleveland. Do you suspect the blackmail of the president may have something to do with the NEST? If so, you'd be right to worry about a Senate inquiry."

Woody dabbed at the corners of her mouth. "There's no relation between the two. I sent Paul to Cleveland because Sheik Tariq Al-Jabori was one of the few remaining members of the NEST. And we both know the deaths of other members didn't stop with the death of Commander Harmon."

Ginny deflated into her chair. "Sheik Tariq Al-Jabori had hundreds of enemies. It could have been any number of factions."

"Not just anyone could pull it off on US soil," Woody said. She sipped her coffee and examined Ginny from afar. For a moment, she was taken back to her childhood and those nights at the dinner table when her mother pondered the appropriate punishment for a common childhood infraction. Then she asked, "If you know I sent Paul to Cleveland, then you know who he interviewed."

"Ibrahim Nassar. Sheik Al-Jabori's security chief."

"No," Woody said, shaking her head. "Ibrahim Nassar turned out to be Malik Saliba." As Ginny stifled a gasp with a palm,

Woody waited for the shock to sink in, then added, "Before you say anything, I want you to hear me out."

"I'm listening." Ginny smoothed her dress and crossed her hands in her lap.

Woody said, "Let's accept as fact someone has been finishing off the NEST for Commander Harmon. Tariq Al-Jabori would be a major target, but so would Malik Saliba. Two high-value targets in the same place at the same time. This is definitely the same person."

"But they missed Saliba," Ginny said, plucking at her fingers with her napkin, one by one, carefully removing muffin residue from each digit.

Woody knew this stalling tactic well. It was her mother's way of packaging a response.

Ginny asked, "What's Paul think?"

Woody said, "Paul's convinced all three of us are on the hit list too."

"Even if Commander Harmon were alive, it wouldn't be the case." Ginny waved the thought away as though it were smoke. "We weren't members of the NEST."

"Neither were Walter Rehnquist or Whitey Garfield. The director of the CIA and the London chief of station—both dead."

"We are not in danger." Ginny paused and caught her breath, then reached across to give her daughter a reassuring pat on the hand. "Trust me."

Woody said, "Are you willing to stake your life on it?"

Ginny said, "Absolutely. I'll even—" But she stopped in midsentence, her eyes spreading to ovals. Drawing in a long breath, she let out, "Where's Paul right now? Tell me he hasn't gotten involved with Toledo."

"He's at home," Woody answered. "I know what you're thinking. He's not tracking the killer. He's meeting with Zilo to have him do some recon, but—"

"When?" Ginny shot back.

"Wednesday at the Hotel Monte. Don't worry. Paul promised me he wouldn't make a move without talking to me first."

"You have to keep him and Zilo out of this, Patricia. It isn't—" But she was interrupted.

Woody said, "Safe? Is that what you were going to say? Paul was a Green Beret and then in the Secret Service, Ginny. I think he knows what he's doing." But when Ginny grinned, Woody stopped. "I didn't come here to talk about Paul. I need your help with the blackmail. Are you going to help me or not?" Woody asked, but Woody didn't need to follow Ginny's gaze to know where she was looking.

Ginny owned two famous paintings. Currier & Ives' Patrick Henry delivering his "Give me liberty, or give me death" speech before the Virginia Assembly, and Peter F. Rothermel's *Patrick Henry Before the Virginia House of Burgesses*, where Henry famously argued against the Stamp Act of 1765, stating, "If this be treason, make the most of it!" Ginny was calling on Currier & Ives.

Ginny said, "BICA has a charter, Woody. Every member takes the same oath as elected officials, to protect and defend the Constitution. But we go a step further, and that is to also defend the founding principles of the Declaration of Independence, which the Constitution was drafted to protect—the only purpose for having a government at all. And BICA is not a hired gun for the benefit of a Progressive. We expose them, then exterminate them." Her gaze drifted to Patrick Henry on the wall as she said with absolute conviction, "We serve to protect the ideals of individual sovereignty, liberty, property, and natural rights. In other words—Americanism—at all costs against every enemy. Even if the enemy somehow got into the White House."

"I'm in the White House," Woody said, then wished she hadn't.

"And if you stand with the socialist Progressives, then—yes—you are an enemy of Americanism. Socialism, by its very definition, is anti-American." But then Ginny smiled as she reached out and touched her daughter's cheek. "You helped to elect a long-shot president to fuel your ego, not because you're a Progressive. You're not the enemy, Patricia. Not on purpose. But you set up your tent in their camp, and now you need to take it down."

"Fine," Woody said. "I'll figure it out on my own."

Ginny said, "I'm sorry, Patricia. But helping you with this issue would be the same as giving aid and comfort to the enemy. BICA won't do that. It's final."

And there were those two words: *It's final.* Woody knew that once those words were spoken, there was no going back. She found her purse and shouldered it, realizing the anger rising in her gut was her own failure to win just one battle with her mother.

Ginny stood and walked her to the air lock. They kissed cheeks. "Take care, Patricia," Ginny said as she glanced toward the glass doorway. "It's getting dangerous out there." An out-of-breath young man caught up with them, a sheet of paper in his hand. He eyed Ginny, then Woody. "What is it, Curtis?" Ginny asked.

"A check," he said. "You won't believe this. It was signed by a dead man." Curtis passed her the note and the image of the check.

Ginny examined the photocopy. The pay to: *Cash.* The name at the top: *Sheik Tariq Al-Jabori.* Ginny said, "San Diego, California? It cleared the bank this morning."

Woody couldn't help but smile as she said, "I'll bet it was written for five thousand dollars."

Ginny and Curtis both looked at her curiously. Curtis said, "That's right. How did you know?"

Woody said, "Four blank checks were taken from the sheik's briefcase after he was murdered. The first one cleared an Oklahoma City bank yesterday. A homeless guy cashed it. Five thousand dollars."

Curtis glanced at Ginny. "This one was cashed by a charity called For the Love of Life."

"San Diego and Oklahoma City," Ginny mused. "That leaves two more checks."

Woody smiled. "I guess you're worried about Toledo too, Ginny. And—"

Ginny interrupted her. "I'm not worried."

"So you say," Woody said. "I didn't come here to get into an argument."

They said their goodbyes, and Woody navigated the streets of DC back to the White House. It wasn't until she passed her credentials to the guard that she realized how badly her hands were shaking. If this was what it felt like for a relative to deal with Virginia Roosevelt-Woodburn, then she never wanted to be a politician. Today, Woody had lost a battle to an adversary she had never beaten. If Ginny wouldn't help her uncover the blackmail, she needed an alternate plan, but she didn't have a clue which way to turn.

# CHAPTER 16

Princeton, West Virginia
Same Day
7:05 p.m.

The chime above the closet door signaled a car had pulled up to the gate and the driver had pressed the silver button. Liam was expecting the visitor but parted the drapes to get a better look. Rental car. Familiar. Single occupant. A dark hand and forearm reached out the window and poked the silver button, and the chime rang again. Liam pressed the button on the intercom panel, and the iron gate lifted, then closed automatically as the car cleared the cattle-stop.

*Welcome back, Agent DeVine.* Liam thought.

DeVine had opted for jeans, sneakers, and a Northwestern University polo instead of his worn suit. Purple letters on his chest against a gray shirt. He strolled easily up the walkway and presented a brown paper sack as Liam opened the door. An offering. It was heavy and glass clinked inside.

"Want one now?" Liam asked, turning away, then heading down the hallway to the kitchen. He could hear DeVine fumbling in the foyer. Liam called back, "Don't worry about your shoes. Mama's not home." At the island, he opened the sack, stared inside, laughed, then pulled out the six-pack and held it up. "O'Doul's?" Liam shook his head at the nonalcoholic beer.

"It's good. You should try it."

"Real beer's bad enough, but fake beer with no alcohol—what's the point?" The six-pack fit easily into the mostly bare refrigerator next to the half-empty gallon of whole milk and two nearly empty boxes of pizza. Liam popped open a near-beer, then placed it on the table in the nook. He then filled a glass with ice and Jack Daniel's and took his place across from DeVine's near-beer.

DeVine entered the kitchen and sat across from Liam. They clinked tumbler to bottle, and after drawing some thin foam from the beer, DeVine took in the room.

"When is Mama coming back?" DeVine asked.

Liam paused a beat, then said, "I'm not sure. Her schedule is nuts." He sipped the Jack.

"Is it serious?" DeVine asked, still taking in the surroundings.

"It's about where I like it. Where's your better half?"

"I never married. Saw the dark side of the institution growing up."

"I wasn't talking about your wife."

DeVine paused, then smiled. "Gillespie worked with the locals all day. He's finishing a report." He then tapped the window, admiring the closed blinds encased between the panes. "Wouldn't it have been cheaper to just not install windows?"

"It's scary outside." Liam gave an exaggerated shiver.

"I'll bet," DeVine said. "For someone so paranoid, you're very open about your relationship with that one student. Rachel, was it?"

"There's no relationship."

DeVine took a cautious sip. "She told you I was at the bar the other night, didn't she?"

Liam nodded.

"And you're wondering why I was there."

Liam said, "You drink O'Doul's, Bo."

"I had a Coke."

"So, it rules out you being a Mormon."

This time, DeVine laughed out loud. "Speaking of worshiping, did Miss No Relationship also mention she's been stalking you?"

Liam's eyes narrowed, and he stopped midsip. "No—she didn't."

*This could be a problem.*

DeVine took a notepad from his back pocket. "Rachel Cruise is the owner of a '95 Acura Integra. Ohio vanity plates. Franklin County. She has two parking tickets, local. No speeding tickets. And her family has big money. Clothing stores in and around the Columbus, Ohio, area."

*Columbus*, Liam thought. He wanted to drop the conversation but decided it was best to let this play out a little. "Is that stalking?"

DeVine said, "She followed you to the bar the other night but waited before coming inside. Then, she followed you home after you left the bar and drove by your place several times before calling it a night. After you and I spoke today, she followed you to your next class, hung out while you played basketball, then tailed you to the gas station. Just now, when I pulled up to the gate, I saw her drive by."

"I have an obsessed fan," Liam said as he thought, *Which could be trouble*.

"You have a stalker, Mr. Curran."

"I'll handle it," Liam said.

DeVine put away the notepad. "Just thought you'd like to know. And a little surprised you didn't."

*Me too*, Liam thought. He shook his head, then checked the time. "What would you like to discuss, Agent DeVine?"

"Call me Bo."

"Can I call you Eugene?"

"I have a gun."

"Point taken," Liam said, then decided it was the right time to offer a token piece of obvious truth to get the lying started. "You're right about one thing. Lacey and I were an item—once—for a short time."

"I suspected as much. Mind if I ask why there are no pictures of you two together anywhere in her house?"

Liam said, "It was brief. We kept it quiet. When we spent time together, we usually met out of town. Dinners in Roanoke or

Charleston. We took a few weekend trips together to beat the winter. The Virgin Islands. The Bahamas. Vegas. It sounds odd, but this is a small town, and the ink on her divorce was still wet."

DeVine said, "I've been in town for three days, and I've run into the same people three or four times. One of them called me by name."

"Did he call you Bo or Eugene?" Liam asked, raising his hands in mock surrender. "Hey, I want to know if I'll be attending any funerals this week."

"He survived," DeVine said. "Why did you and Lacey end it?"

"It was mutual. She was moving back to DC, and it was getting too complicated." Then, he thought, *Because Mika showed up out of nowhere.*

DeVine said, "I've seen pictures of her. Lacey Sullivan was gorgeous. Not too many men would walk away from that without a fight. Casey Conner must be a knockout." He paused a beat as he scanned the kitchen walls, his lips working with no sound. Then he said, "Any photos of Casey around?"

Liam only grinned.

DeVine's eyes narrowed. "Taconelli has Lacey's purse and wallet in evidence. She had a single photo of you two tucked behind a couple of credit cards. A beach somewhere. Red bikini. She was in the bikini, not you."

"That was Rio," Liam said as a breath escaped him in a long, easy, fluid sigh. "We didn't mesh. Politics. Life philosophy. I like meat. She liked plants. And, strangely enough, she talked to both on occasion."

DeVine pursed his lips in thought, then said, "Have you thought about my request?"

"A little. What I really want to do is find the assholes who did this and beat them to death with their own arms." He released a long breath and finished half of the Jack.

"That's what I wanted to hear," DeVine said, then paused for a beat as his gaze turned toward the wall and Lacey's house beyond. "Scott Sullivan showed up today. Forensics finished in the home, so they let him inside."

Liam said, "I saw his car. And the moving van. Lacey isn't cold yet, and he's emptying the place. Is he a suspect?"

DeVine said, "The spouse, or ex-spouse, always is, right? Well, he *was*. Scott has a couple of rock-solid alibis placing him in DC at the time of the murders. Anyway, it doesn't matter now. You'll be happy to know the cops are focusing on Penn and Gallagher."

"That's smart," Liam said.

"Speaking of smart," DeVine said. "This question you want me to answer—where did that come from?"

Liam said, "Louisa called nine-one-one. Last I checked, it doesn't ring the INS in Chicago. That means you and Chaz were well on your way to Princeton before Lacey was murdered. And you already had the names of Angel and Gerardo before you got here. I'll bet you don't know the names of any other illegals who might have crossed the border the same night. You beat the cops to Lacey's by several minutes. You and Chaz showed up—guns drawn—like Butch and Sundance. You knew their names, and you knew where they were, Bo. And if you knew Gerardo was the dead one in the basement, you must have had a description. So—I'll ask again—how did you know?" Liam picked up DeVine's empty O'Doul's, then headed to the kitchen.

DeVine called out, "Lacey called me the morning she was murdered."

Liam stopped what he was doing. "She called *you*?"

DeVine nodded. "She told me about Angel and Gerardo—that they had witnessed the murders in Arizona and claimed the Border Patrol had done it. She told them if they could get to Princeton, she would help them."

"That would be harboring criminals," Liam said. "It doesn't sound like Lacey."

"Which is why she called me and asked if I would meet her here to take them into custody," DeVine said. "She wanted to be with them when I did."

Liam popped another O'Doul's open and caught DeVine's gaze as he walked into the kitchen and greeted it with a cautious squint. Liam slid the bottle to DeVine as he realized for the first time DeVine's and Angel's stories showed signs of coming together.

"When did you know about your AWOL border agents?" Liam asked.

DeVine said, "The day before Lacey called. That's why when she accused two of our agents of committing the murders, I knew she had something. But I didn't know their names until Chaz told us about the BOLO today. You and I found out at the same time."

Liam nodded. "How did you and Lacey know each other?"

DeVine said, "We met about a year ago during an immigration case in federal court for the Northern District of Illinois. A Somali man and his family had made it to Canada, then stowed away in the back of a truck as they crossed into the states at Sault Ste. Marie. Eventually, they were picked up in Milwaukee and faced deportation. Somehow, Lacey's firm got involved, and they sent her to Chicago to represent the defendant. We were on opposite sides of the court that day, but still, there was mutual respect. She remembered me and had my business card."

"Did you ever find out if she called Castille about Angel and Gerardo?" Liam asked.

DeVine said, "It wasn't in her phone records."

"You've seen them?" Liam asked.

DeVine paused midsip as if he'd wet himself. "Look, I came here because I need your help finding Angel."

"C'mon, DeVine. I'm a local yokel. I've got a hobby farm, and I teach history, math, and economics at a small college."

"You know the people and the area. And, I hate to admit this, but you're smart. I'm not sure where your instincts come from, but they're good."

Liam sipped more Jack and said nothing.

"Okay, okay," DeVine said. "I'll admit Penn and Gallagher are probably the shooters in the desert. Maybe even at Lacey's. But they're Taconelli's problem now. Mine is finding Angel."

DeVine would have a valid point if Liam hadn't heard Angel's side of the story—but he wasn't about to bring it up. His gut wanted to help DeVine, but his brain told him not to risk getting involved. And if Taconelli was concentrating on Penn and Gallagher, Liam would have some breathing room. And as long as he could keep the cops away from the pole barn—and Angel chained up in his RV—he'd be fine.

Liam picked up his drink and stood, prompting DeVine to do the same. "Let's get comfortable." He led DeVine to the den, where he poured them both a glass of eighteen-year-old Macallan from the ornate oak bar. He fell into the oversized leather chair, while DeVine took the sofa. They toasted from across the room. Liam sipped while DeVine admired the aroma of the fine Scotch but elected to place his whiskey on the coaster.

"Don't like Scotch?" Liam asked.

"I'm a beer guy."

"I thought we'd established O'Doul's isn't beer."

DeVine paused a beat as he studied Liam from across the room. "Mind if I ask you what you did after college?"

Liam said, "Traveled around Europe. The Middle East. Asia. I rode a motorcycle for most of it. I'd been in school my whole life and needed to do something different."

"For eight years? Where'd you get the money?"

"Inheritance," Liam said. "I lost my parents young. I lived with my grandparents while I was in college, then they both passed away. You mean Chaz didn't get that far?"

DeVine said, "To go deeper, we'd need a warrant."

*Was that a warning or a threat?* Liam wondered. He said, "Playing devil's advocate here, what if you find Angel before Taconelli finds Penn and Gallagher?"

DeVine said, "They're two different issues. If I find Angel, my work is done. It's Taconelli's job to determine who did it."

"But you want it to be Angel," Liam said.

"I want it to be the guilty," DeVine said.

Liam drew in a breath and said, "Okay. I'm in. But I have two conditions."

"Great!" DeVine said, a smile beaming. "What's it going to cost me?"

"First, complete anonymity. No one knows I'm helping you, and if I find Angel or Penn or Gallagher or Jimmy Hoffa, I don't want credit."

"I can live with that," DeVine said. "What else?"

"I want to see the phone records."

DeVine sighed. "I don't know if I can do that. The records are evidence, and the investigation is still open."

"Then let me whet your appetite," Liam said. "You told me about Lacey, so now, it's my turn. Angel, Penn, and Gallagher."

"What about them?"

"They are still here."

DeVine's eyes went wide. "How the hell do you know that?"

Reaching beside the chair, Liam felt for the item he had placed there earlier. After reshaping the bill, he wedged it onto his head and let DeVine see him do it. DeVine did, and his eyes narrowed as he squinted at the cap as if it were the sun.

DeVine asked, "What do the Dodgers have to do with anything?" Liam spun the hat to him like a Frisbee, and DeVine fumbled the catch, then examined it. "I still don't get it."

"Look inside the band," Liam said.

DeVine did, turning it over and over until he found the words *Te amo. RA* handwritten in black Sharpie. "I love you too," DeVine said. "So?"

"I found the cap on my property—*after* Taconelli questioned me. *RA* are the initials of Rolando Alvarez. Whoever dropped that cap took it off Rolando in Lukeville. There's still sand in the band."

DeVine fondled the cap, divining all he could from the texture. "Where are they?" he asked, then spun the cap back to Liam, who wedged it back on his head.

"I don't know, but I've been hunting these woods for a long time. There are places."

DeVine, his gaze locked onto Liam, asked, "How will the phone records help to find Angel?"

"I never said they would."

DeVine said nothing at first. He only sat, staring at Liam and the Dodgers cap. Finally, he stood and said, "I'll get my briefcase."

# CHAPTER 17

DeVine returned with his briefcase and a manila file folder in his grasp. Liam met him at the nook, where DeVine lay both items down but let ten of his fingers tap the folder like a silent piano tune. Something important was inside, something DeVine was still battling internally to reveal.

Liam understood the gravity of the situation. A federal agent was about to show a person of interest evidence in a murder case. Liam said, "I'm not the killer, Bo. And you know that."

DeVine nodded. Then, after a few more taps, he slid the folder across to Liam.

Inside was a single page of laser-printed phone records in a miniature font. At the top of the first page were two phone numbers indicating the ones involved in the search.

SULLIVAN, LACEY J. 304-555-5368.

SULLIVAN, LACEY J. 703-555-2875.

With DeVine pointing at the page from across the table, they started down the list, line by line. Liam recognized the *304* number as the one for Lacey next door. The *703* number was her private cell phone—a number she rarely gave out. He asked, "What about the records for her condo in Virginia? Or Scott's place? Or her office phone? Or her work cell phone?"

DeVine shrugged and said, "This is what homicide gave me."

Liam nodded as he started down the list in chronological order. He touched each line as if a little bit of Lacey could be absorbed from the pulp and the print. In the right-hand margin, notes had been scribbled.

Most of the calls were labeled as dry cleaners or take-out pizza or Chinese restaurants. There was one for an insurance company and one for another attorney (maybe her divorce lawyer). The first call to stand out was from this past Friday, August 23, 1995, at 3:45 a.m., made from a pay phone in Lukeville to Lacey's personal cell phone and lasting fifteen minutes and forty-five seconds.

082395 03:45 520-555-8114 TO 703-555-2875 15:45   Pay phone Lukeville to LSM

DeVine interjected, "This is a pay phone outside a truck stop in Lukeville. We think Angel or Gerardo called Lacey right after they killed Rolando and the baby."

Liam glanced at DeVine. "You mean right after they witnessed Penn and Gallagher commit a double murder."

"Sure," DeVine said as they went to the next call from Lacey's mobile.

082395 04:20 703-555-2875 TO 310-555-2525 5:03   LSM to Sierra

"Is that who I think it is?" Liam asked. "Lacey called Sierra, the singer?"

DeVine nodded. "You didn't know they were friendly?"

Liam shook his head. "Maybe to tell her about her brother?" DeVine only shrugged, and Liam continued to the next line of interest.

082395 12:02 520-555-8114 TO 703-555-2875 3:12   Pay phone Lukeville to LSM

DeVine said, "Gillespie and I think Angel or Gerardo called Lacey to let her know they made the bus."

Liam nodded, then swallowed hard when he saw his own cell phone number—the first in a long series from Lacey to him he never answered because he had been in Toledo and left the phone in Princeton—on purpose.

082395 16:34 703-555-2875 TO 304-555-4960 0:00   LSM to L Curran cell
082395 18:56 703-555-2875 TO 304-555-4960 0:00   LSM to L Curran cell
082495 09:03 703-555-2875 TO 304-555-4960 0:00   LSM to L Curran cell
082495 13:43 703-555-2875 TO 304-555-4960 0:00   LSM to L Curran cell
082595 09:00 703-555-2875 TO 304-555-4960 0:00   LSM to L Curran cell

DeVine said, "Taconelli had the cellular company investigate the tower data. It's less than a mile from here, and your cell phone stayed connected to the same tower from Wednesday until you left for the bar Saturday night."

Liam let his gaze fall back to the page, where his thumb touched the next three lines, then stopped at the fourth, where Lacey had called Louisa.

082595 10:18 703-555-2875 TO 304-555-8854 10:12   LSM to Louisa (maid)

Liam's finger stopped moving, and DeVine said, "Louisa told Taconelli that Lacey called her Friday morning and asked her to stock the fridge because she would be coming in for the weekend with a guest."

For the rest of Friday, there were several more inconsequential calls to names and places in DC and one to Scott's cell phone. Nothing of interest showed up until early Saturday morning and the five calls Liam remembered too well.

082695 01:12 703-555-2875 TO 304-555-4839 0:00   LSM to L Curran home

082695 02:20 703-555-2875 TO 304-555-4839 0:00   LSM to L Curran home

082695 02:35 703-555-2875 TO 304-555-4839 0:00   LSM to L Curran home

082695 02:49 703-555-2875 TO 304-555-4839 0:00   LSM to L Curran home

082695 03:35 703-555-2875 TO 304-555-4839 0:00   LSM to L Curran home

When Liam looked at DeVine, their eyes met, but DeVine said nothing; his pressed lips and faint nod spoke volumes.

Liam shook his head and whispered to the page, "I wish I'd picked up the damn phone." He let his finger touch the next line.

082695 05:02 304-555-2287 TO 304-555-3798 05:02   Bus to LS home

DeVine said, "We think they called Lacey to let her know they had arrived. It matches the schedule the bus station provided." He caught Liam's gaze and said, "The next one's going to sting."

082695 05:31 304-555-3798 TO 304-555-4839 05:31   LS home to L Curran home

DeVine was right, and Liam felt it from his gut to the pounding in his head. The last call Lacey had made before she was murdered was to him.

DeVine said, "The ME believes Lacey's TOD was about the same time."

Liam touched the ink on the page, remembering he had intended to return the call. It wouldn't have mattered. Lacey was dead by then.

"Sorry," DeVine said, then touched Liam's forearm.

"She needed me," Liam said. "She had four strangers in her house, and she was terrified. He shook his head. "I sure fucked this up."

"You didn't know," DeVine said. "Think of it this way—you could have been murdered too."

Liam shook his head, then glanced down at the last line of interest.

082695 09:31 304-555-3798 TO 911 09:22   LS home to 911

"Louisa's call to nine-one-one," Liam said, grinding his jaw. He studied the sheets again, going down the list and the notes in the margins over and over until something finally jumped out. It wasn't what he saw but what he *didn't* see.

"It's not here, Bo," Liam said. "Lacey's call to you the morning she died."

DeVine took the pages from Liam and studied them. "Hmm. I didn't notice, but I guess she didn't call me from either of these phones."

"Was she at her condo or was she at Scott's?" Liam asked with urgency.

"I—I'm not sure. I don't have those records."

"Where's *your* cell phone?" Liam asked. "We can check the log."

DeVine shook his head. "She didn't call my cell phone."

"Where else would she call you that early in the morning?" Liam asked.

DeVine let out a long sigh and leaned back against the bench. "You have some real trust issues, you know that? Do you still have my business card or did you shitcan it?"

Liam retrieved the card from the windowsill in the kitchen. "What about it?" he asked.

"I gave Lacey the same card. Do you see my mobile number?"

"No. Office and fax," Liam said.

"That's right," DeVine said. "If she called my office, it forwards to my home phone in the evenings. Not my cell phone."

"Sorry," Liam said as he closed his eyes and washed his hands over his face. "Castille's number isn't here either. I wonder why she didn't call her partner."

"You're asking good questions," DeVine said. "Which is exactly why I want you helping me." He drained the O'Doul's, then asked, "So—what's our first move?"

Liam chuckled. "I don't know about *our* first move, but *mine* is to go to bed. It's late. Tomorrow I—"

There was a faint ringing from another room deep in the house. Liam checked his watch. DeVine checked the rooster clock above the stove: 10:33 p.m.

DeVine asked, "Is that a phone?"

"Yeah. It's in another room."

"The one on the wall isn't ringing."

Liam said, "The ringer's off."

"You have a strange technology phobia for a man with a degree in electrical engineering," DeVine said.

"That's exactly *why* I have the phobia," Liam said. DeVine grabbed his briefcase, then Liam led him to the front door, where DeVine paused before committing to the door handle.

Liam anticipated what was coming and said, "Look—I'm sure a rogue Mexican in this town will stand out, but Penn and Gallagher might be tougher to spot. Do you have any photos?"

DeVine opened the briefcase, removed two color photos, and handed them to Liam, who held them up, one in each hand. DeVine said, "You can keep the phone records but not the photos. They're my only copies."

Liam studied the two headshots of agents in olive-green Border Patrol uniforms posing before a backdrop of the US Border Patrol seal and an American flag. Both men wore shiny black leather utility belts complete with .40 caliber Beretta pistols on their hips.

Penn's face was narrow, with a protruding chin and a slight dimple. His eyes were dark, brown maybe, and his smile was toothy and bright. Gallagher sported a rounder face with a wider chin. His eyes appeared to be green or hazel, and his smile was tight and toothless. Penn wore the lone wedding band.

Liam passed the photos back to DeVine, then opened the front door, and DeVine swatted away a diving moth as he stepped outside. Liam said, "In all seriousness, I'd be careful if I were you. Penn and Gallagher are still out there, and they know who you are and *why* you're here. You're looking for Angel. And so are they. Remember, they knew Angel and Gerardo were going to be at Lacey's—*before* you did."

"We can get started tomorrow," DeVine said. "I kept my end of the bargain."

"And I haven't made up my mind yet," Liam said. "Good night, Agent DeVine."

Frustrated, DeVine turned away and started down the stairs. Liam waited until DeVine's taillights had disappeared before heading to the safe room and the phone that had rung earlier.

This phone didn't connect to the local phone company but rather to a device in the attic and then the satellite dish on the roof. Only one person called this number, and before he dialed, he flipped the toggle switch mounted to the side of the phone, engaging the encryption device. He waited for the white noise on the line to clear before he spoke to the party on the other end.

"Hello, Ginny. It's a little late in the evening for you, isn't it?"

. . .

Ginny Woodburn let out a long breath. "Can you talk *now*?"

"I have a moment."

"Good. I had a visitor today. The White House is asking questions about Toledo. I know it was you, so don't bother with your bull. This vendetta has to stop."

Liam massaged his temples. "So—who's pissed at me now?"

"Patricia came to see me," Ginny said. "She suspects someone is finishing what the ghost of Trevor Harmon didn't."

"Everyone needs a hobby," Liam said.

"Seems Paul Kelvington has one now. She sent him to interrogate the man who survived your little operation," Ginny said.

"No one survived!" Liam snapped.

Ginny said, "You missed Saliba."

"The hell I did!" Liam shot back, but his mind drifted back to Toledo. Saliba would have been Mika's target, not his. "Okay—it's possible."

Ginny said, "Why Saliba? He wasn't part of the NEST."

"His boss was," Liam said, then asked, "and you're sure he's still alive?"

"Who would know better than Paul Kelvington?" Ginny said.

"Kelvington talked to Saliba," Liam whispered back. "Listen—if you're calling to order me not to pursue Saliba, you can forget it. I've got a little side project with the school PTA, but when I'm finished—"

"You don't have any children," Ginny said.

"We don't know that," Liam said.

Ginny said, "Toledo wasn't the only topic Patricia wanted to discuss. Are you familiar with HR6363, the Renner-Kline Bill?"

"Refresh my memory."

Ginny said, "The law would give amnesty to any illegal in the country without a felony criminal record and would lessen the sentences of those who voluntarily turned themselves in for deportation. Then, if they returned, the slate will be clean. It would also allow any legal immigrant the right to citizenship within four years. It all but dissolves our borders and creates a scenario allowing foreigners the ability to vote in our elections."

"That's a big problem," Liam said. "Just have Patricia fix it."

Ginny said, "She had it stalled in committee, but now there's pressure to get it to the floor for a vote. And—she believes the president is being blackmailed to sign it."

Liam said, "Where's it coming from?"

Ginny said, "What do you know about the murders in Lukeville, Arizona?"

Liam stood, causing the monitors to tremble in their mounts. "I—may have heard something about it. Border Patrol agents murdered two illegals?"

"That's the one," Ginny said. "The murders are high profile for two reasons. One, they killed a baby, and two, Rolando Alvarez—the man who was murdered—was the brother of Sierra. She and her lawyer are putting the full-court press on the media, and that is putting gigantic pressure on the HIBSS committee to push the bill through. I hate to sound callous, but the murder couldn't have happened at a better time to push the bill through."

"You think it *was* deliberate," Liam said.

"Bingo," Ginny said. "And I need you to find out who is behind the blackmail."

"How much does your daughter know?" Liam asked.

"Nothing," Ginny said. "And she *can't* know. She asked for my help, and I refused. To be honest, I don't care about the president, but when someone blackmails the office of the president, they blackmail the country."

Liam sat back down. If Rolando Alvarez's death had been engineered, then Lacey's probably was too, and Angel's story just gained another truth point. He and his brother didn't drag Lacey into anything. Lacey was a target, and Angel and his brother were in the wrong place at the wrong time. And now, Liam had resources and carte blanche. Bo DeVine was going to be thrilled. And, if Paul Kelvington was in any way involved—well—that offered up another opportunity.

"Are you still there?" Ginny's tinny voice spilled from the earpiece.

"Yeah. Sorry," Liam said. "I'm in, but I need to do something you're not going to like."

"Like what?" Ginny asked.

"I have to talk to your daughter."

"You know that can't happen!" Ginny said.

"Sure, it can," Liam said. "But I need to know their itineraries for the next few days."

"No. I can't do that," Ginny said.

Liam said, "Then I'm out. Find someone else." He hung up, then turned off the encryption device, wondering how long it would take her to call him back. She didn't, but he knew she would.

It was getting late, and his mind was foggy. But on his way to the bedroom, passing headlights pulsed through the front windows, painting the walls in fading whites and grays. He parted the drapes and found a car had stopped in the street near his gate. Then, it backed up. Stopped. Adjusted. Eased forward, then finally stopped at the bottom of the drive.

An arm appeared from the driver's side, and a finger poked at the button several times. Finally, the doorbell chimed. Illuminated by the overhead light at the gate, the beige Mercedes coupe stood out by damn near blending in. Liam eyed the noisy box through two ring cycles. Exhausted, his patience waning, the last thing he wanted to do was to talk to this idiot, but his mind kept going back to his conversation with Taconelli.

He needed something from this man. And to quote Sun Tzu, "In the midst of chaos, there is also opportunity," so now might be a good time. His finger pressed the Talk button.

"Who is it?" he said to the speaker.

"It's—it's…Scott," the voice said. "Scott Sluvilan. We need to talk."

# CHAPTER 18

---

Princeton, West Virginia
Tuesday, August 29, 1995
12:42 a.m.

Liam checked the grandfather clock in the corner—12:42 a.m. Scott, his voice clearly slurred from liquid courage, had also grown a pair of booze balls. *This ought to be good.* Liam opened the gate and waited until the uncertain Mercedes was parked and Scott was stumbling to the porch before opening the door.

"A little late for a chat, don't you think, Scott?" Liam asked.

Scott Sullivan stopped walking, but his head missed the message, and he nearly walked into the edge of the open screen door. Missing it by inches, he staggered, then steadied himself with a grip on the porch swing chain. Liam stepped outside to meet him.

"Whoa, big fella," Liam said, taking an extra step to catch the stumbling drunk.

Scott, still clinging to the chain, spun onto the swing as his grip slid down. His eyes were bloodshot pools over alcohol-reddened cheeks.

Liam sniffed. Vodka. Most likely laced with a couple of olives and vermouth. Letting Scott have the swing, Liam opted to lean against the railing. "You need some coffee."

"I need my Lacey back." Scott reached out and found the swing chain again and steadied himself as he leaned forward.

"We all do," Liam said instead. Their eyes met, but Scott was unable to hold the stare for more than a few seconds.

"You—you took her from me." Scott tried to point, but his left hand ended up in his lap.

"I didn't kill Lacey, Scott."

"I know. But I think she loved you."

"You're just drunk."

"Bullshit!" Scott barked.

Liam let his eyes search the slurring Scott Sullivan for any bulges in his clothing where a gun might be hiding but saw nothing obvious. At this point, if Scott did have a weapon, he'd be lucky to get to it.

"She was moving back home," Scott said.

Liam shifted his stance. "I didn't know you two had worked it out."

"We were together the night she came here." Scott covered his face and leaned back in the swing, letting it rock. A mistake, as he lurched forward and blew chunks onto the porch.

*"Really?"* Liam said, watching Scott wipe his mouth on the tail of his shirt. Liam moved from the railing to the downwind rocker.

"Soorrry," Scott slurred.

Liam asked, "So, you knew she was coming here?"

"Mm-hmm. Said she was meeting clients in the morning. We argued 'bout it. Told her I thought she was coming to see you."

"Did she mention their names?"

"No." Scott squinted through bloodshot eyes. "Cops asked me the same thing." After a belch, and catching it before it became more, he pointed toward Lacey's and said, "The cops didn't even clean it up. Blood and that—that—black dust is everywhere. They just took their yellow tape and went home. Pricks. Blood smells bad. Bet you didn't know that." A crooked finger poked at Liam as Scott lost his balance. One foot found the porch, the other found vomit, then his ass found the floor as the porch swing returned and hit him in the head. He rolled onto his side through the puke.

*Keep that up, and I won't have to hose that spot down,* Liam thought. He hovered over the lump of Scott, wondering how much more sympathy he needed to dish out. He turned Scott around until he was sitting on the stairs. Scott lay back and covered his eyes with a forearm.

Liam asked, "What time did Lacey leave DC?"

"Oh shit! Bed spins," Scott moaned as he sat up. "Something like eleven o'clock Friday night." His head twisted slowly toward the front door. "Lacey said you were living with a woman?"

A question, not a statement, and Liam cracked a smile. "Don't worry. She's not home."

Scott nodded. "Cops asked me if I had an alibi. Pricks! Good thing I went to the office Saturday morning and used my key card."

*Yeah. Good thing, pussy,* Liam thought.

Scott said, "Now, they think maybe two Border Patrol guys did it."

"I heard that too," Liam said.

Scott slapped his thighs and said, "I'm sorry for bothering you. And for throwing up on your porch and—you seem like an okay guy to me."

*Sorry to hear that,* Liam thought, but said, "Forget it. We cleared the air."

"I suppose. I always hated you, you know?"

*Get in line,* Liam thought, then said, "I won't hold it against you." He stood and pulled Scott to his feet. "C'mon. Let's get you back home." He held out his hand, but Scott just stared at it. "I need your keys," Liam said, snapping his fingers. "Friends don't let friends drive drunk."

Scott said, "I drove myself here, and I can drive myself back."

Liam didn't budge. His goal had less to do with getting this pansy-ass home than it did with getting—something else.

He waited until Scott had dug the keys out of his pocket and slapped them into his palm. "Sit tight. I'll be right back," he said, then opened the door and went back to the safe room, where he picked up a small thermal printer. On his way out, he slipped on a lightweight jacket and shoved the thermal printer into a pocket.

"A jacket? It's gotta be eighty degrees," Scott said.

Liam pulled the door open. "I get chilled in the night air."

They climbed into Scott's Mercedes with Liam behind the wheel, and moments later, they were parked behind the moving van. Liam followed Scott into the house, where he dropped the keys into the mosaic bowl on the hall table, just as he had done with Lacey many times before. He drew in a breath of nostalgia but received a whiff of bleach and lemon-scented something instead. Hidden beneath it was the too familiar stench of death and dried blood.

"Want to see it?" Scott asked with an undertone of scandal.

"See what?" Liam asked.

"Where it happened." Scott paused near the basement stairs.

Liam didn't answer but followed Scott downstairs, where fluorescent lights flickered to life, exposing the residue of fingerprint powder on light switches and along the edge of the pool table. The cue ball was powdered, and he assumed the other balls might be too. Scott stood by the bar near a half-empty glass of clear liquid and an uncapped bottle of Grey Goose.

"They found the dead Mexican here," Scott said, pointing to the fresh carpet stains. "He was lying on his back. His head was near the bar, and his feet were at the pool table. He was shot in the face." Scott grimaced, then glanced toward the stairs and the two stains the size of deflated basketballs. "Lacey was over there. Face down."

Liam knelt between the two stains, resisting the urge to touch them. Lacey was here. Shot in the back. Shot in the head. Why did someone so innocent have to go out this way? Finally, he did let the tip of his finger touch the edge of one stain. Under his breath, Liam said, "Don't worry. I'll find them. I promise."

Liam put himself into Angel's version of the story. If they had all been lined up at the pool table and Gerardo had been shot first—and was found lying on his back between the table and the bar—Liam must have imagined it wrong. Rather than facing the bar, they must have been lined up facing the pool table. That meant the two border agents must have been on the other side, between the pool table and the wall. Or, at the ends of the pool table. But if they were at the ends, Gerardo's body would have fallen at some angle instead of straight.

Kneeling, Liam searched the green felt for gunpowder residue but found nothing. The forensics team could have pulled it. What he found instead were a few crimson droplets on the edge of the pool table on the bar side. Gerardo must have been leaning against it.

Liam imagined the rest of the events unfolding as he slid the patio screen door to the right, then let it go. A spring mechanism forced the door closed. He slid it open again, pressed on a lever, and the screen caught. He rewound the scene in his mind. *Two shooters. One shoots Gerardo in the hand and face, and the other shoots Lacey in the back when she runs while Angel escapes through the screen door.* He stepped onto the patio. From this vantage point, DeVine said he had looked inside and seen the two bodies. All Liam could see was Scott Sullivan, confused and staring back at him from the bar. Liam stepped inside and closed the screen.

"What are you doing?" Scott asked.

"Just trying to imagine the scene." He sat on the edge of the pool table, remembering it was something Lacey hated because it knocked the table off level. Then, he smiled as he recalled the last time he was on this pool table. He had been naked. Lacey had been naked too.

Liam asked, "When are you going back to DC?"

"The movers will be here early, and the cleaning crew should finish by tomorrow night. Then, I'm out of here." Scott eyed the clock. "I gotta get some sleep." Stretching, he started for the stairs, but Liam wasn't quite finished.

"I almost forgot. I loaned Lacey some tools."

Scott's eyes narrowed. "Tools? What sort of—"

"You know, screwdrivers, wrenches, a hammer. They were in a little green metal box with a silver handle the size of a lunch pail."

"Tools," Scott said again as if translating the word from a foreign language. "Where would she keep something like that?"

"The garage, maybe? The little outbuilding? Is there a utility room?" All questions Liam knew the answers to.

"Yes to all three," Scott said.

"If you check the outbuilding, I'll check the garage and utility room."

"Fine," Scott said. "I need a flashlight." While Scott knelt behind the bar to check the cabinets, Liam refrained from suggesting he check the top drawer beside the dishwasher in the kitchenette. Scott finally found the flashlight, then, after turning on the patio light, he gave the misty backyard a good once-over, then started his trek to the outbuilding.

Liam raced up the stairs, and by the time he reached the utility room, the thermal printer was in his palm. It took a few seconds to hook up the power adapter to the outlet over the dryer and to insert the nine-pin data cable into the port at the bottom of the master security panel. Using the keypad, he entered his six-digit code, then cycled through the menu, entered the date range he needed, then pressed Print. A minute later, the thermal printer softly whirred and spat out a continuous, narrow strip of slick paper—as if giving the home an EKG. When it stopped, Liam ripped off the strip and stuffed it into his jacket pocket along with the printer and cables just as he heard the basement door slam shut.

"Any luck?" Scott called out.

Liam turned to the row of white cabinets above the washer and dryer, opened the far-right door, and found the green toolbox Lacey had purchased herself. "Found it," Liam announced and held it up as Scott appeared at the utility room door.

"It's smaller than I thought," Scott said and turned away. When Liam caught up with Scott, he was holding the front door open.

They shook hands, then Liam stepped onto the porch, Scott closed the screen, and they stared at each other through the mesh.

"I still think you two had a thing," Scott said timidly.

"I don't know how to change your mind," Liam said. "And I frankly don't care at this point. She's gone and we both lose. End of story."

An uncomfortable silence fell between them, neither man knowing what to say next. Scott appeared as if he didn't want to be alone, and Liam couldn't wait to leave. It was late and he had more work to do.

"The wake and funeral are tomorrow morning. It's closed casket," Scott said.

Liam stepped off the porch. "I'll send fresh flowers."

"She'd like that," Scott said.

Liam remained blank, but inside, he was shaking his head. *Lacey hated people who cut real flowers.*

Scott closed the door, leaving Liam on the porch staring at the moths buzzing in the light with the small green toolbox in his hand: his consolation prize. The one thing of Lacey's he could keep. A toolbox. Not even a good one.

He lingered where the walk met the driveway, stopping to look at the Audi. He touched it again as if making up for the funeral he would miss. Inside the Audi were coffee cups from McDonald's and shopping bags from Neiman Marcus, Macy's, and—the Victoria's Secret bag intrigued him. There was another from Bath & Body Works—he could smell her skin now. In the back, seat-belted no less, was the stuffed Snoopy he had won for her at Disney World. He thought she had thrown it away.

# CHAPTER 19

---

Liam jogged the half mile home. In the safe room, at the computer table, he unrolled the thermal paper and flattened it next to the phone records, using tape to keep it from curling.

The time stamp from Lacey's security system wouldn't match his or the phone company's, but it shouldn't matter, and he spent the next hour transferring the information from the thermal paper to an Excel spreadsheet.

The start date he had chosen was the week prior, and as he'd expected, there was a line for Monday, August 21, 1995, at 4:53 p.m., when Lacey had entered her security code to activate the system when she'd left for DC.

Like his own security system, every event was recorded and stored. Doors opening and closing. Windows opening and closing. Motion detectors. Smoke alarms. Even if the alarm was disabled, the system still logged events but didn't send them to the monitoring company. Additionally, every person had their own four-digit code. It took a six-digit code to enter the admin system, and that code belonged to Liam.

Lacey's four-digit code had been entered multiple times on the days before August 21, with Louisa's sprinkled in. But hers lessened dramatically when the house went on the market and Lacey returned to DC. The last favor Liam had performed for Lacey was to set a new code for the realtors to use. So far, up until Friday, August 25, no activities had been recorded. No Louisa. No realtors. And no Lacey.

Liam opened the spreadsheet on the left monitor, the camera

system on the right, and the phone records on the desk, creating a triangular reference. The problem with the camera was that he couldn't see Lacey's house—only the field between them and a little of the main road. He scrolled down the spreadsheet and put the date, *08251995*, at the top—the Friday before the murder and the day Louisa said she shopped for Lacey and a guest.

At 11:12 a.m., Louisa's code disarmed the system. The detectors showed she moved through the den to the kitchen, reversed course, armed the system, then left. Her code was used again at 2:15 p.m. This time, it showed she had also gone into the basement, most likely to put groceries in the kitchenette fridge. She left as expected and armed the system as she should have. Once again, the house went completely quiet until the next morning when Lacey's code was used to disarm the system.

    4:45 a.m. FRONT DOOR OPEN
    4:45 a.m. FRONT DOOR CLOSED
    4:46 a.m. SYSTEM DISARMED BY L. SULLIVAN
    4:46 a.m. DEN MD
    4:48 a.m. UPSTAIRS HALL MD
    4:49 a.m. MASTER BED MD
    4:50 a.m. UPSTAIRS HALL MD
    4:50 a.m. DEN MD
    4:51 a.m. SYSTEM ARMED BY L. SULLIVAN
    4:51 a.m. FRONT DOOR OPEN
    4:51 a.m. FRONT DOOR CLOSED

Because it was still dark, he forwarded the video to those same times and saw the hint of headlights across the field, most likely belonging to Lacey Sullivan arriving from DC. If she had left when Scott said, the timing was about right. Lacey had entered the house, gone to her bedroom, done something for a couple of minutes, then immediately left the house again. Checking the phone records, he figured she was probably on her way to the bus station to pick up Angel and Gerardo. He fast-forwarded the video to 5:29 to match the activity log.

5:29 a.m. FRONT DOOR OPEN
5:29 a.m. FRONT DOOR CLOSED
5:29 a.m. SYSTEM DISARMED BY L. SULLIVAN
5:30 a.m. DEN MD
5:31 a.m. KITCHEN MD
5:31 a.m. UPSTAIRS HALL MD
5:32 a.m. MASTER BED MD
5:32 a.m. BASEMENT MD
5:33 a.m. BAR MD
5:34 a.m. UPSTAIRS HALL MD
5:35 a.m. DEN MD
5:35 a.m. KITCHEN MD
5:36 a.m. BASEMENT MD
5:44 a.m. PATIO DOOR OPEN MD
5:45 a.m. PATIO MD

It all made sense initially until the motion detector in the kitchen tripped before the one in the upstairs hallway. It was a physical impossibility for one person to trip those two in that order without first tripping the den's motion detector. The same phenomenon occurred when the master bedroom and the basement tripped at the same time.

Lacey was no longer alone.

He then traced to the last line to where the bar door and patio motion detectors had tripped, one after the other, at 5:44 and 5:45. This must have been Angel and the shooters running from the basement, and the video showed spooked animals in the field. Then, the house went quiet, and Lacey Sullivan was most certainly dead.

Liam fisted his eyes to clear them before continuing, but at this point, the activity log coincided with Louisa's return to Lacey's,

where she would shortly after discover the bodies. The log indicated
Louisa was running all over the house. The last subset seemed
to match exactly what he would expect from Louisa finding the
bodies and DeVine doing the same.

    9:15 a.m. FRONT DOOR OPEN
    9:15 a.m. FRONT DOOR CLOSED
    9:16 a.m. DEN MD
    9:17 a.m. KITCHEN MD
    9:20 a.m. BASEMENT MD
    9:21 a.m. BAR MD
    9:21 a.m. BASEMENT MD
    9:21 a.m. KITCHEN MD
    9:29 a.m. PATIO MD
    9:31 a.m. BAR MD
    9:33 a.m. PATIO DOOR CLOSED MD
    9:33 a.m. PATIO MD
    9:35 a.m. DEN MD

After printing the Excel sheet and closing the videos, he considered his next move—if there was going to be one. And that was
when his BICA-modified PagSat pager vibrated across the desk.

Liam picked it up and opened the text from Ginny—and smiled.
Now, his next moves had been decided.

Liam gathered every TV dinner from the upright freezer in the
garage, the upstairs kitchen, and the kitchenette in the basement,
then dumped them into a green garbage bag. He added a couple of
bottles of soda, three bags of chips, bread, peanut butter, Doritos,
and toilet paper, then hauled it to the pole barn, hoping it wouldn't
rip along the way. Without knocking, he opened the door to the
RV and found Angel in the recliner, watching an episode of *Little
House on the Prairie*. Liam dumped the contents of the garbage
bag on the counter and loaded up the RV's freezer.

"*Lo que está sucediendo?*" (What's happening?) Angel asked. "I saw headlights earlier."

"You'll be on your own for a day or two," Liam responded in Spanish. Angel spun around in the recliner, his face—pitiful. "There's enough food for a week. The RV is connected to the garage power and water, so you'll have plenty of television, air-conditioning." As Angel gripped the thick chains around his waist, Liam added, "It won't be much longer. Even the government is looking for Border Patrol agents."

"You could take me to another city. I could disappear."

"It's an option," Liam said. "When I get back."

Liam returned to the safe room, where he picked up a go-bag and a 9 mm Glock 26 from the pegboard. For what he was about to do, he needed something concealable.

In the bedroom, he stuffed a few items into a gym bag, went back downstairs, found his keys, then threw everything into the BMW and opened the garage. It was 3:25 a.m. and still dark, but a spill of orange lit the mountaintop. Liam turned on the headlights at the bottom of the driveway. While waiting for the gate to close, he glanced toward Lacey's. How things had changed since Saturday morning. He dropped the BMW into drive, then sped away.

An hour later, he was on I-81 heading north. He popped a Journey CD into the player, then settled in for the long drive. Just past Harrisonburg, he called the college to let them know he would be out for two days. At 8:45 a.m., Liam took the Arlington exit off of I-66. Figuring DeVine was awake by now and enjoying his complimentary hotel breakfast, Liam decided to give him a quick call.

After a few niceties, DeVine asked, "Feeling guilty about stiffing me?"

"I'm calling to let you know that I changed my mind," Liam said.

"That's great," DeVine said. "When do we start?"

Liam said, "I already have."

DeVine said, "That wasn't the deal. I need to come by and…"

"Don't. I'm not home. I'll call you later." Liam clicked off and ignored the two callbacks.

In downtown Arlington, he found a meter on the main drag, then walked the two blocks to a café, where he bought a donut and a black coffee, then took a seat near the window to get a good look at the five-star Hotel Monte. Outside, college-aged kids were placing flyers on windshields—something about anti-car, pro-environmental nonsense. People zigzagged the streets from building to building.

Satisfied he'd seen enough, he left Arlington and followed the outer loop to Alexandria, where he parked, then hoofed it several blocks to a gated condominium community surrounded by a ten-foot white-painted brick wall with one way in and out. He watched several cars make the trip through the orange boom gates. A key card would raise the bars, but if it didn't work, a tired old guard would make a call before raising the boom gate from inside. Liam had more legwork to do, but—having been here before—recalled the only cameras were at the gate and each corner of the white wall.

Confident nothing had changed since the last time he was here, he decided to stick with his original plan. Timing was the key now, and he hoped the information Ginny had given him was correct.

# CHAPTER 20

Arlington, Virginia
Wednesday, August 30, 1995
11:45 a.m.

Paul pushed against the brass plate of the Hotel Monte's revolving door, spun through, then crossed the empty, sunken mosaic-tiled lobby and scanned the area until he spotted the lone man sitting at the hotel's bar. When Paul's reflection hit the booze-lined mirror, the man glanced his way, then turned back to the bar.

Taking a seat at a high-top put Paul in a great spot to see the mounted televisions and the two analysts miming their predictions for the upcoming UCLA football game. The barmaid placed a small square napkin in front of him, followed by a whiskey sour, just as the man from the bar approached, a beer in his grasp.

Zilo Bauer sat, sucked the foam off the top of his beer, then eyed the whiskey sour. "Did I get it right?"

"Perfect," Paul replied.

Zilo and Paul had been best friends since West Point. After graduating, they both became Green Berets and served in Delta Force, where Paul had been Zilo's commanding officer. Both men left as majors after six years and joined the Secret Service. When Paul left the service two administrations ago to form PeKay, Inc., a private military contractor (some called them mercenaries), Zilo had been Paul's first hire. Once again, Zilo was Paul's number-two man and the one person Paul trusted with his life.

"Thanks for meeting me off-site," Paul said.

"You're buying, so what's the downside."

"The downside is the favor I'm about to ask."

"Oh shit! This better not be someplace cold."

"It's about the murders in Toledo," Paul explained.

"Oh—that," Zilo said. "It was a thing of beauty, if you ask me. If you're going to take out a terrorist, you might as well get them all."

"I don't disagree," Paul said. "But whoever did it missed a big fish—Malik Saliba." He took the next few minutes to detail his trip to Cleveland.

"Malik Saliba," Zilo said as if the name were an incantation. "What will the feds do with him?"

"I'm counting on them to turn him loose," Paul said.

"Are we killing him or tracking him?"

"Tracking," Paul said.

Zilo studied his friend's face. "You think whoever missed him in Toledo will be looking for a second chance, and you want to use Saliba as bait. So, we're after the cleanup team?" Zilo asked.

Paul leaned in closer. "Two years ago, I was involved in something I thought was over."

"Wait a minute," Zilo said. "Is this about that CIA agent who ended up getting killed by the IRA? A bomb in his private plane, right?"

Paul nodded. "It's coming back to haunt me, I think."

"What's a dead CIA agent have to do with Toledo?"

Paul drew a breath and said, "Look, I love you like a brother, but that's exactly why I can't divulge too much yet. It's best you don't know—for now."

Zilo let out a breath. "Fine. What's the plan?"

"I need Saliba tailed when the FBI releases him. He'll likely go back to Turkey, so use the PeKay office in Rome. Pure surveillance for now. When someone does take a shot at Saliba, I want that person snatched or taken out, whichever is easier."

"I don't see this working out well for the bait," Zilo said.

Paul said nothing.

Zilo reached across the table and smacked Paul's shoulder. "I'm on it—boss. We'll keep Saliba in our sights until someone takes the bait."

"Thank you," Paul said.

The waitress returned, and they ordered lunch, then spent some time talking about the financial health of PeKay and upcoming contracts with the State Department's Diplomatic Security Service. After finishing, Zilo checked his watch and said, "I have to be downtown in an hour. I hate to eat and run, but I love leaving you with the check. Tell the folks in Kansas City I said hey."

Paul left the hotel for the parking garage. As he approached his Trailblazer, he immediately noticed a ten-penny nail protruding through the vinyl cover over the spare tire. He cursed out loud as he turned in circles, hoping to find the culprits. When he realized he was alone, he pulled the nail and made his way toward the driver's side, where another nail was sticking out of his tire's sidewall.

Paul pulled out *that* nail, then circled the vehicle, looking for more damage. Beneath the windshield wiper, he found a trifold flyer warning about the dangers of fossil fuels and a list of vehicles ranked in order of their carbon emission offenses. He gave it a cursory review, then panned the garage and found several other vehicles with flat tires and flyers on their windshields. All SUVs. He cursed again, then pulled out his cell phone. AAA answered on the third ring and gave him an ETA of forty-five minutes.

He hung up with AAA, then hit a speed-dial button but got Woody's voice mail. Paul said, "You won't believe this, but some tree-hugging flunkies went through the parking garage driving nails into the tires of SUVs. I know we planned on spending some time together before our trips, but it looks like I'll be at a dead sprint by the time I get to the condo. If you're still there, we can get a quickie in. Love you, Pattycakes."

Paul took the stairs to the street level and the café, ordered a black coffee, then found a seat at a table on the sidewalk, where he watched the entrance to the parking garage and waited on the tow truck. Then he thought about the other SUVs in the garage with flats. *It's a good day to be in the towing business.*

# CHAPTER 21



Woody arrived at the White House early that morning, and by 6:30, she was thinning out her inbox. At 7:15, she spoke briefly with the president about their trip to Naples, Florida; the party fundraiser; his speech to a Cuban American organization; and their late dinner at the governor's mansion in Tallahassee. It would be a long day. In the morning, they would meet with electric utility executives on clean air regulations, then end their trip with eighteen holes of golf at a resort with the attorney general and a potential large donor to the president's upcoming campaign. She left the White House at 11:15 to pack and hopefully spend time with Paul before heading to Andrews to catch Air Force One.

At the condo, Woody swiped her card, and the gate went up, but she was stopped by the elderly guard who let her know that Carlos, one of Paul's men, would be waiting.

"I gave him a key card. Just as Mr. Kelvington requested," the guard said.

"I know." She thanked the guard and continued on to the condo.

At the unit, an empty, unfamiliar car was parked next to the garage. She pressed the button on the remote, and the garage door opened to her first clue that something was wrong. Paul's Trailblazer wasn't there. Maybe he was still with Zilo. And where in the hell was Carlos?

She parked her Suburban in the far-right spot and remotely closed the overhead door, but as the garage dimmed, she noticed light spilling from the storage room door. Filled with boxes and plastic bins, the door was normally kept locked, but now—it was wide open.

"Carlos?" she called.

No response.

She crossed the garage and peered through the open door. The space was empty, but she still called out, "Carlos?"

Again, no response.

Stepping inside, she navigated the narrow aisle between stacks of boxes to where a chain hung from the single-bulb fixture overhead. As her hand reached up to tug the chain, she noticed a string had been tied around the bulb. Her eyes followed the string to the ceiling and over a bent nail in a joist and back to the open door—and that was when the string went taut, the bulb exploded, and the storage room went black.

Startled, she screamed as her balance failed her, and she tumbled hard into a stack of boxes that collapsed under her weight. One split open, releasing the musty memories of Christmas decorations. As her mind ran through possible causes, she learned the truth soon enough, sending her heart into palpitations. The space beneath the overhead garage doors allowed enough light to pass that she could make out the silhouette of a man blocking the open storage room door.

Woody gasped, then managed a weak, "Carlos?" When the shadow didn't respond, she retreated deeper into the storage room but fell again.

"Stop doing that!" the shadow said.

"Carlos, what are—?"

The shadow interrupted her. "Carlos is unavailable for consultation. We need to chat."

"Please. Don't do this," she cried, desperate to melt into the blackness. Something sharp and pointy bit into her palm, and she pulled away only to fall back once again.

The shadow sighed. "Are you finished?"

"Where's Carlos?"

"I'm covering his shift."

"What do you want?" Her chest heaved as her breaths battled her heartbeat. Hugging herself, she said, "If you're planning to rape me—" But she was cut off again.

"Why would I want to rape you *and* talk to you?"

As her eyes adjusted, the shadow shifted from left to right in the doorway. She could make out jeans gripping a narrow waist and the outline of a mane of hair settling on broad shoulders.

"Why are you asking questions about a dead CIA agent?" the shadow asked.

"I don't know what—" But she stopped when the shadow hurled something that whistled by her ear.

The shadow said, "I'm not much for conversation. Normally, I just say *fuck it* and shoot people. Sometimes I don't even say *fuck it*. Once again—why are you asking questions about a dead CIA agent?"

Her lips trembled and so did her words. "Someone is murdering his enemies."

"Like Sheik Al-Jabori? A dozen *living* people want to shoot that bastard. Why are you asking about a *dead* one? Is the White House chef putting cocaine in the sugar bowls again?" A beat of silent tension passed before the shadow said, "Two years ago, you sent your boyfriend to kill Commander Harmon. He missed, but an IRA bomber didn't. Now, someone is taking out his enemies, and you're afraid of being next."

"How do you know all this?" she said. "Are you the one taking out the NEST?"

The shadow leaned against the jamb. "Do you really want to know the answers to questions that could get you killed?"

Woody swallowed and whispered, "So—you're here to kill me?"

The shadow scratched his head. "I've never killed a woman

before, but it's an item on my bucket list I was saving for last. Now, are you going to stop asking questions?"

"Who are you?" she asked.

"That didn't sound like a *yes* to me."

"Who are you working for?" she demanded.

"I'm a greeter at Walmart," the shadow said, then checked his watch. "I'm afraid I need an answer right now." The shadow's arms moved, and the silhouette of a pistol appeared.

"Yes," Woody finally spat out. "For Christ's sake, don't do me like you did the sheik."

"Thank you," the shadow said, tucking the pistol away. "Now, let's talk about the murders in the desert. Is the Justice Department certain that Agents Penn and Gallagher are the shooters?"

Her lips fell open and she drew in a breath. "Those names have not been made public and—" Woody stopped talking when the cell phone in her pocket vibrated and a dim glow filtered through the material of her slacks. "Can I get this call?"

The shadow's head shook. "Let it go to voice mail."

Her hand pressed against her pocket and the vibrating phone. It had to be Paul. She could feel him through the device, and when it stopped vibrating, she knew he would be listening to an electronic voice announcing he had reached her number. Then, as a wave of courage filled her, she found herself oddly glad Paul wasn't here. Until…

"Play it," the shadow said. "And put it on speaker."

She hesitated but then dug the phone out of her pocket and played the message. Paul's voice filled the storage room.

*"You won't believe this, but some tree-hugging flunkies went through the parking garage driving nails into the tires of SUVs. I know we planned on spending some time together before our trips, but it looks like I'll be at a dead sprint by the time I get to the condo. If you're still there, we can get a quickie in. Love you, Pattycakes."* Woody closed the phone and waited for the inevitable questioning. But what

she heard was worse.

The shadow said, "I wouldn't count on that quickie." He checked his wrist again. "I'm sorry to say our time's running out. Your limo will be here before Paul."

"How do you know about Paul? Or my trip? Or anything?" she asked, unsettled by the shadow's knowledge of her plans.

"Not your concern," the shadow said. "Now, is Renner the one blackmailing the president?"

"Who said anything about blackmail?" Woody snapped, then realized her tone might have given it away.

The shadow said, "I didn't just fall off the turnip truck. I'm going to ask a simple question: If the bill gets past Congress, would the president veto it?"

"No," Woody said.

"So, he either *wants* to sign it or he *has* to sign it. One more time—who is it?"

Woody sighed. "The truth is—I'm trying to find that out myself." Her pocket vibrated again. After eyeing the display, she said anxiously, "It's the guard at the gate. My limo—"

"Ignore it," the shadow said. "Who do you *suspect* is behind the blackmail?"

She paused, then said, "You have to believe me; I don't know."

"I believe you," the shadow said, then turned in the doorway.

"Where are you going?" Woody asked. It was a reflex, like a burp.

"I got what I came for. Stop asking questions, and I won't come back."

"Are you serious?"

The shadow shook his head. "Would you feel better about this if I shot you?"

As the shadow turned to leave again, Woody felt a fleeting moment of relief, but the wheels spinning in her mind prevented her from enjoying it. An opportunity had presented itself, and she couldn't believe what she was about to do.

"Can I make you a proposition?"

The shadow paused. Looking back over his shoulder, he said, "You thought I was going to rape you thirty minutes ago, and now you want to *proposition* me?"

"I want to hire you."

"To do what?"

Woody said, "Help me find out who's blackmailing the president."

The shadow faced her, and it appeared a finger went to his chin. He asked, "To expose them or to stop them?"

"Maybe both."

The shadow chuckled. "Didn't you try this same thing two years ago? You know—putting a hit on an America citizen?"

She said, "Yes. Of course, I need to know who is behind it first, but if that's what it takes to stop treason—then yes, take them out."

The shadow paused for a beat, then said, "I already have a sweet gig, and Walmart frowns on double-dipping. It's unethical."

Woody said, "You're joking, right?"

"Not at all. And that reminds me." The shadow fumbled with something in the dark, then tossed it to her. "It's Carlos's wallet. I took the credit cards and cash. I'm wearing gloves, so you won't find any prints."

"You robbed him?"

"He has to tell Paul Kelvington something when he admits he got his ass kicked but you didn't get a scratch? It's a couple of hundred bucks. You can reimburse him. His license and photos are still there." The shadow started to turn away.

Woody stared down at the wallet. It was a brilliant move. And against every instinct, she tried once more. "What's to stop me from calling the police?"

"That's a fair question." The shadow appeared to dig into his pocket, and whatever he found, he held it up high and it made a clicking sound. Then another. Then another. Then, the storage room filled with regurgitations of their digitized voices.

*"Can I make you a proposition?"*

*"You thought I was going to rape you thirty minutes ago, and now you want to proposition me?"*

*"I want to hire you."*

*"To do what?"*

*"Help me find out who's blackmailing the president."*

*"To expose them or to stop them?"*

*"Maybe both."*

*"Didn't you try this same thing two years ago? You know—putting a hit on an America citizen?"*

*"Yes. Of course, I need to know who is behind it first, but if that's what it takes to stop treason—then yes, take them out."*

*"I already have a sweet gig, and Walmart frowns on double-dipping. It's unethical."*

The shadow pressed a button, then pocketed the device. He said, "Now—I'm no lawyer, but that sounds a lot like the White House chief of staff soliciting murder for hire—on a US citizen—again."

Deflated, she ran trembling fingers through her matted hair. "Is that why you came here? To frame me? You son of a bitch." She let herself collapse onto the box she had fallen over earlier. It took on the shape of her bottom and gave a little more than expected. *Stupid! So stupid!* she scolded herself. But then, the unexpected came.

"Is that how you talk to all your employees?"

"Employee…? You're going to help me?"

"I have some conditions."

"Like what?" Her pocket buzzed again, and this time, she ignored it completely. "We need to hurry. Paul's going to be here soon."

"No—he won't," the shadow said. "That's the guard again. Here's my conditions. I'll look into this, and you are going to cover my fees. Ten thousand per week, plus travel, hotels, meals, maybe a payoff or two along the way. I'm sure you want to avoid the optics that this investigation is coming from the president's own chief of staff."

She said, "I'll make it work—somehow."

The shadow laughed. "The government does it all the time."

"Not anymore," she said, "Presidential Order 12333. December fourth, '81. Section two-point-one-one. No person employed by or acting on behalf of the United States government shall engage in, or conspire to engage in, assassination. Yes. I've read it."

"Very good," the shadow said. "I'm impressed. Eidetic memory?"

Her eyes lowered. "To me, it's like a birthmark. It comes in handy sometimes. Card games. A conversation piece, mostly." She drew in a fresh breath. "I'll find a way to pay you."

"I have that figured out. PeKay's going to hire me as a contractor, and your company, Relational Excellence, will reimburse him. This is nonnegotiable or the deal's off."

"Paul's company? Are you crazy?" Woody said.

"Wait till you hear this: Paul can't know about me or this conversation." He paused, then added, "C'mon. It's how you contracted to kill Commander Harmon, remember? I'll fax my info."

She asked, "When should I expect—?"

The shadow cut her off. "I'll contact you. As a good-faith gesture, I'll need ten thousand wired in advance."

"That's—doable," she said. Part of her wanted desperately for this visit to end, but another never wanted this man leave. "Why did you come here? I don't think it was to scare me into stopping asking questions about Trevor Harmon."

The shadow said, "I thought it was a job interview. It sounds like I got it. Are we done here? I'm in a hurry."

Taking a long step over a box, then another, she stopped a few feet from the shadow. She expected him to move away, but he didn't. It was like offering the back of her hand to an angry dog.

"That's close enough," the shadow said.

Woody stopped. "When this is over, maybe we can meet and—"

The shadow cut her off. "If that happens, you'll take your last breath. Is that clear?"

She nodded and took another step but stopped when the shadow closed the storage room door. "What are you doing?" she called out.

"When you hear the garage door open, then close, you can come out. I'll leave the remote in the driveway. If you come out before—our agreement ends with your life."

"What about Carlos?"

"He's around—somewhere."

"You're a cold bastard, aren't you?" Then, the door suddenly opened and the shadow was there again.

He said, "I'm hurt. I love dogs. Sushi. Spotted owls. They taste like chicken."

Woody couldn't help but burp a laugh.

"I have to admit, for the White House chief of staff to make this kind of deal with a lunatic she met in her garage storage room, you must be desperate."

Woody didn't reply to the question. Instead, she tried once more with the basics. "Who are you?"

"Someone you'll be glad to have on your side." He closed the door and left her in the dark. Then, through the door, she heard, "As long as you never know who I am."

. . .

Woody waited until she heard the garage door close before feeling her way to the door. The handle felt hot and forbidden as she turned it and eased it open to find the garage dark except for a sliver of light beneath the two overhead doors.

The shadow was gone.

After pressing the button on the wall to open the garage door and shielding her eyes from the sting of reality, she found the remote in the driveway. She returned it to her car's visor while her heart and hands calmed. She needed a drink. She still needed to pack. But first, she needed find Carlos. The driver could wait.

After a five-minute search, she found him hugging a pine tree deep in the brush near the high wall behind the condo. He had duct tape over his mouth, zip ties around his wrists and ankles, the imprint of bark on his cheeks, and was coated in sap.

"I found this in the driveway," she said, handing Carlos the wallet.

Carlos opened it, frowned, then pocket it. "Cash and cards are gone."

In the condo, Carlos cleaned up while she phoned the guard-house. "The driver has been waiting here for some time, Miss Sullivan," the guard said. "Is everything okay?"

"It's fine," she said. "By the way, did you happen to see a man leave the neighborhood in the past twenty minutes? He might have been on foot?"

"No, ma'am. No cars either. It's slow this time of day. You know Mrs. Amherst jogs about this time, and she—"

Woody cut him off, thanked him, hung up, then returned to packing. The limo arrived and the driver rang the bell. Carlos answered it. While descending the stairs, she found the driver in the foyer and Carlos returning from outside.

"I was checking the limo. I'd feel better if you'd let me drive you to Andrews," Carlos said with little regard to the annoyed looks from the limo driver.

"I'll be fine. You can follow us," she conceded as the driver took her bags outside.

Carlos whispered, "Paul's going to be pissed."

"Because you were mugged?"

Carlos said, "Whoever did this was a pro. It's my first day, and whoever hit me had to have known that." He eyed her suspiciously.

"And you didn't see anything?"

"Nothing," she said. "I'll be back late tomorrow night and will have Secret Service protection the whole time." She held the front door open for him, and Carlos stepped onto the porch. She set the alarm, then closed the door.

"Carlos was rubbing the back of his head and the ligature marks on his neck from where he had been duct-taped to the tree. He asked, "Mind if I ask why you're getting private protection instead of the Secret Service?"

"Maybe you should ask Paul," she said as she checked her watch. "He should be here soon. You can pick me up at the airport tomorrow evening."

Carlos paused a beat. "That would be Jeff's shift."

"I see. Then Jeff can give me a lift." When Carlos looked down, she said, "I won't tell Paul, if that's what you want."

Carlos checked out his shoes, then hers. "I appreciate that."

She sent Carlos away, met the limo in the drive, and then apologized to the driver for the delay. She waited until they were on the highway before calling Paul's cell phone. No answer. Then, her cell phone buzzed in her hand. The number was from the condo.

Paul was home.

# CHAPTER 22



You're home?" Woody said, her surprise laced with a little guilt. "What's the story with your tires?"

"Carlos called me, by the way. You want to talk about it now?"

Woody turned and found Carlos was still behind the limo. *Just stick to your story*, she thought, then said, "Not much to tell. I found him in the bushes, tied to the tree. I tried to call you, but you didn't answer. It looks like he was mugged."

"The man I assigned to protect my fiancée gets mugged in a gated community the same day I get three tires nailed full of holes? This was no coincidence."

*And you'd be correct*, she thought, but then said, "If someone wanted me dead, they missed their best chance."

Paul said, "You know, for the White House chief of staff, sometimes you can be naïve."

"And you're paranoid," Woody said. "I'm almost sorry I sent you to Cleveland." Silence deafened the line, so she decided to change the subject. "I have something I'm working on for the campaign, and I need to hire an investigator."

"Let me switch phones so I can pack and talk." There was a click, then Paul was back. "You want to use one of my guys?"

"No. I want *you* to use one of *my* guys."

"You don't have guys. What's going on, Woody?" Paul said with suspicion. "Pekay hires professional soldiers, not ex–mall cops."

"This person is not a security type."

"And Relational Excellence is reimbursing PeKay? Can I interview the candidate?"

"No. He's not for you. You're just handling the paperwork."

"Maybe. But if this guy gets into some shit that comes back on me and my company—What if I say no?"

*The shadow didn't ask for permission,* she thought, then said, "Nothing can come back to you."

"This smells," he said. "Does he have a name?"

"Of course," she said. "I'll get the info to you as soon as I can. It might take—" But her sentence was interrupted by piercing tones in her ear. Loud. And fast. "Did you just chin dial someone?" she asked.

"I don't think so," Paul said. "There's nothing on the display. Not sure what that was. Anyway, I'm taking the red-eye to—"

Their conversation was interrupted again by another sound, rhythmic beeps she recognized as coming from the security system. Paul cursed.

"What is it?" she asked as the driver took the exit for Andrews. "Paul? Answer me, dammit!"

"Calm down," Paul finally said in a whisper. "I think the front door just opened and closed. Let me call you back."

The call ended, and Woody closed the phone. Then, she nearly dropped it when it vibrated in her hand again. In the mirror, the driver lowered his eyes. On the phone's display was a number she didn't recognize.

"Hello?" she answered.

"I have your cell phone number, and now you have mine." The voice of the shadow sent a new chill through her body, and she crossed her legs in defense.

"It was you, wasn't it? In the condo just now. You pressed the redial on our phone. All you had to do was ask me for it."

The shadow said, "It's important you know that I could have

killed your boyfriend but didn't."

Woody's stomach churned. "What's the point?"

"Trust," the shadow said. "You needed to know you could trust me, and I think we've established that."

Woody pinched her eyes closed. "Paul needs to know—"

"I heard," the shadow chimed in. "Tell Paul he'll be hiring a man named Brian May. I'll fax you Mr. May's necessary account info later. Remember our deal. Paul can't know the circumstances. The last thing you want is for him to come looking me. Understand—Pattycakes?"

The call ended, and she dropped the phone into her purse. The limo turned into the entrance to Andrews Air Force Base, and she spun around to watch Carlos continue on. Woody flashed her trembling credentials at the guard, and he waved her through. At the hangar, she was escorted inside by the Secret Service to where the upgraded Boeing 707 was parked. She met the president and Attorney General Rittenger at the bottom of the Boeing's stairs. Rit smiled and kissed her cheek as her cell phone went off again. She stepped to the side to take it.

"Paul?"

"It's all good," Paul said. "It was an open-door alarm, but I checked the whole house. Nobody is here. By the way, did you know the storage room light is busted?"

Across the hangar, Rit was tapping his watch.

"No. I gotta go. I'll call you when I land. I love you."

"Love you too, Pattycakes. Oh wait. You left a pile of twenties and fifties on the coffee table? It's two hundred and thirty bucks."

"Oh," she said, surprised, but grinned when she thought about the shadow mugging Carlos. At least the shadow wasn't a thief. Or maybe it was a test of trust. "I can't believe I did that. Go ahead and take it. If I need cash, I'll get it from Rit. Bye, Paul."

Woody put her phone away and started toward the plane as she fought off more chills. Pattycakes—Paul's term of endearment, and now the shadow's—sounded tainted and cold.

"Are you okay?" Rit asked as she approached. "Your face is—flushed." He reached out to take her carry-on, but she shouldered it instead.

"I'm fine," she said, then followed the president up the stairs with Rit close behind. Now that the president was on board, the Boeing 707 officially became Air Force One.

# CHAPTER 23

Washington, DC
Same Day
3:30 p.m.

Ginny handed the clerk a five-dollar bill, refused the change, then took her Earl Grey tea and blueberry Danish to the second floor of the café, where she found a window seat overlooking Connecticut Avenue and Farragut Square. She loved to watch the people below flow like a river of humanity and wondered what it would be like to be one of them again, to not know what she knew about DC, the most powerful—and power-mad—city in the world.

Two bites into her Danish, her daydream ended when the handsome man with long and wavy black hair tucked under a baseball cap ascended the stairs, biting into a scone as he walked. Two years ago—she recalled—his hair had been so short, it had looked like a black beanie, the mark of a disciplined patriot. Now, his longish locks had become a suit of rebellious armor, but necessary to complete his new disguise, which was, oddly enough, his real self.

She swallowed back her surprise as the man sat in the adjacent chair and stared down at the DC streets with her.

. . .

"Hello, Ginny," Liam said after taking another bite of his scone.

Ginny wetted her throat with coffee, her gaze back toward the window. "Do you know how many enemies you have in this town?"

"No. How many?" he asked facetiously, then said, "It was a

judgment call."

"It was poor judgment," she scolded.

Liam answered her with an insulted glare. "I wanted to stop by and thank you for the information in person."

"Which you're never supposed to do. I hate myself for giving you their itineraries," she said. "Can I ask about Toledo first?"

"The Mud Hens are undefeated."

She shook her head, then glanced at the cap. "When did you become a Dodgers fan? You hate baseball."

Liam ignored the question. "Toledo wasn't a BICA op, so it's not your concern." He turned and their eyes met.

"Everything you do is my concern," Ginny said with a gritted smile. "You're paid to support BICA, not satisfy personal vendettas." She sipped, then said, "You realize the White House pressed to have the sheik's visa approved."

"Of course. And I got that information during a conversation with you," Liam said. "Stop pretending you didn't let it slip out on purpose."

She whispered, "You tortured him, didn't you?"

"He's gone and I got a new name."

"Really? Which bird?" Ginny asked as she held a breath.

"Owl," Liam said. "His real name is Rufus Carmichael."

Ginny let out a long sigh. "The British financier?"

Liam said, "Now I know who provided the seed money and the financial network for the NEST, and I'm one step closer to finding Eagle. But first, I have to finish some business."

"You're too late," Ginny said. "Malik Saliba left the country this morning. We lost him in Istanbul."

"A hundred bucks says Kelvington is having him followed," Liam said.

"Why would you say that?" Ginny asked.

"It's what I would do," Liam said. "Kelvington wants to know who's taking out the NEST again. Saliba is the perfect bait." He bit into his scone, then changed the subject. "By the way, I have a new job."

"What does that mean?" Ginny leaned closer to him.

"Your daughter *hired* me because you refused to help her. It fits nicely with what you want me to do." They both let a moment go by before Liam said, "She must be desperate. I cornered her in her storage room. She never saw my face and still hired me to help her. She says this is about forcing the president to sign the Renner-Kline Bill. But you and I both know it's more than that."

"What makes you think that?"

Liam whispered, "Lacey Sullivan was murdered, Ginny. She was lobbying Congress *for* Renner-Kline, but it sounds like she switched sides and someone killed her for it. Funny you didn't bring it up during our phone call."

"You're right. I knew Lacey and a Mexican immigrant were murdered in her house," Ginny said. "I was waiting for you to bring it up. I agree that there might be a link."

"There's *definitely* a link," Liam said. "That dead Mexican has a brother, and they were both witnesses to the Border Patrol murdering Rolando Alvarez and the baby in Arizona. And those same border agents murdered Lacey and the Mexican." He then pointed to the Dodgers cap. "One of the border agents took this from Rolando Alvarez and dropped it on my property."

Ginny drew in a breath and faced him. "How do you know that?"

"The dead Mexican's brother's name is Angel—and I have him chained up in my RV."

"You're not serious," Ginny said.

Liam spent the next minutes bringing Ginny up to speed. At times, their hands touched, and she gripped his fingers tight enough to cut off the blood. When he finished, she leaned back and pulled in a long breath.

Ginny said, "Don't take this the wrong way, but—you're right— and it's bigger than Renner-Kline and a few murders. I'm not trying to negate the loss of Lacey Sullivan, because I know you two were close, but BICA has been tracking some new subversive, Progressive, globalist groups dropping billions in support of amnesty, open borders, and racial unrest. We suspect that a few of the Mexican cartels are involved."

"Can't say as I give two shits about this president. He's a Progressive, and your daughter helped to put him in office."

"The president is not a true Progressive. He courts the leftists for votes because it's easy to target the mindless groups they put people in. Still, he tends to float with the moderates."

"You know what the difference between a Progressive and a moderate is?" Liam asked.

Ginny replied, "A moderate uses an eraser on America, and a Progressive uses a match. You heard that idiom from me," she said. This time, his eyes were soft and warm, almost motherly. "What's your plan going forward?"

"Your daughter thinks she hired a man named Brian May." Liam paused a beat, then added, "I have to admit, I'm impressed by her ability to think on her feet. She was rattled at first but recovered nicely. She's definitely your daughter." This made Ginny grin. Liam continued. "She wants to find out who's blackmailing the president and how."

"Basically, what I asked you to do," Ginny said.

"With one addition," Liam added. When he saw the question on her face, he said, "She asked if I would be willing to kill whoever is behind it. Sound familiar?"

Ginny's forehead crinkled as she pursed her lips in disbelief. Her eyes begged.

Liam said, "I didn't commit to anything. But if I find it leads to Lacey Sullivan's murderer, then all bets are off."

"What about your guest?" Ginny asked.

"He'll keep, for now. I can't afford to let him get himself killed."

"You also can't afford to have the cops find him either," Ginny said.

Liam nodded and started to get up, but Ginny put her hand on his leg and stopped him. He saw real fear in her eyes. "Don't worry. I'll keep you updated."

Ginny turned away and glanced around the café. She whispered, "Be extremely careful with this, Liam. Whatever someone has on the president, if it gets out, it could damage more than him."

Liam nodded. "Like your daughter?"

Ginny ignored the shot. "Where will you go first?"

"Lukeville. It's coyote season. Can I use the BICA jet?"

"When is Brian May leaving?" she asked. "Which one is he, again?"

"The lead guitarist for Queen. You'd like them. Beats Lawrence Welk."

Ginny said, "I know who Queen is. I'm not that old. Keep me informed of your progress. I don't like it when you go dark."

Liam smiled, then touched her wrist. "I know we have our differences, but I promise you, we're on the same team."

"I know," Ginny said. "But you worry me. You're too much like your father. But you're the bigger smart-ass." She gripped his elbow and pulled him closer. "I almost forgot. What's going on with the two mysterious five-thousand-dollar checks?"

"What checks?" Liam said with a wink. "I'll call you from Lukeville." He then kissed her on the cheek before leaving the café.

# CHAPTER 24



As the limo crept down the alley, the owner of La Elección del Comensal cracked open the service door, searched left and right for paparazzi, then waved the driver forward. The coast was clear except for the bum sleeping on the newspapers next to the dumpster, so he opened the rear passenger door with one hand while holding the service door with the other, and the woman seated in the back put two feet to the alley, then lifted herself out. With her face covered by a scarf and her chin tucked low into her chest, she blindly tossed a hundred-dollar bill in the direction of the bum before hurrying inside. The owner slammed the limo door closed, then the service door.

Once inside, the owner escorted Sierra through the kitchen.

What better way for a woman who was worth millions to enter an upscale restaurant than through the same door the trash was removed from. She stopped to speak with the kitchen help, chatting them up in their native Spanish, and cautiously accepting a few hands. She then followed the owner to one of the private dining rooms, where a single round table had been set for three.

As instructed, two settings had one wine glass, and the one in the middle had two. Bathed in the light from the dozens of candles perched around the mahogany ledge, the private room resembled the drinking scene from *Raiders of the Lost Ark*. The owner touched the dimmer, and the recessed bulbs brightened just enough to negate the effect of the candles. After all, this wasn't a romantic lunch. It was business.

Soft Tejano music dripped from the ceiling speakers. The porter arrived with a bottle of Nickel & Nickel Cabernet Sauvignon, pulled the cork, and passed it to Sierra. She sniffed, nodded her approval, and the porter started the decanting process.

She said, "I also want a bottle of the Merlot I had last time." The owner frowned at the request, so she added, "But I'll still take the Cabernet."

Confused by the request, the owner nodded, then left the room, returning moments later with the cheaper Merlot. "Shall I open the bottle now?"

Sierra instructed him to fill the glass to her right with the Merlot, the one on her left with the Cabernet, and her glasses with one of each. Once the porter finished and had vanished, Sierra picked up her glass of Merlot and touched it to the glass to her right and said, "I'll miss you, Lacey."

"Miss Sierra?" the owner's voice said from the doorway, snapping her from her melancholy. "Your party has arrived."

Sierra didn't get up when Manuel Castille entered. He took her hand for a cordial kiss, but she removed it before he could. Sierra was in no mood for idle chitchat. Not today. Only yesterday, she had returned from Hermosillo, Mexico, after attending her brother's funeral, and it was the last subject she wanted to discuss.

From her purse, she retrieved the folded newspaper clipping she had gotten from her personal assistant and slapped it on the table in front of Castille. "When were you going to tell me, Manuel?"

Castille, surprised by the less-than-cordial greeting, hung his suit coat on the back of the chair as he picked up the clipping and ready the headline.

LOCAL RESIDENT SLAIN IN DOUBLE HOMICIDE

Castille gave the article a cursory glance, then said, "I wasn't aware you and Ms. Sullivan had grown so close."

"Well, we had," Sierra spat out as she dabbed at an eye and

sipped her wine. "It was you who introduced us a year ago."

"Has it been a year?" he said. "Time has gotten away from me. I thought you had met only the one time. Lacey was like a sister, and I will see to it that her husband and children are well taken of."

"She was divorced and had no children," Sierra said. "I think she would have eventually married Liam Curran—had something not come between them."

"Who?" Castille asked.

Sierra eyed him with contempt. "Lacey was in a serious relationship with her neighbor for almost a year before it ended."

"You've met this man?"

Sierra lowered her eyes. "No. But girls talk."

Castille said, "I never pried into Lacey's personal life." He swished the Cabernet and took a sip. His lip puckered with approval. "She had insurance through the company. I will see who her beneficiaries are."

Sierra switched to the Cabernet. "Do they know who did this thing?"

"Not yet." Castille fumbled with his napkin and silverware. "I am hearing it was likely the same men who murdered your brother and the child. The same caliber pistols were used. They are waiting on the ballistics reports."

"Bastards!" Sierra said. "I don't understand any of this. Why would they kill Lacey?"

Castille said, "Nothing in America makes sense."

The waiter returned and they ordered. Salads. Shrimp. Tomato basil soup.

"What of our lawsuit against the INS? Will Lacey's murder strengthen our case?"

"It will," Castille replied. "I have to be honest. It would work in our favor if the two border agents are never found. It has already been established that the guns used in the desert belonged to them, and without defense witnesses, and because this is a civil matter and not criminal, the INS will appear guilty as sin. The government will want to settle."

Sierra considered it, then said, "But you don't want to settle?"

"No. We *want* this to go to court. We *want* a jury—and the public—to see what the INS did to your brother and the child."

"And to Lacey," Sierra added, then backtracked. "Of course, we don't know for sure."

"No—we don't. And neither will a jury. But they'll suspect it because I'll plant it in their minds."

She searched his eyes. Kind and conniving. A lawyer. Yes, they would win, and the government would pay for what they had done. Sierra dabbed at the corners of her mouth with the cloth napkin, folded it, then placed it next to her plate as she locked eyes with Castille.

"I want no money from this lawsuit, is that understood? My share will go to Lacey's parents, and Catarina Guzman can keep the rest. She lost her baby, for God's sake."

Castille raised his chin and said, "That's incredibly altruistic. Can I ask why?"

"I'm rich enough," Sierra spat out as if she had burped. "Where is Catarina now?"

"She's staying with me," Castille said. "She has no other family, as her husband is serving a prison sentence for murder."

Sierra said, "Lacey told me—" But Sierra stopped talking when her voice cracked and the tears came. She buried her face in her hands.

Castille leaned closer but refrained from touching her. "Will you be okay?"

After wiping her eyes, she glanced toward the full glass of Merlot. "I never told you this, but I instructed Rolando not to call you but to call Lacey the moment he crossed into the US."

"I see now," Castille said. "The empty place setting is to honor Lacey Sullivan." He then reached across the table to clink glasses, but Sierra stopped him.

"Don't. Lacey hated you," Sierra said.

Castille retreated slowly. "I—I didn't realize."

"I should have listened to Lacey and never let Rolando use the coyote," Sierra said. "I swear, if those border agents were behind her murder, I want them to burn."

"Of course," Castille said.

Their lunch arrived, and they nibbled in awkward silence. It was Castille who broke it. He said, "We didn't have a choice. Your brother did have a criminal record, so there was no other way to get him across. Once he was on US soil, there was more I could do for him."

"But he *was* on US soil!" Sierra screamed. "And so was Lacey, and they are both dead!" She tossed her napkin onto her plate.

At the door, the owner appeared, but Castille waved him away. Sierra dabbed at her eyes and toasted with Lacey's glass once more.

Castille said, "Sierra, this isn't healthy. Can I offer some help?"

"No," Sierra shot back. "My grief is my own." She gave herself a few more beats to recover, then said, "Tell me about the Renner-Kline Bill."

"It is currently stalled, but I promise it will move to the floor soon and the president will sign it."

"Your promises mean less than shit!" Sierra said, her anger choking off the tears. "I'm sorry, Manuel. I'm being rude and I've lost my appetite."

Sierra finished her glass as she stood. Anyone belonging to her normal entourage would understand immediately this was a signal the meeting was over. When Castille started to rise, she put out her hand. He stopped and slowly returned to his seat.

She shook her head. "Please, don't. I need to get back to the studio." The owner appeared, and she asked him to get the limo ready. She then stuffed a one-hundred-dollar bill into his hand. "That's the tip for the porter and waiter," she said, then shot a glance toward Castille, who was still sitting at the table. "Thank you for meeting me." Sierra left the restaurant in reverse order, but once she was in the limo, she instructed the driver to take her home.

Back in Malibu, standing on her deck, Sierra took in the Pacific Ocean and its pulsing breeze reeking of broken promises. She recalled her father's quote the night before she and her mother had left for America. *You'll only find what you take with you*, he had said. The gulls screeched their agreement.

A small boat drifted a bit too close to shore, and she raised a middle finger for the camera. She whispered an apology to her press agent, who was vacationing in Bermuda with one of her backup singers—neither of their spouses had gone with them—then Sierra turned her back to the beach. *"Why?"* she screamed as she buried her face in her hands. She screamed it over and over until she became hoarse, then fell into one of the teak deck chairs as a tinge of guilt filled her. Lacey Sullivan had been right, she had ignored her, and now both Rolando and Lacey were dead. Her guilt soared as she realized that, by sending him the money for the coyote, she had inadvertently killed him.

Her maid cracked the French doors and popped her head through. "Shall I run a bath, ma'am?"

"Please." Sierra forced a smile until the maid was gone, then quickly let it drop. All these people at her beck and call. She could pick up the phone and have a hundred people over in an hour with champagne and wine and drugs. Producers and artists and directors—and she had never felt more alone in her life. And in the burning Pacific breeze—so cold.

# CHAPTER 25

Two hundred dollars for wine!" The waiter said nothing as Castille dropped his card onto the plastic plate. *She stuck me for an hour of billing too.* He paid the check and left the tip line blank.

Back at the firm, Tiffany, his assistant, peppered him with questions before he finally escaped to the quiet of his office. Standing over his credenza, he gazed through the fifth-floor window at the field. And beyond that were three blocks of shining buildings before the waves of the Pacific coast and the horizon. He fumed.

*That bitch!*

Lacey was not to become Sierra's best friend and work with her on Rolando's case. Sierra was a rich bitch singer who was to look sad for the cameras, raise money, and play the role of a successful, law-abiding Mexican immigrant who'd lost a brother to the Border Patrol. And Lacey Sullivan was supposed to lobby Congress for the Renner-Kline Bill, not the Senate TABS Bill. That was it! How hard was that to understand?

It was clear Sierra's demeanor toward him had changed, and he had gone from master to slave in record time. Had it been purely from grief or Lacey's lingering disdain for him? Whatever Lacey's influence, it was now silenced, and for a moment, he considered his former partner's mind and her beauty—a beauty that rivaled Sierra's. But where Sierra could win indifferent hearts with her voice, Lacey could win crucial battles with her mind, a far more valuable talent. His loss and the loss to his firm were far greater than Sierra's loss of a brother. Rolando's death was the loss of a pawn. Lacey had been a field general, one who had switched sides.

Castille collapsed into his chair as he recalled his promise at the restaurant. He picked up the phone and pressed the IC button.

"Can you come in here, please?" he said.

A beat later, Tiffany had entered and taken a seat, notebook at the ready, tanned legs crossed, and a short skirt pulled over hard thighs toward distant knees. A dime a dozen in LA.

"Can you check on Lacey's insurance beneficiaries?"

"I have," Tiffany said. "It's her parents."

"Really?" Castille said. "We may need to set up a trust for them in Mudburg, West Virginia."

"Mudburg?" Tiffany asked.

Castille delivered a scolding glare as if she should know what he meant. "That shithole in West Virginia where Lacey was living after dumping her husband. I guess she had a redneck boyfriend there too."

Tiffany scribbled a note that had more to do with defusing Castille's frustration than updating her to-do list. "I'll take care of it," she said, then left the office.

It was quite a sight. Not as nice as it had been watching Lacey Sullivan, but she was never an option. Plus, it seemed she had a thing for farmers in—Dirtville. That was okay. Tiffany had her advantages as well. Her looks camouflaged her intelligence, loyalty, and—discretion. And Castille paid her quite well for those attributes. Most people thought they were sleeping together anyway. They weren't, but it wasn't as if he hadn't thought about it. Maybe he'd try—eventually. Truth was, he needed her loyalty and abilities more than he needed sex. Great sex, he could buy at a bargain price of $1,000 per hour. He couldn't afford love. If there was one thing that lovers were not, it was loyal.

He snapped out of it when his pocket started to vibrate.

Castille fished for the cell phone, then clenched his teeth when he saw the number. He even straightened his tie and hair before flipping the phone open.

"Castille." His voice squeaked, which infuriated him further.

"He wants you in Miami," the voice said frankly. It was calm and refined. Foreign. Dignified and used to getting its way. "The plane is waiting for you at Orange County."

Castille said, "It's not a good time."

"My apologies if it sounded like a request," the voice said, and it sent chills through him. "A helicopter will arrive in the field across from your office in ten minutes. Be on it."

As the sound of chopper blades beat the quiet, the door to his office opened and Tiffany stuck her head in; her eyes volleyed between the window and her boss. She said, "Do you want me to cancel your appointments for today?"

Castille gathered his belongings. "And tomorrow as well."

# CHAPTER 26

Naples, Florida
Same Day
6:18 p.m.

Woody let the wedge do the work, sand flew, and her ball landed on the lip of the green, finishing eight feet from the cup. The president, Attorney General Rittenger, and Primo Ruqur—a Greek billionaire—all raised their putters, cheering her shot. Even the Secret Service agents along the edge of the course clapped. She smiled sheepishly, but inside—she loved sticking it to the boys. After putting out, she had a four-stroke lead over the president. An agent picked up the flag and placed it in the cup.

"Twelve—coming up," the president said as he lit the Cuban that Primo had given each of them. "Short par three. A thousand for closest to the pin. Who's in?"

Everyone took the bet. Woody couldn't help but think that the grand Primo was about to give away (because he sucked at golf) the man earned in interest a second. The president spun a tee, and Primo won the honors. After raking stubby fingers through a mane of gelled receding hair, he swung the 8 iron to put his ball twenty feet from the cup.

"Very nice shot," Woody said when Primo returned to stand between her and Rit. The president was up.

"Thank you, Madame Chief of Staff," Primo said.

"It's Woody—please."

Primo smiled, thanked her graciously, then whispered, "I hear someone is buying up the Russian and American small arms left over from the Contra-Sandinista conflict."

"Yes. In Nicaragua," Rit said. "I've heard that too."

"The aggregation is complete, and someone has purchased the entire lot," Primo said.

Rit and Woody glanced at each other as the president swung and put his ball on the fringe of the green. He turned to the Primo, and said, "I've never lost a grand that fast."

Rit and Woody both hit their shots. Rit's hit high and rolled backward, past the hole, but Woody's ball stuck the green, spun forward, and stopped on the lip of the cup. She wondered how she would spend her $3,000. Then she thought about the money Brian May had left behind. She guessed Paul made out too. On the green, she putted out and took the birdie, then waited for Primo and Rit to finish.

Rit picked up his ball and marched to Primo. "If there was a buy, do you know which bank was used?"

Primo said, "A bank in Belize, I'm told. Away from your cyber snoopers." Primo pinched his cigar between square, flat teeth and winked at Rit, an innocent gesture with dangerous undertones.

Woody asked, "Where are the weapons now?"

"On a ship in the Caribbean," Primo said.

She chuckled but kept her eyes on the president as he teed off. "That was an evasive response."

Primo said, "You need the name of the vessel and the destination. It's an expensive answer."

Rit said, "Can Woody putt you for it?"

Primo laughed. "That would cost me a lot more than a thousand dollars, I'm afraid."

The president bagged his driver and joined them by the ball washer. Rit filled him in on the conversation.

Primo turned to face the others. "The peso is in crisis and the twenty-billion-dollar aid package you signed in April was a good first step to help counter the negative impacts of NAFTA on the

Mexican economy. But we all know the source is corrupt politics, and more money only fuels it. Presidential Candidate Luis Colosio was assassinated eighteen months ago, and now many conspiracies are bubbling up to the surface. Drugs and assassinations and corruption can't be solved with a twenty-billion-dollar aid package. What El Presidente needs is confidence from his people. He needs a win."

"What does this have to do with weapons?" Woody asked.

Primo said, "Consider the benefits to El Presidente if these weapons were confiscated in port. It would increase public confidence in his abilities as El Presidente. As you know, El Presidente is a strong ally of the United States."

Woody said, "Mexico has not convinced us they are dedicated to bringing down the cartels and controlling their borders."

Rit jumped in. "We know the drugs coming from Columbia to our borders are protected—and even escorted—by the Mexican military. We also know the CDG cut a sweet deal with the Cali Cartel to distribute their cocaine. This has the Juárez Cartel more than a little angry."

"All the more reason El Presidente needs a win," Primo said.

Rit said, "This sounds like a brewing drug war."

Primo was quiet for a beat, then said, "This isn't about drugs, Mr. Rittenger. It's about guns and mortars and ammunition and explosives—weapons that could be used against your agents. The CDG has little interest in SA-7 shoulder-fired rockets, but Islamic extremists are also sneaking across your southern border—and they have money."

"So—the CDG purchased the weapons," Woody said. "I'm sure that wasn't a slip. What are you selling, and for how much, Mr. Ruqur?"

"In all truth, it will cost you nothing," Primo said. "It is money you are already planning to spend. My request is very simple. My companies do business all over the world in multiple currencies.

At present, I have several companies holding Mexican bonds that I would like to swap for dollars."

Rit jumped in. "What you are looking for is a foreign exchange swap. What is your position at present?"

"Fourteen billion pesos," Primo said. "The exchange rate this morning was six and a quarter pesos per dollar, but I'm willing to let you take them at seven pesos even."

Rit said, "Two billion dollars."

"Yes," Primo said. "I believe nine billion has been earmarked for swaps. All I'm asking is that you dedicate two billion to get the Mexican bonds off of my books."

Woody studied the stocky Greek for a few beats, trying to get a sense of what he was really up to. At present, the peso's value against the dollar was half of what it was eight months ago. She said, "I'm assuming you are willing to swap at a slight loss to improve the bond rating of companies held by your Hermes Corporation, lowering the premium of new bonds?"

"That is very astute, Ms. Woodburn," Primo said. "Perhaps a gentleman's agreement would do to begin."

"Once the swaps are complete, then you'll give us information on the ship and the destination," Woody said. "How much time do we have?"

Primo grinned. "Forty-eight hours to place the order. The ship will still be on the water, of course. The port could be anywhere between Belize and Taiwan."

Rit nodded, "You understand we'll need to discuss this—in private."

Primo said, "Of course. I trust that the help I gave your government during the negotiations could help move things forward. The Mexicans gave up much in exchange for the aid package."

The president walked away to the tee, and Primo followed him. They hit their shots, then climbed in the president's cart and relit their cigars. Woody took a practice swing but stopped when she caught a glimpse of Rit's face, ashen and squashed. "What is it, Rit?"

He put his back to the president and Primo, and said, "That little gyro is holding us hostage. Two billion dollars? In exchange for what? Information on some old guns from the Sandinista-Contra skirmish a decade ago?"

"He's only asking for us to direct the currency swap," Woody said. "That's it. A Mercedes for seven Fords. It's money we were going to spend anyway. And, it might help loosen his wallet for the president's reelection."

Rit said, "The Mexican peso hovered around three dollars and change until the crisis eight months ago. If he's willing to let go of pesos at seven, he's losing his ass. What's going to happen to the peso when the market finds out the US bought it at seven dollars when we could have bought it at six and some change?"

Woody shook her head. "I don't know. But I think he's right about corruption being the drain on the economy more so than their interest rate policy. Ultimately, it costs us nothing. Why not take the pesos off his hands for the intel?" She waggled and Rit stepped back. Playing her drive from the men's tees, her ball stopped only fifty yards behind the boys'. It felt great to compete with the boys on their terms—and win. Golf, intel on illegal guns, money for the campaign, and Brian May. Maybe, just maybe, she had scored four good wins in a forty-eight-hour period. Brian May being the only wild card.

The ride home aboard Air Force One that night proved to be relaxing. And the last one she would ever have.

# CHAPTER 27



The helicopter had touched down at John Wayne Airport twenty minutes after picking up Castille at his office, and by the time he was on the private jet with his cocktail, they were rocketing upward. (JWI's noise ordinance required planes to climb steep and fast.) After leveling off eastbound, the steward took his mud-caked loafers (from the field across from his office) to clean them. With the sun escaping behind them, and the plane at a comfortable twenty-five thousand feet, Castille glanced in the direction of his beloved Mexico, finished his drink, then closed his eyes.

The squeal of the plane's wheels against the still warm Miami International runway woke him up. The attendant gave him a hot towel, returned his shined shoes, wished him well, then escorted him off the plane, where another helicopter waited. This one sported distinct baby-blue markings and a woman's name stenciled on the nose. Clearly, part of a set. Ten minutes later, they touched down on the deck of a yacht whose lifeboats and dingy matched the color of the helicopter. A low-voltage beam lit up the name stenciled on the bow: *GRETCHEN'S EMERALD.*

A familiar and unnerving man met Castille on the helipad, while two men with machine guns walked the perimeter. The man was sinewy, almost skeletal, and tall, with a square T. rex jawline. Plate-size hands protruded from a sliver of white sleeve beneath the cuff of a crisp black jacket.

Still ducking below the slowing blades, Castille called out, "Mr. Rockman, it's good to see you," though both men knew it was a lie. After a dozen meetings and not more than four dozen words between them, he knew better than to try to shake Rockman's hand. Castille checked his watch: 12:10 a.m. "Is Primo still awake?"

"Mr. Ruqur is on the upper sundeck," Rockman said in Albanian-accented English, increasing his words-per-visit average.

Rockman let Castille pass, and the man's presence unnerved him. Castille quickened his steps as he went down one level of stairs, through a set of glass doors, and into the most beautiful room he had ever seen. This was his fourth visit to the yacht, and it still took his breath away. In the world, there was rich and filthy rich, but this was downright dirty, rotten, stinkin' filthy rich. With his own net worth approaching $100 million, the familiar inadequacy rushed over him as he stood in the center of the mahogany-trimmed main cabin. Glass doors led to the sundeck, which jutted out over the sea. His host was out there, leaning over the railing and accepting the wispy breeze.

Castille fixed a drink from the bar, then joined his host in gazing at the awe-inspiring Miami skyline while the ocean lapped gently against the hull. On the lower sundeck, a topless woman moon-bathed in a deck chair, a glass of something red chilled nearby. She stirred, found the two men staring at her, then lowered herself into the hot tub.

"It's good to see you again, Primo," Castille said as if his visit were voluntary. When Georgius Primo Ruqur summoned, you came.

"She's beautiful, isn't she?" Primo said without looking up.

"I love Miami," Castille replied while gazing down on the woman. She had taken her bottoms off now and wasn't shy about bobbing in and out of the bubbles.

"I was speaking of my boat."

Castille said, "Yes. It's nicer than my home."

Primo finally turned to face Castille. Seeing where Castille's real attention had drifted, he smiled and said, "That is Alexandria, my personal nurse." He clenched his drink between palms as if in prayer. "My ship is *Gretchen's Emerald,* named after my mother."

Castille said nothing but sent another glance toward the naked woman, who was now out of the tub and moon-bathing again. Castille asked, "Is Gretchen a Greek name?"

"No. My mother was Irish." Primo turned toward Castille while leaning against the rail. "She died on this boat. Have I told you this?"

Castille shook his head and said nothing. Instead, he studied the man's face. Round and bold. He wore his receding, coarse black curls long in the back. Blue eyes fought off sagging lids.

Primo said, "It was here," and he pointed at his feet. "We were off the east coast of Greece when a storm came on us." He then pointed inside. "I was in the main cabin with my half-brother and half-sister. My father was there with my uncle and my aunt. And my mother—God, she was beautiful. We were playing a board game, but the pieces kept moving. My half sister vomited. She had snuck alcohol when the adults weren't looking. Practice for her later addictions. They sent us below to wait out the storm. It was the last time I ever saw my mother. I was told she came out here and the storm swept her overboard. Her body was found two days later."

Castille remained silent and let the man spill. Not for the information, but he knew that disturbing him could prove unhealthy. He touched the drink to dry lips while Primo reminisced.

"That was eighteen years ago this very night." Primo paused for several beats before finally facing Castille. "The yacht was willed to me by my father, and I changed the name." This time, in his pause, his smile was genuine. "So, you like it, do you?"

"It's magnificent."

"Yes," Primo said, dissecting Castille with his eyes now. Castille shifted uncomfortably until the man moved away and to the high-top table. "I trust your trip was comfortable?" His Greek accent was more pronounced now.

Castille knew the man could have cared less about his comfort, so he responded with, "Expeditious."

Primo smiled, then washed it away with his drink. "My apologies for bringing you here at the last moment, but I have many things on my mind these days. First, there has been a new development. Juan Garcia Lopez will not be receiving the weapons he purchased. The FBI and Mexican military will seize these weapons in Matamoras."

Castille said, "The CDG paid a two-million-dollar deposit and—"

Primo interrupted him. "I know all this, of course, but I am not interested in the squabbles between the CDG and the Juárez Cartel for control of the Mexican-American border. Our concern is the continuation of refugees and drugs coming to American streets. The seizure of the weapons will stop the CDG's planned war and keep them focused on our cause."

"I will let Mr. Lopez know," Castille said.

"You will do no such thing!" Primo barked. "We will let the Mexican army quarantine the weapons, and the CDG can find out on their own. Once the Renner-Kline Bill passes, the CDG will be instrumental in recruiting more Latinos to populate America, and you will be one step closer to achieving your goal of repatriating the land your country lost in the Treaty of Guadalupe. Afterward, if your conscience requires it, you may remind the CDG of their place in this effort. Now—tell me about the bill."

Castille said, "The deaths of Rolando Alvarez and the infant have created immense public sympathy and increased the pressure on Congress to debate the bill."

"And the president is still with us, correct?"

Castille nodded. "Ms. Woodburn has effectively stalled the bill, but it is only a matter of days before Congressman Trent bows to the pressure."

Primo rubbed his chin. "Trent is from California, Mr. Castille. And so is Sierra. He will bow to the pressure of his easily manipulated constituents." Primo turned back to the Miami skyline as he spoke. "We have the momentum in government and the sympathy of the American people, and with the media slapping the hands of the INS, and Sierra sobbing on the Sunday talk shows, everything will move in our favor. Perhaps we could even get Mr. Trent replaced as chairman." Primo paused for a beat, then said, "What of the death of your partner?"

Castille said, "The authorities are focused on the missing border agents. They will, of course, never find them. However, I recently found out that Sierra had befriended Lacey Sullivan. I don't know how much they discussed. I am also hearing that the homicide detectives have a minor interest in a man Lacey was seeing."

Primo said, "If you can find a way to keep their focus on the missing agents, that would be more in our favor. Who is this neighbor?" Primo asked.

Castille thought about it, then said, "Sierra said his name is Liam Curran." Then, he took a step back, as the effect of his words on Primo was like a gut punch. The man had physically bent over and nearly lost his cocktail to the sea. "Something the matter?" Castille asked as Primo recovered slowly.

"Liam Curran?" Primo parroted. "Are you certain of this name?"

"Yes. Why do you ask?"

"Is it possible"—Primo looked away in thought—"that the name might have been Ó Corráin?"

After some thought, Castille said, "I am certain Sierra said it was Curran."

Primo held Castille's gaze for an uncomfortable stretch before turning back to the ocean as it lapped the side of the yacht. "Our business for this evening is complete. Good night, Mr. Castille," Primo said as he snapped his fingers. Moments later, Rockman slid the doors open, then paused as he waited for Castille.

Castille took the hint but was still puzzled by the sudden ending of the meeting.

Rockman escorted Castille from the deck to the helipad. As they climbed the stairs, Castille asked, "Could I possibly sleep here? It's late and—"

"Sleep on the plane," Rockman said coldly, raising a finger, and the chopper blades stirred to life.

Castille calculated his flight time. Six hours put him back at Orange County around eight a.m. Eastern and five a.m. Pacific. Thankfully, he had a change of clothes in his office.

# CHAPTER 28



CIA Director PJ Sanchez (*PJ* was short for *Paul James*) delivered the President's Daily Brief (PDB) in person to select members of the president's national security team this morning—an unusual occurrence—but times were not normal. As requested, late last evening, when the topic of Mexico came up, PJ had passed the ball to Rit, who'd run with it.

Rit said, "We found out late yesterday that a group has procured a large number of Russian and US legacy weaponry leftover from Contra times. We were told a Belize bank was being used, so the buyer is probably the CDG. And, because we leveled their headquarters six months ago, we can safely assume the weapons are earmarked for use against the Juárez Cartel, our agents, and our Mexican partners. Our source indicates the weapons have shipped and are on the way to a port—we assume in Mexico. What we don't know is the name of the ship, where it is currently, or where it will dock. And this, ladies and gentlemen, is the information for sale."

Woody watched the eyes in the room. The president appeared concerned, but she knew that expression. It was his *you handle this and I'll watch how it goes* look. Rit knew the look too, which added to his stock of forehead wrinkles; he would have to turn up the heat if he were going to get a response from the president. Secretary of State Manchin appeared befuddled, knowing this could lead to the release of more compartmentalized information to an audience whose need to know wasn't there.

"Who is the source?" PJ asked.

"Primo Ruqur," Woody said, sending eyebrows up and butts deeper into cushions.

"What is his price?" PJ asked.

"It's free, but it's—complicated," Rit said. He laid out the details of the plan to rid Primo Ruqur of his pesos. He then said, "Full disclosure here—Mr. Ruqur was instrumental in brokering the aid package to Mexico."

PJ leaned forward and asked, "Why wasn't I made aware this had occurred?"

"I wasn't aware the CIA needed to know," the president said. "If you're suggesting Mr. Ruqur is calling in the favor, I'd say that is true." The president then paused and waited for his senior staff to respond.

Manchin asked, "How does Mr. Ruqur know about these weapons?"

Woody said, "I'm less surprised he knows about the weapons and more surprised he offered the information to us." She paused, then said, "We have to go after those guns."

Rit said, "And the FBI-Mexico Joint Task Force is still in place."

Woody said, "Plus, it's a political positive for their president."

Manchin said, "Are we actually going to do this thing?"

The president chimed in. "With the FBI in an advisory role only—yes. There's no downside."

Everyone agreed. Only Manchin's head didn't bob.

Woody stood, signaling the national security team to do the same. The president thanked them but walked with Rit and Woody to the curved door.

"Woody," the president said. "Can I have a couple of minutes?"

She knew this was coming. After a cursory smile to the aides in the outer office and Rittenger, she ducked back inside the Oval Office, where the president had moved to the Resolute Desk. After stopping a foot from him, she said in a hushed tone, "Is this about

Renner-Kline?"

"I—" But the president stopped to gauge his words. "Put a leash on Connie Perdew. No more lobbying for the Senate TABS Bill. There's too much at stake."

She heard his words, but more importantly, his hand gripped her wrist. Glancing down, then back into the eyes of the president, she waited until he let go to respond. "By *at stake*, are you referring to my baggage or yours?"

"Perhaps a little of both," the president said.

"I see," Woody said. "Hypothetically, what if I could eliminate the pressure? We could then let Renner-Kline die in committee and TABS could go through."

The president said, "You don't—understand."

Woody said, "I can't fix what I don't know is broken."

The president asked, "Fix it? How? With Paul's mercenaries? Could you imagine the press if that got out?"

Woody said, "I have another resource. So independent you couldn't possibly believe it."

"Stay out of this issue, Woody!" the president said, his tone excited and booming. He calmed himself, then said, "It's best to play ball now." He straightened his jacket, then added, "Hell, it's just an immigration bill. When I'm out of office—in five years—the next president can change it."

Woody's blood boiled. "By then, millions of illegals will have gained the right to vote. The damage can't be undone."

His smile melted to a scowl. "We're riding on Renner-Kline. That's final."

Woody gritted her teeth, bit her tongue, then uttered a half-hearted, "Yessir." Then, she changed the subject. "I owe the Treasury an answer about Primo Ruqur. What do we tell them about the swap?"

"Tell them to make it happen—by tomorrow," the president said. He straightened his jacket, and then, in a louder tone, he asked, "So, any plans for Labor Day?"

"None," she said. Then, mercifully, her cell phone rang. It was Connie, and she stepped into the hallway to take it.

Connie said, "How'd the meeting go?"

"We can talk about that when you get here. What's up?"

Connie said, "I stopped by the RE offices this morning to go through some of the mail, and I found an odd fax on your machine. Do you know a man named Brian May?"

# CHAPTER 29



Liam had landed in Phoenix the day before and leased a low-key gray Ford Tempo for his ninety-minute drive south to Lukeville. At the 1960s-era motel less than a mile from the Mexico point-of-entry (POE), he'd rented two back-to-back rooms at the far corner of one wing. After dumping his bags in the rooms, he'd gone back to the lobby, where he faxed Brian May's social security and bank information to Patricia Woodburn using the number from her business card that he had taken from her condo. Then, after getting the general lay of the land, he scarfed down some chips and a soda from the machine, then hit the sack in the room facing the front of the motel.

Breakfast this morning had consisted of a complimentary apple from the lobby's fruit bowl and coffee from the vending machine. He spent the morning in the room at the back of the motel double-checking the go-bag and planning his next moves.

With the curtains drawn and pinned closed, he recounted the cash, matched the three passports with the phony driver's licenses and credit cards, then opened the case holding the .308 Sauer 200 takedown rifle. He assembled it, twisted the Leupold 6X scope onto the mounts, screwed on the suppressor, and then loaded the two clips. After checking the functionality, he disassembled it and placed everything back inside the foam-lined case then worked the slides on the pistols. He tucked the Walther into his pants before stowing the bag and the case in the closet and heading next door to the truck stop. It was time for some lunch.

"What are you drinking?" the waitress asked as she wiped the counter.

"Coke," Liam said, admiring her form as she sauntered away. She returned a minute later, and after dictating his order, Liam dug into his jeans pocket and took out the folded phone records and the security log from Lacey's, smoothing them out on the counter. He'd made it halfway through when his food arrived, and he decided to strike up a conversation. Liam raised his half-empty glass.

"What's your name, hon?" she asked, refilling the glass. The badge pinned to her apron strap near an impressive chest indicated she was *DINAH*.

"Brian May," Liam lied.

"Nice to meet you, Brian May."

They exchanged a few more pleasantries before Liam decided to go a little deeper. "How long have you worked here?" Dinah was older, maybe forty-five—a bottle blonde, but not at the roots. Her hair was well sprayed, glued into a bun, and losing the battle with the humidity left by the recent rain.

Dinah thought about it. "My daddy moved the family to the Ajo company town back in '60 to work for Phelps Dodge at the copper mine. I started working here in '75. Daddy retired when they closed the mine in '83, and—here I am. Twenty-two years later. I bought the place five years ago."

"Good for you," Liam said, then spilled Brian May's elevator story about being in sales for a computer company and his made-up exploits from the road, then wondered how many times Mika had told the same lies on her travels while flirting for information. The bell over the door rang as more people left. "Doesn't it get a little dull sometimes?"

"It's a POE truck stop," Dinah said. "I meet people from all over the world. Mexico, Columbia, Peru, Afghanistan—take your pick." She paused, then added, "We did have some excitement about a week ago." She leaned on the counter, drawing him in closer to receive some scandalous secret. It took her ten minutes to tell the story about the murders of two illegals by border agents.

"That's awful," Liam said. "A man and a child?"

"A *jumper* and a child," she corrected him. "And you know what else? The jumper was the brother of Sierra. You know…" And she started humming a song Liam had never heard.

He said, "Come to think of it, I did hear something about it on the news. That was *here*?"

"Yep. They blew up tunnel two days ago," she said as her gaze drifted to the window and the desert beyond. "You can still see where the ground is caved in. They've collapsed so many tunnels around here, we're starting to look like that movie—" She paused in thought. "You know, the one with Kevin Bacon and the worms."

*Didn't every movie have Kevin Bacon?* he thought. "*Tremors*?" Liam finally said.

"That's the one."

Liam said, "Did you know the two agents?"

"Sure. Zach Penn and Isaac Gallagher," she expounded. "They used to sit where you are now. Then one day—poof—gone. They just disappeared."

"Probably right before the murders," Liam said.

Dinah's answer came quickly. "A day or two. That's what I told the investigators. We had a breakfast special that day, trying to get rid of some bacon and sausage coming due. Zach loved the bacon."

"Are they the only two border agents around here?"

Dinah's posture stiffened. "You're not a salesman, are you?"

"Why do you say that?"

"You don't look like a salesman, and you don't talk like a salesman. Or maybe you do, a little too well." She poured two fresh cups of coffee. "Is this about the CDG?"

"What do you know about them?"

"More than *they* know I know." Their eyes locked. "I knew it! You're a government type."

"Actually, I'm not," he said, "but I *am* investigating the murders—privately."

"For who? It's that Sierra woman, right?"

Liam didn't answer. The silence was always filled with more questions than answers.

"What's she like?" Dinah pried.

Liam shook his head. "I've never met her."

"So, you've been hired by her handlers. People like her have—people."

Liam said, "Something like that. Have you seen CDG around these parts?"

Dinah laughed. "All the time. It's not a big secret who they are. The ones who hang out here are the same four or five guys. They drive a black Ford Explorer."

"How do you know all this?"

"Everyone *knows* about it. Doing something about it is another story, and *that* depends on what side of the border you're on." She leaned on the counter and whispered, "Hey—listen. You can't go around asking questions about the CDG. They'll cut your head off. If I were you, I'd leave it alone."

"Not an option," Liam said.

"Then you have a death wish, Brian May. They will cut your throat and feed you to the hogs. No one will know where you went—or that you were ever here."

"But you'll know," he said.

She smiled. "It's funny. You have this delicious boyish innocence, but at the same time…"

"What?" Liam prodded.

"Satan. You're theologically bipolar," she said.

"Impressive," Liam said. "Now you're a priestess?"

"I'm Tohono on my mother's side. We call them shamans. And

you're going to need one if you keep looking into the CDG." She slipped away long enough to take a few orders and refill some glasses before returning.

Liam asked, "Ever hear of Angel or Gerardo Lopez?"

Dinah gave it serious thought before shaking her head. "Should I have?" The bell rang as three men entered. Jeans. T-shirts and tanks. Worn caps. Truckers. "I should probably get back to work," Dinah announced. "And you should probably go back to where you came from."

"Before you go," Liam said. "Where's the tunnel you were talking about?"

Dinah gave a proud nod toward the wall of windows. "It's on the other side of Route 85. Right by the big boulder. It's a waste of time, if you ask me. Nothing to see but a long dent in the ground extending beneath the border fence. The murders happened behind that big dune," she said, pointing toward the windows and the open desert beyond.

Liam turned to look, and he did see the dune. A few hundred yards at least. "I'm going to take a walk and move this food around, then I'll be back for some pie. What do you have?"

"I have all kinds. What do you like?" She winked.

"Surprise me."

"The pie will be waiting for you right here. I'm trusting you not to stiff me on the bill," she said, then strutted away.

Liam watched her with some admiration before leaving the restaurant. He crossed the parking lot, dodged a semi as he crossed Route 85, then started his trek into the desert, searching for this famous boulder. Then, in the distance, it was there, appearing like a pimple on the horizon.

*A few hundred yards, my sweet petunia,* he thought. *More like a half mile.*

It took better than twenty minutes, but he eventually made it, and he clearly wasn't the only one, as the soil around it had been recently disturbed. Traces of footprints, now smeared by the wind, encircled the giant stone littered with cigarette butts and candy bar wrappers. Behind the boulder, a dent in the earth ran in a straight line toward the border fence almost a quarter mile to the south. The tunnel had been imploded, as Dinah had said.

Angel popped into his head as he turned west and headed toward the dune, and Liam wondered where Angel and Gerardo had been hiding that night. Behind the dune, there were boot prints everywhere. After an unsuccessful search for blood or the signs of the murder, he found a narrow indention in the ground that might have been the door to the tunnel. *Ballsy*, he thought as his eyes wandered back eastward, toward the diner. He decided to look around a little more, but came up empty. Still, somewhere inside, he needed to walk on the same ground where baby Esmerelda had spent the last moments of her short life.

Shorter than Lilliana's had been.

He turned east toward the distant POE straddling Route 85. Two lanes south, two north. Most of the vehicles in line were semis, with some pickups and sedans sprinkled in. Certainly not in the same numbers as San Ysidro or El Paso or Tijuana or Brownsville. He made a few mental notes before starting back toward the truck stop, careful to count his steps back to Route 85. When his hiking boot hit the asphalt, the clicker in his head hit 915. He did the math: a little more than half a mile.

A slice of cherry pie hit the counter at the same time his butt hit the red vinyl stool. A scoop of chocolate ice cream shared the plate and was already dripping over the side.

As Dinah watched him put away the dessert with a motherly smirk, he felt a tinge of guilt at his first impression of her as a song popped into his head: *"Brandy, you're a fine girl. What a good wife you would be."*

He finished the pie, wiped the corners of his mouth, then announced, "I need to go." Her grin melted like the ice cream.

Liam stood and tossed two twenties on the counter while she scribbled on the green sales check.

"What's the extra twenty for?" she asked.

"Ten for your tip and ten for admission to the tour of the dune," he said.

"Where are you off to? Just in case I have to send out a search party."

"Caborca, Mexico." He folded the receipt for $18.60, pocketed it, and toyed with the thought of submitting this meal expense to PeKay.

"How's your Spanish?" she asked.

"Passable."

"You coming back?" The pencil now jammed into her hair bun.

Liam smiled. "I have to. I'm staying next door."

"There are better places in Sells."

"Sells is too far," he said.

"If you're thinking about tangling with the CDG, it's not far enough."

He ignored her concerns, but another thought occurred to him, and he realized that Dinah might be useful after all. "Someone might show up looking for me. Gringo types," he said.

"Oh? Let me guess—you're a spy and I haven't seen you?"

"Not exactly. But if they *do* show up, I'd like you to call me." He wrote down Brian May's burner phone number on the sales check.

"Do I tell them where you're staying, or is that top secret?" she asked.

Liam said, "If they show up, they'll already know where I'm staying. Call me and let me know they are here, okay?"

"I'm not here twenty-four seven, you know."

"I know. But if you hear anything, you'll tell me. Right?"

"Because it's you," Dinah said, then touched the back of his hand before strutting away.

# CHAPTER 30

---

It was too late in the day to start anything of consequence, but a little light recon might prove beneficial—like finding the other end of the imploded tunnel. Liam pointed the rented Ford Tempo south on Route 85 and arrived at the POE before ever touching fifty miles per hour. He wasn't sure the piece of crap could get there at all. He'd trade up for something with more balls later.

At the border, he flashed Brian May's passport at the Mexican guard, who checked him out and gave the back seat a cursory glance as a pickup stopped behind him. In the mirror, a dark-brown face with a straw cowboy hat gripped the wheel.

The guard asked, "Mr. May? What is the nature of your business in Mexico?"

Liam knew better than to hesitate or look confused or concerned. "Just heading over to shop."

The guard nodded, checked a computer screen, then handed Brian May's freshly stamped passport back. "Have a nice day." He signaled and the gate rose.

"You too." Liam checked the stamp, then put the rental into drive and pulled away. Behind him, the gate closed, then opened almost immediately as the pickup passed through without notice by the guard.

The sign read: *Welcome to Hombres Blancos, Mexico.*

He slowed the rental to let the pickup pass as he took in the truck stop and the supporting restaurants, strip clubs, and single-story motels ahead. Rather than continue on Route 85, Liam took a sharp right down a side street running parallel to the border wall, where the structures were mostly prefab mobile homes—rusted clean through in some sections. What few stick-built or adobe houses remained were partially caved in somewhere. Lawn chairs were considered landscaping and filled with the occasional sleeping male, whose work started after sunset.

Liam kept track of the trip meter, and after half a mile, he slowed, found the nearest side street, creatively named Thirteenth, then headed north to another colorfully named street, B, that ran parallel to the border.

He parked at a wide spot on the shoulder, tucked the Walther PPK into the small of his back beneath his shirttail, then walked toward the border. At the intersection, he stepped off the remaining distance, about a hundred steps, where he found the dent of the imploded tunnel running south in a straight line between two mobile homes, then between two more on B Street.

Liam followed the indention, looking for an actual house. Then, on the other side of C Street, he found it, and the indention would have T-boned the house square in the side like the trail of a torpedo into a ship's hull. He turned the corner onto Thirteenth, then again onto C, and found the house with a dilapidated porch and a woman rocking on a rusted glider. It squeaked an awful tale. She was ancient. Seventy-five, maybe. Liam checked his surroundings, then took two steps up the walkway before stopping. The old woman had stopped gliding.

Liam cleared his throat and said, *"Buena noches."*

The old woman said nothing. Instead, she let her hand drop between the glider and a moldy white plastic table with a wilting geranium in a chipped terra-cotta pot. When her hand came up, it was wrapped around the pistol grip of a sawed-off shotgun.

Even from this distance, about thirty feet, the size of the barrel's twin tunnels gave it away immediately. A twelve gauge. Liam raised his hands—slowly.

The woman was old, and the weapon that lay across her lap—

powerful. A pistol grip on a sawed-off twelve-gauge shotgun made for good maneuverability, but in her condition, she might be able to fire it once before picking it up off of the porch. He could probably get to the Walther in time to shoot her if he had to. But only if he had to. He was the intruder, and the old woman was scared. And in this neighborhood—he couldn't blame her.

In Spanish, Liam said, *"Yo no soy la policia."* (I'm not the police.) Geez, it was like talking to Angel all over again.

The woman didn't budge. "What do you want, gringo?" she said in good English. "Are you FBI? INS? Or another lawyer?"

"I'm a businessman." He let his hands drop to his waist, keeping them out and away. They remained in a standoff for over a minute.

"What is your name, gringo?" she asked.

"Brian May," Liam replied.

"Okay. Come, Mr. May," the old woman said. Still holding the shotgun, she cradled it like a child as she leaned back in the glider.

A small crowd had gathered. Hole-filled jeans. Dirty shirts. Filthy faces. On the kids too. One woman held a baby in her arms and nursed it openly, and it reminded him of Nicaragua. He accepted the invitation and took the final steps to the front porch as the crowd grew behind him. When he reached the first step, he was careful to plan his ascent, as what was left of the steps was pocked with holes. He made it to the porch, where the 12-gauge was now following his every move.

Rather than take a chair, he leaned against one of the posts, careful to apply his full weight in stages. He also wanted to keep his distance from the old woman. If he was too close, she would be nervous. At this distance, she could relax but still blow a hole in him.

"Perhaps a smaller shotgun would be easier to handle," he said.

This time, she grinned. "This one shoots through walls."

Liam chuckled. "I understand." As the crowd began to disperse, he focused his attention on the old woman and her pet geranium.

"I need workers."

"Is see," she said. "Why do you think I can help you?"

"You have a tunnel that goes to your basement." She didn't answer, so he said, "I have an operation in Arizona sponsoring migrant workers. I bring people in, house them, then hire them to work for my clients."

"Your clients?" the old woman said, the shotgun cradled in her lap now.

"Not sex," Liam said quickly. "Pickers. Watermelons. Oranges. Apples. I'm looking for more workers right now. Autumn is coming soon, and I..."

"Why not use a temp agency?"

Liam grinned. "We both know why, don't we?"

The old woman said nothing but stood, using the shotgun as a cane. Passing by him, she pulled on the screen door, then held it open. Liam took the hint, and after he was inside, she closed both doors and propped the shotgun in the corner before taking a seat on a sofa that was, at most, a year old. He took the chair across from her. Somewhere, beans were simmering.

"Five thousand American dollars," she said bluntly and with an open, crooked palm.

"Five thousand?" he repeated. "Doesn't sound like much."

"Each," she added.

*There we go,* he thought. It was a lot of money, but Liam knew he couldn't accept that as the final number or the old woman would know he wasn't legit. He said, "No. Your people already get money from the migrants."

She said, "Yes. The price to get across. You want dedicated workers."

She had a point, and Liam couldn't argue. The numbers Angel had given him were accurate. Still, nothing was set in stone. "Have you ever provided fifty pickers at a time?"

Her smile faded, and Liam knew she was doing the math. "You

can pay this?"

"Yes. But I should not be charged full price for that large of a number. I'll pay—two thousand per head." It was a nice round number he pulled from thin air. Mostly because the cash he'd brought to play with was in two-thousand-dollar bundles.

"That is less than half! No deal!" she said, but still didn't ask him to leave. She also didn't give him another number. This was where negotiations always went wrong. It was bad enough to be the party who gave up a number first, but to lowball and then raise the number was worse. "Okay. Thanks for trying," Liam said. He then turned to leave.

The old woman said, "Four thousand. Dollars."

"Twenty-five hundred." His finger touched the doorknob.

"Thirty-five."

"Three thousand."

"Okay," the woman said quickly.

Fifty heads at three thousand each for a total of one hundred fifty thousand dollars. Having worked with the Contras in Honduras, the Peshmerga in Iraq, the Mujahideen in Afghanistan, and the local tractor and feed supply company, Liam knew what to ask next. "How quickly can I get them?"

"Two weeks," she said. "I'll need the money today."

*Of course, you do*, he thought, but said, "No, you can have ten percent now and the rest when they reach the other side. If they get caught, I'm out fifteen grand, but you still get paid. That's all I'm willing to risk."

Her eyes raked him from head to toe. "Where is the money?"

"I didn't bring the money across the border because they might have searched me at the POE. Have someone meet me at my motel, and I will have fifteen thousand dollars ready by tonight."

She said, "You will bring the money to me. Here. Then we'll talk. She pushed the screen door open, and when its squeaky spring pulled it back, Liam caught it. She leaned on the shotgun again, like Yoda from *Star Wars*.

"No deal," Liam said. He stepped onto the porch and let the screen door close between them. "I'm staying at the motel next to the truck stop in Lukeville if you change your mind."

Through the filth of the screen, the two stared at each other. He decided to give the issue a hand and turned away from her, starting toward the stairs. It was less about walking away from a deal than showing her the pistol's bulge beneath his shirt at the small of his back. It forced second thoughts.

"I will make a call," she said hoarsely.

He said over his shoulder, "Tell your boss there is ten times more business if we can come to terms. Have them look for a gray Ford Tempo. We'll find each other." At the bottom of the stairs, he jumped to the fractal-filled walkway. Liam didn't need to look back to know the big door was closing and her crooked fingers would be punching buttons on a phone within a minute.

The crowd was gone. He found his car and drove to the truck stop on the Mexican side anchored by a Circle K gas station, a mirror of Dinah's on the US side. Liam went in and took a seat in a booth at the restaurant. He ordered coffee and played gringo tourist.

The booths were ripped brown vinyl with darker-brown Formica trim, cigarette and neglect stained. He wondered how many coyotes and jumpers had sat at these same tables over the years. Liam checked his watch. It was getting late, and the sun would be down soon. His eyes wandered to the crud-covered windows and ultimately the shape of his rental outside, where an SUV had pulled in two spaces away.

It was new—and black. A Ford Explorer. Like Dinah had described earlier. It was this year's model, with all the bells and whistles, most likely. Four dark-skinned men jumped out. Decked out in fresh-off-the-rack cowboy garb, three of them started toward the restaurant, but one stayed outside and examined Liam's Tempo, circling it like a vulture. Liam nibbled another fry as he watched the three men enter through the side door, then meander toward a booth in the restaurant. They peered around the room, looking past him, over him, beyond him, then turned and headed toward the bathrooms.

*About time*, Liam thought.

He dropped a five on the table—gringo money spent well here—as a quote from General George S. Patton came to mind: "Never let the enemy pick the battle site."

Back at the motel, Liam started his preparations. The numbers he had thrown out to the old woman, and the interest her four stooges had shown in him at the Mexican truck stop, ensured the coming visit. Most likely, they had followed him back but elected not to confront him—yet. He also knew the men would be less interested in doing business than they were in relieving him of the cash he had mentioned to the old woman.

And that was okay with Liam.

In the back-facing room, Liam dug into the go-bag and swapped the Walther for the silenced .22 Ruger and two extra clips, which he shoved into his back pocket. Then, he found the silencer for the PPK and screwed it into the barrel before putting it back inside the go-bag. Next, he used the hotel stationery and pen to write a note, then he took the phone book and ripped a small square from the thick cover. On his way out of the room, he placed the paper square on the table next to the door, turned off the light, then closed the door behind him.

Outside, on the second-floor walkway, he reached up to the soffit and busted out the recessed light. He then followed the walkway around the corner between the front and the back, and he broke the lamp there as well. It could be months before maintenance made the repairs—if ever. He followed the walkway to the front, where he passed his other room, then continued the length of the wing to the machines, then down the metal stairs. He crossed the parking lot, where he found his Tempo parked as far away as possible; slipped the note he had written beneath the wiper blade; then went back to the front room.

Liam changed into dark clothing. Black jeans. Black sneakers. Black socks. And a long-sleeve black shirt. He put a spare clip into each hip pocket, then wedged the Dodgers cap on. For ambiance, he found a classic rock station on the clock radio and kept it low as he settled into the chair next to the window. He placed the Ruger on the table, then parted the back edge of the drapes so he could see outside. He propped his feet up on the other chair—then waited.

# CHAPTER 31

After passing the motel for the second time, the passenger in the Explorer ordered the driver to whip a U-turn. When the tires hit the median, the two men in the back seat were thrown in every direction; one nearly took out the sunroof with his head. The driver slowed the Explorer to a crawl, while the passenger leaned forward and scanned the empty parking lot. The gray Tempo hadn't moved.

"Let's do it," the passenger said, and they pulled in and parked in the spot next to the Tempo. He had counted twelve other cars in the lot before noticing something on the windshield of the Tempo. Something that hadn't been there earlier. He pointed. "What is that?"

A man from the back jumped out and removed the folded note from beneath the Tempo's wiper blade. When he returned, he read the note out loud: *"Puedo verte. Dos quince."* (I can see you. Two fifteen.)

"He knows we are here, Jesus," the driver said, his eyes trained on the second floor of the wing. Only one window at the end of the row had a light on. He reached into the floorboard and brought up a pair of binoculars, then pointed. "The room on the end is two fifteen."

"He wants us to go to him," one man said, then worked the shotgun's pump.

"Yes," Jesus said.

"The walkway circles the building. He could be hiding in the back."

"Then we will surround him," Jesus said.

After jogging across the lot, they stopped at the set of metal stairs and vending machines. Jesus pointed to the two men already on the first and third stair. "When you get to the top, go toward the front. Luis and I will go around the back. He will have no escape. Meet us by his room door. Do nothing until we get there."

Everyone nodded.

At the top of the stairs, Jesus and Luis took a left, then a right, then stopped to take in the long row of even-numbered dark rooms. Luis pulled his pistol and heel-toed his way toward the far end, where the walkway turned right behind the wing. After reaching the next-to-last door, they slowed to a tiptoe, and Jesus put his hand on Luis's shoulder, then pointed at the broken lamp at the corner and the glass on the walkway.

The driver swallowed and nodded. Readying his pistol, he leaned against the railing and eased forward, keeping the pistol trained on the darkness ahead. Rounding the corner, he found nothing but a dark walkway, an overgrown tree branch, another busted lamp, and the next corner. He waved for Jesus to follow, then stepped quickly forward. At the next corner, he stopped and said, "It's Luis and Jesus. Don't shoot."

Luis rounded the corner and found the other two waiting for him by the door of 215. Then, his foot crunched another pile of broken glass, and when he looked down, he heard another sound, like feet shuffling, coming from behind him. Maybe Jesus was battling through the tree branch, but when he turned the corner to look, no one was there.

"Jesus," he called in a whisper.

No answer.

"Jesus," he said louder. Luis readied his pistol and started back the way he had come.

"What are you doing?" one man said as he poked his head around the corner.

Luis raised a hand. "Go back and see if Jesus is coming the other way?"

The man disappeared, and Luis started toward the corner, leading with the pistol. Instead of easing around the corner, he popped out quickly, leveled the pistol, and stared down an empty walkway.

"Jesus," he called out again, this time loudly. Then, a room light came on, and he ducked back around the corner and made his way to the other side, where the two CDG thugs were leaving and another light had come on; fingers pulled the drapes back to look.

One man called back as he jogged away, "Where is Jesus?"

Luis said, "I think he left us here."

----------

*"Un chillido y acabare tou."* (One squeak and I will end you!) Liam whispered to the Mexican as he drove a knee into the man's back, pinning him to the stained carpet, until the footsteps of the frantic search party faded. He then wrapped duct tape around the Mexican's head and zip-tied his wrists. Yanking him to his feet, Liam delivered an open-handed blow to the man's chest, sending him flying onto the queen bed, his skull banging against the headboard.

Liam pulled the wooden chair from the desk and sat in it backward, facing the Mexican in the dark and leveling the barrel of the silenced .22 Ruger on the man's crotch.

"I talk—you listen," Liam whispered. "Nod if you understand the game."

The Mexican, wide-eyed and sweating, nodded.

"Do you speak English?"

The Mexican nodded.

"We'll see," Liam said. Laying the pistol aside, he turned on a penlight long enough to reveal the ratcheted PVC pipe cutter he now held. He clicked off the light, then picked up the Ruger.

"First, the rules," Liam said. "I'm going to ask you some questions I may or may not know the answers to. If you lie to me, there are no second chances. This PVC cutter will take off a joint like it's spaghetti. I'm pretty sure your testicles and penis count as joints. Nod if you understand."

The Mexican nodded, then started to sob.

Liam said, "If you cooperate, there's a chance you will live and walk away with cash and other valuable prizes. Have you seen *Let's Make A Deal?*"

The Mexican's eyes narrowed before he nodded.

"Good. You'll have five seconds to answer. After that, you lose something. *Comprendo?*"

The Mexican nodded.

Liam drew in a deep breath. Beneath him was a man who worked for a group that trafficked drugs, illegals, and young girls into sex slavery. He could get past the drugs and illegals for a while, but the last item was going to be damn near impossible to ignore.

"Do you know about the three people murdered in the desert last week?"

The Mexican nodded, but his widened as he let out a muffled, "Two."

"That's very good. You're up to fifty dollars. The old woman I spoke to, did she tell you I was looking for workers?"

The Mexican nodded.

"But you decided to kill me instead?"

The Mexican moaned through the duct tape and shook his head vigorously.

"Shut up!" Liam said. "The questions get tougher but are worth more points. The man who was murdered in the desert, did you bring him across the border?"

This time, the Mexican hesitated until Liam pressed the pistol against his knee. He twisted sideways, nodded vigorously, then squinted in anticipation of the coming pain. Nothing happened, and he opened one eye.

"I told you," Liam said. "Tell the truth and you'll live." He pulled the Mexican into a sitting position, removed the Dodgers cap from his head, and dropped it in the man's lap. Liam went to the window and checked for his friends. They were gone. He turned on the desk lamp and asked, "Do you recognize this cap?"

The Mexican hesitated again. Liam went to the bed, and, unsheathing the tactical knife from his thigh, he cut a slit in the duct tape between the corners of the Mexican's mouth. Liam thought he looked like Iron Man. "One word above a whisper, and *Let's Make A Deal* is over."

The Mexican nodded.

Liam said, "Now, do you recognize the cap?" He then drove a knee into the man's side.

The man grunted. "I know it."

Liam pursed his lips. "You should, because the guy you murdered was wearing it."

"I did not kill the man," the Mexican whispered.

Liam asked, "What's your name?"

"Jesus."

"Nice to meet you. I'm Brian," Liam said. "So, Jesus, how many people did you send through the tunnels that night?"

"Twenty. The van was full."

"That's a hundred thousand dollars. I'd say you had a pretty good night," Liam said. "Next, I'm going to *give* you information. The man who was murdered was also the brother of Sierra. I assume you've heard of her."

"Yes. Of course."

Liam said, "Good. You should do well with the questions on American pop culture when they come up. Do you know who murdered Rolando Alvarez and the baby?"

"I did not see the murder," Jesus sobbed. "I can only tell you what I know. I was given specific instructions to call someone once Rolando was out of the tunnel. The man asked for Rolando's description."

"And that he was the one wearing the Dodgers cap," Liam said, his gaze locked on Jesus. Finally, something concrete. "That means the man you called had never seen Rolando. What did you do after the call?"

Jesus tried to swallow, but nothing happened. "Nothing. I went home. We always wait until the next day to come to the States."

"A baby was murdered, Jesus." Liam willed his finger not to squeeze the trigger as he inched the barrel closer to Jesus's nose. "Did you tell the man about the baby?"

"No, please! The man did not ask about the baby—there are always children. I didn't kill anyone. I think it was—" But he stopped midsentence, choking on his own spit.

"You think it was who?" Liam prodded, knowing Jesus had been sorry he had said it. "The Border Patrol?"

"*Sí*," Jesus said, his chin pounding his chest as he nodded.

"You're too agreeable," Liam said, pressing the Ruger into the man's gut. "Give me a name."

"No—please. They might kill me."

"They might. But I *will*."

Jesus fisted his eyes as he drew in a breath. "Penn and Gallagher," he said.

"I need more. What's Penn's first name?"

"Zach, I think," Jesus said. "He is the man I called."

Liam lowered the pistol as he collapsed back into the chair. Jesus was telling him the truth, and the US Border Patrol had murdered Rolando and the baby. "Our own people," Liam said.

Jesus, still gasping for his breath, said, "It is just a game. I bring workers across, and we pay the Border Patrol to look the other way. They will catch a few, but most they let go."

"The ones they send back will pay you more money to try again.

That's good repeat business," Liam said, and Jesus nodded. "How can these people afford to keep paying that kind of money?"

"Most do not," Jesus said. "The money is paid to us by groups in the United States. They send a list of names and the money; I bring them across."

"What groups?" Liam asked.

"It doesn't matter," Jesus said. "They only exist for a short time before closing their doors and renaming themselves."

"It's a dangerous way to get into the country," Liam said.

"The danger is not the Border Patrol but the journey across the desert. Dehydration. Hunger. Snakes. The border agents usually treat migrants well when they are caught."

"Only, not this time," Liam said.

Jesus's gaze dropped to a spot on the bed.

"I have one last question. When did you last see Penn and Gallagher?"

Jesus looked up, found Liam's eyes, then said, "They disappeared after I saw them—"

Liam gripped Jesus by the balls. "Want to keep 'em?"

"We would always meet Penn and Gallagher at the truck stop the night before a crossing. But, this time, they didn't show up. My men and I waited for an hour, but we had to leave because we were driving some workers to Phoenix that night. On the way, I passed their Tahoe parked on the side of the road near Ajo and the old copper mine. When I stopped to have a look, I saw the keys were inside and there was a roll of plastic in the back. Then, a flash of light caught my eye from the desert, and when I turned to look, I saw two shadows, so I got closer. It was Penn and Gallagher kicking a roll of plastic into a ditch."

"Now they're burying immigrants in the desert?" Liam asked.

"I don't know," Jesus said. "I went back to my truck and left before they came back. That was the last time I saw them. I tried to call him later, but Penn doesn't answer his phone now."

*Because they drove to Princeton to murder Lacey Sullivan and Gerardo Lopez*, Liam thought. Angel's story was coming together, but questions remained. Why would they murder a baby—but let the mother live? Had they known Angel and Gerardo witnessed the murders and tracked them to Princeton? If they had, Lacey was the innocent bystander. If not, Lacey had been the target all along. And if that was the case, what was the link?

Liam grabbed Jesus by the shirt and pulled him from the bed. "C'mon. We're going for a drive."

"Where?" Jesus asked.

"You're going to show me those graves," Liam said. "Any idea where we can get a shovel at this hour?"

Jesus said, "We won't need a shovel."

# CHAPTER 32

Princeton, West Virginia
Saturday, September 2, 1995
5:58 a.m.

Bill Shipman stopped at the bottom of the drive, entered his code, crossed the cattle stop, then backed the fifth-wheel livestock trailer up to the open gate and dropped trailer's ramp. He then coaxed his new calf and its mother into the field before locking it. Shielded his eyes from the rising sun, he yawned, and wiped his brow. He checked his watch again and realized he had made the trip from Oklahoma City in just over nineteen hours. Time to head for home. But first—a good piss.

At the garage, Shipman entered another code and waited for the door to rise. He disabled the alarm using the mudroom panel, then used the half bath before continuing to the kitchen. In the refrigerator, he found old pizza and one of Mika's overpriced waters. Then, a hint of light shimmered through the glass in the man door of the pole barn. Peeling back the flowery drapes, he waited for a moment until he saw it again, and then, realizing he hadn't imagined it, he decided to investigate.

When his foot hit the driveway, he realized he should check in first, having already committed three acts that sent three text messages to Liam's pager: the gate code, the garage code, and disabling the house alarm. Using his phone, he typed out the text message: IT'S BS. DROPPED OFF 2 NEW FRIENDS. He hit Send, then retrieved a snub-nosed .38 caliber Colt from his truck and approached the pole barn—slowly. He pressed the combination on the five-button lock, a motor whirred, and the twenty-foot door rose, flooding the barn with sunlight.

To the right, by the stalls and blacksmithing equipment, was only shadows. To the left, the dirt bikes and workbench, and taking up the back left corner, Liam's new RV.

Shipman took a step closer and noticed an extension cord had been run from the RV to the plug on the pole barn wall. The RV was equipped with blinds covering the front and side windows, and they were all down. But the door to the RV was cracked open, and a vertical slice of light spilled into the garage.

Certain that some local kids had broken in, he relaxed his grip on the pistol and started toward the open door, looking forward to scaring religion into some unsuspecting teens whose state of dress or undress might come into question. But then, the door burst open, and a short man spilled out, half in and half out of the door. Open palms smacked smooth, hard concrete, and his legs disappeared somewhere into the RV. And—what was that rattling noise?

Shipman steadied the pistol as the man tried to right himself and reverse crawl back into the RV. "Stop right there!" he said, and the man froze. Then, the man rolled over and stared up at Shipman pitifully.

Shipman cocked his head and squinted at the dark-skinned man, whose face and nose had seen better days. And around his waist, a padlock and heavy steel chain had worn through the man's T-shirt; faint strips of crimson painted the fabric. Shipman's eyes followed the chain into the RV until it disappeared. From inside, he could hear the television, and he saw that the floor was covered with empty microwave pizza boxes.

"What in the fuck is going on?" he said, then stepped closer and put his foot on the man's hand. "Who in the hell are you?"

The man didn't answer, but shook his head instead.

Shipman checked the man for weapons, ignored the sweet stench of booze, then went inside the RV. It was empty. He recognized the chain as being one of his, and it had been snaked through one of the small access panels in the floor.

He went back to where the man was now lying face down, his cheeks against the concrete. "Well, you didn't do this to yourself," he said. "Do you speak English?"

The man shook his head again while Shipman scratched his own. He helped the man up and led him back into the RV, then let him fall onto the sofa. Shipman left the RV, then took out his cell phone and dialed.

*What in the hell had Curran gotten himself into now?*

# CHAPTER 33

North of Lukeville, Arizona
Same Day
3:05 a.m.

When they reached the parking lot, Liam noticed Jesus's Explorer was gone.

No doubt his friends had made a break for it, but the shitty part was now Liam and Jesus had to take the Tempo—a vehicle not known for its off-road bragging rights.

Liam drove while Jesus navigated. The Mexican's hands were still zip-tied behind his back and had to be rubbing him raw by now. An hour later, after passing the first sign for Ajo, Jesus pointed to a wide spot in the road and a washed-out gully.

"That's not a road," Liam said.

"It is in Ajo," Jesus said.

Liam patted the dashboard, wished it luck, then pressed the gas. The car bottomed out about every twenty feet, and a few times, the front bumper bit into the dirt and kicked up dust so thick, he ran the wipers to clear the windshield. Not having the advantage of free hands, Jesus's head pounded the side glass and roof more than once. Two hundred yards in, Jesus pointed at a pair of cacti, their arms bent up and waving. Liam parked, and they walked the last few yards to a spot where the soil had been recently disturbed. Jesus sat and worked his legs through his zip-tied hands until they were in front of him.

"What are you doing?" Liam asked.

Jesus said, "Digging." Then he started scooping earth barehanded.

Liam joined in and they dug like dogs; the soil was so dry, it should have blown away. Less than six inches down, Liam's hand hit a mass of heavy plastic. Using the tactical knife, he sliced open a section and exposed hair. Minutes later, there were two faces, both beaten so badly, they were more like maggot-covered steaks from a butcher shop's trash bin. After slicing the plastic further down the torsos, Liam found the bodies had been stripped to their underwear. Both corpses were men. The stench and horror of burnt, peeled, beaten, and rotting flesh was nothing new—but it didn't make this any easier.

Penn and Gallagher's body count was now up to six, and given the timeline, these two men were probably their first victims. The question now was: Who were these guys, and why were they murdered the night before Rolando and the baby?

Liam retrieved the PagSat pager from his pocket and turned it on. After it had synced up, a notification flashed. He had a new text message. He read it. Thought, *Oh shit!* Then ignored it, for now. He typed a message to Ginny, which simply read, `note this long and lat`, then pressed Send.

"Okay. Let's cover them up," Liam said and began refilling the graves.

"Are we leaving them here for the hogs?" Jesus asked.

"I took care of it," Liam said.

After topping the graves with stones, he led Jesus back to the Tempo while watching the sun crown the horizon.

"What will we do now?" Jesus asked.

"I keep my promises. I'm taking you back to Lukeville." When Jesus's face faded to white, he asked, "What's wrong?"

"I can't go back. Not now," Jesus said, his head bouncing against the side window as Liam steered the Tempo into and out of its first hole.

"Why not?" Liam asked.

"The CDG will kill me."

Liam had been in this situation before in Iraq and Afghanistan when using local interpreters who also knew about the opium smuggling operations. There was no way they could ever go home. But Jesus was no interpreter. He was just a foot soldier and had not come willingly.

"Why would the CDG kill you?" Liam asked.

Jesus said, "Because I am not Mexican."

"You're shitting me! You're an American?" Liam said, resisting the urge to flatten the man's nose with an elbow.

Jesus said, "My mother was pregnant with me when she and my father immigrated to Tucson in 1970. In Mexico, my family had worked for the CDG, but there was some kind of trouble and my parents fled for their lives. After a few years, my father attempted to get my grandmother away from the CDG and into the States. He failed." When his gaze met Liam's, he added, "Two months later, a box was left on our porch. My father's head was inside."

Liam said, "And you found it."

"Yes," Jesus said. "I don't remember much of it, only the stories from my mother. But she is dead now."

They had reached the main road, and Liam parked in the wide spot. "What happened to your mother?"

"When she found out I was working as a coyote with the CDG, she"—Jesus stopped talking, then went back to watching the signs go—"took some pills."

Liam nodded, but still, something wasn't adding up. Maybe an American-born Latino working as a coyote for the CDG was an oddity, but it would also have its advantages, and they must have known he was an American when they brought him on board. At the end of the day, he was at the bottom of the food chain. There had to be more to it.

Liam said, "What are you not telling me, Jesus? You're a coyote who got his ass kicked, as far as the CDG will ever know. Now would be a good time to let me in on the story." When Jesus didn't respond, Liam pulled the pistol from beneath the seat and aimed it at Jesus's knee. "Do we need to do this again?"

Jesus said nothing, but a bead of sweat tracked from his hairline to his ear.

Liam said, "You have ten seconds."

"Okay!" Jesus screamed. "Please. I'm afraid for my grandmother."

"Your grandmother?" Liam asked. "The one your father tried to get out of Mexico? Is she the old woman with the shotgun?"

"No. My grandmother is in Puerto Peñasco. She works for the CDG. She's all I have left."

"And they would kill her because of what happened to you?" Liam said. "Try again. What does your grandmother do?"

Jesus turned away, then touched his head to the glass. "She's—an accountant."

Liam said, "An accountant? For the Cartel Del Golfo?"

Jesus sighed. "No. My grandmother is *the* accountant for the CDG."

"Holy shit!" Liam said. "No wonder you're afraid. If the CDG thinks you're spilling your guts—" *They'd kill you*, Liam thought. And if Jesus was telling the truth, he couldn't let this opportunity get away. But he had a big problem now—a *time* problem. They may want Jesus dead, but they weren't about to kill their accountant. They'd secure her. And if they moved her, Liam would lose one hell of an opportunity to get the grandmother to the Lake and let Babbs and Bailey pick her brain.

Leaning over Jesus, Liam found a map in the glove box and unfolded it across the steering wheel. Puerto Peñasco was in the armpit of the Gulf of California and at least a two-hour drive from Lukeville. But what other choice did he have? He had to get the accountant. If the CDG knew about Jesus, it was already too late. But if they didn't, he might have a chance.

Then, there was the other issue. His second reason for coming to the border. It was still a little early, and he hadn't heard anything from Dinah. Liam checked his watch and did the math. If he played it right, this could work in his favor. But he had a lot to do.

"You're right," Liam said. "You can't go back. But your grandmother can't stay in Mexico either. I can help you both, but you have to trust me."

"Are you with the government?" Jesus asked. His chest heaved, and his zip-tied hands were tucked between his clenched knees as if he had to pee.

"No. Better than that," Liam said, then reached into the go-bag for the burner phone. There was no signal. He pulled out and drove south, watching the bars on the phone until they had climbed to three. He pulled to the side of the road, took the keys from the ignition, then got out to make the call. It was picked up immediately.

"Brian?" Ginny said as she answered. "I received your text. What was that about?"

After bringing her up to speed, he said, "I need to extract Jesus, and we need to get those bodies from the desert. Their GPS location is embedded in the text message I sent."

"I'll put Curtis on it," she said.

He heard voices in the background, and Ginny used the word *stat*. Sometimes, he loved this woman.

Ginny asked, "Now, about your friend—what's your level of confidence he's telling the truth?"

"Unknown. But I'm not going to find out *after* the CDG moves her. I have to get there first. If I do find her, I won't be able to drive her out of Mexico. Can I get a seaplane out of Puerto Peñasco?"

"That's an easy one. We have an asset in San Diego who can help us. If there's a chance we can score the CDG's accountant, I'll make it happen. As for Jesus, this can get tricky. He's an American citizen."

Liam turned toward the car, where Jesus was still rocking back and forth. "He'll do something stupid. Let's get the accountant first. Then, if Jesus wants to be an idiot, he's on his own. I think he understands he's the consolation prize."

"Okay," Ginny said. "Where's the closest runway?"

Liam said, "I noticed Sells has a strip of asphalt they pass off as an airport. We could get a light jet or prop in there."

"Okay. Give me a minute," Ginny said, then the phone went to hold. Liam decided to use the time to open the rear door of the Tempo and retrieve his personal cell phone from the go-bag. The phone found a tower, and it immediately vibrated, telling him he had a missed call. It was Bill Shipman's number from an hour ago.

Ginny's voice came back on the burner phone. "I got it. Sells has a fifty-eight-hundred-foot runway, and it's operational. Michaels is in Dallas and can be there in two hours."

"I'll make it work," Liam said. "Also, I'm ditching this burner phone." He thanked her, then clicked off. That sealed it. He was officially in love with Ginny Woodburn.

At the passenger door, he tapped on the glass until Jesus looked up. Liam held up a single finger, stepped away, then pressed the Redial button on his personal phone. It rang once and was answered.

"Where in the fuck are you?" Shipman's voice was scolding. "I've been entertaining your new pet for the past hour. Why didn't you let me know?"

"Uh—surprise. I have a pet Mexican," Liam said. "I fed your animals while you were gone, so can you return the favor? I named him Angel, by the way."

Shipman said, "Your pet was drunk and fell out of the damn RV. I sobered him up with some coffee and restocked the icebox with more frozen pizzas. This guy isn't going to shit for a month."

"While you were in Oklahoma, Lacey was murdered, and Angel is the only living witness," Liam said. "I'll explain the details later, but you have to do me a favor and make sure he stays chained up and out of sight. There are two lunatic border agents named

Penn and Gallagher trying to kill him. Oh yeah, the INS *and* the state police want him too."

"So, we're protecting this Mexican from the good guys, the good guys, and the other good guys? Makes sense to me."

Liam chuckled. "I'll be back in a couple of days."

"I'll treat him with all the love I give to my other livestock," Shipman joked. "And if the authorities come calling with a warrant?"

"Play dumb," Liam said. "You were in Oklahoma."

There was a long pause before Shipman said, "I'll brush up on my Spanish. Where are you?"

"Arizona heading to Mexico. Those border agents are on a killing spree, and I just dug up two more bodies."

Shipman said, "And we're keeping the cops away because—"

"Because I don't want to go to jail for kidnapping. The INS has two agents in Princeton right now. A skinny Black guy named DeVine and his partner, Gillespie. I'm supposed to be helping DeVine find Angel."

"And you found him."

"But DeVine doesn't know that yet. Keep him away from Angel. And—you and I have not spoken."

"You're a lunatic. You know that?" Shipman said.

"Thanks for caring," Liam said, then clicked off.

When he got back in the car, he found Jesus with his forehead pressed hard against the dash. Liam smacked the man's cheek. "I need your grandmother's address."

Jesus didn't answer the question but instead said, "How did this happen to me?"

"You were doing bad shit and you got caught," Liam said bluntly. "Now, let's get your grandmother out of Mexico."

"I was thinking," Jesus said absently. "Why are you so concerned about my grandmother?" He turned toward Liam, his eyes sunken and sad. "This thing you are doing, it isn't about the CDG, is it?"

"Not entirely," Liam said. "Do you know a man named Manuel Castille?"

Jesus considered this, then said, "I have heard that name, but all I know is that he is an important man."

Liam nodded, then started the car and headed south again. The Y in the road for Route 80 east was ahead, so Liam slowed and took the left. The sign said that Sells was sixty-two miles away, and he wondered if he had enough time to bring Jesus back around. The man was having second thoughts.

"What is in Sells?" Jesus asked.

"I'm putting you on a plane to DC. My people will take care of you there."

"You can't do that to me. I'm a US citizen. It would be kidnapping."

*Which I seem to have a knack for*, Liam thought, but said, "I could take you to the cops instead."

Jesus said nothing.

"Thought so," Liam said. "Now, how do I find your grandmother?"

"What does it matter?" Jesus said.

"Your father tried to bring her out before and failed," Liam said. "I'm going to finish the job."

"Because you want the CDG's accountant," Jesus said, his voice laced with accusation.

"And to save her life," Liam said. "Can't I have both?"

"And if the CDG is there?"

"I'm not leaving Puerto Peñasco without her," Liam said.

"Then I should talk to her first," Jesus said. "Maybe I can convince her to—"

"Not a chance," Liam said. "If you're telling the truth, then her phones are tapped, and I'm not giving anyone a heads-up I'm coming."

Jesus smiled weakly, then said, "You promise to take care of my grandmother?"

"I will do everything in my power. I promise," Liam said.

Jesus said, "There is something you should know. My real name is Stephan. I only use Jesus when dealing with the CDG. It's a matter of survival, but I don't expect you to understand."

Liam chuckled inside, then said, "I'll bet it's tough."

They said little else before pulling into the tiny airport lot. They both got out and stretched, and Jesus-Stephan made the comment they were in Tohono Indian territory now and the Tohono Nation owned and operated the airport.

"If we need to name-drop, I know a Tohono shaman priestess," Liam said, thinking about his earlier conversation with Dinah. He texted Ginny for an update, and she replied that Michaels was a half hour out. It was going on ten o'clock now, and the urgency to get on the road weighed heavy. And he still needed to get rid of the Tempo in favor of something speedier.

The Cessna Citation CJ2 landed a few minutes later than expected and taxied up to the tarmac. The door opened, and a young man Liam didn't know lowered the stairs. Behind him, the familiar face of Rick Michaels appeared. He spotted Liam standing by the cyclone fence, then sent him the middle finger.

Liam and Jesus-Stephan entered the terminal, where they both hit the restroom. They stopped at a counter, where Jesus-Stephan jotted down his grandmother's address on the back of a ticket jacket.

"Your grandmother's name is Araseli?" Liam asked. "How old is she?"

"She's in her seventies," Jesus-Stephan said.

*Perfect*, Liam thought as he imagined pushing a screaming old woman in a wheelchair down the streets of Puerto Peñasco while lugging an oxygen tank behind.

Another set of glass doors later, and they were on the tarmac, where Liam and Rick shook hands, then slapped backs. Liam rubbed Michaels's blond buzzcut. Michaels was still an active Navy

SEAL working with Team Six out of San Diego, and he gripped Liam's hair near his shoulder and tugged hard.

"You nasty civilians," Michaels said. "How long did it take you to sprout this fern? You look downright sexy."

"Your beard's coming out," Liam said. "Where are you deploying?"

"Kuwait. But not for a few more weeks." Michaels introduced the younger man with him as Ensign Luke Wilhelm. A SEAL hopeful who hadn't started BUD/S training yet. Then he turned to the Mexican standing behind Liam, his gaze dropping to the man's zip-tied hands. "Is this my passenger?"

"Rick," Liam said grandly. "This is Stephan. Stephan, this is Commander Rick Michaels. And he's not as patient as I am." Liam waited until after Ensign Wilhelm had escorted Stephan onto the plane to fill Michaels in on everything but his little project.

"You're in over your head, amigo," Michaels said. "Ginny asked if I could hang around and give you a hand. It's Saturday and I'm bored anyway."

"I appreciate that, but this is something I have to do on my own. It's more important to get Stephan to the Lake so Babbs and Bailey can take a run at him. Don't worry. In a couple of hours, I'll be having a margarita with a seventy-year-old Mexican woman."

Michaels said, "You have no idea what you're walking into down there. Somebody needs to at least watch your six."

"It's a drag and drop, Rick. Trust me." Liam thanked Michaels again, and by the time Ensign Wilhelm had retracted the stairs and closed the Cessna's door, Liam was back on the highway.

Turning down Michaels's help was more difficult than he had let on. Two SEALs working together would all but ensure the extraction of the grandmother. But after she was safe on a seaplane, Liam had one more objective to complete, and there was no way in hell Rick Michaels, or anyone else, could be involved in that.

# CHAPTER 34

Alexandria, Virginia
Same Day
7:45 a.m.

His eyes fluttered when the security system beeped, and Paul Kelvington rolled over and reached for the cool, empty spot in the bed. With one eye, he checked the clock and surmised the beep must have been Jeff leaving his shift. Andrew would have followed Woody to the White House.

Paul had returned from his trip late last evening, never once considering checking in at the office, and when he entered the condo, he found Jeff eating a sandwich in the kitchen. Woody was already asleep. He and Jeff had exchanged some pleasantries and some banter before Jeff provided Paul with a short list of what *hadn't* happened. Boring was good. The subject of the mugging came up briefly before Paul tiptoed up the stairs, showered quickly, then slid beneath the covers. Woody had stirred long enough to smile at his kiss on her cheek.

This morning, he toasted two bagels for breakfast and carried them to his private study, where he sifted through the mail. The item on the bottom was the manila envelope addressed to *Paul* on the front in Woody's handwriting. He broke the seal and removed the three-page fax.

The top page was simply a cover, where the name *Woodburn* had been scribbled. The second page was simple as well. Three lines. Brian May's name, a number appearing to be a social security number, and a nine-digit number followed by a ten-digit number. Paul suspected they were a routing and account number. The last page had the word *BLANK* scribbled in the center with a Post-it note from Woody. $10,000 ASAP.

*Son of a bitch. She wasn't kidding.*

Paul bit into his bagel, fired up the laptop, and wrote a quick email instructing his HR manager to put Brian May in the system as a 1099 contract employee and to pay him a $10,000 advance for expenses. He was about to run the fax through the shredder when something else caught his eye—something so standard and so normal, he nearly let it slip by.

Paul held the fax up to the light and laughed. Whoever this Brian May was, the idiot had made a rookie mistake. Paul wondered if Woody knew how incompetent their new contractor was and what service the man would be performing. One thing was for certain, for her sake and his own, he was going to find out.

Paul picked up the phone and called Mandy, his assistant; apologized for bugging her on a Saturday; rattled off the information from the fax; ensured her it was important; then hung up and waited for the return call. Ten minutes later, she gave him the information he was looking for, and Paul thanked her, hung up the phone, then immediately phoned Zilo.

"Morning, boss. It's Saturday," Zilo said.

"So what," Paul shot back.

Zilo replied, "I just—thought it was important you knew. What's up?"

"Something's come up, and we need to go to Arizona—today. We need to go by the office in Quincy first."

"Arizona? Today? Are you joking?"

Paul said, "United has a direct flight leaving from Dulles in two hours."

"Fine," Zilo said after a long pause. "I'll meet you there."

Paul hung up with Zilo, then called United's one-eight-hundred number and made the reservations himself before darting up the stairs for a quick pack job. When he finished, he phoned Woody to let her know he was leaving again, but told her he was going to PeKay's Phoenix office to deal with a personnel situation, which, as it turned out, wasn't a total lie. He then went back downstairs to his study, where he had left the faxed pages, took one last glance at them, and smiled at the dumb luck providence had afforded him.

In the margin of each faxed page, the sending fax machine had printed its phone number. Using his cell phone, Paul entered the digits and hit Send. He received the expected warbling tones of a fax modem trying to sync up. "Gotcha! Dumbass!" Paul said. He folded the pages and tucked them into his jeans.

# CHAPTER 35



At nine thirty that Saturday morning, Detective Wallace Taconelli made the forty-five-minute drive from Beckley (his home detachment) to the Mercer County courthouse in Princeton. He unlocked the door to the cramped visitor's office assigned to him by the sheriff, gathered the Sullivan case files, then retreated to the conference room across the hall, where he could spread out.

He wouldn't have made the drive on a Saturday had it not been for the interview scheduled for eleven thirty, and there was no way he'd miss this one. With the primary suspects in his case shifting to the missing border agents suspected of committing two murders in Arizona—and the FBI about to take over—this may be his last interview. But, without a doubt, it would be the most interesting.

Across the table, he splayed out every notated photo, document, interview, phone record, and handwritten note—which, together with the coffee he'd thrown away earlier, added up to zilch. According to agent DeVine, the dead John Doe was a Latino named Gerardo Lopez, the brother of a man DeVine called Angel, who he swore was the shooter. But the latest ballistics report, which DeVine hadn't seen, proved there were two separate .40 caliber pistols used in the Sullivan home, and they matched the rounds found in the victims in Arizona. Plus, after running both names through the state and federal databases, neither came back. As far as real evidence was concerned, all he had was the victim's name—Lacey Sullivan.

However, no one could find information for agents Penn and Gallagher either. Their vehicle was missing, and there were no credit card receipts, no tollbooth videos, no calls to loved ones from pay phones or pings from their cell phones to towers. On the Angel and Gerardo side, all he had was two bus tickets purchased in Lukeville but no record of them ever getting on the bus. The two bus drivers interviewed recalled more than a dozen Latino passengers on the route, but none had gotten off in Princeton. Penn's and Gallagher's pistols were absolutely guilty, but how had they gotten to Princeton?

Taconelli found the color photos in the pile and studied them. What could have turned two model border agents into serial killers: Drugs? A tumor? Lunacy? And what were the odds of two psychopaths being partners? Still, ballistics didn't lie. Perhaps he had to admit the two border agents were the murderers and help to locate the only witness to all the murders—DeVine's infamous Angel Lopez.

After tossing the photos into the pile, he went to the window for a little sunlight and saw Deputy Zeller climbing out of his patrol car. Then, a young woman met him on the sidewalk, and together they disappeared around the corner. Taconelli sighed, certain he was about to waste another hour interviewing this woman. But he would change his mind in a matter of minutes.

There was a light tapping on the conference room door, then Deputy Zeller poked his head inside, his Smokey Bear hat in his hand. "You ready for us?" he asked.

"Absolutely," Taconelli said, and Zeller opened the door and let the young, lovely redhead lead the way. Zeller closed the door and showed her to the conference table while his eyes were glued to her blouse, tight jeans, and impressive backside.

Zeller said, "Ms. Cruise, this is Detective Taconelli."

"Nice to meet you, Ms. Cruise." Taconelli held his hand across the conference table. She took it, shook it, then pulled hers back quickly as she turned and took in the voluminous room and the litter of documents on the table. "Thank you for spending time on a Saturday to help us out. May I call you Rachel?"

"That works," Rachel said as she sat and a red nail tapped the table.

Zeller sat beside her and asked, "Would you like something to drink? There's a machine down the hall."

"No, thank you. Do I need a lawyer?"

Taconelli said, "Let me do all the talking first, then you can decide. But you haven't done anything wrong." He held up a small digital recorder, pressed Play, then placed it at the center of the table. "We are recording, okay?"

"Fine," she said.

"Good. First, have you heard about the murder of Lacey Sullivan and a Mexican man?"

"Yes. It's all over the papers," she said.

Taconelli passed her the photos of Agents Penn and Gallagher. "Have you ever seen these men before?"

Rachel shook her head and passed them back. "Is this about Li—" Rachel started to ask, then said, "Professor Curran?"

Taconelli said, "Not directly. Why do you ask?"

"We haven't slept together," Rachel said, her tone defiant.

"Not my business, unless you're under eighteen, which you're not," Taconelli said. "However, it's our understanding that you may know a good deal about him."

"Why's that?"

Measuring his words, Taconelli said, "You have developed quite the—what's the word—fascination with him."

"I guess," Rachel said.

"Let me be direct, okay? Your interest in Mr. Curran is border-line—obsessive—and we know you follow Mr. Curran around." When she started to object, he stopped her. "Once again, this isn't about your crush on an older teacher, and I'm not your father. It's Dr. Curran we're interested in, and—"

"Professor," Rachel said, correcting him.

Taconelli glanced at Zeller, who suppressed a grin. "I'm sorry," Taconelli said, "*Professor* Curran. We have a few questions, and you'll be out of here."

"It's a waste of time," she said. "I happen to know that Professor Curran was in Columbus, Ohio, two days before the murders. He met his girlfriend at the airport, and they were going to Put-in-Bay for the weekend."

"Really?" Taconelli said, surprised at the revelation. It might be nothing, but anything new was good. He remembered that the girlfriend, Casey Conner, had flown out of Roanoke the same morning Lacey Sullivan was murdered. So, if they had gone to Put-in-Bay, they didn't stay the whole weekend.

Taconelli said, "Rachel, I have to ask this. It has nothing to do with you personally. Do you understand?"

She nodded.

"Good. Now—can you verify any of what you just told me?"

Rachel recrossed her legs under the table. "You promise this isn't about me."

"Cross my heart," Taconelli said.

"Okay. I know because I followed him."

"You followed him where?" Zeller asked.

"To Columbus."

Zeller said, "That's a little—"

Taconelli raised a finger and interrupted him. "Sorry, Miss Cruise. Keep going."

She said, "I know what you're thinking, but my family lives in Columbus, and when I heard Professor Curran wouldn't be back until Monday, I decided that if he wasn't teaching the Friday class, I'd go home for a long weekend too."

"And you followed him?" Taconelli asked.

Rachel studied her interlaced fingers and said, "Kinda like that."

"Okay," Taconelli said. "So, Curran left Princeton—when?"

"Wednesday night," Rachel said.

"What time?" Zeller asked.

"Around seven o'clock."

Taconelli said, "So that had you guys in Columbus around…"

"Midnight," Rachel said. "My plan was to follow him as far as the 270 bypass because my parents live in New Albany and, if he was going to Put-in-Bay, he'd stay on 71. But when Professor Curran took the bypass too, then took the airport exit, I got curious."

"Of course," Taconelli said. "What happened next?"

Rachel said, "I followed him to the short-term garage. He parked next to his girlfriend's SUV, then entered the terminal. I parked on the other side. I waited for a few minutes and was about to leave when another car pulled in and parked beside his BMW. When Professor Curran got out of *that* car, I stuck around. He moved some luggage from the BMW to the new car. Then, about fifteen minutes later, his girlfriend drove up in another SUV."

"So, they had four vehicles there," Taconelli said as he closed his eyes and tried to make sense of what he had just heard. "Casey Conner drives from Princeton to Columbus to catch a flight for her job. She returns a few days later, and Curran meets her at the airport to pick her up for their trip to Put-in-Bay. None of that seems odd until the two new SUVs show up. Maybe Curran leased an SUV to do some off-roading, but why had his girlfriend rented one too? Or had she? Plus, Casey Conner already owns an SUV."

"What happened next?" Taconelli asked.

"They kissed, talked for a few minutes, got into the two SUVs, and left the garage—separately. I waited and followed them out until they got to Route 67. That's where they went west, and I went east toward New Albany. It was good timing because I passed a bunch of emergency vehicles coming in. I heard the next day there had been a fire. The next time I saw Professor Curran was

Saturday night at the bar in Princeton."

Zeller asked, "Why did you go back to school on a Saturday?"

Taconelli, when he heard *interrogation* in Zeller's tone and saw Rachael cross her arms, he raised his palm and asked, "What type of SUV did Professor Curran rent?"

"I'm not sure." Rachel's gaze dropped to the table. "I don't know one from another."

Taconelli knew he had stumbled onto something, but what did it matter, when he already knew both Curran and his girlfriend were home at the time of Lacey's murder? He had spoken to Curran at his house just after ten a.m. The ME put Lacey's time of death between five thirty and six thirty Saturday morning, and Curran already admitted they were both home at that time and that Ms. Connor had an early flight out of Roanoke that day. With the evidence mounting in favor of Penn and Gallagher being the killers, pursuing this too far might be a big waste of time. Still—this was just too weird to ignore.

Taconelli wrote a note, then passed it to Zeller, who, without a word, grabbed his Smokey Bear hat and left the room.

Rachel strained her neck to watch the man leave, then turned back to Taconelli. "Where's he going?"

"To run an errand," Taconelli said. "Is there anything else you can tell me?"

"My parents can prove I didn't leave Columbus until Saturday afternoon," Rachel said.

"I believe you," Taconelli said. "Like I said, you're definitely not a suspect. Do you mind if I ask how you've developed such an interest in Professor Curran when you've only taken one of his classes and this is your first semester?"

Rachel said, "I took classes this summer, and that's when I first met him. I know it seems weird, but when I see something I want, I go after it." She checked the floor again, then added, "I know what you're thinking, I'm a girl who dresses a little provocatively, but God gave me this body, and it doesn't matter what I wear, I'm going to get attention. But I've only had two boyfriends my whole life. One moved away in high school and the other went to the military last year. That's why I transferred to Concord—to get away. Then, I met Professor Curran in the student union. He's smart, handsome, and mysterious, I guess."

"But he has a live-in girlfriend," Taconelli argued.

"And I'm giving him options. I know what you're thinking, he's fifteen years older than me," she said with some pride. "I'm trying to get to know him better, you know—"

"To give him—options," Taconelli finished for her.

"Is that illegal?"

"No, it isn't," Taconelli said, pressing Stop on the recorder. He stood and Rachel stood with him. He held out his hand and they shook. "If we have any more questions, we'll give you a call. I want you to know how appreciative I am you gave us your time today."

He showed her to the door, then went back to the table. He found a new file folder and wrote *Rachel Cruise* on the tab. This girl wasn't obsessed—she was fanatical. Still, her infatuation with Liam Curran didn't put Penn's and Gallagher's bullets in Lacey Sullivan and John Doe.

Zeller returned fifteen minutes later with several faxed pages. "I talked to your friend, Detective Braden Willis, with the Ohio State Highway Patrol. You are not going to believe this shit." He slid the fax to Taconelli. "You wanted rental car data from all the companies at the Columbus airport for August twenty-third and August twenty-fourth? Well, here it is. And not just the rental car data, the manifests for the commercial flights are there too. He asked that we not share this."

"I get it. We'd need our own warrant to use it." Taconelli took the faxed pages and started running a thumb down the columns. "How in the hell did he get this so quickly?"

"Because he already *had* it," Zeller said. "The Ohio State

Highway Patrol and the FBI are working on the Toledo mass shooting."

"I'll be—" Taconelli said, his thumb still running down the columns and rows.

Zeller said, "Let me save you some time. You won't find Liam Curran or Casey Conner anywhere. Not for car rentals and not on the passenger manifests."

"Son of a bitch!" Taconelli dropped the pages on the table, then rubbed his temples and said, "Deputy Zeller. I was always taught the absence of evidence is not evidence. I'm starting to think that's a load of bullshit. What about the airport security tapes?"

"We chatted about that too," Zeller said. "Looks like your absence-of-evidence theory is accurate. Ms. Cruise was right. There was a small fire at the airport that night."

"And the recordings were destroyed, right?"

"The whole security office was destroyed," Zeller added. "Official ruling—faulty surge suppressor."

Taconelli said, "I have the strangest feeling we've stumbled onto something huge, but it has nothing to do with the murders in Princeton."

Zeller said, "Detective Willis said the same thing."

# CHAPTER 36

---

Princeton, West Virginia
Same Day
12:15 p.m.

DeVine's phone rang as he was spooning dressing onto his salad and Gillespie was squirting ketchup on his fries and Philly cheesesteak. He eyed the unfamiliar number, plugged one ear with a finger to block out the restaurant noise, then answered, "Bo DeVine."

"Hello, Eugene," Curran said.

"It's been four days," DeVine blurted out. "We had an agreement."

"And I'm keeping my end of it," Liam said. "I'm in Lukeville, Arizona."

"Lukeville? I told you that I had to be involved," DeVine said.

There was a long pause, and DeVine wondered if the connection was lost. Finally, Liam asked, "Do you want the info or not?"

"What info?" DeVine removed a pen from his pocket and tested the ink on a napkin.

Liam said, "I made contact with the CDG coyote who brought Rolando Alvarez over the border."

DeVine's eyes shot to Gillespie, who was eyeing the napkin. "That is extremely interesting. Go on."

Liam said, "I also know Penn and Gallagher murdered two more people and buried them in the desert the day *before* murdering Rolando Alvarez and the baby."

DeVine said, "Really? Tell me where?"

"Don't worry. I took care of it," Liam said.

"How did *you* take care of anything?"

"Trust me," Liam said.

"Like hell," DeVine said. "Two of my men are now accused of murdering six people. I'm not going to just sit—"

Liam interrupted him. "There's more. The coyote told me that he was instructed to call Agent Penn to give him Rolando Alvarez's physical description. Does that sound like premeditated murder to you? It does to me."

"What are you trying to say, Mr. Curran?"

"That Penn and Gallagher are hit men, and you have a mole in the INS, Bo. I told you I was going to solve this thing, and I meant it." He paused, then said, "Oh yeah. I found the CDG's accountant."

"You what?" DeVine stopped writing. "All I wanted was for you to help me find Angel," DeVine said.

Liam said, "Penn and Gallagher should be our focus."

DeVine dropped the pen and massaged his temples. "That wasn't our deal."

Liam said, "Give me a day, maybe two. Oh, and, Bo—I need the call records for Lacey's and Scott's condo in DC? Any chance you can get a copy from Taconelli?"

"Why do you need it?" DeVine asked.

"I have a hunch."

"What kind of—hunch?" But the phone went dead, and DeVine stared at it as if it would ring again.

"Where is he?" Gillespie asked.

"Lukeville, Arizona," DeVine said absently.

"Is he running?"

"I'm not sure," DeVine said.

"Why would he call you?" Gillespie asked.

DeVine ignored the question. He stood and dropped cash on the table. "I'm going after him, but I need you to stay here and keep looking for Angel. I won't be more than a day or two. You're driving me to the airport."

Gillespie drove back to the hotel. On the elevator, DeVine pressed the 2 button, then the 4 button. When the elevator doors didn't close, DeVine pounded the 4 until they did.

"Something the matter?" Gillespie asked.

"Curran's trying to pull something," DeVine said. Floor two came and the doors opened.

Gillespie said, "I'll meet you in your room in a few."

"Fine," DeVine said. The doors closed, Gillespie stepped off, and DeVine stabbed at the 4 button several more times. *Did that actually do any good?* he wondered. Didn't matter. It made him feel better.

Back in his room, DeVine tossed his suitcase on the bed and started filling it. He scooped everything from the drawers, then emptied the hanging clothes in the closet. In the bath, he stuffed toiletries, minus his toothbrush, into the travel case, then made a second call to the office. The plane was in Charlotte and could be in Bluefield in an hour, but he needed to get the clearance. Then came the knock on the door. "I'll call you back," he said, then hung up.

DeVine checked the peephole and found Gillespie standing there. He opened the door and invited him inside while he finished brushing his teeth.

Gillespie sat on the unmade bed and called out, "What makes you think you can find Curran?"

"Lukeville's nothing but a wide spot in the road. I'll find him." DeVine zipped his bags and expanded the handle on his suitcase. They left the room and the hotel without conversation. DeVine stowed his luggage in the trunk, then opted for the passenger seat while Gillespie drove.

After pulling onto US 460 west, Gillespie asked, "What do you think he's doing?"

DeVine said, "He's trying to do my job, I think. I need to make sure he stays out of trouble."

"Did he ask you to come down?"

DeVine glanced between Gillespie and the road. "Not exactly."

Gillespie said, "I had a bad feeling about the guy from the start. I mean, he's a college professor, for Christ's sake. And he lives in that huge house. The guy said he was touring Europe for eight years. Who does that?"

They drove for a few miles with neither man speaking. In the end, bad judgment got the better of them.

Gillespie said, "I could talk to Taconelli about a warrant and—"

DeVine interrupted him. "We'll brief Taconelli when it's time, understood?"

DeVine had Gillespie drop him at the curb in front of the tiny terminal. Rather than endure any further interrogations from Gillespie, he decided to wait inside the terminal. He gathered his luggage from the trunk, then leaned in the passenger window.

"Remember. Not a word to Taconelli until I tell you," DeVine said. "If he's still running a search party, see if you can get yourself on the team. We have to find Angel, and we have to do it before Penn and Gallagher do. Keep me updated."

"I will," Gillespie said as he dropped the car into gear and drove away.

DeVine shouldered the bag and pulled the suitcase into the terminal, where he went to the back and watched the single-engine planes sit idle on the tarmac in the late-summer heat. One plane did a touch-and-go on the runway. DeVine fished the cell phone from his pocket and dialed a number from memory. It was time to update his superior. Three rings and two hard swallows later, it was answered.

"*Hola*, Senor DeVine," the Latino said. "It seems we have a problem in Lukeville."

"Is the problem named Liam Curran?" DeVine asked.

"No. The problem is with one of my coyotes. Jesus. And he was taken by an American."

"And the name of the American is Liam Curran," DeVine said, "I'll be there in a few hours."

He hung up and dialed the Chicago office to secure the INS plane.

. . .

After dropping DeVine off at the airport, Gillespie decided not to go back to the hotel but to drive by Curran's farm instead. The place was quiet, except now there were *two* trucks parked in the drive instead of the one rust bucket. He remembered one truck belonged to a Mr. William Shipman, and it hadn't moved since the day he and DeVine arrived. A second newer and larger black pickup was parked nearby with a fifth-wheel livestock trailer attached. Then, out of the pole barn, a tall and lean man with a leathery skin and snow-white hair emerged. He walked with a slight limp, but for the most part, he appeared fit for his age.

Gillespie slowed to get a better look before continuing to Lacey Sullivan's place, where a moving van was being filled. The man he knew to be Scott Sullivan was standing in the front yard, pointing at the workers and cursing at his cell phone. This time, Gillespie didn't slow but drove on until he reached the main road into Princeton. His cell phone rang as soon as he reentered coverage. He recognized the number as the INS's Chicago office.

"Agent Gillespie here."

"Good morning, Charles." It was the sweet voice of the director's administrative assistant. They exchanged a few pleasantries, and he welcomed the sense of normalcy she brought. Then, she asked, "Can you hold for Director Minton?" She didn't wait for a response as the line clicked and rang again.

"Agent Gillespie? This is Raymond Minton. I'm trying to locate Agent DeVine. Is he nearby?"

"No, sir. He's at the airport waiting on the jet to fly to Arizona."

"I just hung up with him. I have new information on the bodies recovered in the desert. They have been exhumed and are being taken to Tucson, not Phoenix."

"What bodies?" Gillespie asked.

Minton, seemingly frustrated now, said, "I approved the use of the INS plane so you guys could meet with the Arizona State Troopers and the ME. I originally thought the bodies would go to Phoenix, but they are taking them to Tucson instead."

"Sir," Gillespie said, "I'm completely in the dark here. If you told DeVine in the last thirty minutes, I had already dropped him off."

"Fine," Minton said. "The Arizona State Troopers received a tip that two bodies had been found buried in the desert not far from Organ Pipe Cactus National Monument. The tip was accurate, and the bodies are being taken to the ME's office in Tucson."

"Two more dead immigrants?" Gillespie asked.

"No. Two dead Caucasians," Minton said. "If you talk to DeVine, tell him to get his ass to Tucson, not Phoenix."

Gillespie swallowed hard, trying to keep his question in. He failed. "DeVine told me he is going to Lukeville to find Liam Curran."

There was a long pause, then Minton asked, "Who the hell is Liam Curran?"

Shocked by the question, Gillespie said, "Curran is the next-door neighbor of the murder victim, Lacey Sullivan. He's been in every report I've turned into DeVine. Have you not—"

"I've read every report from DeVine," Minton barked. "Don't remember any Liam Curran."

"I think DeVine had asked him to help locate our missing illegal as well as Penn and Gallagher. But Curran left town abruptly for Lukeville, and now Agent DeVine—"

"I see," the director interrupted. "What I'm hearing is this Curran person may know more than you two. I thought I was pretty clear when I told DeVine to shift his focus to finding the missing illegal and leave Penn and Gallagher to the marshals. I don't know what's going on down there, but from what I know, the dead illegal is a John Doe. Who told you his name was Gerardo Lopez?"

Gillespie said, "DeVine is certain of it."

"And how does he know?"

Gillespie paused. "I—That was not my understanding. DeVine told me Lacey Sullivan gave him the names of the two illegals."

Minton said, "That's nice. But it still doesn't tell me how DeVine can make an identification." In the background, paper rattled, then Minton said, "I've got the homicide report in my hand. Tell me you've met Detective Taconelli."

Gillespie's eyes went wide as his mind went into overdrive. How *did* DeVine know the missing illegal was Angel and not Gerardo? Then, he recalled what Curran had asked DeVine while leaning on the car that day. He asked it again in the restaurant. *How did you know?* Curran had asked. Was this what Curran had been wanting to know?

"Yessir. I've met Detective Taconelli," Gillespie said, then something else came to mind. "Sir, are we certain Penn and Gallagher are the guilty parties?"

Minton's voice became hot and to the point. "If you've met Taconelli, then you've seen the ballistics reports. I sent them to DeVine, for shit's sake!" After a brief episode of paper shuffling, Minton read, "The bullets found in the body of the child in Lukeville match the bullet found in the John Doe Mexican in Princeton. And the bullet found in the body of Rolando Alvarez matches the two found in the body of Lacey Sullivan. All rounds were .40 caliber. And all fired from the two pistols belonging to Agents Penn and Gallagher. We have the signature of their weapons on file."

*And Curran knew*, Gillespie recalled.

Minton continued. "Am I certain our guys did all four killings.

Well, their guns sure as hell did. What we don't have are the guns themselves. I don't know what DeVine and this Curran guy are doing, but everyone needs to get back on point. And you need to communicate with your partner. If he calls in, tell him to get his ass to the ME's office in Tucson."

"Yessir," Gillespie said through a cottony throat. "I will."

After a long pause, Minton said, "Until DeVine returns from Tucson, I want you to report directly to me."

"Yessir," Gillespie said.

The call dropped, and Gillespie steered the rental into the nearest lot, shifted into park, then stared at his quivering hands. Was that fear or anger? Or both? Why would DeVine keep the ballistics information from him? He felt like an outsider, but one thing was for certain: he now had Director Minton's attention and approval to skip over DeVine and communicate directly to him—and to work with Taconelli. From here on, that was exactly what he would do.

# CHAPTER 37

Hombres Blancos, Mexico
Same Day
2:35 p.m.

The Range Rover crossed from the US into Mexico at the Lukeville POE. The guard on the Mexican side recognized the driver immediately and did not ask for either of their passports. The driver pulled into the parking lot at the Mexican customs offices, and the two men entered through the back door, where an agent at the desk leapt to attention and greeted them.

"Senor Lopez," the agent said, surprised to see the leader of the CDG standing in his offices. "Good afternoon. What can we do for you?" His gaze shifted between the powerful Mexican human trafficker and the slender Black man standing with him.

"Let them pass." The voice came from an armed Mexican border agent at the end of the hallway. "I'm expecting them."

Juan Garcia Lopez said nothing to the man at the desk as he and the Black man walked by, then disappeared through the open door held by the Mexican border agent. Once inside the security office, the agent closed and locked the door.

Rows of computer monitors adorned the operations desk, where a man was seated, typing and clicking. He shifted in his seat to get a good look at the visitors as if they were from another world, then turned back toward the twin monitors and started typing again.

It was Lopez who spoke first, and he addressed the border agent by name. "Pascal, what did the old woman say?"

Pascal replied, "Said she had spoken with Mr. Brian May on Friday and that he needed laborers. She surmised he had a great deal of money in his motel room. She sent Jesus and his men to take care of it, and it was the last time she heard from him. But we've been looking into Brian May and have found something interesting."

Pascal nodded toward the console. The operator punched a button, clicked a mouse, and photos tiled the monitor on the left, seemingly of the same man. "This camera is mounted at the first gatehouse and captures vehicles as they approach. Another catches them as they pass. These are from yesterday afternoon."

All four men studied the tan face. The long, dark, wavy hair. The image was clear. The man was smiling.

Pascal pointed at a particular photo showing the gray Tempo and its California license plate. He said, "We checked and it is a rental. The driver was Brian May." Pascal put his hand on the operator's shoulder and said, "Now, on the other monitor, bring up the photos from an hour ago."

The operator pressed buttons and clicked the mouse, and the second screen came to life and more photos tiled the display. The same driver's face, the same car, and the same plate were again clear. All eyes darted back and forth, comparing the license plates and faces on each screen.

Lopez said, "Why is this a problem?"

Pascal explained, "The problem is the passport. The man on the left is Brian May. The man on the right is Steve Walsh."

Lopez stepped away and ran his fingers through his jet-black hair. "This bastard posed as a man looking for laborers, kidnapped Jesus, my best coyote, and is now going back and forth across the border on different passports? He is obviously an American agent. I will kill this Brian May or Steve Walsh."

"That's not his real name." Bo DeVine stepped forward and spoke directly to Lopez. "This is the man I told you about on the phone. His name is Liam Curran. And if he's with the government, I have no idea which agency. I've checked. One thing is for certain—he has your coyote and quite possibly is going after your accountant. And, he's been investigating"—DeVine paused midsentence as he glanced around the room—"the men involved in our little project." DeVine turned to Pascal and asked, "Where did this man say he was going?"

"Mexico City," Pascal replied.

"That is a lie," Lopez said, flipping open a cell phone. "He is going to Puerto Peñasco. I am sending men there now." He left the security office, screaming into the phone as he walked.

DeVine followed Lopez out of the building to the parking lot. When Lopez clicked off his call, he was still fuming and walking in circles. DeVine said, "What's happening, Juan?"

Lopez said, "Jesus is also the grandson of my accountant."

DeVine shook his head. "How quickly can your men get to her?"

"Thirty minutes, maybe," Lopez said. "They will kill this Liam Curran when they find him." He paused, then asked, "Do you have a problem with this, Mr. DeVine?"

DeVine shook his head. "No. But we have another problem. The Arizona State Troopers have recovered the bodies buried near Ajo. That's why I was in Tucson. You and I both know I didn't need to see the bodies to know who they were." He paused until there was understanding on Lopez's face, then said, "Your boys fucked up, Juan."

"No!" Lopez yelled and jabbed a finger at DeVine's chest. "It is you who has fucked up! They were to kill the lawyer, and you were to kill them. This Liam Curran is not here by accident. And that means that fucking Jesus is talking."

# CHAPTER 38



After leaving the airport, Liam checked out of the motel. Jesus-Stephan's disappearance had made Brian May a target, and given what he needed to do in Mexico, he couldn't come back. It was time to change identities. Not that it was a big deal. Getting rid of Brian May was critical to his side project anyway. From the go-bag, he gathered the new items and burner phone, then, at the POE, he used Steve Walsh's well-stamped passport to cross into Mexico. Ninety minutes later, he passed the exit for the Puerto Peñasco international airport.

He located the marina first, then continued until he found the address Jesus-Stephan had given him for Araseli. He parked the Tempo on the street, and even from a distance of about a hundred yards, the peeling paint and warped boards on the building screamed of years of neglect.

The layout reminded him of his motel in Lukeville, only five stories taller. A single set of stairs around an elevator accessed the floors of the two wings. The sidewalk leading to the building was mostly empty, but the town bustled with tourists in shorts, workers in orange vests, and kids playing baseball in a vacant field. Waiters were writing their menus on the windows of restaurants. And there were no obvious signs of the CDG yet. But they'd be here, and the last car he wanted to rely on then was a Tempo.

Liam drove back to the airport and parked the Tempo in the long-term lot. Across the street was a Hertz, where Steve Walsh rented a car with more muscle: a white 1995 Ford Mustang GTS convertible with a five-liter V8 and tons of "scalded dog" under the hood. Then, he drove back to the Tempo, transferred his bags to the Mustang, and left the Tempo behind. He followed the signs to the marina, where he parked in a gravel lot near the dock, shut off the engine—and waited.

Opening the convertible's roof allowed the cry of gulls, the tat-tat of distant rivet guns, and the screeching of steel cables against iron pulleys to fill the car. A welcome sense of normalcy. In the distance, the waves of the Gulf of California rocked the row of docks, mast tips of fishing vessels stabbing at the bright sky while multimillion-dollar yachts stayed safely anchored outside the breakwater. Then, appearing over the distant hill, a seaplane swooped in, contouring the topography. Its pontoons hit the water between the yachts and the breakwater, and it taxied to a dock, where a worker tied it to a mooring. Liam recognized the red tail, white lettering, and the large black letters—*PH*—against the blue rudder's trailing edge. What other organization besides BICA would place the initials of Patrick Henry on the tail of their aircraft?

The pilot climbed out onto the dock, where he negotiated with the dockmaster before making his way up the ramp to the landing. Liam waved until the pilot waved back. After instructing the pilot to wait for him to return, Liam went back to the Mustang and drove the ten blocks to the back side of the apartment complex. He parked in front of a hair salon in a spot close to a T intersection. Between him and the apartment building, a dirt path wound through a bare field pocked with weeds.

To keep from drawing attention to himself, rather than take the path back to the other side of the building, he took the long way around and used the cracked sidewalk. Then, just as he arrived at the front of the building, a black SUV screeched to a stop next to him, and two Mexican men leapt out. Liam started to reach for the pistol at the small of his back, but the driver and passenger—both in jeans, with one in a blue sport coat and the other in a white one—ignored him completely and ran toward the apartments.

Blue Coat had been driving, and White Coat had been the passenger. Therefore, White Coat was most likely the leader, especially as it was White Coat who took the elevator to the third floor, while Blue Coat took the stairs. Blue Coat flung the door open and held it, revealing a dark hallway. White Coat passed by, and Blue Coat slammed the door closed.

Liam doubted they would kick in Araseli's apartment door. Too loud and too disrespectful. They would knock, and Araseli would have little choice but to open the door. Once inside, they would order her to get dressed. She might resist, as questions would fly about her grandson, but she would comply. They would help her gather important documents, maybe a computer, then escort her from the apartment and down the elevator. They would both walk her—or push her—to the SUV. Blue Coat would drive, while White Coat would sit in the back with the woman. Mission accomplished.

Liam couldn't let it get that far.

Having a plan was useful, but the ability to improvise was far more valuable. His SEAL Team commander once told him, *Every plan works perfectly every time—until it begins.* SEALs weren't trained to follow the letter of the plan but to navigate it and adapt to potholes. Liam checked his watch. Blue Coat and White Coat had been inside for five minutes now, and it was time to move. But first, Liam needed to assemble his team.

He jogged to the vacant lot where the boys had been playing baseball earlier. They were still there, and he approached them with money and the promise of a better game. They agreed to the game, and he left the vacant lot with twelve pairs of curious eyes anxiously watching his signal. His team was ready to go.

Liam crossed the street to the SUV and peered inside, making certain he hadn't missed someone. The SUV was empty, and he jammed his hands into his jacket pockets, then started toward the apartments. Once in the alcove, he ran through the plan once more and all the moving parts that could fall apart. Angles. Corners. Actions. Reactions. Odds. Unknowns. When he was certain he had covered everything in his power, he gave the signal, and his Vacant Lot Gang went to their places as Liam bolted up the stairs to the third-floor walkway and the railing overlooking the SUV.

With one eye on the street and the other on the door to the hallway, Liam gave the thumbs-up, and the group of boys bolted from the shadows and started rocking the SUV back and forth. Laughter filled the air until the SUV's horn blared and its lights flashed angrily. The boys then scattered back to the safety of the shadows between buildings, no doubt chuckling and peeing themselves in delight.

Liam pulled the silenced PPK from his waist, then squatted in the stairwell—and waited.

The plan went to hell immediately...

# CHAPTER 39



In his mind, Liam saw the event unfolding differently. The SUV's alarm should have drawn the two men out to the landing together, giving Liam a known quantity at a known time on a battlefield he had chosen. But when the SUV alarm sounded, and Blue Coat crashed through the steel door to scream at the kids—without White Coat—the need to improvise also dictated their fates.

Blue Coat followed the original script—partly. He did stop at the railing to raise a fist and curse at the scattering kids. The problem now was this: if Liam came out of the stairwell, he'd put himself into a position where he'd be surrounded. Blue Coat in front, White Coat in the rear. But not acting was not an option, so he tucked the pistol into his jeans and sprinted toward Blue Coat while the man's back was still to him. A hard blow to the back of the neck would drop the man immediately. And *that* would have worked had it not been for the gunshot that came from inside the building. Meaning, it came from behind both of them.

When the shot rang out, and Liam's focus changed to the shot's origin, Blue Coat reached for his pistol and spun around as his gaze went immediately to the door first. But after a fraction of a second, he found himself face-to-face with Liam in full charge. His eyes bloomed white as his aim shifted from nothing in particular to Liam—and fired.

The shot hit—but not Liam. A metal-on-metal ping sounded

behind him as Liam lunged forward, grabbed the man's gun hand, and at the same time plowed his shoulder into the man's chest, driving him back several steps before taking him down and snapping his head against the concrete landing. Liam got his left hand on the pistol, then, raising his body above Blue Coat, drove his right elbow into Blue Coat's temple. The man's eyes rolled back, and the pistol fell from his hand. Liam drove another elbow into the man's head for good measure.

Blue Coat was out of the picture, but the sound of his shot introduced another dynamic, as now there had been two shots fired. At present, he was more concerned with the shot from inside the building, curious residents, the ultimate arrival of the police, and the chance a very pissed-off White Coat would be exploding onto the landing at any time. Ducking behind a corner, Liam drew his pistol and waited…

And nothing happened. No sirens, and no White Coat.

Picking up Blue Coat's pistol and tucking it in his waistband, he dragged the man to the stairs and zip-tied his wrists to the railing. Liam then turned his attention back to the still unknown possibility of White Coat.

The rusted door Blue Coat had body-slammed through had settled at a nearly forty-five-degree angle, and Liam used it as a shield while taking in the long hallway, the intermittent lights, and the row of doors on each side. The hallway was empty. A face poked out from one door, then changed its mind quickly, like a game of whack-a-mole. But the second door on the left, Unit 306—was wide open.

Time and surprise were no longer his, so Liam darted inside, pulling the steel door closed. The hallway was still empty. Maybe the residents were used to random gunfire and their best course of action was to stay inside and ride it out. With the silenced Walther leveled, he heel-toed it to the door of Unit 307 to get a better angle on the open door of Unit 306. But all he could see was a sliver of the inside wall.

Still—no White Coat. Only silence.

Now that he had a decent view inside Unit 306, Liam eased to the right and found something fleshy and rounded against the black-tiled floor. As he leaned sideways in small increments, the object became longer and organic. A fingertip. Then fingers. Then knuckles. Then a gold ring and a palm at the end of a wrist and a man's watch protruded from beneath the sleeve of a white sport coat.

Darting to his right, he pressed against the door of Unit 305 and stared directly into Unit 306 and a short hallway that opened into a larger room. There was one end of a sofa and the back of a recliner. Behind the sofa, two half-open windows behind gathered drapes revealed murky glass and a distant field of weeds. And at his feet, the body of White Coat, lying on his side. A black puddle had formed, draining toward the rubber trim in a single line.

Liam called out, *"No soy CDG!"* (I am not CDG.)

*Good, Liam,* he thought. *Who coming through this door would admit they were CDG?*

He continued: *"Estoy aqui para ayudar."* (I am here to help.) Then, he said the magic words, "Stephan sent me."

After a train of silent moments, a reply squeaked back from somewhere inside. Tiny. Spanish. Raspy. And female.

*"Quién eres?"* (Who are you?)

Liam took two steps forward, then pressed his back against the wall. *"Por favor, deja que te ayude."* (Please, let me help you.)

Then, there was another sound. Fabric against fabric. Then, over and above his own breathing, he heard, *"Vamos por delante, gringo."* (Come ahead, gringo.)

*Gringo,* she had said. How did she know? Was his Spanish that rusty? More concerning—she had told him to *come ahead.* Liam eyed White Coat and wondered if those had been the last words *he* had heard, minus the gringo part.

*"Tira la pistola,"* he said. (Toss the gun.)

*"No. Tú primero."* (You first.) She gave a wasn't-born-yesterday chuckle.

Wow. A true Mexican standoff. The old woman wasn't stupid.

Liam decided to comply, sort of. Reaching beneath his jacket, he pulled out the Colt he had taken from Blue Coat and slid it across the floor to the middle of the room where he could still see it. *"Yo vengo a cabo,"* he said. (I'm coming out.)

Keeping the Walther low to his waist, Liam took a quick peek around the corner and caught a glimpse of a frail form sitting on the sofa wearing something red and beige. Brown skin. He let a sliver of his arm and body show around the corner, along with an empty hand. In front of him was the back of the recliner, and he kept his one hand with the Walther low and behind it.

"Araseli?" he asked.

*"Sí."*

Araseli was seated upright on the sofa—regal, her frame so small, her legs poked straight out. His first thoughts went to Dr. Ruth. She was old but not as ancient as he had first imagined. Brown hair with graying roots capped a once pretty but now leathery face. Suspicious eyes burned through him, glaring over the barrel of a stainless-steel Smith & Wesson .357 magnum revolver. It would have punched a serious hole in White Coat—and left Araseli with five more tries.

Araseli, switching to surprisingly good English, said, "Where is the other man?"

"On the landing. But I need to bring him in here. Okay?"

Araseli nodded.

Sprinting back to the landing, he found Blue Coat on the ground and still bleeding from the nose. Liam cut the zip ties, freeing the man from the railing, then dragged him by his feet down the hallway and into the apartment. Making sure the pistol that he'd slid across the floor was still there—it was—he finagled Blue Coat into the recliner before closing and locking the front door.

On the sofa, Araseli hadn't moved, and she kept a crooked hand on the giant revolver, though the barrel had drooped somewhat. Still, Liam elected to stay behind the recliner as the old woman's gaze drifted from White Coat on the floor to Blue Coat in the chair to Liam.

"Are they CDG?" Liam asked.

"*Sí.* And now they will send more."

"They were sent to find you before I did," Liam said. "Do you know them?"

She motioned toward White Coat. "He was related to Juan Garcia Lopez."

"Oh yeah. You're screwed now," Liam said. "My name is Steve Walsh, by the way."

"You are lying, gringo. Your name is Liam Curran. These men were asking about you—if you had contacted me."

Liam let out a long sigh, which Araseli must have heard, as she dropped the pistol and said, "Stephan calls me at three o'clock, every day. He did not call today. Can you tell me why?"

Liam started to respond, but his words were stuck behind his surprise. If anyone had checked up on him, maybe talked to the old woman with the shotgun or consulted the motel registry or the Mexico POE, or even Dinah at the restaurant, they would have heard about a man named Brian May or Steve Walsh—but not Liam Curran. So, how had the CDG come up with his real name?

Liam said, "You're right. My name is Liam Curran. And Stephan hasn't called because he is in protective custody. The CDG wants all three of us dead. I am here to stop that." Then, from the chair, Blue Coat groaned, his wrists straining against the zip ties. Liam stepped around the recliner to get a better look. Blue Coat's nose and cheek looked worse than Angel's had. He smacked the man's face until his eyes opened.

"Welcome back," Liam said.

Blue Coat said nothing; his eyes shot toward the pistol on the floor, then to his dead partner nearby. His hands began pulling against the zip ties.

"Relax," Liam said, picking up the Colt. "Your buddy made a bad decision."

Blue Coat said nothing. Through a groan, Liam made out, *"My jaw."*

"There's more I can break if you don't answer my questions," Liam said. "Now, who sent you?"

As if his jaw was wired shut, Blue Coat's eyes watered as he spoke. "Lopez."

Liam said, "Did Lopez tell you my name? Liam Curran?" He put a foot on Blue Coat's ankle.

"Aaaagh! Yes. Lopez told us."

"Okay. So, who told Lopez?"

"I—I don't know," Blue Coat said. "We were told to take the woman to Matamoras, then to find you."

"And do what? Kill me?" Liam asked.

"Only if we had to," Blue Coat said. "They want you back in Hombres Blancos to talk to a man there."

"Who? Lopez?"

"No. Some man called Devin."

Liam lifted his heel from Blue Coat's ankle, then steadied himself. Was this true? Bo DeVine was working with the CDG and had been playing him the whole time? Which—oddly enough—made sense. If Penn and Gallagher had been working for the CDG, that meant DeVine had to know about it. That could explain why he had been less interested in finding Penn and Gallagher than he was in finding Angel. And, if Angel had witnessed the murders of Rolando, the baby, Lacey, and his brother, DeVine wasn't just trying to find Angel—he was trying to kill him. But did that mean he had lied about Lacey calling him? Or had he already known about Gerardo and Angel? Or even Penn and Gallagher?

*Christ, what is going on?*

Pulling the Colt from his waist, Liam pressed it against Blue Coat's knee. "Tell me how Manuel Castille is involved."

Blue Coat groaned and, through clenched teeth, said, "I know he is—" But that was all Blue Coat got out. He might have chosen more eloquent words had he known those were the last words he would ever speak.

An ear-piercing boom came from behind Liam, and a large hole bloomed opened in the center of Blue Coat's forehead as the man's brains painted the leather upholstery of the chair. The momentum sent Blue Coat and the recliner rocking, and Liam spun around with the Colt leveled, searching for the source of the shot. All he found was Araseli, still on the sofa, gripping the now smoking .357 revolver.

"What in the fuck?" Liam said, lowering the Colt.

The recoil had taken the pistol up and over her head, but she recovered nicely and let the pistol fall to the sofa as she tapped out a cigarette from a pack, then searched the general area, presumably for a lighter or match.

*This woman is a piece of work*, he thought as he kicked the .357 revolver, and it slid into the collapsing heap of Blue Coat as he melted from the recliner. There were now two dead CDG thugs and the Mexican police were certainly on the way, and Araseli was acting like they were waiting on a pizza. "We have to go!" Liam said. "We'll need to stop by your office on the way out."

"Give me a minute," Araseli said. Dragging on the Marlboro, she rose from the sofa and disappeared into the bedroom.

"Why did you kill him?" Liam asked. "He was about to tell me about Manuel Castille."

"Yes," Araseli said. "I know."

Liam went to the bedroom but stopped at the door. "You know how Manuel Castille is involved, don't you?"

She grinned slyly at him. "If we live through this, I'll tell you all you need to know."

Liam now understood. By killing Blue Coat, she had ensured herself a huge bargaining chip.

In addition to the lone twin bed and a dresser, there were file boxes everywhere like stalagmites from a cave floor. A small desk hugged one wall, and filing cabinets lined the other. Stepping inside the room, Liam picked a cabinet and opened a file. "You keep the CDG's files here?" he said. Then, in the distance, he heard the cry of a siren. "Damn! We only have time to grab the most important stuff. What do I need to get?"

"Nothing," Araseli said as she shuffled toward the computer. The mouse brought the screen to life, and after a few clicks, she dropped a CD into the external drive.

One siren grew to many.

"We don't have time to—"

"Patience," she said, cutting him off. The horizontal bar on the screen indicated: *40%*.

Liam sprinted to the front door and opened it. People were starting to vacate their apartments. He went back to the bedroom, where Araseli was standing with a pocketbook over her shoulder.

Indicator bar: *74%*.

The sirens grew louder still, and Liam could tell at least one car had stopped somewhere outside. A voice from the hallway asked if Araseli was coming, and she replied calmly: "*Sí*."

Indicator bar: *100%*

She removed the CD, snapped it into a jewel case, then, with a few more keystrokes, ordered the machine to format the C drive. *Are you sure? Y/N*. She jabbed the *Y*, hooked Liam's arm, then started toward the front door.

In the hallway, they mixed with the others. At the landing, Liam jabbed at the elevator's Down button several times. Beyond the railing and across the field, his Mustang seemed a planet away. People were lining the sidewalk, pointing toward the building.

Behind him, metal squealed as the elevator doors parted, and they stepped inside with six others.

On the ground floor, people rushed out, but not fast enough for Liam's liking. Everyone was either heading toward the main street to the west or the field to the east, which was the direction Liam steered Araseli. "That's my Mustang," he said, pointing.

Behind them, the sirens had stopped, replaced by clusters of flashing lights. Ahead, more lights and more cops were cautiously duckwalking through the field with pistols drawn. One of them yelled at Araseli.

"Where are the shooters?"

"I think they are on the top floor." Araseli came off as pitiful and helpless, but Liam was laughing inside and awarding her the Oscar for her performance. This little old fart of a woman had killed two men today with a pistol the size of an armadillo. Mika would like her.

Liam imagined the scenario inside the apartment complex and calculated how long it would take them to find the bodies of Blue Coat and White Coat and then alert Juan Garcia Lopez that the relative he sent to pick up an old woman was now dead. He estimated maybe an hour.

After reaching the street, they waited for the traffic to halt before inching across the faded crosswalk. At the Mustang, Liam opened the door for Araseli and helped her into the passenger seat. He fired up the five-liter engine, pulled out, and less than ten minutes later, they were back at the marina, where the pilot of the seaplane was waiting. The pilot opened the Mustang's passenger door and reached down to let the old woman take his arm.

The pilot said, "Did you hear those sirens? Something's going down." After a beat of silence, the pilot asked, "Or was that you?"

Liam eyed Araseli instead, who was clutching a purse in one hand and the arm of the pilot in the other. "Take care of her," Liam said. After escorting her to the dock, he helped her into the seaplane and buckled her in. "Once you get to San Diego, you'll fly to Washington. From there, you'll go to a nice place called the Lake. You'll meet two very smart women there named Bailey and Babbs. Stephan will be there too."

"When will I see you again?" she asked with a smile.

"Very soon." Liam kissed the woman's wrinkled cheek. "Thank you, Araseli." Liam left the plane for the dock and closed the door, then slapped the plane like a bronco.

"Where the hell do you think you're going?" the pilot asked through the cockpit window.

"To run an errand," Liam said.

"My orders from BICA are to get you both out of here."

"I'm not going back with you," Liam said, then sprinted across the dock and up the plank to the Mustang. Stomping the accelerator, he let the tires burn and smoke as the Mustang fishtailed to the street.

Liam checked his watch. It was after eight now, and he still had about an hour of sunlight left. One thing was certain—Brian May, Steve Walsh, or Liam Curran wouldn't be able to cross back into the United States without getting stopped at any POE. But it wasn't in his plans anyway.

He still had one more mission to accomplish, one more piece of revenge to exact. He needed to find his target, then lure him in. Assuming his plan was working and Paul Kelvington was smart enough—or stupid enough—to find him. But first, he needed sleep, so he found a wide spot in the road, pulled off, and closed his eyes and fell asleep repeating the phrase he had memorized in training: *Never let the enemy pick the battle site.*

# CHAPTER 40

Lukeville, Arizona
Same Day
9:18 p.m.

Paul and Zilo arrived at the motel late. The rang the bell on the counter—twice—before a young Latino man appeared from the backroom, rubbing his eyes and holding a finger in the air.

"Sorry to wake you up," Paul said. "Do you have rooms available?"

The clerk yawned and started typing. "Sure."

Zilo spoke up. "Separate rooms. He's paying."

Paul chuckled and passed the clerk his American Express. While the clerk typed on the computer, Paul asked, "Do you have a business center?"

"No. I have a fax machine," the clerk said. "It's twenty-five cents per page."

"What's the number?"

The clerk pointed to a stack of business cards in a clear holder, then went back to typing.

"By the way," Paul said, "could you tell me if Mr. Brian May has checked in yet?"

The clerk paused, gave an annoyed sigh, then typed some more. "He checked in and he checked out."

"That's rude," Zilo said, glancing toward Paul.

Paul addressed the clerk: "Do you remember what he looked like?"

"You don't know?" the clerk asked. When Paul didn't respond, the clerk said, "I remember he was a big white guy. Muscular. Longish, dark, wavy hair." He typed again. "He registered a Ford Tempo. I didn't check him out. Do you still need the rooms?"

Paul said they did, and the clerk went back to typing.

"What time does the restaurant next door close?" Zilo asked.

"It's twenty-four seven," the clerk said without looking up. "The food is good." He then passed two brass keys to Paul and Zilo. The engraved numbers indicated they were probably next to each other.

They thanked the man, then drove the short distance to the truck stop, where they sat at the counter and an attractive older waitress placed two laminated menus in front of them. Zilo took the motel's business card from his pocket and sent it spinning over to Paul.

"Is that the right fax number?" Zilo asked.

"That's it. My boy Brian May sent his info from that machine," Paul said, then took the folded pages from his breast pocket and gave them to Zilo.

"Ah—the infamous fax," Zilo said, picking up the pages. "Definitely social security, routing, and account numbers. It's gotta be the thinnest resume I've ever read. Any idea about this account number?"

"Not yet. I'll put Julie on it in the morning," Paul said as the waitress returned.

"Something to drink?" she asked.

"Yeah"—Paul eyed her name tag—"Dinah. I'll have a Coke."

Zilo ordered the same, then waited for the waitress to leave. "I understand your concerns about this Brian May guy, but don't you feel a little like a dog chasing a car? Let's say that tall, dark, and muscular gringo is sitting at the end of the bar, right now. What do you do? Walk up and ask him if he's working for the White House chief of staff? Do you really want to muck it up for her?"

Paul's gaze softened the more he thought. "I just want to get a look at this guy," Paul said. "Maybe tail him a little. Get a photo. Woody wouldn't tell me anything."

Zilo said, "She's been neck deep in the immigration bill, and then all of a sudden, there's a murder down here in Lukeville. It can't be a coincidence."

"You're probably right," Paul said. "I'm just—I don't know—watching her back."

Zilo lay his hand on Paul's shoulder and said, "You're a good egg, Charlie Brown." They both had a chuckle, then stared at the menu. It was late, and Paul started to feel his efforts were pointless until Dinah arrived with their drinks and started talking.

"Hey," she said, pointing at the fax on the counter. "Are you looking for Brian May, by chance?"

They glanced at each other, then Paul said, "Actually, we are. Do you—know him?"

"Sure. He came in here Friday afternoon."

"You talked to him?" Zilo asked.

"Sure. Like we're talking now," Dinah said. "Everyone always asks about the murders." She pointed to the window, and they both turned. "He said there might be a couple of guys looking for him. Would that be you?"

Paul decided to roll with it and said, "That would be us. You don't happen to know where we can find him, do you?"

Dinah's eyes narrowed. "Don't you know?"

"Well—we thought he was staying at the motel next door," Paul said. Then, with a faux-embarrassed chuckle, he added, "But he checked out."

Dinah squinted, then shook her head and said, "Without leaving a note?"

"Uh—yeah," Paul said. "Look. We came a long way to meet him."

"He said he was going to Caborca. But that was on Friday. Are you guys going to eat or not?" Her tone was less than cordial now.

"Sure," Paul said. They ordered, and she sauntered away. She jammed the order into the clips on the steel wheel and spun it around before disappearing into the kitchen.

"That was weird," Zilo said.

"*Fucking* weird," Paul said as he pulled out his cell phone. "Crap! I missed the call." He hit the Redial key, the SPKR button, then placed the phone on the counter. Carlos answered after two rings.

"Hey, Carlos," Paul said. "You're on speaker. It's me and Zilo."

"Hey, guys," Carlos said. "I thought I would report in on the *I Love Woody Show*. "She went to work early, worked late, and now she's home. In bed, I guess. Basically, ain't shit happening."

"Boring is good," Paul said. "How's your neck?"

"A little sore still," Carlos said.

Paul said, "Again, I can't tell you how sorry I am. How much dough did the guy take? I'll reimburse you."

"Not necessary," Carlos said. "It was my fault."

"No, really," Paul said. "It will make me feel a lot better."

Carlos paused, then relented. "It wasn't much. Two hundred and thirty bucks."

"Two hundred and thirty?" Paul repeated. "What denomination of bills?"

"I think—a couple of fifties, and a ten. The rest twenties. Look, it's not—"

"No, no. It's coming out of the company kitty, so it's fine," Paul said. "Go get some sleep." Paul clicked off, then turned to Zilo and said, "That little bitch!"

Zilo did his best Desi Arnaz impression and said, "S'plain it to me, Lucy."

Paul said, "Carlos's money. Two fifties, a ten, and twenties. That's exactly what I found on our coffee table the same day he was mugged. When I asked Woody about it, she said the money was hers and that she accidentally left it on the table." Paul dug into his trousers, pulled out his wallet, then fanned the bills on the counter. "I still have them. Son of a bitch. Two fifties, a ten, and six twenties."

Zilo's mouth dropped open. "Are you suggesting Woody mugged Carlos?"

Paul chuckled. "No. The cash wasn't there when I walked in. But the door alarm went off while I was packing, and when I went downstairs, it was there." His eyes watered and the veins in his temples pulsed wildly. "What the hell is going on? Woody lied to me, Zilo, and she's covering for the fucker who clocked Carlos." Then, they both turned to look at the swinging doors where Dinah had disappeared.

Zilo said, "We really gotta find Brian May now."

"You're damn right," Paul said as he whipped out his cell phone and pressed a speed-dial button.

"Who are you calling?"

"Someone who owes me a favor," Paul said. A few beats later, the party answered, and after a few moments of chitchat, Paul got straight to the point, clicked off, then stood.

"Where are we going?" Zilo asked.

"About two thousand feet," Paul said.

. . .

Dinah watched from the kitchen as the men left—in a hurry. They backed out of the parking spot, then squealed away south.

"Watch the counter," Dinah said to the other waitress as she slammed the door to the tiny office. Searching through a batch of sales checks, she found the one from Friday afternoon and dialed the phone number scribbled there.

Brian May picked up after two rings.

Lukeville, Arizona
Same Day
10:15 p.m.

They made the trip from the diner to the POE in less than a minute. When they entered the building, they were met by an anxious salt-and-peppered officer identifying himself as Field Operations Supervisor Duncan. The man led them down a corridor into a low-lit security office filled with computer monitors. Duncan asked the man at the console to take a break, then pulled Paul and Zilo aside for a quick briefing.

Duncan said, "I don't need to tell you gentlemen how unorthodox this is, and, if ever asked, we never met."

"Understood," Paul said. "I appreciate the help."

Duncan breathed a sigh, then said, "My boss said I am to get you any information you need, but without a warrant—"

"This will never see a courtroom," Paul interrupted. "I'm at a crossroads in an investigation, and this is simply a guide."

"Okay, then," Duncan said. He sat at the console and started typing and clicking. "Who am I looking for?"

Paul said, "Brian, with an *I*, and May, like the month."

"Like the guitarist for Queen," Duncan said.

"If you say so," Paul said, shrugging at Zilo.

Duncan typed, and the hit was immediate, filling a monitor with the man's passport number, time of entry, time of exit, travel history, a photo of the car, plate, leasing company, and, most terrifying—the man's passport photo side by side with his actual photo behind the wheel of the gray Ford Tempo.

Paul's mouth fell agape as he stifled a gasp and absorbed the shock of seeing the face of a man who had died two years earlier. "I'll be a— And this was Friday afternoon?"

"Yessir," Duncan said. "He reentered the US two hours later, and—wait a minute—it looks like he tried to pull a fast one. Brian May has two records in the system, but his car has three."

"What's that mean?" Zilo asked.

Duncan clicked and filled three computer monitors. He said, "The first monitor has Brian May and his Tempo crossing into Mexico. The second is Brian May and the Tempo returning two hours later. The third monitor is the same Tempo from earlier today. Same plate, only driven by a man named Steve Walsh. Your man, whatever his name, is still in Mexico."

Zilo squinted at the screen. "Any chance the car was returned and then rented out again?"

"Not in that amount of time," Duncan said. "Walsh told the Mexican side he was going to Mexico City. That was probably a lie."

Paul scribbled down the information, thanked Duncan for his trouble, then he and Zilo left the building. In the parking lot, Paul leaned against the hood of the Suburban.

Zilo said, "Our friend has a fetish for classic rock musicians. Brian May and Steve Walsh," Zilo said.

"How so?"

"I missed the question on Brian May, but Steve Walsh is the lead singer for Kansas. I'm from Topeka. We know that shit. If this guy is messing with the CDG, then he's probably right here in Hombres Blancos or Sonoyta."

"Maybe. But we aren't looking for Brian May or Steve Walsh anymore."

"We're not?"

Paul let out an insane belly laugh. "I'm sorry, but I dragged you into a shitstorm."

"You're losing your mind," Zilo said.

"Yep," Paul said. "Because I just saw a real, honest-to-God ghost. The man in those photos died two years ago when a bomb exploded and his plane went into the English Channel. His real name is Commander Trevor Harmon. Ex-SEAL. Ex-CIA. And a deadly SOB."

Zilo said, "Same guy, same story as before, right? You think he murdered the CIA director?"

"And others," Paul said. "But that's not the worst part. My fiancée—the chief of staff—tricked me into hiring him. She's working with same man she sent me to…" But he stopped midsentence as his eyes met Zilo's. He changed the ending to: "Find two years ago."

Paul held his watch to the sodium lights, then fished his cell phone from his breast pocket and said, "Perfect! She'll be in a deep sleep, and I get to wake her ass up."

# CHAPTER 42



After hanging up with Dinah—and working out the crick in his neck from sleeping in the Mustang's front seat—Liam got out, stretched, then smashed Brian May's burner phone on the curb. Burners weren't traceable to an individual, but their ping data could be tracked. Besides, Dinah had already called.

Kelvington had no doubt traced the fax to the motel, found the money Liam had taken from Carlos and left on the table, and was hot on his scent. And, if Kelvington was half as good as he thought himself to be, he'd know by now that Brian May, Steve Walsh, and his old nemesis—Commander Trevor Harmon—were one and the same. Maybe he could tie the name Liam Curran to the batch. None of that would matter after tonight, and Liam could check one more box on his list.

He pulled into the Circle K on the Mexican side to gas up and take a leak. A rotund Mexican cop entered the mostly empty station as Liam exited the restroom. The cop was chatting up the adolescent clerk about a recent soccer match, and the clerk became annoyed at Liam's rude need to purchase some jerky and a bottle of water.

Firing up the Mustang, he pulled out of the Circle K heading north but kept his speed to a crawl, as the POE was just ahead. He retrieved Steve Walsh's burner phone from the go-bag, checked the bars, then dialed. It was twelve thirty a.m. in DC, but Ginny picked up.

"Where are you?" Her tone—scolding.

Liam replied, "Did my packages arrive?"

"Everyone is at the Lake. Jesus and Araseli are settled into one of the cabins. Why did you turn down Rick's offer to help?"

"If I would have waited, you wouldn't have Araseli right now," Liam said.

"You were supposed to be on that plane," Ginny said.

"I have some cleanup, but I'll be back in a couple of days." Ahead, the sodium lights of the POE lit up the low clouds with a yellow haze. Liam turned off the headlights and eased off where the road started to widen to multiple lanes. From this point, he could see the US Customs office.

Ginny said, "About the bodies you found. They've been identified as Zachary Penn and Isaac Gallagher. The missing border agents. The ME dates their death to August twenty-second. They were beaten to death, their faces carved up and their fingertips removed. Their uniforms and guns were taken, and their vehicle was recovered in Lukeville in a vacant parking lot and—are you still there?"

But Liam wasn't. His mind was spinning at light speed, doing the math. The murders in Lukeville had been on the twenty-third, and Lacey on the twenty-sixth. If Penn and Gallagher had died on the twenty-first, they couldn't have murdered anyone. And now, knowing DeVine was the CDG mole inside the INS, Liam couldn't figure out how Angel fit. DeVine had been hell-bent on finding him, but why? Then, it all became clear…

"Holy shit!" Liam said. All along, he knew he had been missing something. And now it hit him—Angel's story was complete bullshit.

"Liam? Are you there?"

"Hang on," he said into the phone.

Digging into the go-bag, he pulled out the Excel sheet containing Lacey's security system data and spread it out on the hood of the

Mustang, then his finger indexed each line, each moment, and his mistake glared back at him. He shouldn't have been looking for what *was* there but what *wasn't* there.

From the beginning, he had used Angel's story as his base, correlating the movements of Lacey, Louisa, Angel, and Gerardo with the motion detectors in the house. But Angel's own story had been laced with the biggest clue of all, and Liam hadn't caught it. Angel had said the Border Patrol agents had been waiting for them in the basement. But Liam's finger traced each line on the spreadsheet, and there was no unaccounted-for movement in the house. Why? Because there was no one waiting for them. Penn and Gallagher were already dead.

Liam closed his eyes in thought. *Angel, you lying fucker! You and your brother killed Penn and Gallagher and assumed their identities; you killed Rolando and the baby, then you killed Lacey. But why would kill your own brother? If he really was your brother. Or was that another Bo DeVine lie? Or Lacey's call to DeVine? But why is DeVine hell-bent on finding Angel? That means I'm one up on you—asshole!*

Liam put the phone to his ear. "I know who the murderers are, Ginny. I know everything. Everything except why." Liam retrieved the spotting scope from the go-bag, and with the phone still to his ear, he focused it on the US Customs office while he filled Ginny in on everything he knew so far. When he found the dark-colored Chevy Suburban, he had to smile. But when Paul Kelvington and his blond crewcut buddy came bounding out of the office door, Liam had to laugh.

"What's so funny?" Ginny's voice asked.

"Nothing," Liam said, still peering through the scope. "You should get Babbs and Bailey working with Araseli right away."

"They already are. When you get back, we can look to see if there's a link—"

Liam didn't hear the rest of Ginny's sentence. He had already clicked off. He powered down the burner phone and the PagSat pager while his growing rage and trembling hands made him lower the scope and take in long, deep, calming breaths. When he could focus again, Kelvington was pacing and stabbing at a cell phone. Liam thought, *It took you guys long enough. Why do you act like you've seen a ghost?*

He tried to focus on Kelvington, but his mind kept drifting back to Angel, wondering how he and Gerardo had gotten to Lacey. Had they pretended to witness Rolando's murder or had they simply posed as the living Rolando Alvarez? Liam rubbed his eyes and thought, *I'm still missing something, and the answer is in my RV eating microwave pizzas.*

After a long, frustrated breath, Liam checked the spotting scope again. Kelvington and his buddy were still there. He powered up Steve Walsh's burner phone again and dialed another number. A groggy Shipman cursed a greeting: "Who the fuck is this?"

"It's Liam, Bill. Sorry to wake you, but something big has come up." He gave Shipman a beat to come around, then said, "I don't have time to get into the details, but Angel is Lacey's murderer."

"Damn!" Shipman said. "You want me to drive over and put one in his head tonight?"

"No," Liam said. "Keep him comfortable, for now, and don't let on that we know. But he may have stashed a pistol or two on the property. See if you can find them. Most likely .40 caliber Berettas. If you find them, don't touch them. And double-check his chains. I have a lot of questions for him when I get back."

After clicking off the phone, Liam went back to the spotting scope, where he saw that Paul Kelvington had wandered away from his buddy, still screaming at the cell phone.

What Liam *didn't* see was the Range Rover that had doused its lights and parked on the shoulder halfway between him and the Circle K. The driver picked up his own cell phone and dialed, and when it was answered, he said, "Find your partner and come to the Circle K at the POE. And bring the monster."

# CHAPTER 43

Alexandria, Virginia
Sunday, September 3, 1995
1:02 a.m.

When her cell phone rang, it startled Woody from a deep sleep. Her heart raced but calmed when she recognized the number.

Still groggy, she said, "Hey, babe. How's Phoenix?" The response she received was less than cordial.

"How could you *do this* to me?" Paul's words came through like daggers.

"Do what?" Woody asked. She swung her legs over the side of the bed, her heart racing. "What's happened?"

"I just got fucked by my girlfriend! And not in a good way."

"Calm down. Please."

"The hell with calm," Paul said. "I found our new employee. I traced the number on his fax to a motel in Lukeville."

"You what?" Her tone was less surprised than disappointed. "You said you were going to Phoenix, not—" But she was cut off.

"I went to Phoenix. Then I went to Lukeville, and then to the motel where he was staying. You knew I'd recognize him. That's why you kept him from me."

"You've lost me," Woody said, pacing now. "How do you know Brian May?"

Paul screamed, "You know damn well Brian May is Trevor Harmon. I tracked him to Lukeville and saw his face at the POE security office. He's the guy who clocked Carlos, then left his money on the table—which you lied about. For two fucking years, you've made me believe Harmon was dead."

Her mouth agape but unable to take in air, Woody struggled with what she was hearing. Could it be true? She had been alone in the storage room with Trevor Harmon? She felt a chill and the burn of nausea.

"Paul, you have to believe me. I—I had no idea."

"You actually expect me to believe you didn't recognize him?" Paul said, his voice cracking.

"I never saw his face, and—it's complicated," Woody said, then explained what had happened in the storage room. When she finished, a wave of relief washed over her; she felt happy to get it off her chest and grateful they were both still alive. She said, "I know it doesn't make much sense."

"I'll tell you what doesn't make sense," Paul said. "He could have killed us all—but didn't. And—you lied to me. I can't believe you did this."

Woody found herself in the kitchen with no memory of coming down the stairs. She said, "The only reason I didn't tell you was because of *how* I met him."

"How much did you tell him about me?" Paul shot back.

"Not a word. This wasn't about you." A lingering stretch of silence arrived, so she let out a long sigh to fill the void.

Then, Paul asked, "What else are you not telling me?"

"Only that he recorded our conversation," Woody said. "It's— incriminating."

"He's framing you?" Paul said. "Then you need to start practicing these four words: *I can't recall, Senator.* Or, how about: *On advice of counsel?*"

Paul had gone cold, and a long silence ensued. Woody could imagine Paul on the other end, his eyes fisted and rubbing his temples. But as much as she wanted to scold herself for unknowingly hiring a killer from their past, she had—no matter how strange it was—hired the best man for the job.

"What are you going to do?" she asked.

Paul said, "He screwed up again. He crossed twice in the same car as Brian May, then crossed into Mexico again as Steve Walsh. He's somewhere in Mexico. And if he tries to cross back, I'll know. And that gives *me* the upper hand."

"What are you saying? You're hunting him—again?"

"This time is different. It's a freebie; technically, he's already dead. Now, tell me how to contact him."

"I don't know. He's supposed to contact me, and so far, he hasn't," Woody said.

Paul's voice came back clear, calm, and concise. "At this point, I have to assume you are lying to me. Goodbye, Woody."

She wanted to jump through the phone and strangle him, but she had two problems. One, he had hung up, and two, he was right. She *had* lied. The shadow—or Trevor Harmon—had called her on her cell phone, and she had saved the number. She found it in her contacts and let her finger hover over the phone's Send key. Never had she been so terrified to press a button. What would she say? What name would she call him? Finally, she forced herself to press the button, the phone dialed, and was answered immediately.

A female voice said, *"The number you have reached is no longer in service. Please check the number and try your call again. Message eight, nine, eight, four..."*

Woody clicked off.

She went back upstairs and collapsed on the bed, staring at the textured ceiling, wondering which was worse: not being able to contact the shadow or lying to Paul—again. Then, a voice called out from downstairs. *Oh shit!* She thought. *Jeff had been downstairs the whole time. He must have heard the argument.*

"What is it, Jeff?" she called back as if she weren't surprised at his presence.

"I—I'm leaving now. Paul called and—he's pulling us off."

A lump formed in her throat. "Thank you, Jeff. I appreciate

everything. Can you let yourself out? I'm not presentable."

"Sure," Jeff called back.

Downstairs, a door opened, then closed. The security panel briefly came to life, and she reset it. How would the White House chief of staff handle this crisis? And this was the very definition of a crisis. She flipped open her cell phone and dialed. Surprisingly, it was answered on the first ring.

"Good. You're awake?" Woody said.

Ginny said, "It's been a hectic night, Patricia. Can this wait until morning?"

"No. It can't," Woody said. "I screwed up—big-time." She then started from the beginning, filling Ginny in on what had happened, what she had done, and Paul's reaction. But when she got to the part about Trevor Harmon, Ginny stopped her cold.

"Don't say another word," Ginny fired back. "Not over the phone."

"Fine," Woody said. "I'll come to your place."

"I won't be there," Ginny said.

"Are you at your office?" Woody said.

"No. I'm somewhere else." Ginny dictated the directions.

"I'll be there in an hour," Woody said, and she was about to end the call when the events leading up to her meeting with the shadow suddenly became clear. Paul's meeting with Zilo, his tires getting punctured, her trip to Naples, Carlos—there was only one way the shadow could have known.

"Oh my God!" Woody said. "You knew he was coming to see me." She paused, expecting to hear commentary or denial. But that's not what came back.

Ginny replied, "You're right, about everything. We'll finish this when you get here. I think we could use your help."

"So—it's true?"

"We'll talk later," Ginny said, then clicked off.

Woody dressed in haste, then found the atlas in Paul's study and traced the directions her mother had given her to a small dot on the map near Germantown, Virginia, about an hour outside of the city. It was nothing but farmland in the middle of nowhere. Why would her mother be there at this time of night?

While checking the mirror for the last time, her tears finally came as she realized Paul's last two words to her. He had said, *Goodbye, Woody*. Paul hated that nickname. He thought it sounded too much like a hard-on. And, in their many years together, he had never once used it. And, Paul had pulled her protective detail. She knew now—she had lost Paul Kelvington.

The Lake
Germantown, Virginia
Same Day
3:00 a.m.

Woody followed Ginny's directions while still second-guessing her own sanity. State Route 28 was eerie enough to navigate in the dark, but when she found herself on County Road 649, visions of the movie *Children of the Corn* started to haunt her. Eventually, she found the turnoff, which put her onto a darker and narrower gravel road flanked by cornstalks, which only increased her anxiety.

After about a quarter of a mile, she came upon a dimly lit guard shack manned by a serious-looking ex-military type, who stopped her with a flashlight, took her driver's license to the shack, then returned it and waved her forward. After a sharp left-hand turn through the stalks, the massive Colonial-style plantation home seemed to appear out of nowhere, lit up warmly and bustling with activity. By the time she parked and reached the stairs, Ginny was stepping out to greet her.

Ginny descended the stairs and met Woody at the bottom. "Welcome to the Lake," she said, then kept walking.

Woody followed her beneath a willow next to a white Ford Explorer and asked, "How long have you known that Trevor Harmon was still alive?"

"He's not. Commander Trevor Harmon died. I can give you the plot number in the cemetery in Hilliard, Ohio."

Woody sat on the bumper of the Explorer and massaged her

temples. "I can't believe you're trying to spin your way—"

Ginny interrupted her. "I'm not spinning anything, Patricia. Trevor Harmon is dead."

"I talked to him, Ginny," Woody said. "Paul saw his photo at the POE in Lukeville. And if there is anyone who knows Trevor Harmon's face, it's Paul. How can you—?"

But Ginny interrupted again. "The man in your storage room," Ginny started, "and the face at the border, they were not Trevor Harmon. His name is Liam Curran, and he works for BICA."

"How could he be dead and alive?"

"It's a long story, and I don't have time tonight," Ginny said. "But I will say that BICA arranged to kill him off—his identity, anyway. It was the only way to stop the contracts on his life. One of them was yours."

Woody said, "The IRA claimed responsibility for the bombing of his plane."

"And BICA worked with the IRA to make it happen."

"Why would you protect the man you know killed William Rehnquist—my own godfather, for Christ's sake—and the director of the CIA?"

"Because I know *why* he did it," Ginny said sternly, then turned away. When she turned back, she said, "When you asked for my help with the blackmail of the president, I told you BICA would not get involved. That was to give *you* deniability. But we *did* get involved. Now, do you want to know what Curran's found out or not?"

Woody listened to Ginny weave the most unbelievable tale: dead border patrol agents, murders in Lukeville, Lacey Sullivan, and a corrupt INS agent. Then, she added in a Latino pop star and a possible link to her lawyer, who operated the American Latino League.

"You knew Curran would contact me. You gave him my itinerary?"

"Yes," Ginny said.

"He could have killed me," Woody said.

"No, he wouldn't have," Ginny said. "Curran has let it go."

"Paul hasn't," Woody said. "He's in Mexico right now."

Ginny's face melted to terror, and she gripped Woody's shoulders with both hands and said, "Tell me you're not serious."

"Paul tracked him to Mexico and is waiting for him to come back across the border." Then, Woody watched as her mother, the cool and calm and sophisticated Virginia-Roosevelt Woodburn, began to pace while hugging herself. "Relax, Mother. This is what Paul does."

"How could he have gotten this close?" Ginny asked.

Woody said, "I guess Curran slipped up when he sent me a fax. Paul traced it to a Lukeville motel. Then, there was the thing at the POE and—"

Woody stopped talking when the Ford Explorer started to rock. One of the doors opened and slammed shut, and a large, muscular man with a crewcut wearing navy-blue khakis appeared and put a boot on the back bumper. Even in the dark, the urgency in his eyes was visible. In the starlight, the silver oak leaf clusters at the corner of his collars, the four rows of ribbons, and the SEAL Trident on his chest gleamed.

Ginny introduced the man as Commander Rick Michaels. "He's the man who brought Jesus here," Ginny said. She then turned to Michaels. "I didn't realize you were out here."

"Catching some bunk time," Michaels said. "But I overheard you saying something about Curran slipping up. Care to elaborate?"

Woody said, "Curran sent me a fax with his banking information on it. My fiancé, Paul Kelvington, traced it back to the sending fax machine at a motel in Lukeville. He also said that Curran was using two aliases, Brian May and Steve Walsh, but crossed the border in the same car using both passports. It sent up a flag, I guess." But as she spoke, Michaels started shaking his head. "What is it?"

Michaels said, "Those stupid rock star aliases." He then turned to Ginny. "This is why he's still in Mexico."

Woody said, "I'm afraid that if Paul finds Curran, he'll—"

But Michaels cut her off. "You don't get it, do you? Curran doesn't make those kinds of mistakes by accident. The fax. The passports and the cars."

"What are you getting at?" Woody said, her wrinkles deepening with every syllable.

"Sweetheart. Your boyfriend isn't hunting Curran. Curran is hunting *him*. He dropped a trail of bread crumbs, and Kelvington pecked them like Hansel's birds."

"You should never have sent Paul to Cleveland," Ginny said.

Woody pursed her lips and said, "When Curran told me to stop asking questions about dead CIA agents, I knew he was the one who pulled off the Toledo hit." Then, she turned to Michaels and said, "He could have killed Paul in the condo. Why lure him to Mexico?"

Michaels said, "Killing the boyfriend of the White House chief of staff in his own home would bring the world down on him. But the owner of a paramilitary organization murdered in Mexico would look more like an occupational hazard. Curran is selecting the battlefield, and your boyfriend is walking right into it. If I were you, I'd tell my fiancé to get the hell out of Mexico."

Woody nodded, fished her cell phone from her back pocket, and dialed Paul's number. It went straight to voice mail. "Shit! He's still pissed off. Can you call Curran and tell him to stop?"

"No," Ginny said. "He's gone dark. Let me try something else."

Ginny went to her car, found her purse, then produced a PagSat pager. She typed a message, then waited for several seconds. A flash from the device painted her stern face, and she said, "His satellite pager is turned off." But then, her cell phone buzzed. "Oh. Thank God! It's him," she said, staring at Steve Walsh's burner phone number.

Ginny answered the call by saying, "Please tell me you haven't done something stupid."

# CHAPTER 45

Hombres Blancos, Mexico<br>Same Day<br>1:45 a.m.

Liam rubbed fatigue from his eyes, then went back to the spotting scope. Kelvington was no longer on the phone but was giving it to his buzzcut buddy. Finally, Kelvington stopped talking, and they both jumped into the Suburban and headed north toward Lukeville.

*Shit! Did I spook my prey?* Liam thought as the taillights faded. But then the Suburban pulled a U-turn and the headlights glared back. A minute later, the Suburban stopped at the POE, and two minutes after that, it was accelerating into Hombres Blancos. Liam gave Kelvington some breathing room, fired up the Mustang, then pulled out behind him.

On the Mexican side of the border, US Route 85 changed to Highway 8, and Liam, keeping a traffic light between them, followed Kelvington as he zigzagged the side streets until the man stopped at a soccer field to take a leak. Kelvington continued the pattern until he ran out of side streets in Hombres Blancos. Then, he simply turned south on Route 8 and continued the process through the tiny burg of La Copa. When he finished, Kelvington entered the larger city of Sonoyta.

*Are you looking for a gray Ford Tempo, Kelvington? Good luck.*

For the next hour, Liam tailed Kelvington through the Sonoyta side streets. Soon, he would run out of city, and the closer they got to the south side of Sonoyta, the greater the odds Kelvington would need to pee, fill up the tank of the guzzling Suburban, then start the process of heading back north. Liam knew there was only one good spot on the south side. Finally, after almost two hours, the Suburban gave up.

South of Sonoyta, all semblance of civilization stopped as Route 8 continued to Puerto Peñasco, and in between, there was nothing but desert, mountains, and Gila monsters. No gas stations. At first, Liam thought the Suburban might keep going, but then it did another U-turn and pulled into the last gas station for at least seventy miles.

On either side of Route 8, cliffs rose sharply, with webs of access roads cut into them. Liam saw his chance, so he cut through the median, bottoming out the Mustang in the process, then crossed the northbound lane and sped up on one of the access roads, winding his way up the hill. Halfway up, he cut back toward the gas station. In less than a quarter of a mile, Liam found a wide spot where a quarry access road took a hard left. He parked the Mustang, doused the headlights, and cut the engine.

From the go-bag, Liam removed the black case, then started the process of assembling the Sauer 200 takedown rifle, the Leupold 6X scope, and its suppressor. Chambered for a .308 round, at this distance perched above the target, the Sauer had more than enough accuracy and punch to take care of a target less than 250 yards away. Liam liked to shoot over the top, but as the Mustang was a convertible, that was not an option. He slammed home the four-round magazine, dropped the bipod, then rested the rifle across the hood.

In the clip, he was using Hornady 150-grain rounds and had zeroed the rifle at 50 and at 200 yards. Using the spotting scope, he ranged the Suburban at 230 yards, did the trig in his head, and determined he'd need to hold two inches over the target. In this case, the forehead would work fine. Putting the spotting scope back to his eye, he watched the scene below.

A single pickup occupied one of the three islands of pumps,

all well-lit by mast-type lamps with no canopy. Kelvington had stopped at the pump closest to the building and had control of the handle. He was visible from the chest up, partially hidden by the angle of the windshield. The blond man said something to Kelvington, then entered the store. A motorcycle pulled up to the center island, the pickup pulled out, and Kelvington turned to look.

Setting the spotting scope down, Liam moved behind the rifle scope, reacquired Kelvington, then settled the crosshairs on the top of his left ear. Liam touched his index finger to the trigger and prepared to say goodbye to the man who had tried to kill him two years ago.

This position was absolutely perfect. Downward shot. Lit up like it was high noon. His target was stationary and staring at the rolling digits on a gas pump. He drew another breath, let it out, then put tension on the trigger. Nothing could go wrong, except—

The roar was deafening, as if from concert speakers at a Motörhead show. And the lights that came with the sound were blinding. Initially, Liam couldn't tell where it was coming from, but when he turned and looked over his shoulder, it was just in time to catch a glimpse of the huge beast barreling at him, rearing up on its hind legs. It wreaked of gas, oil, and rage. His first instinct was to roll to his right, toward the front of the Mustang's hood, but the bulk of the beast was already there, so instead, he rolled to the left, up the slope of the windshield, then down into the seats. Looking up into darkness, his last vision was of a hot transmission and two massive tires—coming down.

Liam's world went black.

. . .

Two men leapt from the cab of the black Ford F-250 monster truck, then leveled their machine pistols on the mangled Mustang. Juan Garcia Lopez took his time getting out, keeping his own machine pistol tethered to his shoulder. He caught up with his men, then knelt to examine the Mustang. Reaching inside, he gripped the hair of the pinned man, studied his bloody face, then let it drop.

"I hope you enjoyed your beef jerky and piss, gringo!" Lopez said, then spit in the man's direction.

Bo DeVine climbed from the rear passenger seat as Lopez waved him forward to show off his prize. The driver knelt, reached through the crumpled metal, and took Liam's wrist in his hand. Then, he pressed two fingers against his neck.

DeVine asked, "Is he dead?"

"Not yet," the driver, whose name was Dante, said in accented English.

"Pull him out," Lopez demanded.

Dante climbed into the cab and backed the F-250 off of the Mustang. His partner—Pedro—gripped Liam beneath the shoulders and dragged him from the twisted car and into the gravel road. From a cut above his hairline, Liam's head bled profusely, pooled at his temple, then ran down his face.

Lopez checked Liam's pockets and came up with a passport, a driver's license, an American Express card, a pager, and a crappy cell phone. Dante, basking in the truck's headlights, started rummaging through the Mustang's interior, tossing anything loose into a pile. An empty bag of jerky took to the breeze, and a bottle of water gathered dust as it rolled.

Lopez, still examining the documents, said, "Steve Walsh and Brian May," to no one in particular and then tossed the passport to DeVine, who gave it a cursory read.

DeVine kicked the water bottle away, then knelt next to where Curran lay motionless, touching the man's blood-caked cheek. "I always knew there was something wrong about you," he said, then looked up at Lopez. "He must report to one of the three-letter agencies."

Lopez chuckled. "They will be looking for a replacement, yes?"

Dante approached and aimed his Uzi at Liam's head. "Want me to finish him?"

Lopez was about to answer when his cell phone rang. He cupped the device in his palm and turned away.

DeVine said to Dante, "Leave him for now," then he stepped toward the Mustang and the pile forming around a canvas bag. Scooting the bag into the monster truck's headlights, he felt inside and pulled out a paper-wrapped stack of twenties. Then another. After more rummaging, he counted thirty-six additional stacks. Then, from the darkness, Lopez screamed.

"They took my fucking guns!"

"What are you talking about?" DeVine asked.

Lopez said through gritted, "Two million dollars—gone! The Ejército Mexicano raided my ship in Matamoras. Someone talked!" He then turned to DeVine. "How much is in the bag?"

DeVine said, "Thirty-eight thousand. Some clothes. Boots. There's more junk in the bottom." He started tossing the cash into the bag.

"Small compensation for my losses." Lopez went to where Liam lay and examined him as if he were a deer in the road. "I think this man is involved." Lopez lowered his Uzi toward Liam's head.

"Do you want to kill your only bargaining chip?" DeVine asked.

"What do you mean?" Lopez asked.

"I mean, if his three-letter agency took your guns, you can make a trade," DeVine said. "I can assure you it's not the INS."

Lopez mulled it over while the barrel of the Uzi bobbed in the night air. When Liam groaned, Lopez kicked him in the gut, then turned to DeVine and said, "You'd better be right. Keeping him alive may be more trouble than it is worth. So, how do you suggest we do this thing?"

From the pile, DeVine picked up the burner phone and the PagSat pager, then passed them to Lopez.

Lopez said, "This man is clearly a spy." He turned on the burner phone. The signal was weak. He put a finger on the Redial button.

DeVine said, "Before you do that, let's think about it."

Lopez nodded. "What's to think about? I will tell them I have this man's money and his life in my hands. They will return my guns and my accountant and that coward Jesus."

"Really?" DeVine said. "Who do you have? Steve Walsh or Brian May?" When a question wrinkled Lopez's forehead, DeVine shook his head. "Tell them you have Liam Curran."

Lopez smiled and pointed toward DeVine, then pressed Redial. It rang once, and a woman's voice answered.

"Please tell me you haven't done something stupid."

# CHAPTER 46

The Lake
Same Day
4:02 a.m.

t is *you* who has done something stupid," the Latino voice on the phone said.

"Who is this?" Ginny asked, putting the cell phone on speaker as she led Woody and Michaels toward the house.

"I have Liam Curran beneath my boot and will break his neck. Unless we can trade."

Ginny asked, "Trade what?" She climbed the stairs to the porch, and when Babbs appeared at the door, Ginny held a finger to her lips, then mouthed, *Get Curtis on the phone.*

"You have my guns, bitch!" the Latino man screamed.

"You must have the wrong number," Ginny said. Michaels shrugged, but Woody drew in a breath and stepped away. Ginny pressed Mute and asked, "Any ideas what this guy is talking about?"

Woody said, "I think so. The FBI and the Mexican military raided a ship carrying guns from Nicaragua bought by the CDG. Millions of dollars' worth."

"Where are the guns now?" Ginny asked.

"Still on the ship, last I heard."

Ginny went back to the phone as a barrage of Spanish flew from the speaker. She pressed Mute and said, "Is this Raul? Not funny, Raul."

"This is Juan Garcia Lopez—and I want my fucking guns!"

"Juan," Ginny said calmly. "Can I speak with Mr. Curran?"

"No!"

"Why not?" There was a pause, so Ginny said, "I see. Could you have him call back when he's available?"

"He'll be dead, bitch!"

"I suppose our trade is out of the question." Ginny hung up then said to Woody, "He has Liam's phone, so—"

Babbs returned, holding the front door open. She pointed to the multiline phone on the wall and the flashing light. Ginny nodded understanding. Curtis was on hold.

"I can't believe you hung up on him," Woody said. "Are you crazy? He's going to kill Curran."

"Maybe he has already," Ginny said as she stepped inside, then pressed the flashing button on the wall phone. "Curtis, I'm going to give you a phone number. Can you see if you can find it?" Ginny read the digits from her cell phone's display.

Curtis said, "I'll be right back."

Ginny's cell phone vibrated. She placed it on a table, answered, then pressed SPKR.

"That was another stupid move!" Lopez screamed.

Ginny asked, "Can I help you with something?"

Michaels grinned and shook his head.

Lopez said, "Your man for my guns."

"It isn't that simple," Ginny said. "I mean, if he did find some guns, how would he know they are yours? Also, how do we make the trade? I'm probably a long way from where you are, and—this is most important—how do I know you have Liam Curran?"

From the wall phone, Curtis's voice came over the line so Woody muted the cell phone.

"What did you find out, Curtis?" Ginny asked.

"The number is a burner and doesn't appear to be in the US," Curtis said. "Can I ask what's going on?" Ginny explained it to Curtis, who then said, "Have Lopez use Curran's PagSat pager to send you a text message. I'll at least have the GPS location."

Ginny pressed Mute on the cell phone, opening the line again.

"Okay—Juan. If you can prove you have my man, I'm prepared to make a trade."

Lopez said, "How do I know *you* can make this trade?"

Woody leaned in, then said, "This is White House Chief of Staff Patricia Woodburn. I'm the person who had the FBI and the Mexicans quarantine your ship."

Lopez said, "You could be a prostitute for all I know."

"The ship's name is—*Carlotta*," Woody said.

Several beats of silence passed, then: "You bitch!"

Woody pressed Mute. "I think he's ready to deal." She pressed Mute again, then said, "First, the proof. Find Mr. Curran's pager, turn it on, then send a text message to the number I'm going to give you." Ginny scribbled the number on a napkin, and Woody read it off. "Did you get that?"

"Yes. I'm sending the message now," Lopez said.

Michaels pressed Mute, then said, "Hey, guys. We have an asset in Mexico right now."

"We do?" Woody asked. But when she saw the look on their faces, she said, "You've got to be kidding. Even *if* Paul would answer my calls, he's trying to kill Trevor Harmon or Liam Curran or whoever the fuck he is. If Lopez doesn't kill him, Paul will."

"He won't," Ginny said. "He won't, because Paul is a professional."

Woody chuckled. "Ginny, he's really pissed. And why would he save a man who's trying to kill *him*?"

Michaels said, "Paul doesn't know Liam's trying to kill him—right?"

Woody volleyed glances between the two of them as Lopez's voice came back.

Lopez said, "I sent the text. You know we have him."

Ginny felt the pager vibrate, and she read it out loud. "Fuck you," she said, and Woody couldn't help but burp a laugh. Hearing her mother use that word was like watching Snow White fart on a dwarf.

Curtis's voice came from the wall phone. "I got it. They are four miles south of the Lukeville POE and just east of Mexico Route 8. Here are the coordinates." He rattled them off, and Michaels wrote them down.

Ginny turned to Woody and said, "Please, try Paul again."

"Okay," Woody said. She found her cell phone and pressed a speed-dial button. It rang five times, then went to voice mail. She tried again. Same result.

Michaels said, "What's the damn number?" Woody dictated the number, and Michaels entered it into his own phone.

Lopez said, "What are we going to do, ladies?"

Ginny pressed Mute. "We're going to make a trade. Let me speak with Curran."

Lopez said, "I'm afraid Mr. Curran was in an accident and is unconscious. If he wakes up, I will put him on."

Ginny was about to speak, but Michaels pointed to his phone and mouthed, *I got him*.

"I need to put you on hold, Mr. Juan. My associates would like to have a discussion." Ginny pressed Mute while Juan cursed her. She turned to Michaels and said, "Put Paul on speaker." Michaels did, then placed his cell phone on the table next to Ginny's.

"Paul? It's Ginny."

"Hello, Ginny," Paul said. "Using a different cell phone to call me is deceitful. I guess it runs in the family."

"You know that's not true," Ginny said. "But I need your services, and I understand you are somewhere in northern Mexico at present."

Paul said, "In the general area."

Ginny said, "BICA has an asset there who was involved in—an incident—with the cartel and is in a bad way," Ginny said. "BICA is willing to pay you a hundred thousand for the recovery."

Paul said, "You're lying again. You're talking about Trevor Harmon. Let me assure you, I'm already close. A hundred grand won't keep him alive."

Michaels stepped away, his face a ticking bomb. Grabbing a metal folding chair, he hurled it across the room, swearing under his breath that he would kill Kelvington if it was the last thing he did. Babbs palmed her lips to hide her gasp as Woody shook her head, then leaned over the phone.

"Paul? It's Patricia," she said. "Please—don't hang up. The man you are after is not Trevor Harmon." Ginny was shaking her head, but she continued anyway. "His name is Liam Curran. He's ex-military. Ex-intelligence. I was lied to about who he was. Had I known the truth"—she stopped long enough to send a scolding glare toward Ginny—"none of this would be happening. If you kill him, you'll be murdering an innocent man."

The line went stone quiet. Not even a hiss, so Woody knew Paul had muted his phone. Ginny stepped away in frustration but turned back when the line clicked and Paul's voice came through. "Your promises don't mean shit! But I'll make you a deal. The price is two hundred grand. That's the hedge to cover the odds that I'm being screwed with again."

Woody eyed Ginny, who nodded her approval. "Okay, Paul. Two hundred. Now—"

"Wait a second," Paul said. "There's no guarantee I'll find him. But if I do, I want the money wired to PeKay's account before I bring him out of Mexico. Is that clear?"

Michaels returned and was unfolding the note with the GPS coordinates.

Woody didn't wait for him. "We'll get you the money as long as Curran is still alive when you have him," Woody said. "Now comes the easy part. We know *exactly* where he is." She rattled off the coordinates from memory, causing Michaels to glance at Ginny, who pointed a finger at her head. Woody continued. "Curran is being held by a man calling himself Juan Garcia Lopez."

Paul said, "The head of the CDG? I should have negotiated a

bigger number." There was silence for beat, then Paul came back. "Jesus Christ, Woody! Zilo just entered the coordinates into the Garmin. We were sitting on top of him not fifteen minutes ago." The squeal of rubber against asphalt dominated the phone's speaker. "I'll call you back." The phone went dead.

Ginny hit Mute on her cell phone. Woody said, "Mr. Juan. Are you still there? Mr. Juan?" There were several more beats of silence.

Then Lopez said, "Have you decided to let him die?"

Woody said, "We have agreed to make the exchange. The issue is the logistics. I will need to coordinate with the FBI and—"

"Don't waste your breath," Lopez said. "During your stupid discussion, I have heard the *Carlotta* is no longer docked at Matamoras. Someone has purchased the entire cargo, and the ship was released. So, you see, you no longer have anything to offer. Unless you know who now has my guns."

Woody said, "I—I wasn't aware it had happened. Let me make some calls to see—" But she was interrupted.

"No! It is too late for you and your man," Lopez said.

"We will pay you for your loss," Ginny chimed in. "How much?"

"My price is four million dollars. I don't believe even the great United States would pay that for one man," Lopez said.

In concert, Woody and Ginny both let out a breath, uncertain exactly where to go with the conversation.

"Pay it!" Michaels whispered. "We'll figure out how to get it back. Or tell him we can get him some more guns. I've got sources. Tell him we'll give him the accountant back."

"He doesn't want the accountant. She's damaged goods," Ginny said and lowered her head, her lips pursed. Woody turned and found Michaels's eyes burning.

"What's your decision?" Lopez asked. "Or have we agreed to disagree and—"

Before Lopez could finish, a series of pops came over the speaker. Then a volley of cracks that were clearly gunfire. While Ginny and

Woody huddled over the cell phone, animated Spanish overtook the static. Metal pinging off of metal. Thuds like wet laundry. More pinging. Woody paced frantically as she jabbed the Redial button on her cell phone.

Michaels was the only calm one. "What are you doing?" Michaels asked.

Woody said, "I need to talk to Paul, but he won't pick up."

Michaels reached out and stopped her finger before it could jab again. "If you'll listen closely, Paul is talking to us right now."

# CHAPTER 47

Sonoyta, Mexico
Same Day
5:12 a.m.

From their position overlooking the monster truck and the crumpled Mustang, Zilo and Paul had clear views through their night-vision sniper scopes of the five men below. Three, maybe four, Mexicans and one, clearly not.

One Mexican paced a rut while stabbing wildly at a cell phone as he passed in and out of the truck's high beams. Two more Mexicans stood on either end of a Mustang. Near the Mustang's passenger door, a dark-skinned and lanky man hovered over a fifth man, pointing a pistol at his head.

It was clear to Paul that the man on the ground was the once deceased, now very much alive Commander Trevor Harmon. The man Woody called Liam Curran. He also recognized the lunatic on the cell phone as Juan Garcia Lopez. Paul raised a palm, signaling for Zilo, who was now fifty yards to his right, to hold.

Lopez stopped pacing near Curran's feet, then stomped on his knee. Curran didn't move, and Paul wondered if this whole exercise was pointless now. A passing thought suggested he could wait it out and let the lanky man put a bullet in Curran's brain, removing all doubt.

Zilo had gone prone behind the scope of his H&K SR9 rifle, but was looking Paul's way. Paul sent him three tactical hand signals. One for *ENEMY*, followed by four fingers. Then, Paul put his hand to his throat, which meant *HOSTAGE*. He then went to one knee and lay his SR9 overtop a boulder. His finger touched the trigger as his cell phone buzzed. Paul ignored it, put his eye to the scope, let out a breath, then fired—only a half second before Zilo.

Below, the two Mexicans standing guard both collapsed in twin heaps. Lopez, now in the headlight beams and shocked by the sight of his men dropping, dove behind the bumper of the Mustang. He tried to reach a dead man's Uzi, but Paul fired another round that missed Lopez's hand by an inch, and he snatched it back.

Paul couldn't see Lopez but fired at the Mustang anyway, and the round clipped the bumper. The lanky man, now in the open and confused, lost interest in Curran and followed Lopez behind the Mustang. One of Zilo's rounds punched a hole in the Mustang's fender.

*Damn it!* Paul thought. *Now they're both behind that car. Time to change our angles.*

He motioned for Zilo to move farther right, and he moved left, which would take the Mustang completely out of the equation and give Zilo a clear view of both Lopez and the lanky man. Zilo could choose his target, and Paul would get the other when he bolted.

Lopez must have predicted his coming predicament. Before Zilo could get into position, Lopez sprinted toward the truck, then dove to the passenger side behind a giant wheel. If Zilo moved a few feet more, he'd be able to see Lopez, but the man didn't wait for that either. He climbed into the cab and lay prone in the seat.

The lanky man attempted the same maneuver, but Zilo pinned him with a couple of close rounds. Paul put three more rounds into the bed and cab of the truck.

Lopez had had enough. The truck had been running, and Paul figured Lopez must have rolled onto the floorboard, pressed the brake pedal with one hand, and shifted the truck into drive with the other. It lurched forward, sending a suitcase and two shovels from the bed into the gravel. The truck took out several small trees and scrub as it started down the steep embankment toward the gas station. Lopez's head popped up in the rearview window just in time to avoid taking out an entire island of pumps where Paul had filled up earlier.

The lanky man, now completely exposed, stood frozen—his hands raised high and a pistol at his feet.

Paul gave Zilo the signal for *COVER ME*, then started down the hill. He stopped long enough to yell, "Kick the pistol away!"

The lanky man did.

"On your knees!" Paul said as he stepped from the darkness, his assault rifle hungry for a stupid mistake. The man was skinnier than Paul had anticipated. And darker. Not a Mexican. "Who the fuck are *you*?" Paul asked, shining a light into the cowering man's face and holding the SR9 by the pistol grip. Zilo arrived, checked the two dead men, then started dragging them into the scrub.

"I'm with the INS," the Black man said. "I have ID."

"On your stomach," Paul ordered, then put a boot between the man's shoulder blades as he zip-tied his hands. Searching him, he found a wallet and a .357 Smith & Wesson revolver in a holster. He tossed the revolver to Zilo, then rolled the lanky man onto his back. Paul then retrieved the Beretta the man had kicked away and tucked it at the small of his back.

Paul opened the wallet, found the shield, and read the ID out loud. "Agent Eugene DeVine." DeVine was struggling to sit as Paul shone the flashlight beam in his wide eyes, then back to the ID. "What are you doing here, Agent DeVine?"

"Was about to apprehend the man lying over there until you started shooting. He's an American working with the CDG."

"Oh," Paul said. "I thought you were about to put a bullet in his head. Is that the definition of *apprehend* in the INS handbook?"

"Who the hell are you?" DeVine asked.

Paul didn't answer. Instead, he went to where Zilo had finished with the bodies.

"Both are dead," Zilo said. He then shined his light on Curran and whispered, "He's alive—but barely. His breathing is raspy, he's bubbling blood around his lips, and his pupils are unresponsive."

Paul trained both the SR9 and the flashlight onto Curran and thought, *Dead, my ass.* Finally, right in front of him lay the man he was certain had murdered the CIA director, the national security advisor, the CIA's chief of station in London, an Iraqi general, his wife and daughter, and probably others. He'd had his chance in the condo. So, why were he and Woody still alive?

"See what you can get out of the other guy," Paul said absently. "His ID says he is Eugene DeVine. INS. But don't trust it." He then flicked off the SR9's safety.

"Boss," Zilo said. "Whatcha doin'?"

Paul turned and barked, "Check on the INS guy!"

"He can wait."

"Go!" Paul screamed, but Zilo didn't budge.

"It's cold-blooded murder, and you know it," Zilo said. "But if that's what it takes for a Green Beret to beat a SEAL—hell—what do I know?" Zilo turned and left Paul alone with Curran.

Paul shouldered the SR9, then pulled out the Beretta he had picked up. The pistol was warm, and it gleamed in the moonlight. He checked the chamber and found a sliver of brass shining back at him. The safety was off, and he lowered the Beretta to Curran's forehead. He moved his finger to the trigger. *Why didn't you do it in the condo?* he thought.

More pressure on the trigger.

"Why didn't you do it?" he screamed this time. Then, the shakes showed up.

They started in his shoulder but ended in his wrist. The last time he'd felt this way, he was fourteen and had his first deer in the crosshairs of his 30-06 rifle. And he had missed.

Lowering the pistol, Paul knelt to Curran's ear and whispered, "I had you. Son of a bitch, I had you."

Paul cursed as he got to his feet; his eyes went to the ground, then to Zilo, who was standing nearby, shaking his head. He was about to speak when headlights appeared from the access road to the quarry. It was a pickup, and the driver got out and started toward the Mustang. Zilo fired a shot in the air, and the driver turned, ran back to his car, then drove away.

Zilo turned back to Paul. "We're on borrowed time now. They'll stop us at the border for sure."

Paul pulled out his cell phone, and Woody answered, her voice broken and urgent.

"Paul? Paul? Are you okay?" she asked.

"Fine," he responded coldly.

Woody said, "Ginny can still hear you on her phone."

Paul turned to Zilo. "Lopez must have dropped his cell."

Paul rummaged through the crushed Mustang while Zilo searched the ground. "Got it," Zilo said as he held up the phone. "Bye, Ginny," he said, then disconnected the call.

Paul put his own phone to his ear and said, "Lopez got away. We have his cell, so he's searching for a pay phone to get some more boys. A civilian spotted us, and I know he's calling the cops."

Woody said, "You don't have Lopez's phone. It was Curran's burner."

"Shit! We gotta move," Paul said. "Take DeVine's Suburban, then meet me back here." He went back to Woody. "INS Agent Eugene DeVine. Ever heard of him?"

There was a pause, then Woody said, "Ginny said Curran had mentioned him. Why?"

"Well—I kind of have him in custody," Paul said. "And I don't have enough favors banked up to get us back across the border with a hostage."

Woody asked, "And Curran?"

Paul knelt and checked Curran's pulse. "He's—uh—hanging on."

"Paul?" It was Ginny's voice now. "If you can get to Puerto Peñasco, I can send you the same seaplane Curran used to smuggle the CDG accountant out. I'll have a medic on board."

"CDG accountant?" Paul asked. "Never mind. Just send it. We're about ninety miles out. Put Woody back on."

"Paul?" Woody said from the speaker.

"Did you hire Curran to smuggle the CDG's accountant out of Mexico?"

"Not specifically. But it was a huge win."

Paul looked down at Curran, then to the headlights bouncing his way. "I'll call you back," Paul said, then closed the phone.

Zilo stopped the Suburban as Paul lifted Curran in a fireman's carry and propped him up in the driver's side passenger seat with DeVine next to him, buckled in and still zip-tied. After salvaging everything they could from the site, Paul took the front passenger seat and slapped the dashboard, and Zilo floored it.

"Where are we going?" DeVine asked.

Zilo said, "I'll let *you* know when *I* know."

Paul said, "Puerto Peñasco. Go south on Route 8."

"Could you at least free my hands?" DeVine asked.

"I *could*," Paul said. "But I'm not going to." A mile later, Paul adjusted the rearview mirror, found DeVine's eyes, and asked, "Is that your suitcase in the back?"

"Yes," DeVine said.

Paul and Zilo exchanged knowing glances before Paul leaned between the seats to check on Curran. A mist had formed where Curran's lips pressed against the window. Anyone could have mistaken him for sleeping if it weren't for the blood caked on his mouth and face. Paul returned to his seat, glanced in the mirror again, let out a satisfied sigh, and said, "Okay, Eugene. Let's hear your story."

# CHAPTER 48

North of Puerto Peñasco, Mexico
Same Day
6:06 a.m.

It's not much of a story," DeVine said. "And call me Bo."

In the mirror, Paul caught a glimpse of DeVine's eyes and didn't like what he saw. "C'mon. An INS agent keeping company with Juan Garcia Lopez. We have an hour to kill."

DeVine let out a bored breath. "I've been chasing two illegals who jumped the fence in Lukeville and murdered several people. One of the victims was the neighbor of Mr. Curran here. When I requested his help locating them, he ran down here to Mexico to hook up with the CDG. I came to get him. He got on the wrong side of Juan Lopez, and I suggested a trade for his confiscated guns."

Zilo chuckled and said, "Good thing we showed up when we did."

"The situation was under control," DeVine said.

Zilo said, "I couldn't help but notice the Sauer 200 sniper rifle. I hope it isn't yours. It's in two pieces now."

DeVine shook his head. "No. It was Curran's."

Paul said, "Where was Curran's neighbor murdered?"

"A small town in West Virginia," DeVine said, gazing through the window.

"West Virginia," Paul repeated. He smacked Zilo on the arm and said, "You tracked your illegals there, met Curran, then asked for his help." He shifted his eyes back to the mirror and said, "And you think maybe Curran had something to do with the murder?"

DeVine said, "Not at first. He was just a local who knew the area. When he ran to Mexico, I got suspicious. It was Lopez who beat him up like that. If I hadn't shown up, Lopez would have killed him."

Paul asked, "Who was Lopez talking to on the phone?"

"I'm not sure. He found Curran's phone and hit Redial," DeVine said.

Zilo asked, "Speaking of that—how much do you know about Curran?"

DeVine said, "He has a few aliases; I can tell you that much."

"Whoever he is, he doesn't look too good," Paul said just as his cell phone buzzed between his legs. He checked the display. It was Ginny, and he had a single bar of reception. "Pull over here," he said. Zilo did, and Paul stepped out to take the call. A few minutes later, he was back inside telling Zilo to *floor it*.

Paul let the silence percolate for a few miles before he adjusted the mirror to see DeVine again. "Sorry about that. When the office calls—"

"Which office is that?" DeVine asked.

"FBI," Paul said. "And we know about Lopez's guns. That's why we're in town."

"FBI?" DeVine said as his shoulders relaxed and his forehead crinkled with concern. "How will your director respond when my director tells him you kidnapped a fellow officer?"

"You ask the most interesting questions," Zilo said, then turned back to the road in time to see a glowing set of surprised red eyes scurry into the weeds.

"You'll have to let me go before we cross back into the US," DeVine said.

Paul leaned back and found that Curran's cheek was flat against the window with his neck bent at an awkward angle. "We're flying out," Paul announced.

DeVine held his zip-tied hands up in the mirror. "Please?"

Paul ignored him and said, "You found Curran pretty quick."

DeVine said, "I had a good idea where to look."

"Good job," Paul said. "I doubt *we'd* be able to find a person that fast."

Out of DeVine's sight, Paul flicked Zilo's thigh again. Zilo grinned. Something wasn't meshing, and they both knew it, and Zilo was trying to blindly support Paul's game.

Thanks to Ginny's call, Paul now knew about the gun shipment, and he also knew why the INS had sent DeVine to New Mexico. And it wasn't to find Curran. He wanted to let DeVine dig himself into a hole but needed to provide him with the tools to make it a deep one. He had an idea, but Zilo was going to have to be in the dark on this one.

Paul bent over and removed the small 9 mm pistol from its ankle holster and fumbled it in his lap before placing it on the console between the SUV's seats. Paul stretched back and lay his hands in his lap and said, "How much did you get out of Mr. Curran?"

DeVine said, "He never regained consciousness."

Paul said, "I imagine your director will be less upset that we kidnapped you than the fact that you disobeyed his orders."

"His orders?" DeVine asked.

Paul flicked Zilo's leg again and said, "You know—to view the remains of the two dead border agents in Tucson. Penn and Gallagher were their names, right?"

Paul never adjusted the mirror, but he could feel DeVine squirming in the back seat. And he could smell the odor of sweat, like a cologne. Paul had just flipped over a big hold card, and now DeVine had three options: come clean, embellish on his bullshit, or…

The one he chose.

DeVine explained, "I was ordered to Tucson because I was already on my way to Mexico."

"But you went after Curran anyway."

There was silence for a beat, then DeVine said, "Curran's trail was too fresh, so I decided one live man runs faster than two dead ones."

"Do you mind if I used that one?" Zilo asked. "I like it."

Paul let out a breath. "I'd say you're just as lucky to be alive as Curran."

"Why's that?" DeVine asked.

"I saw the Mustang, Eugene," Paul said. "If Curran was driving, then whoever was in the passenger seat is a lucky bastard. And it must have been you, right?"

DeVine said nothing.

"Or maybe, you were riding with Lopez," Paul said. "Your suitcase *did* roll out of the bed of his truck when old Juan left your ass." Paul glanced into the mirror and added, "You see where I'm going with this, Eugene? You didn't walk to the quarry."

"It's—complicated," DeVine said.

Paul said, "I'll bet you have no clue how long we were watching your little charade. If we hadn't started shooting, Mr. Curran might be on his way to the morgue."

DeVine leaned forward, his head between the seats. "It was an act."

"Then you deserve an Academy Award and—" But Paul stopped talking when he realized the 9 mm was missing from the console. In the mirror, a gleam of the stainless-steel pistol flashed from DeVine's zip-tied hands.

"What are you doing, Eugene?" Paul asked calmly.

"Changing our travel plans," DeVine said.

"You prick!" Zilo said.

Paul said, "Just everybody be easy. How long have you been a mole for the CDG?"

"Long enough to get rich," DeVine said. "Now, turn this car around."

Zilo eyed Paul, who nodded, and Zilo performed a quick U-turn through the median. In the mirror, Paul saw Curran's limp body bang against the window, then slide onto the floorboard. When he saw DeVine glance toward Curran, Paul said, "You're the cleaner, aren't you?"

DeVine smiled. "If that's what you want to call me."

"The two illegals you're looking for are actually the killers, and you were sent to kill them."

In the mirror, DeVine glanced at Curran on the floor, then said, "If you knew who Curran really is, you wouldn't have stopped me from killing him."

"Now, that interests me," Paul said. "Why don't you fill me in?"

"My partner did some digging and found some very interesting tidbits about Mr. Curran's past. He may be an American, but he was born in Ireland. And his father was once with the CIA and—"

A flash lit up the interior as an explosion splintered the night, sending bolts of lightning into every ear. Paul turned in his seat as Zilo swerved off the road, the bumper clipping a guardrail before he jerked it straight and sent it bouncing across the median. It crossed both lanes, coming to a stop on the shoulder of the southbound lane. Zilo drew his pistol from its holster. Glancing in the mirror, he saw DeVine melting against the passenger seat in a crumpled heap.

Zilo turned to Paul. "Are you okay?"

"Yeah," Paul said as he patted down his body for holes. "How about you?"

Zilo asked, "What the hell did you do?"

"Not a damn thing." Paul leaned over the seat and found the 9 mm pistol DeVine had taken from the console on the floor. Zilo felt the barrel.

"It's cold," Zilo said.

"It had better be," Paul said as he placed six rounds on the console. "I unloaded it first. It was a ruse for DeVine, and he fell for it." Turning in the seat, Paul reached into the back and pinched DeVine's neck, looking for a pulse. Nothing. When he pulled his hand back, he found it covered with blood. Zilo jumped out and yanked DeVine from the back seat and onto the shoulder of the road. DeVine had been shot. The bullet entered at his jawline and left a cauliflower exit bloom at the crown of his head. Trajectory—low to high.

"Did he drop the pistol and it went off?" Zilo said as he used his pinky to gauge the bloody hole. "This is not a nine millimeter entry wound—" He stopped talking and turned toward the back seat and the open rear door. Curran was there, still slumped on the floorboard. That's when Paul gasped, his hand frantically searching for the Beretta he had taken from DeVine at the quarry.

Zilo tore open the driver's side passenger door and caught Curran's body before it spilled out. He set him back up in the seat and felt for a pulse. It was there and a lot stronger than before. Then, there was a thud as something heavy landed on the toe of his boot. He reached down and picked up the pistol by the trigger guard between his thumb and forefinger, then held it to the moonlight.

Paul nodded, then grinned. "Remember—at the quarry—I threw Curran over my back?" Paul gripped Curran's cheeks and said, "You sneaky bastard."

# CHAPTER 49

---

Puerto Peñasco, Mexico
Same Day
8:15 a.m.

After moving DeVine's body to the hatch of the SUV, and they were back on the road, Paul reached over the seat and smacked Curran's cheeks. "Hey. Anybody home?" Curran groaned, so he smacked him a few more times.

"You can stop now," Liam croaked through blood-caked lips. He opened an eye; the other had clotted closed.

Paul asked, "Do you know where you are?"

"Taco Bell?"

"Close enough. We're heading to Puerto Peñasco."

"Been there already." Liam let his eyes close. "Overrated."

"Do you know who I am?"

"Just another fucker who wants me dead."

"Bingo," Paul said. "Tell me what hurts."

"Easier to tell you what doesn't," Liam said. "Feels like I've been hit by a truck."

"Funny you say that," Paul said, as Liam's eyes rolled over and his head lay back against the window. "Oh no, you don't," Paul said, smacking Liam awake. "If you die, I don't get paid and my workers' comp premiums will go through the roof."

"Take it out of my check."

"I can't. I fired you already."

When Liam coughed, another blood bubble popped at the corner of his mouth.

"There's a seaplane waiting for us," Paul said.

"Guess I'll get to ride on one after all."

Paul couldn't help but laugh as he asked, "Why did you shoot DeVine?"

A cough. Blood. "He talks too much. And, he was going to shoot you. By the way, you owe me."

Paul shook his head. "The gun was empty. How long were you playing possum?"

Liam wheezed and coughed blood. His words whistled as he spoke. "You shouldn't leave loaded pistols tucked into your ass."

Zilo laughed this time.

Liam grinned and his eyes closed again.

Paul smacked him. "You're not screwing me out of my money." He pinched Liam's cheeks, then said, "I hear you have a recording of Woody from the condo."

Liam nodded.

"What are you planning to do with it?" Paul asked.

"Let me die and you'll find out." He licked his lips, then asked, "I know you're tracking Saliba. Where is he?"

"Son of a bitch! It *was* you in Toledo," Paul said, smacking the seat. "I'll trade you. The recording of Woody for Saliba."

"You know where he is?"

Paul nodded, then turned to Zilo, who confirmed, "We do."

"I thought you might. Your offer is under advisement," Liam said.

Paul found a half-full bottle of water on the floorboard and put it to Curran's lips. Half went into his mouth, and the other half down his shirt.

"How long have you been working for BICA?" Paul asked.

Liam said, "It seems like forever. Even longer now." Then he coughed up more blood.

Paul said, "The plane has a medic."

"Oh good. Silver nitrate," Liam said.

Paul asked, "What were you doing in Mexico?"

Liam said, "Working for your fiancée and waiting to kill someone."

"Who?" Paul asked.

"You," Liam said. "I left a trail Ray Charles could follow."

Paul leaned back and washed his hands over his face, answering a question he had never asked before: Was it possible to hate this guy more than he did? Paul said, "You're serious, aren't you?"

Liam leaked a bloody grin. "DeVine was telling the truth. The Sauer is mine. The .308 in the chamber was yours."

Paul shook his head while Zilo chuckled, then eventually broke into a laugh.

Fifteen minutes later, they reached the marina. The pilot of the seaplane and the medic were waiting, and both helped walk Curran aboard. Paul found a stack of folded white sheets in the back of the plane and took one to the Suburban to wrap up DeVine like a rug. DeVine got to fly out riding with the luggage.

Paul spoke with the pilot while Zilo returned to the car for the rest of the gear. Ten minutes later, Paul exited the plane and met Zilo coming down the plank. Zilo's mobile rang in midstride. The look on his face forced Paul to quicken his pace.

"What's going on?" Paul asked as Zilo closed the phone.

"It's Saliba. He went into a hotel in Ankara and never came out," Zilo said. "Two days later, an ambulance showed up and carted him out. Someone popped him."

"Shit! Who did it?" Paul asked. When Zilo shrugged, Paul rubbed the coming beard on his chin and turned toward the plane, where his prize was being tended, and thought, *Doesn't this guy know how to die?* Once more, they had both lived to hunt another day. Paul pointed toward the plane and said, "At least we know who *didn't* kill Saliba." He smacked Zilo's shoulder. "Would you mind driving the Suburban back to Phoenix? Give it a good scrubbing before you take it back to the office? We'll turn it into the insurance later."

"And DeVine?"

"Let me take care of him." They said their goodbyes, and Paul watched his friend drive away before boarding.

Paul took the first seat ahead of where the medic had Curran on a gurney secured to a notch in the aisle floor. After the plane had leveled off, Paul maneuvered the cramped quarters to watch the medic work as memories of Iraq flashed in his mind.

Curran had an oxygen tube pinched to his nostrils, and an IV snaked from his arm to a swinging bag. Paul turned away when the medic inserted a long, fat needle into Curran's chest, and, in a hushed tone, the medic said, "He has a punctured lung. The needle is to remove the air between the lung and the cavity of the chest wall. I don't have a chest tube or else I'd use it. He'll need surgery as soon as we land, but it's the head wound that concerns me."

"It doesn't look that bad since you cleaned it."

"It's not the cut," the medic said. "Four or five stitches, maybe. But his skull is cracked below the cut, and he's showing signs of intracranial pressure. What I don't know is if the pressure is from blood pressing in or out."

"He was talking to us in the car," Paul said.

The medic thought for a few beats. "How long was he unconscious?"

"I'm—not sure. Thirty minutes, maybe."

"Moving around could have provided momentary relief of the pressure. Did he vomit? Have trouble focusing?"

"Once, I think. It was dark," Paul said. "He was blinking a lot."

The medic was nodding. "All symptoms of pressure on the brain."

"And the morning after a hot night in Tijuana," Paul said.

The medic didn't answer. Instead, he went back to work on Curran, and Paul took the seat across the aisle. "How long till we reach San Diego?" Paul asked, closing his eyes.

"Ninety minutes," the medic said. "They'll get him stable before moving him to Walter Reed."

"Walter Reed?" Paul asked. "Who approved that?"

The medic kept working and said nothing.

Paul shut his eyes, then said, "Don't let Curran out of those straps—in case I doze off."

# CHAPTER 50



I'm here to see Liam Curran."

The young candy striper behind the counter smiled. "Can I have your name, please?"

"Paul Kelvington."

"You're not on the list. Just one moment." The woman picked up the phone and turned away. When she returned, she said, "Someone will be with you," then nodded toward the rows of chairs before a muted television. Moments later, a brunette woman in camo fatigues, a stethoscope, and a clipboard appeared from the back and approached him without offering her hand. "I'm Dr. Treviana. One of the neurosurgeons here. I operated on Mr. Curran. I'm also his attending physician." It was then he noticed the caduceus patch on her left arm and the blue eagle Velcroed on her placket. A full bird colonel. "Can we speak in private?"

"Sure—Colonel," Paul said. He followed the woman down a vacant hall littered with stores of medical equipment. A door was open on the left, and she paused to let Paul pass first. Once inside, she closed the door, and the room went black—at first. When the fluorescents flickered to life, there were three of them. A man had been standing behind the door and was now very visible and very armed. Paul opened his palms and raised them.

The man with the pistol was in desert camo and sported close-cut blond hair, a backslash scar beneath the beard on his chin, and an eagle embroidered on his cap. On the right side of his chest, the black patch said he was *Commander Rick Michaels*. On the left side, the trident said he was a Navy SEAL.

"I should shoot you right here," Michaels said.

Paul's eyes wandered the bland room, then volleyed between Dr. Treviana and Michaels. "I guess I couldn't be in a better place."

Michaels turned to Dr. Treviana and said, "Thank you, Maggie. I'll come by before I leave."

She smiled at Michaels, then glared at Paul. "I'll check on our patient," she said, then left the room, leaving Paul face-to-pistol with an angry SEAL.

"Can I ask what I've done?"

"Sure. The other night when you were talking to Ginny and Woody, the phone was on speaker. I was there," Michaels said.

"I see now," Paul said. "You're going to shoot me for what I *wanted* to do, not what I *did*."

Michaels took a step forward. "What you *did* was take a two hundred grand payoff *not* to kill him. This would be a preemptive strike."

"If you knew Curran's history, you'd understand—" But Paul never finished his sentence. Michaels rushed him, pinning him against the wall. The pistol pressed between them, but Paul felt the barrel under his chin and heard the hammer thumb back. His eyes clenched tight.

Michaels's words fought through gritted teeth. "I know *everything* about him. We've been together since BUD/S; we served together in Iraq, Iran, and Afghanistan as squad leaders before he became a platoon leader, before he left the navy for the CIA. I know what our own people did to him and—a word of advice—when someone tries to recruit you to the CIA, shoot them."

Paul let his eyes creak open; his breath had still not returned. It wasn't until he felt the pistol barrel leave his chin that he dared to inhale, and even that was a battle until Michaels backed away a fraction. "Wha—" Paul swallowed to rewet his throat. "What do you mean, you know what our own people did?"

"I'm not giving you his classified life history, Kelvington. But I will tell you this much. He was recruited to the CIA by people at the highest levels, and it was a setup from day one. They pulled him into the CIA's Special Activities Division for a single mission, and he was never supposed to return alive. But when he did, multiple contracts were put on his life. Including yours. But man, did you ever pick the wrong person to fuck with."

Paul pulled in and released a breath. "I'm not here to finish anything. I wanted to see how he was doing. And maybe figure out how he got into Walter Reed."

"When the undersecretary of defense says you're in—you're in," Michaels said. "See what I mean? You don't know a gnat's dick what's going on. And to be honest, neither does your girlfriend. I don't know how much Ginny has told her, though."

"Ginny knows?" Paul asked.

Michaels laughed out loud and backed away another step. "Wow! You really don't—I mean—wow!" He opened the door, then clicked off the light. "C'mon. Let's go."

In the hallway, Dr. Treviana was waiting for them. She eyed Paul with more contempt, then sidled up to Michaels. "It's okay," Michaels said. "I have him."

Paul stayed a step behind as they navigated the halls. Treviana spoke as she walked.

"The puncture to his lung and the pneumothorax were corrected, and they took the tube out of his chest this morning. A hole was drilled in his skull to relieve pressure. There was some bleeding in the brain, but his latest MRI looks promising. *If* he wakes up, don't make him think. Complex thought could lead to tension that would lead to—problems. He's on a light morphine drip along with some other drugs."

They took a service elevator to the seventh floor and an isolated waiting area outside a door with a card reader. The nurse at the station glanced up, smiled at Dr. Treviana, then went back to her work. Dr. Treviana swiped her card, and the door opened to a hallway, where a single table and chair had been placed. A guard in khakis stood as his hand dropped near a pistol in a shiny black holster. When he turned to face them, the SEAL Trident on his chest gleamed.

"Commander Michaels, sir," the guard said. "You'll need to sign your guest in."

Michaels flashed his green ID, then signed a clipboard. Dr. Treviana turned to the guard and said, "Give them fifteen minutes." She touched Michaels's hand, then walked away, never once acknowledging Paul.

"You heard the doc," the guard said. "Fifteen minutes." His demeanor was no-nonsense. Paul, being ex-army, knew anyone assigned to a guard position in the military carried a certain authority that trumped rank.

Once in the room, Michaels closed the door. The lights were low, and an episode of *Little House on the Prairie* was on the television. Michaels changed it to VH1, then went to the far side of the bed.

With gauze wrapping his head, Curran's face was only visible from his eyebrows down, and the bedsheet was pulled to his neck. An IV dripped into his left arm. A wire disappeared under the sheet, and beeps pulsed from the monitor at forty-seven beats per minute.

"Isn't that slow?" Paul whispered.

"Not for this heartless asshole," Michaels said. Reaching out, he gripped Curran's shoulder through the sheet and lightly shook it. "You going be sociable? I don't have all day."

Liam groaned. His eyeballs rolled beneath his lids before they fluttered open.

. . .

At first, Liam saw only milky white with flashing silver hues. Then, as the fog cleared, there were indistinct shapes followed by irregular outlines, like ghosts of spilled milk. Then voices, as if underwater. The voice registered as being friendly.

"Ri-Rick?"

He felt a warm hand, and a voice said, "It's me, dipshit!"

Liam tilted his head and brought Kelvington's face into focus. Then, he turned to Michaels. "Did you check him for poison?" A searing pain shot through the back of his head and stabbed his temples as it went.

Liam forced out, "Araseli?"

Michaels said, "Being grilled by Babbs and Bailey."

Liam nodded. Rick found ice chips on the serving table and fed him a few pieces. Liam squeaked out, "How did you—?"

"Long story. Wild Bill set you up in here. Do you remember what happened?"

Liam rolled his eyes toward Kelvington. "Up to the truck rolling over me. After that, I remember pieces."

"Do you remember DeVine?" Paul asked.

Liam nodded. "Where is—?"

"Taken care of," Paul said.

Michaels said, "Ginny sends her best, by the way."

Liam nodded. "Have you talked to Shipman?"

"Was I supposed to?" Michaels asked.

Liam said, "Yes. He needs to tell you a story about an Angel."

"I'll do it," Michaels said.

The door opened, and the guard stepped in and announced, "Two more minutes, gentlemen."

"Roger that," Michaels said, then touched Liam's hand. "I'll bring you some guitar magazines." Michaels walked away with Paul trailing behind, but Liam stopped him.

"Hey! Asshole!" Liam choked out.

"Are you talking to me?" Paul asked. When Michaels's eyes

narrowed, Liam added, "It's okay. Let me have him for a minute."
Michaels nodded, then left the room.

Liam licked his lips as he reached for the container of ice chips.
Paul picked up the container and tapped a pile into Liam's hand.
"What is it?" Paul asked.

Liam finished crunching ice. "Still want to kill me?"

Paul shook his head. "I had one reason to kill you and two
hundred thousand not to."

"Saddam Hussein would have offered you a million," Liam
said. When Paul smirked, he added, "I didn't get to thank you
for saving my ass."

"You should be thankful I didn't shoot you myself."

"I could say the same thing," Liam said. "The cash and the fax.
Dinah in the restaurant. I led you right into my sights. Payback
for trying to kill me and—" Electric agony shot through his head,
and he fisted his eyes until it passed.

Paul said, "Yet here we are. You pissing in a can and me
capable of breaking your neck." He glanced at the floor, then
said, "Michaels—uh—filled me in on some things. We have no
more business to conduct."

"There are a couple more things," Liam said. "Where are
the two Berettas? I took one out of your ass in Mexico, and you
probably found the other one in DeVine's luggage."

Paul said, "I have them both."

"Good. Give them to Michaels—today."

Paul nodded. "What else?"

"Tell Woody you're an idiot and that you're sorry."

"I can't promise that," Paul said. He started to leave but turned
back around. "Has it occurred to you that if your plan to kill me
in Mexico had worked, you'd be dead right now?"

Liam smiled, then gripped the IV line. "Yeah. I'm feeling pretty
lucky."

# CHAPTER 51



Shipman arrived at Liam's with the sun. The four cop cars showed up at the gate twenty minutes later—three with blue and red flashing lights. By the time he took the ATV to the road, three suits and one uniform were leaning on the gate; one man had papers.

Shipman climbed off the ATV, exaggerating his limp, then stopped at the gate. "Can I help you, gentlemen?" he asked, directing his question to the man with the papers.

"Good morning. I'm Detective Wallace Taconelli, West Virginia State Police. We have a warrant to search the premises." Taconelli smiled, but his eyes never blinked. "We brought a few deputies to help out. Plus, the big man to my right is Detective Braden Willis with the Ohio State Highway Patrol. To his right is Agent Charles Gillespie with Immigration and Naturalization Services, and the man to his right is—"

Shipman interrupted Taconelli and said, "You're Martin Zeller. We've done some shooting together out at Triangle Sportsman's Club."

"It's *deputy*—today," Zeller said. "Do you know Mr. Curran?"

"I lease the land for livestock and hay." He turned back to Taconelli. "Mr. Curran isn't home."

"Where is he?" Gillespie asked.

"I'm not sure," Shipman said. "I just got back myself."

"That's okay. He doesn't have to be here," Taconelli said. "Can you open up for us, or do we have to get things scratched?"

Shipman took the papers from Taconelli, read them, let out a defeated breath, then opened the gate. He took the ATV back to the garage and parked in Mika's spot. Four deputies poured out of each squad car, waiting for instructions.

"That's Mr. Curran's copy," Taconelli said, passing Shipman a page. "Detective Willis will start with the house while we go to the pole barn."

Shipman thought about it for a beat, then said, "Help yourselves."

Willis issued the instructions to the deputies, then disappeared into the house. Zeller, Taconelli, and Gillespie stayed outside. Taconelli turned to Shipman and said, "Let's have a look in the pole barn."

Shipman walked around to the side door, went inside, fired up the overhead lights, pressed a button on the wall, and the big door opened, flooding the area with sunlight. Taconelli, Gillespie, and Deputy Zeller stepped inside, their gazes taking in the high ceilings, workbench, stalls, and farm equipment. A John Deer with a hay trailer had been parked in the back left corner—where the RV once was.

"Have at it," Shipman said, then went outside and sat on the ATV in the attached garage while the cops searched the house, the pole barn, and the old barn. After two hours inside, they kicked around the grounds for another hour, then reassembled at the turnaround. Taconelli thanked the uniformed deputies, and they loaded up into the two squad cars and left the property empty-handed.

Zeller approached the garage, then lay his Smokey hat on the trunk of the BMW. Gillespie leaned against the car, shaking his head. Taconelli put a foot on the rack of the ATV and flicked mud away, while Detective Willis stood near the front. Shipman was now surrounded.

Taconelli wiped his brow. "We checked the tax records. This place cost a couple million, and there's no mortgage. How does a college professor afford this?"

Shipman shrugged.

Taconelli said, "Scott Sullivan mentioned an inheritance."

Shipman shrugged again.

Willis said, "Mr. Curran and his girlfriend, Casey Connor, were in Put-in-Bay August twenty-third through Saturday, August twenty-sixth. Can you verify that?"

Shipman shook his head. "I was in Oklahoma City picking up my new cow and calf. Got back this past Saturday, so I haven't seen Mr. Curran since before I left."

Willis said, "Mr. Shipman, my office is investigating the Toledo murders that occurred on the twenty-fifth. Do you have any information that could help us?"

Shipman's face contorted. "Just what the papers say."

Willis asked, "Does Mr. Curran own any firearms?"

"I know he has a shotgun and a deer rifle. Been hunting with him once or twice."

Willis said, "We found a twelve-gauge and a thirty-thirty Winchester in the upstairs closet."

Taconelli asked, "What did you do in the army, Mr. Shipman?"

The question caught him by surprise, and Shipman hesitated, not knowing exactly how much they knew. "I was a warrant officer stationed at Fort Belvoir. Honorably discharged in '89."

"You weren't at the White House?" Taconelli asked.

"No," Shipman said.

"You weren't with the NSC at one time? Maybe training some Contras at Hurlburt Field? Going back and forth to Honduras?"

"Do you have copies of those orders?" Shipman asked.

"There weren't any."

Shipman chuckled. "There you go."

"How'd you get the limp?" Willis asked.

"You have my records. Purple Heart's in there."

"Vietnam. Third Marine Expeditionary Force," Taconelli said. "You fell in a pit of punji sticks."

"That's the one."

Taconelli lifted the tail of his dress shirt, exposing a six-inch scar below his bottom rib. "October twenty-third, 1983. Second Marine Division."

Shipman closed his eyes in silent prayer. "Beirut. We lost a lot of brothers that day. Semper fi."

"Oorah," Taconelli responded. "What about Mr. Curran? Did he serve?"

"Not that I'm aware of," Shipman said.

Gillespie said, "Then where did you meet Mr. Curran?"

Shipman chuckled. "It definitely had to do with brothers-in-arms, but not the military. It was August of '85. Pittsburgh. Met him at the Dire Straits concert. We are both guitar nuts."

Willis said, "I saw his studio. He must have twenty guitars."

"He's good," Shipman said.

Willis asked, "How well do you know Casey Connor?"

"She moved in several months ago, I guess. We're friendly. She's a looker, let me tell you."

"We'll take your word for it," Willis said. "There's not one photo of her anywhere."

Shipman chuckled. "Did you see any of me?"

Gillespie drew in a deep breath and asked, "Have you heard the name Eugene DeVine or Bo DeVine?"

Shipman pursed his lips in thought. "Should I have?"

Gillespie said, "He was my partner. He left here on Saturday for Lukeville, Arizona, to find Mr. Curran. He turned up in Tijuana yesterday morning. His head was missing."

Shipman grimaced. "Sorry to hear that. Gangs, you think?"

Gillespie kicked a rock across the drive and walked away.

Shipman said, "Look, gentlemen, if there's nothing else, I'd like to get back to work."

"We'll get out of your hair, Mr. Shipman. Thank you," Taconelli said.

The officers climbed into their cars and started down the drive. Shipman followed on the ATV and waved as they passed. He even shot Deputy Zeller a salute, but it was Taconelli who returned it. Before Shipman could close the gate, he saw the white Ford Explorer back out of Lacey's driveway and peel out, heading his way, and seconds later, Rick Michaels skidded to a stop. The passenger window went down.

Shipman leaned on the open window. "Chickenshit! Didn't want to meet my guests?"

"Brother Bill—it's great to see you." Michaels reached across the seat and shook Shipman's hand, then lifted the beach towel from the passenger seat, revealing two pistols. "Your guests didn't need to see these."

Shipman led Michaels to the top of the drive and into the house then led him into the safe room. Then, he opened one of the standing gun safes, and Michaels placed the beach towel and the two pistols inside but took the digital recorder from the top shelf. Shipman closed the door, spun the dial, then locked up. They met in the kitchen, where Shipman popped open two beers. "How's our boy?" he asked. Michaels gave him an update, and afterward, Shipman said a silent prayer.

Michaels asked, "How'd you manage to hide Angel?"

"I hid the whole damn RV," Shipman said. "State park."

Michaels closed one eye and studied Shipman. "That means someone tipped you off."

Shipman smirked, then tapped his bottle against Michaels's. "This isn't over, is it?"

"It's just getting started," Michaels said.

# CHAPTER 52

Alexandria, Virginia
Wednesday, September 6, 1995
11:40 p.m.

Woody sprung upright when she felt the floor vibrate beneath the bed. Realizing it was the garage door, she listened for familiar sounds and waited for her own heart to calm. A car door slammed, followed by muffled cursing at the state of the garage. The security panel greened as a good code was entered, and the door to the kitchen opened, then slammed closed.

She tied her robe as she started down the stairs, but paused, wondering if he'd be able to see her heart pounding through the silk. She stopped halfway down as Paul gripped the banister and paused when he saw her. They adjusted to each other as if meeting for the first time. Paul didn't have his suitcase.

"I'm glad you're home," Woody said.

Paul restarted his climb, said nothing as he stepped around her, then disappeared into their bedroom.

When Woody caught up, she sat on the bed and watched him. She didn't ask; she didn't want the answer. His actions explained his intentions, as he had opened several drawers in the chest and was digging around in the closet. He emerged with two empty suitcases and a giant duffle bag.

"You're giving up?" she asked.

Paul stuffed underwear and socks into the bag while he spoke. "Going into this relationship, we both knew who and what the other was—and we accepted it. In politics, and in my business, cruelty is sometimes necessary. But not to each other." He dug into his pocket and produced two folded slips of paper and spun them her way.

Woody recognized them as PeKay invoices. One to Relational Excellence for $87,000 and one to BICA for $200,000. Both with the same description of charges: *CONSULTING SERVICES*.

Woody said, "I never intended—"

"Oh no, you don't!" Paul interrupted as he stormed out of the closet, his finger drawn like a gun. "You used our relationship to launder money for Harmon or Curran or— Screw that guy! You made a deal with the devil, and it nearly got me killed!"

"That's bullshit, Paul!" Woody said, bolting from the bed. "Your ego sent you after Curran. *That's* what almost got you killed."

"You lied about Carlos and the money." Paul caught his breath as he squeezed the next words through tight lips and rage. "I can't believe—Trev—I mean, Liam Curran…" After collecting himself he said, "You hired a man who trapped you in our storage room. Who does that?"

"I was desperate," Woody said. "And BICA refused to help me."

"And you still don't know about the blackmail," Paul said.

"Babbs and Bailey are close."

"Who?"

"Forget it," Woody said. "Curran snagged the accountant for the CDG—and she's talking. It's a huge first step."

"You can thank me later for saving your boy's ass," Paul said.

"You're getting paid for that."

"You're damn right I am! Two hundred grand," Paul said, pointing to the invoices. "How much was Harm—I mean, Curran— getting paid to kill me?"

Woody's brow scrunched. "Nothing."

"I rest my case," Paul said.

"I heard he saved *your* ass in the car," Woody said.

"Did Zilo tell you that?" Paul gritted his teeth. "I've been thinking, DeVine was ready to spill something on Curran and his family's past right before he got a bullet in the brain. What is back there that so many die to keep it quiet? Here's the shit of it all. He's at Walter Reed under the good graces of the undersecretary of defense. Who the hell is this guy? I don't know whether to hate him or worship him. But one thing is for damn certain—he's a dangerous son of a bitch. I hope, for your sake, he doesn't hold any grudges. Especially now that he has a head wound driving his decisions."

Paul went back to packing, but Woody thought about Araseli and the fact that Babbs and Bailey were discovering new links every hour. Information she'd love to share with Paul but couldn't now. It was satisfying to admit that maybe, just maybe, her plan would bear fruit. But was it worth the loss?

"BICA is forming an operations group."

Paul's head peeked out of the closet. "You mean like what my firm does?"

"More like—intellectual dynamics," she said.

"Now there's a spin." Paul went back to the closet and asked, "Why does a think tank need an ops group?"

"The enemy has found its way into government."

"Because people like you get them elected!" Paul called out.

It was an intentional sting, but he wasn't wrong. Perhaps accepting the punishment made her next sentence easier. "Ginny asked me to head it up. And I agreed."

Paul reappeared with more clothes to stuff into suitcases. He said, "Your greatest contribution to this country might be abandoning the president's reelection campaign."

Woody said, "Michaels is on board, but Curran—it's too early to tell."

"I saw Curran. He didn't look good."

Woody took a cautious step toward him. "It's almost midnight. Why don't you stay the night?"

Paul ignored her.

"Where will you go?"

"I'll sleep in my office until I find a new place. I'm in hotels most of the time anyway."

"What can I do to stop you?"

"Do you have a flux capacitor and a DeLorean?"

"A what?"

"Forget it." Paul zipped the suitcases shut, and a smothering finality caused her to reach out and touch his shoulder. He stopped, but only briefly, then shouldered the duffle and yanked the suitcases from the bed.

Then, she grinned and said, "*Back to the Future*. I get it. But I don't have a time machine, and my feelings for you haven't changed."

Paul extracted the handle from the suitcases. "And *that's* exactly why I'm leaving. I can't—" But his sentence was interrupted by buzzing in his pocket. Paul pulled out the phone, eyed the display, flipped it open, then turned away before speaking.

Another sting, on target.

After closing the phone, he said, "Your boy checked himself out of Walter Reed."

"I'm glad he's okay."

"I didn't say he was okay," Paul said, then faced her. "Curran wanted me to tell you that he's sorry." Paul dug into his pocket, pulled out a tiny digital recorder, then tossed it to Woody, who caught it after one fumble.

Woody pinched her eyes and sighed as she gripped the tiny, powerful device. "Where did you get this?"

"From Michaels. I guess you're not going to jail after all. At least, not for conspiracy to commit murder." They were his last words before he walked away.

Woody wanted to run after him, but her brain said no. Downstairs, a door slammed, and the floor vibrated again just as her cell phone buzzed from the nightstand.

"Patricia Woodburn," she said.

"Ms. Woodburn? It's Bailey. I hope I didn't wake you, but—we found something. Something big."

Woody thought about her packed schedule in the morning. "Can you give me a summary?"

"No, ma'am," Bailey said. "Not over the phone."

"If I move my schedule, I can be there by noon," Woody said. Bailey agreed, and she closed the phone, wondering how much she could actually dump on Connie Perdew.

Still struggling to corral her thoughts, Woody eyed the recorder, picked it up, then pressed Play and listened to her conversation with Curran. A shudder of residual fear shot through her. She listened again. Then again. After pressing Stop, she deleted the recording, then pitched the device against the wall, sending shards of plastic and chunks of circuit board flying.

She fell back against the pillows and tried to convince herself that whatever Babbs and Bailey had dissected would make everything better—that, by tomorrow, the world would make sense and she could find a target on which to focus her efforts. Then, she thought, *What lies we are willing to tell ourselves for a little false hope.*

# CHAPTER 53



Woody arrived at the Lake early and parked next to Michaels's now familiar white Explorer, and her heart skipped at the memory of the last time they were both here.

As she approached the house, Ginny stepped onto the porch, and Woody noticed right away she had aged ten years in two days. Still, Ginny forced a smile and said, "Babbs and Bailey have been here all night with Araseli." Then, she took Woody by the elbow and pulled her to the side. "Curran checked himself out of the hospital."

"I heard," Woody said.

"And—he's here."

"Here? Now?" Woody said as apprehension tightened her gut at the thought of facing the man she had only seen in shadowy silhouette.

"Is something wrong?" Ginny asked.

"When we last met, he said we should never meet in person—"

Ginny interrupted her. "Trust me—we have more important issues to discuss."

Woody stepped inside, and her attention settled on the huge whiteboard. Babbs and Bailey were both kneeling with markers in their hands, while Araseli, perched on a footstool behind a podium and computer screen, conducted their efforts. Along an empty wall, two card tables accommodated containers of steaming chicken and sides.

"Hello again, Ms. Woodburn."

Woody drew in a breath and turned and saw Rick Michaels holding the kitchen door open. She almost didn't recognize him in jeans, a US Naval Academy T-shirt, and sneakers.

She said, "You should probably call me Woody now."

"Okay—Woody," Michaels said, and his eyebrows danced. "I—brought you a present. Actually, he didn't give me much of a choice."

When the battered face beneath the baseball cap appeared over Michaels's shoulder, Woody drew in a breath of recognition as anxiety sent a shudder through her. All she could manage to get out was, "It's you."

"What's left of me," Curran said, stepping around Michaels.

He looked younger than she expected, but it might have been his attire. His polo shirt strained against his chest and arms and was tucked into a narrow waistband held tight by a rope belt and faded jeans. His feet were stuffed into worn boat shoes—sockless. A few days of beard peppered a strong jaw, and his piercing blue eyes seemed to balance over high cheekbones, smiling in concert with his lips. The brim of his Dodgers baseball cap rose and lowered with his eyebrows, no doubt wondering why she was staring. He started slowly toward her.

"It's good to finally see you. In the daylight, I mean," she said, then wished she could pull the innuendo back. Or, had she subliminally meant it? Standing before her, wrapped in a single package, were two dangerous men: Commander Trevor Harmon, who she had once tried to have killed, and Liam Curran, a ruthless and handsome shadow of the first. Both possibilities sent tingles through her. Through his shirt, the outline of bandages bulged. The cuts and scrapes and gouges on his face and hands and forearms became tally marks of the cost he had paid—for her. When he was close enough, she could smell the musty, masculine danger.

. . .

Liam said, "I don't remember you being this quiet. If you like, I can turn the lights down." He offered a hand, and she reluctantly shook it.

Woody stammered, "I—I didn't expect to see you again."

Bailey stepped over to the group, wrapped her hands around Liam's neck, and hugged him. Then, she stayed by his side, her arm around his waist.

"You didn't really see me before," Liam said as an electric jolt shot from his neck to his temple, and he clenched his eyes until it subsided.

"Are you okay?" Woody asked.

"No, he isn't," Michaels chimed in.

Woody's gaze had drifted to the ballcap and the hint of a stitch protruding near his ear. Her hand reached out, then stopped. "Can I see?"

Liam nodded. "If you must. It's best before you eat anyway." He removed the cap, revealing his new buzzcut and a postage-stamp-size patch over his left ear, shaved smooth. Seven stitches laddered upward, dividing the patch in half. She grimaced, but still let her finger touch the single stitch, which sent another surge into his temple. He pulled away.

"At least he has a decent haircut," Michaels said, breaking the tension. "Did Paul give you the recorder?"

"As he was moving out," Woody said, glancing at Ginny, who stepped forward to join the circle.

"Liam," Ginny said, "Where is Angel Lopez?"

"Tucked away for now. He still thinks I'm protecting him," Liam said as the room blurred, but he blinked it back into focus.

Liam squeezed Bailey tighter, and she returned the gesture by wrapping her arms around his chest. The two of them went back a lot of years now, and in many ways, Bailey had become like a real sister. Worrisome. Demanding. Scolding. Obnoxious, at times. That was why when she peeled herself away and backed up a step,

Liam recognized the fear.

"We have much to discuss," Bailey said with forced professionalism. Her gaze fell to the floor, and when she looked up, it was at Woody. "I hope you know what you've gotten into." She kissed Liam's cheek, then added, "Both of you."

. . .

They filled paper plates with chicken and sides, then slid metal chairs in front of the whiteboard, where dry-erase boxes had been drawn, each connected by multiple arrowed lines. Using a thicker vertical line, the whiteboard had been divided in half vertically. At the top of each side, an underlined title had been written:

*ARASELI'S WEB*          *BABB'S WEB*

In the dead center of the whiteboard, a simple green box had been drawn. Lines with arrows sprouted in all directions like rays of sun in a Dr. Seuss tale. Inside the green box were the letters *PoP*.

Ginny spoke first, and delivered a brief welcome before introducing Araseli to the group. Then she said, "Over the years, BICA has partnered with financial organizations and intelligence agencies to dissect terrorist money-laundering operations around the globe. This effort increased tenfold after Ramzi Yousef bombed the World Trade Center two years ago. What we've come to realize is the networks engineered by the drug and human trafficking cartels are among the most complex. Thanks to Araseli becoming our cartel Rosetta stone, we've been able to fill in many blanks in our earlier efforts." Using the laser pointer, Ginny spun a red circle around the green box. "This organization, ladies and gentlemen, is a key player. And only last night were we able to put the letters *PoP* in the box."

Ginny passed the laser pointer to Bailey, who hesitated before taking it, as a reluctant runner might take a baton in a relay. Bailey glanced at both Liam and Woody again. More fear. More hesitancy. Whatever information she had, it was bursting at the seams to get out, and Bailey was struggling to keep it in.

Bailey tapped the green box and said, "PoP. We know this organization as the Power of Progress. It's a pro-socialist, anti-Americanism organization that funds subversive groups. Countering this group, and others like it, is why Charles Edward Billings founded BICA. "But for now, I want to work from the bottom up. So, let's talk about money laundering."

Pointing to the left side labeled *ARASELI'S WEB*, Bailey said, "Araseli's laundering mechanism for the CDG is one of the most complex we've seen. Dissecting it has revealed direct links between the Mexican government, the CDG, and Manuel Castille's American Latino League. But we also found missing pieces to a larger puzzle BICA has been trying to solve for years. The link between the cartels and the Power of Progress."

Bailey playfully flash-tested the laser pointer on Liam's shirt. He offered a comforting grin before she said, "The CDG relies on laundering processes; what Babbs and her forensic accountant friends call *layering* and *integration*. They create cash-friendly legitimate businesses like laundromats, casinos, vending machines, restaurants, strip clubs, and the like to make it easy to take in legitimate cash and mix in the bad. Also, having multiple accounts at multiple banks allows for many smaller deposits without visiting the same bank over and over.

"Here's a real-life example. Araseli set up four shell companies. One owns laundromats and vending machines, one has a cleaning company, another has a construction company, and the fourth owns a savings and loan. The money from the cash businesses makes its way to the parent account through the banks, then down to the construction and loan companies. It looks like infused capital. Then, the cleaning company bills for services never performed. The loan company can make a business loan to other shell companies or to individuals, then forgive the loan at a loss. Sometimes, the monies are invested in single premium life insurance policies and the principal taken out as a loan. CDG leaders take on jobs at these companies, or positions on the boards of charities, and are paid huge salaries or consulting fees. Which takes us to Castille's American Latino League." Bailey directed the laser pointer to multiple lines leading to larger boxes terminating into a box at the top center of the whiteboard labeled, *A.L.L.*

"The A.L.L. is a legitimate organization separate from Castille's law firm providing free legal services to immigrants while paying Castille huge fees. From Araseli's data, we discovered that the A.L.L. also collects millions from the Power of Progress and diverts those contributions to other charities known to support illegal immigration. Latinos are not the only migrants crossing. Islamic terrorists do too. And, we know there are lawmakers on the payroll of these organizations willing to pass legislation that aids this treason. If you're wondering how politicians hide these payoffs"—Bailey paused, seemingly to gain Woody's attention—"I have a perfect example."

Bailey shifted to the right side of the board and *BABB'S WEB* while making circles around multiple boxes with the laser. "These are all Progressive fronts that funnel money to socialist candidates at local levels. They corral people with like leftist interests, creating PODs so they can target their messaging. These groups don't necessarily like the others, but their single-issue supporters donate for their cause, and they vote how they are told to vote."

Bailey moved to the center of the whiteboard and tapped the green box. "The Power of Progress. They receive most of their money from various PACs (political action committees) formed by well-known corporations. And some extremely wealthy individuals. In turn, the PoP funnels money to groups whose names contain words like *fairness, labor, change, people's, open, green, social,* or *democracy.*"

Liam said, "Thomas Jefferson said, 'merchants have no country.'"

"Amen," Bailey said. "The PoP is the United Way of money laundering supporting the concept of a one-world government."

Ginny rose slowly and went to the front, studied her hands for a beat, then said, "I think we can get to the point now." She seemed to study the room in an attempt to secure the attention of her audience.

Liam looked to his left at Woody, then to his right at Michaels. Babbs and Araseli were both watching him from their position along the wall. Bailey, from the front of the room.

Ginny said, "What you are about to hear cannot leave this room." She then pointed to the lower-right corner of the whiteboard and a small obscure box labeled only with a dollar amount—*$20 billion*. "Patricia…" Ginny said, and when Ginny spoke, Woody's eyes fixed on her mother's. "This is the information you asked BICA to obtain, and it ties directly to the aid package to Mexico."

Ginny nodded, and Bailey picked up a marker and wrote the letters *CEPHU* inside of an empty box.

Woody gasped, then said, "I'll be damned."

. . .

Bailey tapped the box, then said, "CEPHU is a grocery store conglomerate in the Balkans doing business with a bank in Montenegro. CEPHU's chain of stores is owned by the Sidran family in Bosnia-Herzegovina."

"That's Tracy's husband's family," Woody said, massaging her temples.

"Who the hell is Tracy?" Liam asked.

"The daughter of the president of the United States," Woody said. "CEPHU was founded by Danilo Sidran. Tracy married his son, Filip, two years ago. I was at their wedding."

Bailey continued, aiming the laser at a group of boxes. "The day after the aid package was signed, the PoP initiated electronic fund transfers from their bank into these twenty Progressive US-based charities. That move in itself was not strange, as the PoP is known for infusing these groups with cash from time to time. However, over the course of the next month, each of these charities sent multiple EFTs into a single account in a Belize bank controlled by the A.L.L. Ten days later, the EFTs into the Belize bank stopped. Then, only days after that, five EFTs—forty million each—were sent from the A.L.L. account to the Sidran family's trust in Montenegro. Three days later, the Montenegro bank transferred one hundred and eighty million dollars to a private account in Switzerland, leaving twenty million in the Montenegro bank. The Sidran's trust then moved the twenty million into a CEPHU account in the same bank." Bailey paused, drew in a breath, then said, "Three months ago, regular monthly transfers of twenty million dollars began between a bank in Mexico City—owned by the Mexican government—to the account controlled by the PoP. Three payments have been made so far, and we expect at least seven more, totaling two hundred million, or more."

Liam washed his hands over his face. "What you're telling us is this: the Mexican government used the PoP to front a two-hundred-million-dollar investment in the Sidran family, washing money through charities to do it. Then, they sent twenty million into the bank account of their grocery chain and a hundred and eighty million into someone's private Swiss account."

"Exactly! A one percent fee," Bailey said as her eyes drifted to Woody, who was searching the floor and shaking her head.

Liam said, "We'll have to hack into the Swiss banks to figure out who got the bulk of that cash."

"Maybe not," Woody said, her words distant as she asked, "What's the IBAN on the Swiss account?"

Bailey opened a notebook, thumbed a few pages, then started reading off the twenty-one letters and numbers. After she had rattled off the first eleven, Woody interrupted her and said, "Eight, four, nine, one, five, one, six, eight, zero, two."

"That's right," Bailey said, wide-eyed and in disbelief.

"She did that same trick with the GPS coordinates the other

day!" Michaels said. "And to think I was proud of myself when I finished a sudoku puzzle in the can this morning."

Woody ignored the quips. "I was the one who opened that Swiss account. At the request of the president not long after Tracy and Filip were married. This means Castille not only knows about it but was instrumental in making it work *for* the president."

Ginny said, "And Castille is holding it over the president to ensure he signs the Renner-Kline Bill. If he doesn't, Castille can prove the payoff."

"And now, so can we," Woody said, her gaze drifting to Liam, her eyes smiling. "You did it."

"I just retrieved the rock. Araseli, Bailey, and her team squeezed the water out of it," Liam said. As flattering as the compliment was—and now more in tune with what was missing instead of what was on the page, or, in this case, the whiteboard—he knew information had been purposefully left out of Bailey's presentation. He found her sitting by herself in a chair next to the whiteboard.

She must have felt his stare, because she looked up at him just as he waved for her to join them. The fact that she was taking her sweet time getting there spoke volumes.

Liam said, "The PoP group has a bank account somewhere, and that bank is in a country. You left that information out. Can I ask why?"

Bailey said nothing as her eyes met his, then seemed to plead with Ginny. Ginny stepped back and said, "Ladies and gentlemen, could we please have this room?" After Michaels, Araseli, and Babbs had left, she motioned for everyone to sit and addressed Liam directly. "The Power of Progress operates out of Kalopigado, Greece."

"Primo," Liam breathed out. And there it was. The tie to his past that had been festering below the surface. He had suspected Lacey's murder was somehow tied to him, then he'd convinced himself it wasn't. Her death may not have been linked to his operation in Toledo, but it sure picked an even bigger—and more dangerous—bridge to cross. "The money was sent from the banks owned by the Hermes Corporation, right?"

Bailey nodded. "Liam, I'm sorry. I couldn't bring it up in the briefing—" But Liam raised his hand, cutting her off.

"It's okay," he said. "I understand."

"I don't," Woody said. "Not for one second. I know Primo Ruqur. I played golf with him last week in Florida. He was the intelligence source on the guns that we confiscated. We're buying his peso positions as part of the aid package."

"How much?" Liam asked.

"Two billion dollars."

"Then you just got screwed," Liam said. "Primo's Hermes Corporation owns several shipping companies. One of them is Apollo Oceanic. He uses that company to supply weapons to the Balkans."

"To which side?" Woody asked.

"It doesn't matter," Bailey chimed in. "To support his one-world Progressive agenda, he's supporting the fight, not the fighters."

Woody, her gaze suspicious, turned to Liam. "How do you know so much about Apollo Oceanic?"

"I once owned it," Liam said.

"You owned it?" Woody barked. "So, what—you sold it to Primo Ruqur? Is that your relationship with him?"

"It's more complicated than that, but technically—yes."

Ginny said, "I know what you're thinking, Liam. That thread is so thin, it has to be a coincidence."

"Maybe," Liam said as he stood. "But I'm not waiting around to find out. Ginny, please give Araseli and Babbs my best, but I've got some work to do."

Outside, Liam folded his hands behind his neck and fought off the coming headache. He paced the porch end to end, straining to hear the birds or the breeze through the rising pain. What he heard instead was the screen door fly open and Michaels skidding to a stop with Woody on his tail.

Michaels said, "Hey, amigo. Are you okay?"

Liam turned to Woody and said, "I'm going to fix your blackmail problem."

"You've done enough," she said. "I'll take it from here."

"Take what?" Liam said. "From here on out, Castille will always have something dangling over the White House. And that means you—Pattycakes. Plus, if he's tied to Primo Ruqur, then—"

"Then what?" Woody asked. "How do you know Primo?"

"I can't go into that with you. But you need to check into Apollo Oceanic. You'll find the guns."

"Are you saying Primo would buy back the same guns he sold?"

"You're looking at it wrong. His product was the intel he provided to get his peso positions liquidated. After that, the guns are a side venture," Liam said. "My guess is that he took the CDG's money, tipped you off, then bought the guns back, maybe at a steep discount. Trust me—guns in the Balkans are worth more to him than guns in Mexico."

"Okay—so now what, amigo?" Michaels said.

"How much leave do you have before you deploy?"

"Enough," Michaels said. "What do you need?"

Liam said, "First, I need a ride back to Princeton. Then, we're going to have a meeting with Castille."

Woody's eyes shifted between the two men. "I don't think I like the sound of this. How are you going to get close to him?"

Liam said, "I may have a secret weapon."

"Now I'm worried," Michaels said.

"Will you at least keep me updated?" Woody asked.

Liam said, "I hear you'll be our boss soon. So—maybe."

"There's a lot riding on this, you guys. Letting the chips fall where they may is not an option this time."

"Rick and I have a five-hour drive to iron out the details. We'll give you a call later."

Los Angeles, California
Saturday, September 9, 1995
8:07 p.m.

The LA Forum was sold out, and more than sixteen thousand hormone-drowned teenagers were about to be assaulted with lights and skin and costumes and bodies gyrating to overamplified sound. Along the way, some music might sneak in.

The opening act finished, and as the roadies adjusted the stage for the headliner, people flooded the concourses for T-shirts, cups, hats, shot glasses, and other trinkets. At the entrance of each section, volunteers passed out pamphlets and answered questions about HR6363 and the lies being spread by the government to cover up the murder of Rolando Alvarez and a child.

The trifold slicks were gone an hour before the show, and most of them ended up lining the concrete floor beneath the feet of many too young to vote. They didn't care about government or treason or Americanism. They came to hear their favorite songs and to score some weed, even if it was secondhand.

Two men, too old for the crowd, waded through the sea of adolescents to one of the booths, where they purchased two white XXL concert T-shirts. Turning them inside out, one man dug into his pocket for a black marker, and they proceeded to design their own logos. They slipped down the stairs to the floor, showed security their tickets, then made their way through the masses to the front of the stage, where their age would draw the angst of the youth waiting to see the headliner—Sierra.

At 9:20 p.m., the LA Forum fell dark, twinkling with stars of butane flames as cheers rose in anticipation of the thunder that would pass as music. Then, a drum kicked in, followed by a searing guitar chord, as the stage exploded with reds, yellows, and blues. Confetti cannons went off, dancers pranced, and a scantily clad and quite beautiful raven-haired woman rose mystically from beneath the stage floor belting a song neither of the two older men recognized as they prepared for something called a mosh pit.

Sierra finished her first song, something about a friend's boyfriend's jeans, then immediately went into another drum-heavy song about Rio. The stage layout was a T shape, with the middle leg jutting out into the crowd. The lights came up, and the two older men went into action.

One man unrolled his handmade T-shirt and held it by the shoulders high above his head. The second man, wearing a Dodgers baseball cap, did the same. They both stood firm, waiting for what would come next.

"Hey, old fart," one girl screamed. "Why don't you sit in the balcony with the rest of the dads?" The comment was followed by more complaints and a chorus of boos that eventually caught the attention of two security guards. From the stage, Sierra shielded her eyes and spotted the two men. One had short-cropped hair, and the other wore a baseball cap, but her smile bent to a frown when she read the disturbing message on their shirts in black magic marker.

*LACEY SENT US*

Sierra turned away and stomped down the T to the main stage, motioning for a guard. She whispered in the guard's ear, then pointed to the two men in the crowd. The guard disappeared, and a smiling and waving Sierra returned and started her next song. Less than a minute later, two hulking young men in tight Sierra T-shirts with credentials hanging around their necks waded into the crowd. One guard pointed at the man with the Dodgers cap, motioning for him to come forward. Both men lowered their T-shirts as the crowd around them cheered. The barricade parted, and they were let through.

Sierra sang for another ninety minutes before taking a bow and disappearing stage left. She waited for a couple of minutes to see if the cheers would subside. When they didn't, she went out for an encore. Her set list had allowed for three, but after the first one, she decided something more important was waiting for her in the belly of the LA Forum.

The tour manager and two bodyguards escorted Sierra into the cinder-block caverns of the arena to her dressing room, where the two men waited, flanked by two of her security guards.

. . .

Sierra's manager, a Yorkie of a man struggling for breath, spoke first; his English accent croaked with nervous uncertainty. "Who the fuck are you guys?" The earring on his left lobe bounced with each syllable.

Sierra said, "Shut up, Milo. I asked them to come. The T-shirt thing was my idea." She turned back to Liam. "Are you the man I spoke to?"

"Yes," Liam said. "Lacey Sullivan was my neighbor." He looked past Milo and addressed Sierra directly, putting her in charge.

Her eyes wandered over his body. "Lacey said you were growing your hair out," Sierra said.

"Styles change," Liam said.

"Look," Milo said, "I don't know who you are, but you have upset Sierra. She ditched two encores because of you?"

"Ease up, Milo," Sierra said, her eyes drifting between Liam's gaze and the Dodgers cap. "What happened to your face?"

Liam chuckled. "Car accident. Not far from where your brother died."

Sierra's eyes flashed understanding, and she took a cautious step forward, putting herself between the two guards, Milo and Liam.

Milo wasn't convinced and he reached out and gripped her shoulder. "Don't. Can't you see these men are—lunatics?" Milo flinched as Sierra pulled away from his grasp.

Sierra studied Liam for several beats. Then, cryptically, she asked, "What did Lacey like to eat for breakfast?"

Liam's face contorted at the question, but then he understood. "Cocoa Puffs with chocolate milk."

Sierra turned to Milo. "Leave us," she commanded.

Two gold-clad hands went to narrow hips as Milo protested. "I won't allow this. Insurance won't—"

"Get out!" Sierra said, then turned to the four bodyguards. "You can stand outside the door."

"You're not serious," Milo said. He was pacing now, his fingers knotted in highlighted blond locks.

"Don't I look serious? Now, earn your pay in the hallway."

Milo stopped pacing, and his hands shot frantically into the air. "Fine. Fine. Fine. Do what you want. Get killed. Raped. What do I care?" He stormed out, followed by the bodyguards. The last guard stopped short, frowned at Liam, then turned to Sierra.

"I'll be fine. Really," Sierra said, shutting the door behind the man.

Sierra's leather and lace look was impossible to ignore. Her top was a low-cut bustier that pushed her mocha cleavage up nicely. But most impressive was the heaving in her chest and the fire in her eyes. She had dealt with the pansy-ass Milo impressively, and Liam had to give her points for that.

A red cardigan hung on the mirror of her dressing table, and she put it on, crossing her arms as she sat on the padded bench seat, patting her glistening face with a towel. Her eyes wandered between the two men until Michaels plopped into a wooden chair. She swiveled to Liam. "Lacey told me a lot about you."

Liam smiled weakly. "That's funny. Because I haven't heard

shit about you."

Sierra took a tiny photo from the corner of the mirror and passed it to Liam. "That's me and Lacey on Catalina Island a few weeks before she died. I flashed some of our photos together on the jumbotron."

"I noticed." Liam turned the photo over and read the date. It was a Saturday back in April, and he remembered Lacey had told him she would be in DC that weekend. Lacey had lied to protect her relationship with Sierra, just as he and Lacey had lied to protect their own privacy. He passed it back to Sierra, who dropped it into a clutch.

Sierra said, "When my father died, my brother was all alone in Mexico. I could either leave him to a future with the gangs or get him into the States and into college. Because he had been deported before, I consulted with Castille. He said if we could get Rolando here first, he could help him. But what he couldn't do was get him over the border legally. I paid Castille ten thousand to get Rolando into the States. I guess I paid to get him killed."

Liam shook his head. "The price for the coyote was five thousand. The other five thousand probably got stuck in Castille's bank account."

Sierra's mouth opened in disbelief. She drew a breath, then said, "Lacey and I didn't meet until later. It was by accident, actually. I was in the CHS offices, and she had flown in from DC for a different meeting. We started chatting and grew to become good friends. When I finally confided in her about what Castille and I were doing, she tried to talk me out of it. She said that if Rolando used a coyote to cross, it would make things worse legally and could be dangerous. I guess she was right."

Sierra snatched a tissue from a box, then dabbed at the corners of her eyes. "Rolando took a bus to Hombres Blancos to meet the coyote. Rolando was supposed to call me when he got to Lukeville, and I would arrange to pick him up. If something went wrong, he was supposed to contact Lacey. I sent him Lacey's business card, instructions, and a new Dodgers cap. His first taste of America." Sierra went to Liam, and as their eyes met, she reached out, but then stopped; her hand was only inches from his head. "May I?"

Liam nodded, and Sierra removed the Dodgers cap.

She flipped the cap and ran a finger over the band. "I wrote this before I sent it to Rolando."

Liam smiled, realizing Bailey had been right about the handwriting being female. "I thought maybe it was written by a girlfriend who wanted to say, *I love you, Rolando Alvarez.*"

"No," Sierra said. "The initials are mine. My real name is Rosalyn. Sierra was my label's idea."

"It's—lovely," Liam said, drawing a sigh from Michaels.

Sierra smiled back, and Liam felt his heart skip. Her gaze settled on his head and the shaved spot. She stepped closer, and their knees met, their faces inches apart. Sierra touched the stitches. Beneath her touch, the pressure returned, but not the same as before. His hands went clammy. "How bad was the accident?" she asked.

Liam started to reply, but Michaels beat him to it. "He should still be in the hospital."

Sierra asked, "Did this have anything to do with Rolando?"

"Partly," Liam said. "But it's mostly about Lacey."

Her face reddened and her eyes blazed. "The border patrol will pay dearly for what they did, and—" But she stopped in midsentence when Michaels fidgeted and Liam shook his head. "What is it?"

"You'd better sit back down," Liam said.

The butter-smooth forehead wrinkled as she sat in the swivel chair at her makeup table, her palms pressed together in a sandwich between her knees.

Liam picked up the cap from the table and put it back on his head. He said, "The border patrol didn't murder your brother or

Esmerelda. It was a frame. They were actually murdered by the same two CDG assassins hired by Castille to kill Rolando and Esmerelda to gain public support for HR6363.”

“I don’t believe you!” Sierra said. “You can’t possibly prove—”

“It is and I can,” Liam interrupted. “There is a much greater agenda at play. Manuel Castille runs an organization called A.L.L. The American Latino League. When they aren’t representing immigrants in the courts, they are importing third-world votes to American soil. We know all about his organization and the terrorism they support against this country. Your country—now.”

Sierra’s gaze shifted between the men, but she said nothing.

Liam said, “The assassins were two men named Angel and Gerardo Lopez. They murdered the border agents to assume their identities before murdering Rolando and Esmerelda. Ms. Guzman was left alive so she could tell the story about what the border patrol had done. Angel also murdered Lacey and probably his own brother. And now—I know why. Because Lacey was helping you.”

“If publicity and sympathy were Castille’s goals, why not kill me instead?” she asked.

“You don’t kill the goose that lays the gold eggs. Rolando’s death motivated you to raise more money. You have a huge public platform.”

Sierra stood and paced the small room. “This can’t be true,” she said. “It is a government lie! Castille warned me about this. They have concocted a story to—Why are you shaking your head again?”

Liam said, “The bodies of the border agents were dug up by the Arizona DPS. They were murdered *before* Rolando and the child. I know because I’m the one who found their bodies.”

“No. I don’t believe you!”

“The coyote who met your brother—his name was Jesus, wasn’t it?”

Sierra nodded.

"I found him. He's the one who showed me where the border agents were buried. Jesus is now in protective custody." Then he thought, *Sort of.*

Sierra's eyes fell to the floor. "Lacey was my friend. I just can't—believe—that she died because of me."

"It wasn't your fault," Michaels said. "It all goes back to Castille." Then, the door opened, and the round face of a bodyguard peered inside.

"You okay?"

"I'm fine," Sierra said and sniffed. "We need a few more minutes." The bodyguard eyed Michaels and Liam once, then slowly closed the door. Sierra began stuffing items into a duffle bag. She said, "I have to fly to Dallas tonight for my last show tomorrow. You've given me a lot to think about, but I don't know how I can believe any of this."

"How about this?" Liam reached into his pocket, then placed a business card on Sierra's leather-clad knee.

It took a beat for Sierra to register what she was seeing. Then, she recognized the heavy stock of the card and the company name of Castille, Huerto & Sullivan—the name Lacey Sullivan—and a drop of smeared crimson over the company logo. Her eyes found Liam's, and he answered her question.

Liam said, "Yes. It's blood. Most likely, it's Rolando's."

She flipped it over and found Lacey Sullivan's cell phone number scribbled there. "I remember when Lacey wrote this," she said. "Where did you get it?"

Michaels said, "We believe Angel dropped it in Lacey's basement."

When Liam saw confusion on her face, he said, "To cover up the conspiracy, a man named DeVine, who was a mole inside the INS, was sent to kill Angel and Gerardo at Lacey's, but something went wrong. When he showed up, Gerardo was already dead and Angel was gone. So, he picked up the two murder weapons they had left, and he probably picked up that business card too. That's how Angel got Lacey's private number."

Sierra said, "Why wouldn't he leave the guns at the scene? Wouldn't that implicate the Border Patrol more?"

Liam said, "Not if Angel's and Gerardo's prints were on the guns instead of the border agents'. In this case, no evidence was better."

After a heavy sigh and studying Liam's face for an uncomfortable moment, Sierra asked, "You're not a professor or a farmer, are you?"

"I'm actually both," Liam said. He took her hand and led her back to the chair. "I'm also a man who needs your help exposing Castille."

Her eyes fixed on the patterns in the carpet. "What can I do?"

Liam dug in his pocket and produced the phone log and the Excel sheet, then spread them out on the makeup table. Sierra turned in her seat and read where Liam pointed. "Two days before Lacey was murdered, at four twenty in the morning, Lacey called you. Why?"

It took a few seconds, but Sierra said, "She told me that Rolando had called her from Lukeville and was taking a bus to Princeton. I was going to meet them, but Lacey said I shouldn't. That she had an idea to protect everyone legally."

Liam said, "Lacey had never spoken with Rolando, had she?"

"No," Sierra said.

"One of the brothers posed as Rolando on that call."

Sierra rested her elbows on the table and her cheeks in her palms as she took in the phone records. Her fingers traced a few lines, then she tilted her head toward Michaels, who was now standing behind them and looking over their shoulders. Then, she turned to Liam. "You must have known something was up."

"Why's that?" Liam asked.

"If the notes here are correct, it looks like Lacey called you several times."

Liam swallowed and dropped his gaze. "I never answered those calls."

"Because of the woman who moved in with you?"

Liam said, "How did you know that?"

"Girls talk." Then, she reached out and took his hand. "I may seem like an anomaly, but in the end, I'm just a girl."

"Yeah. I noticed," Liam said, then switched gears. "Where is Ms. Guzman?"

"Catarina is staying with Castille," Sierra said. "Why? Do you believe she's in danger?"

Liam said, "Castille knows by now that his plan is falling apart. Jesus has disappeared and the news media is reporting the border agents were murdered and were not the ones who killed your brother or Esmerelda. There's more that I won't go into, but you and—Catarina—are no longer safe either. The bodies of the border agents have been found. Catarina's story no longer holds up. Castille doesn't need her anymore. Witnesses are disappearing, Sierra."

"So you say." Her eyes drifted to the clock on the wall. "I have a plane waiting to take me to Dallas. Lacey was my friend, and if there was a way to prove Castille had anything to do with this, I'll be the first one to testify against him. But I don't—I don't know either of you. How do I know you two aren't the bad guys?"

Liam and Michaels exchanged glances, and Michaels asked, "If we were the bad guys, why would we be here?"

"I don't know," Sierra said. "Why *are* you here?"

"We need you to help us get to Castille," Liam said.

"Make an appointment," she said.

"That's not what I meant."

Her arms folded across her chest as she chewed on her lip, and her gaze went back to the carpet and the swirling patterns. Then, her stare locked onto Liam's sneaker and traced upward until it ended at his eyes. "I still have—questions," Sierra said. Taking a step toward Liam, she held his gaze for several seconds before he looked away. Reaching out, she touched his shirt and pressed into his chest. "The hearts of most men would be pounding right now. But yours is slow and strong. Like a drumbeat."

"What's your point?" Liam asked, forcing himself to look at her, accepting the dare.

She said, "I think you are here to pay a debt—to Lacey. Or maybe you feel like you are protecting me. You seem eager to have me believe you, but in the end, whether I help you or not, you will find a way to get your revenge."

Sierra smiled for the first time, and Liam found it less sexy than warm and confident—an unspoken signal of understanding that revealed the depth of her intelligence and knowledge of people.

She said, "Give me some time to think about this. I promise, I won't call the police."

"I—could care less," Liam said. "But I am concerned about your safety. When I called you, it was from my cell phone, so you have my number."

Sierra said, "There are only ten people in the world who have my personal number. I trust you understand what that means."

Liam said, "And even less have mine."

Sierra took the Dodgers cap from his head. "May I have this?"

Liam nodded. "It's yours anyway."

She smiled, shouldered the duffle, then knocked on the door, and a bodyguard opened it immediately. "I'm ready," she said, and the bodyguard relieved her of the duffle as she pushed the door wide and sped past him. From the hallway, Sierra's voice rang out: "Okay, boys. Let's move." The bodyguard slammed the door closed.

# CHAPTER 55

The LA Forum
Same Day
11:05 p.m.

I like her," Michaels said after the dressing room door slammed. "Now what?"

"We go to the RV and wait for her call."

"You really think she'll call?"

"She has to. How else will the plan work?" He held up a finger while pressing keys on his cell phone, then his PagSat.

"What are you doing?"

"Entering Sierra's into my address book and putting Curtis to work." He pocketed the devices. "Let's get out of here."

After finding their rental car, Michaels climbed in behind the wheel, followed the concert traffic to the freeway, then headed north. Two hours later, they took the exit for Topanga State Park. Michaels pulled in beside the RV. It was Shipman's face that appeared when the door opened. Angel was on the sofa behind him, bound and gagged.

Liam expended every ounce of restraint he had to keep from ripping the little prick's head off his shoulders and mailing it to Castille. He took a step toward Angel, and the man cowered into a fetal ball. Shipman stepped between them.

"Easy, brother," Shipman said. "I know what you're thinking."

Having been on the road for forty-eight hours straight, Liam, Michaels, and Shipman had driven the RV from Princeton to Topanga State Park. Somewhere around Indianapolis, they'd revealed to Angel they knew he and Gerardo were the murderers, changing his status from protected refugee to shitting-himself inmate.

Liam let his anger cool, then said, "Thanks for babysitting."

"Don't mention it," Shipman said. "We got to know each other a little better. Oh, by the way—the little asshole sprinkles de English after all."

Liam ripped the duct tape from Angel's mouth just as his cell phone buzzed. The display showed *HOT TOMALE*, and he held the device up so Michaels and Shipman could see, then stepped outside to take the call, returning ten minutes later. Before anyone could speak, he held up a finger, then dialed his phone. When it was answered, he put it on speaker and said, "Good morning, Curtis. You have me, Michaels, and Shipman here."

"I suppose two o'clock is technically morning," Curtis said. "I'm guessing you want to know about the phone number you texted me."

"That would be nice."

Curtis rattled some pages and said, "The number belongs to a Rosalyn Alvarez. Over the past two hours, she has made two phone calls. The first was to a company called Challenger and Snow Entertainment. It lasted three minutes and seventeen seconds. We checked, and CSE is an agency that manages big-time artists. The second call was fifteen minutes ago—to your number."

"Great job, Curtis. Let me know if there's any more activity." Liam thanked Curtis, closed the phone, then turned to the group. "She didn't call Castille." Liam grinned.

Shipman said, "And that's good because—"

"Now, we're going to help Angel collect his money," Liam said.

"And you have a plan?" Michaels said.

"Yes, *we* do!" Liam said, then glared at Angel.

"You're going to kill me," Angel sobbed. "Please. I am defense-less and—"

"So were your victims," Liam said. "I'm not going to kill you,

Angel, because I want Manuel Castille's head worse and I may need your help." Liam gripped Angel's face. "Did you know DeVine was sent to kill you and your brother—not to pay you?"

Angel's mouth fell open, but he said nothing.

"Just an FYI, I blew his brains out in Mexico. Here's my point. I liked DeVine, and I hate you. Imagine how much easier it would be for me to drive screwdrivers into every hole in your body if you don't do exactly as you're told."

Angel shuddered, then stammered, "I—I will help you."

"I thought you might feel that way," Liam said. "The way I see it, Castille still owes you money. What was the agreed-upon price?"

"Fifty thousand," Angel said.

"Fifty thousand," Liam repeated, fighting off the coming anger. After fisting his eyes, Liam slapped his thighs with his palms, stood, and said, "Okay—let's get you paid."

Shipman cleared his throat and raised his hand like a schoolboy. "Uh—question. How are we going to pull *that* off?"

"Simple," Liam said. "Angel is going to ask Castille for his money."

"Oh! Why didn't I think of that?" Shipman said facetiously. "And how are we going to get close enough to ask this question?"

"Let's step outside, and I'll fill you in," Liam said, then started dialing his phone. "I need to update my new boss first."

CHAPTER 56

---

The White House<br>
Tuesday, September 12, 1995<br>
9:30 p.m.

It was not standard operating procedure. Still, at Woody's request, the president had scheduled a late-day meeting of the National Security Council to follow up on new intelligence relating to the massacres in Chechnya and the war in the Balkans discussed during the morning's PDB (President's Daily Brief).

In attendance were the president, Secretary of State Manchin, Secretary of Defense Vanderhoff, CIA Director Sanchez, Treasury Secretary Carnegie, National Security Advisor Morrow, Attorney General Rittenger, and Woody. The vice president and the secretary of energy were out of the country. Staring into the tired and pissed-off eyes of the member of the NSC, Woody crossed mental fingers and began with the pleasantries and ignored the grumblings and clock watchers.

"Mr. President, team, we have a development concerning arms shipping to the Balkans." She then turned to Treasury Secretary Carnegie, and said, "But before Rit and I begin, if Stanley could please give the team an update on the status of the peso swaps with Primo Ruqur, it would be most helpful."

Carnegie, taken a little off guard, cleared his throat and said, "The transactions have been settled. I don't have the final dollars and cents, but Primo estimated it was a million or two shy of the two billion dollars. Is there something we need to address?"

Woody shook her head. "Not everyone on the team was aware of this, and context was needed for our discussion." She shifted her gaze to Rittenger, signaling that he was on.

Rit said, "This morning, I briefed the team on the cache of guns and shoulder-fired rockets that were quarantined on a ship called the *Carlotta* in Matamoras and the fact the FBI-Mexico Joint Task Force led this effort."

Morrow interrupted. "You just said *were* quarantined."

"That's correct, Admiral," Rit said. "The FBI has credible intelligence that the Mexican government has sold the *Carlotta*'s entire contents to a single buyer."

Though Rit made no eye contact with her, she understood the man was struggling inside, having just told—no matter how white—his first lie to the president. It was true, the FBI had credible evidence, but that evidence had come from BICA and the girls at the Lake. Had Woody made the same claim, the NSC would have pelted her with questions about her sources. Coming from Rit, it was treated as an absolute.

The president asked, "They sold the guns back to the CDG?"

"No, sir," Rit said. He removed a stack of pages from his briefcase; each had a red cover page marked *Top Secret*. He passed one page to each member, then continued. "The Mexican government, through a bank in Belize, sold the contents of the *Carlotta* to the company that owns the ship—Apollo Oceanic. It is a subsidiary of the Hermes Corporation owned by Primo Ruqur."

"Jesus Christ," Carnegie blurted.

Manchin asked, "Can't we seize it on our own?"

Rit shook his head. "The *Carlotta* is now a few hundred nautical miles east of Bermuda, with its final destination set as Sarandë, Albania."

"The Serbs have an elaborate smuggling operation there," Morrow said. He turned to the president. "Primo Ruqur is arming the enemy of NATO with the same guns we confiscated—on intelligence he gave to us in trade for relieving his peso positions."

"Yessir," Rit said.

Woody sat back and read the room, but no one understood as well as she the real pressure the president was now under. Pressure to do absolutely nothing.

The president said, "Team—I want to know all our options one week from today. Political, military, economic—everything. The *Carlotta* is still a long way from Albania, so we have time. Woody, make it happen."

Woody said, "Sir, I'm not a shipping expert, but in a week, the *Carlotta* will be at least two thousand miles closer to Albania— somewhere around the Azores."

"Woody's correct," Sanchez chimed in. "Sir, I'm sure we can have a working outline by tomorrow."

The president closed his eyes in thought. When he opened them, they burned with anger at Woody. "Fine. Let's make it tomorrow."

The meeting adjourned, and Woody waited until everyone had left the Oval Office and the president was behind the Resolute Desk shuffling papers to keep from looking at her. She knew he wanted to jump down her throat for second-guessing him in front of the team. She also knew the president didn't understand why she had done it, but he was about to find out.

"Mr. President, I need another minute of your time."

"Can't this wait?" he asked.

"No, sir," Woody said as she closed the curved door. "Renner-Kline goes to the House floor in the morning for a full vote."

"And it will pass the House and squeak by the Senate," the president said. "Then, I have to sign it. We've been through this already."

"Things have changed," she said, removing a single page from her portfolio, then placing it in front of the president. He read it in less than a minute, then looked up at her with rage.

She said, "The Associated Press already has it—sir. Tomorrow morning, the world will know that Manuel Castille was responsible for sanctioning the assassination of two border agents; one of his own lobbyists, Rolando Alvarez; and an infant named Esmerelda Guzman. And—they'll know why. They'll also think that the Mexican government paid him millions to do it. The AP has copies of phone records, emails, bank transfer records, and ballistic reports. They have details on the money trail from Mexico to Primo to Castille to numbered accounts in Montenegro and Switzerland. What they don't have are the names on those accounts. CEPHU—and yours." When the president's face went white, she said, "I know about the two hundred million dollars you took from Mexico."

The president collapsed into the chair, leaned back, stared at the ceiling, and said, "You little bitch! Do you know who you are fucking with?"

"Absolutely. I'm fucking with an enemy of the United States that I helped put into the presidency. You've compromised this office with that payoff. Castille is using his knowledge to force your signature on a bill, and Ruqur knows you wouldn't dare stop his guns going to the Balkans."

"And now you're using the same information to pin me from this side. Damned if I do—damned if I don't, is that it?" the president said. He opened his mouth to speak, but the curved door opened, and Press Secretary Carl Mahoney's face appeared. "Give us a second, will you, Carl?" the president said.

Mahoney glanced worriedly at Woody, then said, "Something important has—"

"One—fucking—second!" the president barked, and after the door closed, he turned to Woody. "So, now you have a seat at the big table. What's your price?"

"Not a dime," Woody said. "But this *can* go away."

"Enlighten me."

"The AP *will* release the story they have. But without my information, it won't lead to CEPHU, Tracy, or you. Only Castille will burn. The House will reconsider its vote, and if it still passes, the margin will be small. And, if by some miracle it gets through the Senate, you're going to veto it. Connie has already polled, and there aren't enough votes to override you."

"Veto it?" the president said. "After we've put our full weight behind it?"

"After the news breaks tomorrow," Woody said, "you'll have a change of heart, and the White House will get behind the Senate's TABS Bill."

"I see," the president said. "And if I don't, you release what you know to the press."

Woody didn't answer the question. At this point, she couldn't trust herself to control her own rage. And there was still one more elephant in the room, and she wondered if he was smart enough to recognize it. He was.

"You haven't thought this through very well, have you?" he asked, lacing his fingers behind his neck. "If I veto that bill, Castille will spill the rest to the press. It's coming out, one way or another. So, ask yourself this question: Would I rather go head-to-head with Castille and a billionaire, or you?"

Woody held is gaze as long as possible until she couldn't hold back the smile from forming on her lips, and one on the president's lips melted. She said, "You know me better than that. By the time the story hits the press, I'll be the only player on this side of the net. I guarantee it."

The president crumpled the press release, threw it at her, but missed. He stood and straightened his jacket. "I can't believe you're cashing in a huge chip for one immigration bill."

"I'm not cashing it in," she said. "I'm putting it in the bank until the day you leave office. I'll be resigning effective this November, and I *won't* be running your reelection campaign."

She checked the grandfather clock: 10:10 p.m. Woody picked up the wad of paper from the floor and said, "Carl wants to talk about the AP story. I suggest the White House has no official response. Good night, sir."

Woody opened the curved door to leave but glanced back momentarily at the president, who was fumbling for something in his coat pocket. She smiled and gently closed the door. Mahoney was waiting in the outer office.

"We know about the story," Woody preempted.

"Are you leaving?" Mahoney asked. "You need to be in this discussion."

"It's been discussed," she said.

Mahoney eyed her curiously before slipping into the Oval Office and closing the door behind him. As the latch clicked, she steadied herself against a desk as nausea danced in her gut. She waited until she had reached her car to flip open her cell phone and make the call to Curtis.

She said, "Did the president call him?"

"He did," Curtis said. "At ten fifteen, a call from an unavailable number went to Castille's cell phone. He didn't answer. Then, the same number called Castille's phone in his house."

"Could you hear the conversation?"

"Not from here," Curtis said, then chuckled. "They're taking care of it. Please be patient, Ms. Woodburn. And have a little faith."

"Curtis…" Woody said, "I'm only praying that Curran is half as smart as we think he is. If he's not—I'm dead."

# CHAPTER 57

---

Beverly Park, California
Same Day
6:30 p.m.

On the lanai, overlooking his view of Laurel Canyon, Castille addressed his two dinner guests in Spanish. *"Señoras, bebamos a nuestro éxito."* (Ladies, let us toast to our success.) Castille raised his wine glass, then said, "Tomorrow, the House will pass HR6363 and send it to the Senate." He touched glasses with Catarina Guzman, sitting to his left, who then touched her glass to Sierra's, sitting to *her* left. Castille glanced across the table at Sierra and said, "I'm glad you suggested this dinner, Sierra. And congratulations on finishing the first leg of your tour."

While Castille and Catarina sipped, Sierra fiddled with her goblet, observing the sloshing red liquid against the glass. "I'm not so sure," Sierra said. "The press is reporting that CDG assassins murdered Rolando and Esmerelda, not border agents. Our lawsuit is in jeopardy, and perhaps Congress is no longer so sympathetic."

Castille said, "The momentum is with us, and Congressman Renner has assured me the votes are there."

"Maybe," Sierra said. "But a reporter from the Associated Press called my assistant earlier today asking that I respond to a story being released in the morning—about you."

Castille put the wine glass down. "What are they saying?" he asked, cutting into his filet.

"I haven't called the reporter back."

Catarina Guzman's gaze volleyed between Sierra and Castille as she fidgeted uncomfortably in her new Halston evening gown.

Sierra had dressed down this evening. Skinny jeans and a long green blouse with a thin silver belt wrapping her tiny waist.

Castille said, "Let my office handle the AP."

Sierra's jaw muscles worked as she glared at Castille from across the table. Her body craved the wine, but her now trembling hands prevented her from reaching for her glass. "I need to use the restroom," she announced, leaving the table and closing the French doors behind her.

Castille watched Sierra leave, then turned his attention to Catarina. Still speaking Spanish, he said, "You haven't said much tonight."

"I'm still mourning Esmerelda," she said. "But I am so grateful for all you have done. For taking me into your home—and—for your love." Her eyes dropped momentarily. "It doesn't matter what the press says. I was there when the agent shot my baby."

Castille touched her hand tenderly and said, "We know the truth."

Sierra returned, and Castille's gaze went from Catarina to Sierra, noticing her amazing form in those jeans and then her wonderful brown eyes. Eyes that were looking away from him and toward the French doors and the sudden appearance of a new guest.

Castille's smile melted. He leaned back, crossed his legs, then lay his trembling hands calmly across his knees. He didn't recognize the short, stocky fireplug of a man. But Catarina did.

Catarina leapt from her chair, her back arched against the railing and the hundred-foot drop to the shadowy forest below. "It is you!" she screamed, pointing a trembling finger. "You murdered Rolando." Then, she turned back to Castille for help, but his gaze was fixed on the guest. Picking up a steak knife, Catarina made a move toward the man, but Castille caught her in a bear hug and pulled her into his lap.

"Calm down," he whispered.

"This man is Agent Penn," Catarina screamed.

"No," Sierra said. "His name is Angel Lopez."

Castille picked up his cell phone and started to dial a number but stopped when the man drew a semiautomatic pistol from the small of his back.

In Spanish, Angel said, "Put the phone down."

Castille hesitated, weighing his options. When his eyes focused on the pistol, he closed the phone and slid it across the table, and Sierra stopped it from falling to the floor.

Angel said, "You owe me fifty thousand dollars. I want it now!"

Sierra glanced up, the pistol directly over her head.

Castille said, "If you put the pistol down, we can work this out."

Angel jabbed the pistol at him. "You will get me my money, then I will leave."

"Fine," Castille said. "I have the money in my safe." He guided Catarina back to her chair, then, with his hands raised, started toward the French doors. Angel backed up to let him by, then followed Castille into the house.

. . .

Once they were out of sight, Sierra reached into her clutch and removed a small electronic device, and placed it on the table while a curious Catarina watched. Sierra pushed a button, spun a dial, then pressed an index finger to her lips, signaling for Catarina to remain quiet as Spanish radiated from the speaker.

Castille: "How did you get past my security?"

Angel: "Shut up and get my money."

Castille: "DeVine was supposed to pay you."

Angel: "No. DeVine was supposed to kill me. You owe me for the border agents, Rolando, the child, and the lawyer. I lost my brother too."

In the background, a door slammed closed and a chair squeaked. Something slid open.

Castille: "Where did you disappear to?"

Angel: "Hiding. Shut up and give me my money."

The sound of metal against metal came through the speaker.

Castille: "You were supposed to leave the guns at Lacey's."

Angel: "I did."

Castille: "They weren't found." After a long pause, he asked, "Is that one of the pistols?"

Angel didn't answer.

More metal against metal, then more chair squeaks.

Castille: "Five, ten, fifteen, twenty, twenty-five, thirty, thirty-five, forty, forty-five, fifty thousand. Now get your ass back to Matamoras, call Juan, and tell him what happened."

Paper slid against wood.

More squeaking, then leather against wood.

Castille: "You didn't bring a bag? Here."

Bustling sounds, then a zipper. Then footsteps. Then a door opened.

Angel: "Fuck you, Manuel."

Footsteps trailed off, and the speaker went quiet.

Sierra leaned away to look inside the house and caught a glimpse of Castille and Angel. They disappeared around a corner toward the foyer. Both women eyed the device on the table.

"I—I do not believe it," Catarina said.

Sierra said, "Neither did I."

Then, at 7:15 p.m., Castille's cell phone vibrated on the table. Sierra eyed the number on the display—*UNAVAILABLE*—then tossed the cell phone over the railing. Inside, a door slammed, and Castille approached but then stopped, his head turning toward his office as ringing came through the speaker of the device. Castille held up a finger, then walked away. Then, on the device, Castille's voice answered the call.

Castille: "Manuel Castille."

Pause.

Castille: "This isn't a good time. Our missing man showed up alive and—"

Pause.

Castille: "The press tried to contact me as well. Calm down and let me call you back."

A chair squeaked, a door slammed, and the device went silent.

When Castille returned to the lanai, he did so with a wide grin, returning to his seat while Catarina's eyes burned through him.

Castille announced, "I got rid of our guest." He paused, drank some wine, swished it, then rested his chin on tented fingers. He gave Catarina's fury cursory notice before glancing toward Sierra. "You let Angel inside, didn't you?"

Sierra nodded, then picked up the device and waved it in the air. "We heard everything you said, Manuel."

"What do you think you heard?" Castille said and took a bite of steak.

"You can't spin this. Not with me," Sierra forced out through gritted teeth.

Catarina asked, "Why have you done this, Manuel?"

Castille ignored Catarina, and asked, "Where are my guards and my chef? Seems everyone has suddenly taken the night off."

Sierra stood and let the breeze filter through her hair. It was the first time in months she felt in control and not like a player in someone else's game. Reaching out, she put her hand on Catarina's shoulder as the woman glared at Castille as her hand gripped the steak knife on the table. Then, she lunged across the table, knocking dishes and candles to the floor.

Castille was able to catch Catarina's wrist. He wrenched the knife from her hand, pulled her from the table, then sent her flying across the lanai into Sierra's arms. Satisfied she wasn't coming at him again, Castille laced his fingers behind his head, and said, "You've been busy, Sierra."

"You don't know the half of it," Sierra said. She turned toward the French doors, where a large, muscular Caucasian man now stood.

"*Hola*, Manuel," he said, his voice deep and calm. A silenced pistol in the man's hand dangled near his thigh. The man stepped to the side, and Angel reappeared behind him.

"And who the fuck are you?" Castille asked.

"This is Liam Curran," Sierra said. "He's the man Lacey was dating. I mentioned him during our lunch."

"Are you some kind of investigator?" Castille asked. He picked up his wine glass, which caused Liam to raise the pistol.

"Easy," Castille said as he sipped. "Let's everyone stay calm. What is it you want, Mr. Curran?"

Liam chuckled. "Your head on my wall," he said, staying in Spanish for Catarina's benefit. "The AP has a story coming out in the morning. It should be a good one. CDG assassination of border agents, Rolando, the baby, Lacey. Jesus and his grandmother have given their statements to the reporter."

"Araseli?" Castille hissed, his eyes narrowing with rage.

"That's right," Liam said. "And she's the reason we know about the president's payoff and you helping to launder it for him. And now, you're using the information to blackmail him into signing the bill. And—I know about Primo Ruqur."

"You naïve gringo! Never able to see the war through the battles. It does not matter what you know; it's what you can do. And that is nothing. Every year, my people flood the southern border in the millions regardless of what you know."

Liam chuckled. "When you were on the phone, did the president tell you he would be vetoing the bill?" He paused to let Castille catch his breath, then said, "Yes. I know it was the president. The bill may pass the House, but not the big white one."

Castille sat with his knees crossed and his hands twitching in a perpetual state of shock. Still, the smirk on his face said he wasn't finished. "You have a very powerful enemy, Mr. Curran. Or is it Ó Corráin?"

When Liam heard the Irish version of his family name, he drew

in a breath, realizing his involvement had just been pushed beyond
bringing down Castille. He had bigger issues now.

Liam turned to Sierra. "You should take Catarina to the
bedroom and help her pack."

Sierra glared at Castille as she stood, then spat in his direction.
"I will see you burn, if it's the last thing I do."

Castille said nothing.

Sierra took Catarina's hand and led her around the table.
As they passed Angel, Catarina kneed him in the groin, and he
doubled over in pain. Sierra managed to gain control of Catarina,
and they disappeared into the house.

When the women were gone, Castille turned to Angel, who
was still recovering from the knee. "And you! Juan will take care
of you. Mexico will be the last place you can hide. You will be
running for the rest of your short life."

Struggling to stand upright, Angel coughed as he spoke. "Juan
is my cousin. I have nothing to fear from—"

The gunshot sent crisp waves echoing off the hills and bouncing
down the canyon. Castille dropped to his knees beneath the table,
while Liam dove into one corner as glass shards rained down on
him. Angel, whose back was to the French doors, fell face-first
into the Sierra's dinner plate.

. . .

The shot had come from inside the home. The large caliber
round had taken out a glass panel in the French doors, then entered
the back of Angel's head, sending him violently forward onto the
table, where his chest and face landed in Sierra's unfinished sea
bass. He slid to the ceramic-tiled lanai floor, coming to a stop
next to Liam with a thud. Lifeless eyes fixed on a point beyond.

Through the one open door, inside the house, Sierra stood
frozen in shock, her shaking hands pressed to quivering lips. In
front of her, Catarina Guzman was holding the still smoking

Beretta Liam had left on the dresser in the bedroom. Their plan had worked. She had avenged the death of her daughter using the same pistol. Liam nodded with satisfaction, but now it was time to regain control of the situation.

After Catarina pulled the trigger, the Beretta had recoiled over Catarina's head, but she had recovered nicely and was now creeping closer to the French doors, in search of her next target. Liam knew her heart was set on Castille, but Liam had other plans.

Castille had dove beneath the glass table, where he still cowered. Catarina took another step toward the lanai as she tried to negotiate the angle for the shot. Before she could lock onto Castille, Michaels arrived behind her and wrapped up Catarina in his arms, peeling her fingers from the pistol's grip.

Liam stepped inside, where Sierra was still frozen, her gaze locked on Angel's corpse. He pressed Sierra's face into his chest, and said, "Don't look at him." He helped her to where Michaels had Catarina in almost the same position. Michaels took Sierra in his free arm.

"Where's Shipman?" Liam asked.

"Waiting for the call," Michaels said.

"Good. Get these two out of here."

Michaels nodded. "Roger that, amigo. I'll catch up with you on Mulholland." He led Catarina and Sierra from the room and then out of the house.

Liam raised the silenced .22 Ruger and stepped onto the lanai, where Castille still crouched under the table. The man hadn't moved, and his gaze remained fixated on Angel's corpse.

"Get up!" Liam demanded, switching to English. He stepped around the table, and when Castille didn't move, Liam aimed the pistol at the man's knee. "You're going to lose it in five, four, three…"

"Please, please," Castille cried out as he slid from under the table. Using the railing, he stood with his hands raised in surrender.

His knees buckled as if to keep from pissing himself.

Liam said, "We need to have a serious talk. But first, you need to understand that each lie will result in pain. Understand?" And he stabbed the silencer against Castille's knee.

Castille nodded.

"Good. I know that you sent Angel and Gerardo to kill Lacey. I just don't know why." When Castille hesitated, Liam counted, "Three, two, one—"

"Wait! Please," Castille begged, holding up a palm and drawing in a breath. "I found out Lacey had been lobbying for the Senate bill instead of Renner-Kline. Then, when I found out she was secretly working with Sierra, I realized she was jeopardizing the operation. She was never supposed to get hurt."

"And Rolando, Esmerelda, and Catarina?" Liam added.

Castille closed his eyes. "Rolando's death was for public sympathy. Killing a child was a multiplier. Catarina was left alive to become a witness against the border patrol." Then, Castille began to sob.

"Here's the shit of it," Liam said. "Your plan was working until Jesus showed me the bodies in the desert."

"You?" Castille asked. "Who the hell are you?"

"I'm the ghost in the machine," Liam said. "You know the old saying: If you want God to laugh, make a plan."

Castille glanced over the railing and into the darkness below. "I don't understand how you got involved."

"Your boy, DeVine, begged me to help him find Angel. So, I did." He gripped Castille's jaw and spun him around, glaring into his fearful eyes. "I thought that was damn funny."

Castille swallowed and fisted his eyes. "What do I do now? Get down on my knees?"

"Trust me. I'm showing great restraint in not killing you. But it's not your time."

"And who decides?" Castille asked. "The people pulling your

strings? There is a dead man on my lanai from a gun I do not own. The police will believe what I tell them. You can't just walk away from here. Your plan makes no sense to me. What is it you are not telling me?"

"We're not done," Liam said. "You mention the name Ó Corráin. Where did you hear it?"

Castille shook his head. "Mr. Ruqur mentioned it to me one evening. I didn't know why at the time. It seems you have some history with him. Can I ask what your relationship is to Primo?"

"No—you can't," Liam said. "I'm going to leave now and let you clean up a little." Liam tucked the .22 Ruger into his waistband. "Before I do, I want to put a little bug in your ear. Tomorrow, when the AP releases the story, you'll have nowhere to go. And the information you have on the president? If I were you, I'd sit on it until you need a get-out-of-jail-free card. His reelection is next year, so your prison term will be short and cushy. Now, sit down, finish your steak, and"—Liam glanced down at Angel's body—"enjoy the company."

Liam picked up the electronic device from the table, then backed away through the French doors, and disappeared.

# CHAPTER 58

Paralyzed by fear, Castille existed in the blur between his own life and Angel's corpse in a heap on the far side of the lanai. A man whose life had mimicked his own in many ways. Bookends of the same war. From the time of his youth in Juarez until now, what had they been but manipulators and survivors? Had Angel's end been but a prophecy of what awaited him? And if not, *What in the hell had just happened?*

Struggling to his chair, Castille let his mind clear and realized— once again—that he had survived. And the outcome may prove better than he could have planned. Rolando was dead. Gerardo was dead. Angel was dead. Lacey was dead. The border agents were dead. Even DeVine was dead, which put an exclamation point on the plan. The rest was manageable. It was all optics. It was marketing. It was politics.

Sierra could tell her fabulous tale, play her recording, but in the end, he had been the one who was robbed at gunpoint and had to deal with the mental anguish of a murder committed in his home and the dead man stinking up his patio. He could even prove that Sierra had helped facilitate it.

Castille searched the lanai for his cell phone but soon gave up. Holding on to the railing, he made his way around the lanai, stepped over Angel's corpse, then went inside.

First, he locked the front door and retreated to the safety of his office, where he took the cordless phone from its stand and stabbed the Send button. The dial tone howled in his ear, offering a surprising sense of normalcy. His finger hovered over the 9 button before he changed his mind and pressed the 1 button instead, then ten more digits. Still shaking from the adrenaline, he managed to press the phone to this ear.

"Rockman," the Albanian accent answered. Even through Castille's spite for the man, he found his voice oddly comforting.

"It's Manuel Castille. I need to speak with Primo." A long pause ensued. No doubt the Albanian was himself deciding the importance of the call.

Finally, there was a response. "One moment."

Castille waited for what seemed like an hour before a series of clicks and a hybrid Greek American accent came on the line. "This is Primo Ruqur."

"Mr. Ruqur? It's Manuel Castille. There's been a development."

For the next few minutes, Castille brought the billionaire up to speed on all that had occurred. With every syllable, Castille's breath stammered and his heart skipped as more adrenaline rushed in, his angst building at not being able to see the powerful man's face as he spoke. What he heard was far more terrifying.

"Stay calm, Manuel," Primo said. "You are the victim of a crime and should react as any innocent person would to a break-in and murder in their home. Call the police. And as for Mr. Ó Corráin, he is not your concern. Mr. Rockman is skilled at managing these matters and will arrive tomorrow."

"Rockman?" Castille said. "I see no need for him to—"

Primo interrupted. "It is not a request. Now, hang up the phone and call the police like a normal person."

The phone went dead.

Castille closed his eyes and tilted his head back, wishing away the events to come. Not the police or the questions or the investigation or the AP story. He'd handled much worse before. Perhaps calling Primo Ruqur from his office phone hadn't been the smartest move.

*Where the hell was his cell phone?*

He'd worry about that later. Gjon Rockman would be here in

five hours—to "manage" the crisis. Not Castille's crisis, but the crisis *he* had caused. And that meant one thing: Rockman was coming to kill him.

After staring at the buzzing device in his hand, Castille let his fingers hit 911, then pressed the green Send button, and immediately a man's voice answered.

"Nine-one-one. What's your emergency?" the operator said.

"There's been a break-in and a shooting. Please hurry."

"Okay. Calm down, Mr. Castille. Is the intruder still there?"

"No. They're gone—I think. Just please hurry. A man has been shot."

"Thank you, Mr. Castille. We have police and an ambulance on the way."

"Hurry," Castille said before the phone went dead. He checked his watch to time the arrival of the police. *Ten minutes, maybe*, he thought. After all, this was Beverly Park. And Beverly Park paid high taxes for the best cops. His next call was to his accountant to liquidate accounts and move money around overseas and make arrangements to run. The phone rang several times, but Castille's accountant man never answered.

His next move was not to play his biggest trump card but to secure it. Contrary to Curran's suspicions, he had never intended to use the evidence he had against the president as blackmail. Why would he need to? What Castille needed now—as Curran had suggested—was a way to secure a pardon if need be. And if he couldn't get out of the States by the time the AP story hit in the morning, his US passport could be flagged, severely hindering his movements.

At his desk, Castille swiveled to the credenza, then pressed the hidden button behind a section of trim. Gears whirred, and a section of the wall beneath the credenza opened, revealing a safe. He manipulated the lock and tried it, but it didn't open. Realizing his shaking fingers had betrayed him, he wiped them on his shirt and tried again. This time, the safe door opened, and he reached deep inside, felt for the thick envelope, then pulled it out. For the first time, he felt the energy exuding from the simple rectangular piece of manila pulp, which housed so much power it seemed to radiate. Now, he needed to get his ass to Mexico.

With the envelope in his lap, he leaned against the arm of the chair and pressed to get up but stopped when he sensed the presence behind him and the cold steel pressing against the back of his neck. Castille collapsed into the chair and raised his hands as an icy voice sent chills up his spine. A hand in white surgical gloves appeared over his shoulder and took the envelope from his lap. At the corner of his eye, the demon reappeared.

"I—I thought you had left," Castille stammered.

Liam tucked the envelope under his free arm and dropped a thinner one onto the desk. "I forgot to give you your present." He gripped Castille's shoulder and spun him around in the chair. "It's really more of a trade. One envelope for another."

Castille picked up the envelope in shaking hands, and inside, he found several pages of computer printouts. He thumbed through them briefly, then asked, "What am I looking at?"

"Phone records, mostly," Liam said. "And some emails between you and Congressman Renner and Senator Kline. Between you and DeVine. You and Angel. Angel and Lacey. Angel and DeVine. There are screenshots proving money transfers between banks. The envelope was hand-delivered to your mailbox—probably. You were shocked when you opened it."

"I take it this is the same evidence the AP has?" Castille asked.

"Pretty much," Liam said.

"And why are you giving this to me?"

"It's not for you," Liam said. "It's for the cops. To save them a lot of time and taxpayer money trying to figure out your motive."

"Motive for what?"

"For something you haven't done—yet." Liam reached across

the desk, gripped Castille's head in both hands, and, in one swift motion, slammed the man's forehead down.

. . .

Standing behind Castille, Liam retrieved the Beretta from the small of his back—the same one that had once belonged to Agent Penn, and the same one used to kill Rolando Alvarez and Lacey Sullivan. He placed the pistol in Castille's right hand, gripped a handful of hair, then lifted his head up and slightly back. Wrapping his free hand around Castille's while it still gripped the Beretta, he lifted it until the barrel was beneath the man's chin. That's when he saw the three figures standing in front of the floor-to-ceiling window.

He saw Lilliana first—still in her nightgown and slippers as she had been in Baghdad and always appeared in his dreams. Her sleepy eyes narrowed with condemnation. Lacey Sullivan was there too. She had gathered up her long black hair and draped it over one shoulder, letting it fall over a breast. He loved it when she did that with her hair. It was like an ebony waterfall hiding a buried treasure. Standing between them was a faceless infant girl still attempting to take her first step. One tiny hand held by Lacey, and the other, by Lilliana. He assumed the infant was Esmerelda. His mind's eye drifted back to Lacey, and she smiled, melting his heart all over again.

Then, in an instant, Mika's voice echoed in his head: *Sometimes, I lay awake and listen to you dream. Mostly it is only murmurs, but I already know the story. It's the little girl. Sometimes I want to wake you, but then I think you should let them play out.*

Liam thought, *Now is a great time to wake me. But where are you?*

Mika may know the story, but she didn't understand it. She wasn't in Baghdad when Lilliana and her mother were poisoned. She didn't know what it was like to wake up in the middle of the night, swimming in the sweat of guilt over the death of a beautiful child. And she certainly couldn't understand how baby Esmerelda would only multiply his exhaustion. Two lives never lived. Problems never solved. Joy never embraced. He needed to silence the nightmares—all of them—once and for all. To make amends. Pay the penance he owed. And to ultimately protect Catarina Guzman, who was, without a doubt…the last witness.

# CHAPTER 59

BICA Headquarters
Washington, DC
September 15, 1995
9:30 a.m.

Curtis was waiting for Liam on the other side of the air lock. Even through the smoked glass, he could tell the man's foot was tapping, his eyes checking a watch. When the door opened, Curtis started walking and said, "What did you do?"

"Can you be more specific?" Liam asked.

"The admiral is here."

Liam pulled and held a breath. At the Pentagon, admirals were a dime a dozen. But in the halls of BICA, *admiral* meant only one person. "Wild Bill is here?" Liam asked.

Curtis raised an eyebrow. "How long has it been for you two?"

Liam shook his head, but thought, *At least two years. When I was Trevor Harmon.*

When they reached Ginny's office, Curtis stayed in the outer office and closed the door behind Liam. Today, Ginny was holding court in the sitting area, where four chairs straddled a coffee table, two on each side. Ginny worked the serving cart and smiled when she saw Liam as she served coffee to the two filled chairs with their backs to him. One chair, he could only make out a feminine arm on the rest. In the second, a man's bald Black head protruded well above the back of the Queen Anne.

The feminine arm moved, and Woody stood to meet him. Her eyes were softer and welcoming, and for the first time, he detected a hint of girl beneath the professional and prickly exterior of a woman who had once tried to have him killed. She gave him a light hug before her attention settled on the manila envelope.

Liam held it out, and she took it. He said, "Merry Christmas."

Woody started to speak, but instead, she let her eyes smile, then she drew in a breath and simply nodded.

Ginny placed a coffee cup at the empty chair, and said, "We were starting to worry."

"*They* were worrying," the booming voice said from the other chair. "I came for the free donuts." The imposing bald Black man stood and turned to Liam, his sport coat waving like a tent in the wind around his massive six six frame.

Retired Rear Admiral William Randolph, affectionately known as Wild Bill, was now referred to by DC types as Undersecretary of Defense Randolph. When Liam was still Commander Trevor Harmon, William Randolph had been more than just a mentor and superior officer. He and his wife, Annika, were Trevor Harmon's adopted parents. When BICA had orchestrated the fake death of Trevor Harmon, Wild Bill and Annika had played the part of grieving parents in Oscar-worthy fashion.

Randolph took two long steps and embraced Liam warmly, delivering several pounding backslaps with hands the size of plates. "It's good to see you again. I suppose I have to get used to calling you Liam—again."

"I remember when you had trouble calling me Trevor." Liam poked Randolph in the belly. "Civilian life agrees with you. How's Annika?"

"I told her I was coming to see you, and she cried. She thinks your exile is over and you can visit again."

"I'll find a way. I promise."

Liam took the empty chair, sampled the espresso Ginny had placed there, then pointed at the envelope still in Woody's grasp. "I read it. And it's damning. If it got out, it could convince a lot of congressmen to call for the president's impeachment." Then, he saw Ginny and Woody exchange telling glances, and asked, "What now?"

"We've all heard the recorded conversations from Castille's—the handheld device and the box Shipman put on Castille's phone line," Woody said. "When the president called Castille, he was clearly unconcerned about Castille releasing information on him. But he was terrified by what *I* had on him."

"Meaning what, exactly?" Liam asked.

"The president wasn't being blackmailed by Castille," Woody said. "I think he wanted me to believe he was being blackmailed so I would think he was being forced to sign the bill. That way, I'd stay with him through his reelection campaign. The fact that you uncovered an actual bribe was pure happenstance."

A grin leaked to his lips, and Liam said, "I'll be damned. I was right."

"About what?" Ginny asked.

"Being my usual smart-ass self and suggesting to Castille he leverage the evidence for a pardon," Liam said, motioning toward the envelope. "He intended to take that with him when he left the country."

Randolph cleared his throat. "We also heard Castille's conversation with Primo Ruqur. The world may believe Trevor Harmon is dead, but now, Primo knows Liam Curran isn't. And that presents a whole new set of problems."

"Wait a minute," Woody said. "Are you saying Liam Curran was once dead too?"

Ginny said, "Patricia, there's still a great deal you don't know. We'll talk about all that after you resign from the White House." Then, she turned to Liam and said, "I know you've considered adding Primo to your stupid list. I'd like to beg you to reconsider."

"Primo wasn't part of the NEST," Liam said. "And we both know going after Primo would be more—complicated."

"Good. Because right now, we have to let things cool off," Ginny said, pulling a copy of the *LA Times* from her purse and dropping it on the coffee table. The headline read:

PROMINENT LOCAL ATTORNEY'S DEATH RULED SUICIDE.

Liam gave it a cursory glance. "Dentists and lawyers have the highest suicide rates." He pursed his lips, then pointed to Woody. "Didn't you go law school?"

Woody smiled. "It looks like the typed suicide note and copy of the AP release you left on his desk worked. For now."

Ginny said, "The Beverly Hills police determined the .40 caliber Beretta that Castille used to—commit suicide—once belonged to Agent Gallagher. It was also used to kill Angel, *and* the baby in the desert, *and* Gerardo Lopez at Lacey's. Oddly enough, the police found a second Beretta in Castille's den that belonged to Agent Penn. But not one print was found on the gun, inside or out. The ballistics IDs it as the gun used to kill Rolando Alvarez and Lacey Sullivan."

Liam said nothing. Then, Woody chimed in.

"I'm more interested in the .22 caliber pistol found near Angel's dead hand with his prints all over it. *And* the blank checks and credit cards belonging to Sheik Tariq Al-Jabori found in Angel's pockets. It was the same pistol used in the Toledo killings."

"That's outstanding police work," Liam said. "They should let the Beverly Hills cops take a look at the Jimmy Hoffa case."

"There were two shooters in Toledo, Liam," Woody reminded him.

Liam said nothing, but his thoughts went to Mika, wherever she was. He wasn't worried she'd be found out. She had missed Saliba because he hadn't come out of the building. But every other detail had been met without exception.

Ginny said, "The AP release this morning has Congressman Renner and Senator Kline playing duck-and-cover politics. Inquiries and hearings will follow, but without a certain witness, they'll make it through." She paused for a length, gazing at the croissant on the napkin in her lap. When she looked up at Liam, she said, "I'll only ask you this one time. Where is Catarina Guzman?"

"Who?" Liam replied, causing Ginny to bite her lip.

Woody had just taken a bite of a pastry and nearly choked on it as she stifled a laugh. Ginny turned away, and Randolph changed the subject. He pointed at Liam's head, and said, "You haven't been for a follow-up?"

"Isn't that a violation of a patient's right to privacy?" Liam said.

"Horse-hockey! I was the one who put you in Walter Reed. I've been briefed." Randolph leaned forward, his elbows on his knees and his palms pressed together. He glanced at the two ladies, then back to Liam.

"I'm guessing you're not here to give me a Purple Heart," Liam said.

"I wasn't aware you had been recommissioned." Randolph chuckled, but his demeanor quickly turned somber. "I want you to repeat after me: Lacey's murder case is closed."

"Why is that important, Bill?" Liam asked.

Randolph studied him for a beat, then said, "Detective Wallace Taconelli."

"What about him?"

"He was once Major Taconelli."

"Army grunt?"

Randolph pursed his lips and shook his head. "Marine MP. He served in the Med from '88 to September of '90 before deploying to Desert Storm about the same time Commander Trevor Harmon was playing with the Kurds in Mosul. Taconelli won the Navy Cross for killing a suicide bomber climbing a fence in Kuwait. Probably saved twenty or thirty lives."

"Why are you telling me this?"

Randolph said, "I checked his file yesterday. Looks like the Pentagon owes him a third oak leaf."

Liam said, "They don't give oak leaves for the Navy Cross. Trevor Harmon had one."

Randolph smiled and said, "Oh yeah. I forgot. But they *do* give oak clusters for the DMS. Perhaps a navy commander could deliver the citation in person."

Liam said, "Trevor Harmon is busy rotting in an empty grave. And so is his service record."

"About that," Randolph started. "Trevor Harmon had earned all those college degrees, but Ginny was able to call in some favors and get Liam Curran's name on them. I can make that happen with your service record."

"There's just one problem," Liam said. "Trevor Harmon died with the world believing he was a murderer. The warrants died with him."

"That can be fixed—if it's something you want," Woody said.

"So, the deceased Trevor Harmon would be—"

"Pardoned by the president," Woody interjected. She eyed the envelope on the coffee table, and added, "It needs to happen before my leverage runs out."

"Isn't that blackmail?" Liam quipped.

Before Woody could defend herself, Randolph turned to her and said, "A word of warning, Madame Chief of Staff. What's in that envelope is compelling. But make no mistake—the president is the most powerful man on the globe with unlimited resources at his disposal. Be damned careful."

Woody pursed her lips. "Thank you, Admiral." After he nodded and smiled, she turned to Liam. "Now—Malik Saliba?"

Liam's heart skipped. "What about him?"

"While he was asleep, someone capped him in his hotel room in Ankara," Woody said. "It's a box you no longer need to check."

"Who was it?" Liam asked, aiming the question directly at Ginny.

Ginny changed the subject. "Before we officially cut the ribbon on the new operations group, I want you to take some time off.

You have a PhD to finish, anyway."

"I accept," Liam said. As he stood, so did the room.

Randolph delivered another bear hug, then made Liam promise to stop in and see Annika on his way back to Princeton. When Liam spun around, Woody was waiting, and this time, she shook his hand, strong and professional.

"I want to apologize for—you know—two years ago," she said. "I was wrong about you." Then, she tiptoed closer and kissed his cheek. "Thank you for everything you've done."

"I was on orders," Liam said. "But I'll let you in on a little secret: you're not as *wrong about me* as you think you are." When he saw her take a breath, he added, "Don't worry. Paul and I are even."

"Thank you," Woody said. "By the way, we've decided to name the new group in your honor. We're calling it ICEBRG. Minus the second *E*."

"I'm sure that's an acronym for something," Liam said.

Woody nodded. "In case of emergency, break glass."

Liam laughed out loud. "That sounds like me, alright."

He started for the door, where Ginny was waiting, her hand on the knob. But she kept the door closed.

Liam asked, "What now?"

Ginny touched his hand, her eyes searching his. She leaned in and whispered, "She's on her way back now."

# CHAPTER 60

Concord College
Athens, West Virginia
Monday, September 18, 1995
8:15 a.m.

"You're back?" Julie said with a smile as she looked up from her desk and saw Liam at the door of the office suite. She gave him a long hug, then added, "The pile on your desk is getting— What happened to your head?"

"A little accident," Liam said. After a few minutes of chitchat with Julie and the dean's secretary, consisting of tall tales from a vacation he never took, he explained he was here to check his mail and prepare to take classes back in the morning.

"Dean Parkey is anxious to dump them back on you." Julie handed him a stack of yellow message slips, and for a fleeting moment, he considered investing in an answering machine. But the moment of lunacy dissolved just as quickly.

On his desk, mail and memos had been stacked like 3D bar graphs. Some of the stacks had made it to his chair, which he relocated to another chair. After an hour of filling a garbage bag, the gentle rap on his door mercifully arrived. "Come in," he called out, then saw Rachel Cruise's face peer timidly inside.

"Professor Curran?" she said. "I— Julie said you were in, so I—" Then, her eyes saddened and locked onto his face and fading bruises. "What happened to…? Never mind." Her gaze fell to the slip of paper in her hand.

"What's that?" Liam asked.

"Today's the last day to drop classes, and I figured with all that's happened—"

"You're dropping my class?" Liam asked.

"I'm leaving Concord."

Liam moved a pile of papers from the visitor's chair and offered it to Rachel, while he sat on the edge of the desk. "Tell me why," he said.

"You know. After what happened with the cops and my stupid behavior, it seems like the right thing to do."

"No—I don't know," Liam said. "Enlighten me."

Rachel spent the next few minutes reliving her conversation with Detective Taconelli. In the end, it at least explained the warrant. At the most, he realized Taconelli may be a bigger problem than he had first thought.

Liam said, "I appreciate your candor, but as far as I'm concerned, no blood, no foul. You talked to the cops, and you were honest. You did the right thing."

"So—I should stay?" she asked.

"Only if you understand a romantic relationship with me is off limits."

Her eyes dropped to her fidgeting fingers. "Yeah. I got it. I promise I won't—you know. It's just that when I find something I want, I go after it. You probably wouldn't understand."

Liam pressed on a smile, then glanced toward the shredder. She took the hint, then sent the drop slip through.

She said, "I can't tell you how much this means to me. Thank you."

Liam paused for a few beats, struggling to ignore her raw beauty and the ease with which he could enjoy the company of a sexy, lively woman again. No, not a woman. A student. A gnat's hair past being a teen. He said, "I suggest you put that hate-to-lose attitude into your grades. Which are exceptional, by the way."

When she stood, her arms came up for a hug, but then she held out her hand instead. "Thank you," she said as a tear traced her cheek. She wiped it away as she left his office.

Liam worked for another hour until he had the pile under control. He stuffed as much as one hand could grip into his satchel and called it a day.

He was home by noon.

In the refrigerator, he found some lunch meat, sniffed it, tossed it, and decided to call for pizza. While he waited, he headed to the pole barn to check on the RV, but when he opened the overhead door, he stopped short as the sunlight painted the shape of a woman in jeans sitting on the railing of the same stall where Angel had once hidden. Below her feet, in the straw, lay an oversized yellow gym bag.

Liam caught his breath, and said, "Ginny said you were on your way." He scanned her from head to toe as if it were the first time.

Mika slipped off the rail and stopped a few feet from him as if blocked by some invisible barrier. "You've been—busy," she said, her Russian accent thicker than he remembered.

"Your car isn't in the garage. How did you get here?"

"The BICA jet is waiting for me at BLF. I took a cab here," Mika said. "My car is at the Roanoke airport. A man has agreed to buy it."

"You're selling your car?"

She glanced at the yellow gym bag. "I came to get my things, but I couldn't leave without seeing you."

Liam reached out to take her hand, but she stiffened and took a half step back. "Why are you leaving?"

She dodged the question and said, "I saw Shipman earlier. I—I can't do this anymore."

"Can't do what?"

"Pretend," Mika said. "I can't pretend that you will ever stop avenging the death of a little girl you didn't cause, and that we are"—her eyes dropped to the floor—"more than what we are."

"Why didn't you tell me that you missed Saliba?" Liam asked.

Mika shouldered the gym bag, and said, "Because I didn't."

Liam searched her eyes, then remembered what Woody had said: Saliba had been capped in his hotel room in Ankara. A question formed, but he decided not to ask it.

Liam pulled her in tight. "You worry too much. Toledo worked perfectly."

"I worry because you actually believe that."

"What's that supposed to mean?"

"The clothes you burned—did you get a good look at your trousers?"

"No. I just burned everything in the barrel."

"Not your trousers," she said, then dug inside the gym bag and pulled out a wadded ball, shook it, then held up the wrinkled black Armani slacks. She poked her pinkie through the half-inch-diameter hole punched in the fabric an inch above the cuff. "This—is a bullet hole," she said.

*From Tariq Al-Jabori's desperation shot*, Liam thought, but said, "It missed me." But then he remembered the hundred-dollar bill and the note Mika had stuck on the stove's clock the morning she left: I pray I never win this bet. But I came close this time. Now he knew what she had meant.

"This time," she said, zipping the gym bag closed.

"Where will you go?" he asked.

"If you don't mind, I would like to use the villa in Lapta—for a while," she said. "Most of my belongings are there anyway."

"Use it as long as you like," Liam said. He stepped toward her, but she turned her back on him. "I'm not giving up on us, Mika."

She spun around to face him, smiled, and then touched his chin. It felt almost motherly as she said, "You haven't given up on any of them."

"Them who?"

She smiled and said, "I know all about the loves from your past—and Trevor Harmon's. Tani, Nadia, and Lacey."

*You left out Stephanie Maguire. Thank God*, Liam thought, but it was interrupted by the two cars pulling into Lacey's driveway. Then, he felt Mika's hand touch his stitches.

"Why did you get involved?"

"I didn't have a choice," he said.

"Yes, you did," Mika said. "But you thought Lacey died because of your past. But, sometimes, bad things just happen. You should consider how this might have turned out if you had done nothing." He felt her hand trace his cheek just before she delivered her hardest blow right on his emotional chin. "You thought *I* killed Lacey, didn't you?"

"Nooo—I—" But he was interrupted.

"Stop!" Mika commanded. "You deny this as if it were a bad thing. But if our positions were reversed, I would have wondered about you." She poked his chest. "Addictions and obsessions are not the same. Addictions are internal and can be managed or cured. Obsessions are external and the source must be erased. You can kill everyone from the NEST, but you can't erase a memory without erasing—yourself."

A distant horn punctured the moment, and they both turned to see the yellow cab waiting at the gate. Liam dug in his pocket for the remote and opened the gate. At the top of the drive, the driver got out, smiled, then took Mika's gym bag and tossed it into the trunk. Liam gave the man three twenties, more than enough for a twenty-minute trip to the airport and a serious tip. He put Mika in the back seat, closed the door, then kissed her through the open window. This time, it felt cold and platonic.

"I love you," he said, stroking a blonde strand from her forehead.

"And I love you. This is why I must go."

"Where does this leave us?" Liam asked.

"Where we should have stayed..." She smiled, but a tear leaked as she said, "Bro."

Liam stepped back as the taxi backed up then then navigated

the driveway. As it pulled onto the main road, one of the cars from Lacey's turned in before the gate could come down.

*The place was becoming Grand Central Station.*

The silver Acura stopped, and a too happy woman in a suit climbed out and strutted in his direction. Her hair was up and sprayed heavily. Makeup caked a face that might have needed more, and her eyeliner appeared almost Halloween-like. A business card was out and beat her to Liam by an arm's length.

"Hello there," the woman's voice sang. Her steps were quick, but she paused as she got closer, her eyes scanning his face.

Liam took the business card without reading it.

"I'm Rhonda Stallworth. With Century 21?" Her inflection on the last word indicated the woman expected her sentence to mean more than it had.

"Nice to meet you," Liam said, then passed the card back to the woman. "Let me save you some trouble. I'm not selling my house."

"Oh! I'm not here about your home. I've got the listing for the Sullivan's place." Then her tone soured. "A shame what happened there."

"Yes, it was," Liam said, then thought, *Scott Sullivan isn't wasting any time.* He added, "I tried to buy the Sullivan place a while back. What is Scott Sullivan asking?"

Her eyes widened as she smiled again. "I'm so sorry, Mr. Curran. The house is already in contract, and the buyer is at the home right now. She asked me to come here to see if you might have a moment to meet your new neighbor."

Just then, a blue Jeep with no top and California tags skidded to a stop at the gate, and the owner began waving wildly from the seat. Liam opened it remotely, and the Jeep sped up the drive. The driver's ponytail flipped in the wind, and Liam marveled that her Dodgers cap stayed on. She leapt from the Jeep without opening the door, and her ebony eyes found his.

"Are you Mr. Curran?" she asked with an outstretched hand

while stepping over the gas can and a coil of water hose. "I'm Rosalyn Alvarez."

Liam took Sierra's hand, touching it lightly before letting it go as if testing its temperature. "Mrs. Alvarez. Nice to meet you. I like your cap."

She smiled. "It's *miss*. And I didn't catch your name."

"It's Liam. And I have to warn you, I'm a bit of a recluse."

The realtor lost her smile.

Sierra said, "Then you'll be quiet. I'm buying the place next door as a second home, and I'll be gutting it next week. I hope you won't mind the noise."

Liam shot a glance toward the Jeep and the California plates. "That's a long drive in a Jeep."

"I had some time to kill. Besides, I'll need something to drive here. If you're feeling neighborly, I'll need a ride to the airport in a few days."

Ignoring the request, Liam asked, "What is it you do, Ms. Alvarez?"

"Entertainment," she said, then made a show of drawing in a lungful of air. "Interesting—smells."

"Today's a good day," he said. "Horses. Cows. Sheep. Can you tolerate the fragrances of nature?"

"I grew up in worse." Her eyes went from his face to the healing cuts on his arm to the wad of trousers in his grasp. A sly smile pierced her cheeks.

"I'll buy the place for twice what you paid for it. Plus, the seven percent realtor fee," Liam added and he watched Realtor Stallworth smile.

"Can you afford it?" Sierra asked as her eyes scanned his house.

"Try me," Liam said. "Give me a number."

"The house is a crime scene. That's why I'm gutting it."

"Mine's haunted. Give me a number."

This time, the realtor interjected. "Okay. I'm glad you were able to meet. I've already made the proper disclosures to Ms. Sanchez. Now, if you don't mind, can we go and finish the paperwork?" The realtor walked back to her Acura, then stopped, willing Sierra to follow.

Sierra made sure the realtor wasn't coming back, and said, "It's good to see you again."

"I was serious. I'll double it," Liam said.

"It was Lacey's and I want it," Sierra said. "Now, speaking of money. A mutual friend told me that a million dollars were wired to her account from a trust in Belfast, Northern Ireland. Was that you?"

Liam let the question go unanswered, and asked, "How is Catarina making out?"

"She's recovering," Sierra said. "That was a very generous gesture on your part. I matched it, by the way." Her gaze went past him to his house. "Mind if I ask about—"

Liam interrupted her. "Yeah. I mind."

Sierra nodded. "I think I'm going to fit in around here."

Liam's eyes narrowed. "The last time two Mexicans came here—it didn't end well."

"I'm an American, thank you very much." Her smile faded to pouting lips as her eyes softened.

"We—shouldn't do this," he said.

"Do what?"

"My offer just went to three times."

"I'll think it over. We can discuss it at my housewarming party. Tomorrow around seven."

Liam asked, "Who else will be there?"

"If you're there, then everyone I know in town." Sierra's ponytail flipped as she turned to leave.

The Acura and the Jeep were pulling out as Shipman came from around the barn, wiping wet hands on the thighs of his overalls. He put his arm around Liam's shoulder as the two cars vanished over the rise. "When it comes to women, you're like a bug light—you know that?"

"Thank you," Liam said. "That's comforting."

Shipman chuckled. "Somethin' I've been meaning to ask you." Striking a match against his heel, he lit a cigarillo and asked, "How did you know Catarina Guzman would kill Angel?"

"I didn't," Liam said.

"Okay. What was your contingency if your plan went to shit?"

Liam said, "Who said it was ever *my* plan?" He let his gaze drift back to the rise in the road.

Shipman smiled as he clenched his eyes. "We have a busy day tomorrow."

"We need to start early. I have something tomorrow evening."

"Yeah. Thought you might." Shipman pushed the straw hat back, then tapped away a sleeve of ash. "Are you sure it's a good idea?"

"It never has been," Liam said.

Shipman smacked Liam on the back, then climbed into his truck. Liam slammed the door closed, his hands gripping the window frame. Shipman gazed out over the property. "We need to get the hay up. Fall's comin'."

Liam said, "My bad. I got a little sidetracked."

Shipman laughed as he started the truck. "By the way, Marty Zeller and I are goin' shootin' Thursday over at Triangle. Thought you might like to tag along."

"Would he be *Deputy* Zeller?"

"Yep. You might want to look the man in the eye and say—thank you. Maybe buy him a box of shells."

"For what?" Liam asked.

"Ever wonder why the RV *wasn't* here when the cops *were*?" Shipman asked. "Just tell him *thanks*. He'll know what it's for."

# CHAPTER 61

Beckley, West Virginia
Wednesday, September 20, 1995
3:45 p.m.

Detective Wallace Taconelli carried all six of the evidence boxes from the trunk of his car into the federal building in Fayette County, where they would be logged, copied, and placed in the archives. Afterward, he drove to his place near Grandview State Park, swearing to put the case of Lacey Sullivan far behind.

After a dozen wings for dinner, the news, and a beer, he closed his eyes for an hour, and when he awoke, he peed, opened another beer, then retired to his deck to watch the day leave. The grass needed mowing. Something his ex-wife would have demanded he do with what was left of the day, so he counted his blessings and propped his legs up on the bottom railing as he felt cold steel press against the nape of his neck.

"You're quiet—for a big guy," Taconelli said to the presence, his hands rising slowly; one was empty, and the other still held the beer.

"Put your hands down and keep them on the arms of your chair," a voice commanded.

Taconelli did as he was told as the voice stepped from behind him and showed his face.

. . .

Liam aimed the silenced pistol on Taconelli's chest. "You don't seem surprised to see me."

Taconelli said, "I'm not. But you never struck me as a coward."

"I'm not. I am lazy, though, and my patience is all used up."

"Good. I'd rather get it over with quick."

Liam leaned against the post. "Nope. I have a few questions first."

"Or what? You'll shoot off a finger or a knee?"

Whether Taconelli's bravado was real or fear induced, Liam wasn't sure. But the man had obviously read Sheik Al-Jabori's case file. Liam asked, "What do you know about me?"

Taconelli swallowed hard and found little spit available. "Not much. I know you and Casey Conner enjoy playing shell games with rental cars. And that you're the only human on earth whose paper trail is like picking up litter on the highway, then trying to find the drivers who tossed it." He sipped some beer, and said, "I closed the Sullivan case. The murder weapons were involved in another murder in California. Lacey's murderer is most likely dead. Anyway, it's the FBI's problem now."

As Taconelli spoke, Liam noticed how calm the man sounded. He didn't stammer, and his hands were firm on the arm of the chair as it easily rocked. Wallace Taconelli was not afraid. But he *was* talking, so Liam lowered the pistol barrel to a point at the man's feet.

Liam said, "Tell me about Italy."

"Italy?" Taconelli squinted. "I was in the Sixth Fleet—an MP—before they sent me to Kuwait in '90."

Liam said, "Under Admiral Bill Randolph."

Taconelli stopped rocking. His index finger tapped nervously on the arm of the chair. "How the hell did you know that?"

Liam reached into his pocket and pulled out a large gold pin depicting an eagle clutching a trident, an anchor, and a pistol. He tossed the SEAL Trident to Taconelli.

"You were a SEAL?" Taconelli asked. "How'd I miss that in your service record? Where did you serve?"

"Nicaragua. Iraq. Kuwait. Saudi Arabia. Somalia. Iran. Syria. Other sewers," Liam said. He tucked his pistol away, then said, "Now, tell me what happened at Lacey's. From the beginning— please."

"What is this? A therapy session?"

"Yes," Liam said.

"Fine." Taconelli sighed. "When the locals arrived, they found DeVine and Gillespie already there. After breaching the house, they found the maid huddled in the kitchen, terrified, and two dead bodies in the basement: an unknown John Doe with his pants around his ankles and his brains splattered on the ceiling, and Lacey Sullivan, dead and half naked on the floor. Then…"

"She was raped?" Liam said as he pinched his eyes closed.

Taconelli nodded. "Samples show both brothers had a turn. We weren't sure how it went down, but after the prints and ballistics came back, and we interviewed the man working the bus station that night, a story started to take shape. The two brothers drove from Lukeville, parked a stolen car behind the bus station, then came in and sat like they were waiting on the bus to arrive. It came and went, and that's when they used the pay phone to call Lacey. She picked them up, then took them to her house, where they started raping her. We don't know who started it, but we know how it ended. Lacey was able to get her hands on a pistol, and she splattered Gerardo's brains on the ceiling. After that, she tried to run, but the missing brother—Angel—shot her in the back and the head before he disappeared. Looks like he made it to California and got himself killed. Anyway, we know the brothers murdered the border agents in Mexico and used their guns to commit two murders there before they killed Lacey. All the ballistics match perfectly to that story."

Liam let himself relax against the railing as his knees weakened at the thought of Lacey suffering while he slept next door with Mika, ignoring her calls. "Did you come up with a motive?"

"Not really," Taconelli said. "Given what happened in California, it appears Lacey's law partner may have hired the brothers to kill her. Anyway, that case—and DeVine's—belong to the feds now."

"What about DeVine?" Liam asked, then thought, *Thank you, Paul Kelvington.*

"I guess you hadn't heard," Taconelli said. "He and his head were found about twenty feet apart in Tijuana. His head had a .40 caliber bullet put there by Angel. Or so they think. Ballistics match the gun from Agent Penn. The feds are feeding me bits and pieces now. Sorry."

Liam nodded slowly, studying Taconelli's face. The man's lids drooped, but his gaze remained fixed. "What is it?" Liam asked.

"I guess you know we talked to your little—student—Rachel Cruise. She had quite a tale about rental cars in Columbus. Care to explain that little nocturnal vehicular whack-a-mole?"

"Maybe another time," Liam said.

"I also have a good friend who's an Ohio State cop. He's been working closely with the FBI on the murder of that sheik in Toledo. He told me that one of the pistols used to murder the sheik showed up in Angel's hand in California. Now, there's a link that will take some time to come together."

Liam said, "The FBI has their hands full."

Taconelli chuckled. "It's FUBAR alright."

Liam spilled a grin, not having heard the term since leaving the military. FUBAR was a common military acronym meaning *fucked up beyond all recognition.*

Taconelli drew in a breath, then drained his beer. They eyed each other for several beats before Taconelli said, "Do you want a beer before you shoot me?"

Liam shook his head. "You have any Scotch?"

"I have Jack."

"On the rocks."

Taconelli disappeared into the house, then returned with an

acoustic guitar strapped over one shoulder and two glasses half filled with a golden liquid and three cubes each. Liam took one of the glasses and toasted with Taconelli.

Liam said, "You brought a guitar instead of a gun?"

Taconelli pursed his lips, sipped, then stared into the darkness. "When we searched your house, I saw your collection and thought you might teach me something. I can play something that sounds like 'Wildwood Flower,' but that's about it."

Liam took the guitar and started tuning it. "I suppose I should fill in a few blanks for you."

Taconelli said, "What did we miss?"

"Plenty. You didn't find the murder weapons at Lacey's because DeVine took them before you got there. And you're right about Castille. He hired Angel and Gerardo to kill the border agents, Rolando Alvarez, the baby, and Lacey Sullivan. DeVine was Castille's mole in the INS, and—he was the cleaner. JFK, Oswald, and Ruby all over again. I was the one who found the bodies of the border agents in the desert. That's why DeVine shit himself and went looking for me."

Taconelli said, "I guess there *were* a few holes." He took another sip and started the rocker again. "Did DeVine ever catch up to you in Arizona?"

Liam didn't answer.

Taconelli studied his face for a beat, nodded, then said, "I'm very sorry about Lacey. I know you think it was a big secret, but her mother knew about you two."

Liam stopped tuning and strummed a G chord. "Want to learn 'Take It Easy' by the Eagles?"

Taconelli grinned and said, "In honor of Sheik Tariq Al-Jabori, how about a little 'Rock the Casbah'?"

Liam chuckled and said, "I don't know anything by The Clash, but I do have one more question." He set the guitar against the railing. "Did you ever suspect my girlfriend?"

Taconelli let his head roll slowly toward Liam. "You mean the one who flew from Roanoke to New York as Casey Conner, then disappeared? That girlfriend?" He shook his head. "Why? Did you?"

Liam stood, drained the Jack, then set the glass on the table. "I'm going home," he said, stretching. He still had a half-mile walk to his car—in the dark. "Oh! I almost forgot." Digging in his pocket, he removed a small box and a folded sheet of paper. He tossed the box to Taconelli, and said, "Congratulations on your third bronze oak cluster for your DMS."

Taconelli opened the box, then looked up at Liam. "How in hell did you…?"

Liam unfolded the page and asked, "Want me to read the whole citation out loud? You know, the whole *Major Wallace Taconelli distinguished himself* shit? It's nice of the marines to award it *after* you've been discharged for—how many years now?"

"You're a prick. You know that," Taconelli said. "So, yeah, read the whole citation."

"Screw you," Liam said and left the page between the railing's spindles.

As his feet hit the sidewalk, Taconelli called out, "Sorry. I forgot that SEALs can't read!"

Liam adjusted the pistol in the waist of his jeans. "This is still loaded, you know."

"Is that silencer registered? I could charge you for that."

Liam laughed. "I guess being friends with you is going to suck!"

# ACKNOWLEDGMENTS

I could write an entire chapter of thanks to those who helped shake this debut novel out of my head. Every story from every author is a product of every truth and lie that has touched their ear, and mine is no different. I've heard thousands of tales and have expounded on and manufactured thousands more for no other reason than to entertain—regardless of the therapeutic value I may have received from dumping my soul on an unsuspecting reader, to whom I offer an apology, and a sense of gratitude, for smiling in sympathy and, hopefully, enjoying the story.

First, to my wife, Robin, and my daughter, Allyssa, for putting up with a husband/father who is creative and moody and contrary and isolated (at times). I'm not easy—and I know it.

To my mother, Emma, for her constant encouragement. Perhaps our direct lineage to Sir Thomas Wyatt (poet to Henry VIII) is to blame for my obsession with prose.

As well, to the memory of my father, Trevor, not so much for the artistic gene but for the one responsible for perseverance (or thick-headedness). But certainly, he's behind my ability to BS a good story to death.

A great thanks to Philip Smith, for his feedback and stomaching the raw second draft.

To Deb Thompson, for keeping the Spanish in this novel real and for editing it while relocating from the desert southwest to the southeast coast. Did you happen to check the average humidity before making that decision?

A special thanks to my lifelong friend Harry Bandy. He not only moves me to write but actually stomached two drafts (the first was almost eight hundred pages). I swear, I'll pop out a horror novel in your honor—soon. JoHo say so!

This second edition of The Last Witness would never have

happened were it not for the editing talents of Michelle Hope and the creative magic of Paul Palmer-Edwards who redesigned the cover. You have my greatest admiration.

And, of course, thanks to my new and blossoming readers. If there's no you, there's no me. It's that easy. Writers must be read, or there's no point.

Most importantly, thanks to God first, and our nation's founders, especially Thomas Paine.

# AUTHOR BIO

Michael Shayne grew up in southern West Virginia, served in the Air Force, graduated from West Virginia University (BSEE) and Wheeling University (MBA) before settling in Cincinnati, Ohio with his wife, daughter, and a dog. Goal Number One—check! What's missing from the tale perhaps begins with his 13th great-grandfather, Sir Thomas Wyatt, the official poet of Henry VIII. Or maybe his grandfather who was with the local newspaper. Or being named after Brett Halliday's sleuth. Either way, those Norman and Scotch-Irish genes have compelled him to spin yarns since he was old enough to hunt and peck on Smith Corona. A ravenous reader, he's usually engulfed in two novels, something non-fiction, iced with an audiobook at the same time he's writing. Outside of writing, he found himself working as an electrical engineer, project manager, product developer and business development executive in the electric utility and telecommunications industries.

www.ingramcontent.com/pod-product-compliance
Lightning Source LLC
Chambersburg PA
CBHW021336310726
48971CB00001B/148